"NATHAN, I DON'T KNOW HOW TO DANCE."

"That's easy enough to remedy," he said, pulling Susannah to her feet. He murmured the tempo into her ear—*one*-two-three, *one*-two-three—and she followed, stumbling over his boots whenever she allowed his nearness to interrupt the rhythm. And his nearness was truly an interruption. Nothing in her daydreams had prepared her for the sensation of moving so closely against a man whose mere touch sent her pulse soaring away.

Staring up into his face, she mused, "Well, at least this way I can look at you."

The color of his eyes changed, darkening with desire. "And when you look at me like that, I want to kiss you until you faint, then drag you off to the hayloft."

The warmth in her belly expanded. "What . . . what would we do?"

"We could lie in it, like a young man and a young woman just discovering forbidden pleasures," he answered, running his hand gently over her hip.

"Just . . . just lie in it? Is . . . is that what new lovers do?"

"No," he said on a whisper, "I'd probably shyly touch you here." His fingers grazed her breast, sending the nipple tingling.

"And . . . and what would I do?"

"Ah, being the sweet, young virgin you are, you'd push my hand away, hoping I'd try again, and again."

"And would you? . . ."

Dancing on Snowflakes

Jane Bonander

POCKET BOOKS

New York   London   Toronto   Sydney   Tokyo   Singapore

This book is a work of fiction. Names, characters, places and incidents are products of the author's imagination or are used fictitiously. Any resemblance to actual events or locales or persons, living or dead, is entirely coincidental.

An *Original* Publication of POCKET BOOKS

POCKET BOOKS, a division of Simon & Schuster Inc.
1230 Avenue of the Americas, New York, NY 10020

ISBN: 0-671-50110-0

First Pocket Books printing February 1995

10 9 8 7 6 5 4 3 2 1

POCKET and colophon are registered trademarks of Simon & Schuster Inc.

Cover art by Doron Ben-Ami

Printed in the U.S.A.

For my agent, Denise Marcil

I love you soulfully and bodyfully, properly
and improperly, every way that a woman can be loved.

—George Bernard Shaw to Ellen Terry

~∽ *Prologue* ∽~

Rural Missouri—Early spring 1867

Corey's scream came from inside the cabin.

Flinging the wet sheet aside, Susannah hiked up her skirt and ran to the house, shoving the door open with her shoulder.

"Corey?" Her heart drummed hard. "Corey? Are you all right?"

She heard a whimper from his bedroom. Perhaps he'd fallen. Hand pressed to her breast, she hurried to the door and pushed it open. The blood drained from her face at the sight that greeted her. Harlan was bent over their three-year-old son, a lighted cigar poised at the child's tiny privates.

"Stop it!" Susannah lunged at her husband, throwing herself onto his back and wrapping her arms around his neck. She pulled against him as hard as she could. "Don't you touch him! Don't you *dare!* What you do to me is one thing, Harlan Walker, but don't you *ever* hurt Corey."

Harlan swore and buried his cigar into Susannah's

1

arm. The excruciating pain traveled to her shoulder, then into her neck, but she refused to release her hold.

"Corey! Go to Louisa," she ordered.

Corey had wiggled off the bed and now stood in the corner, shivering with fright.

"Corey, *now!*" She struggled against Harlan, trying to ignore the angry thrust of his elbows and fists against her stomach and ribs.

Corey ran from the room just as Harlan pried Susannah's arms from around his neck. He spun her around to face him. She wasn't quick enough to avoid his fist; he hit her jaw, then backhanded her across the face.

Susannah stumbled away, a bright profusion of stars prickling her vision.

"You *bitch,*" he snarled. "I'll teach you not to interfere!"

"But, Harlan, he's your *son.*" Nursing her jaw, her eyes on Harlan, she started backing away. She tripped over her skirt and fell onto the floor.

Stepping on her hem so she couldn't get up, he answered, "So *you* say. But I figure he could just as well be Sonny's as mine." He punctuated his accusation with a kick to her ribs.

Susannah swallowed a moan and rolled into a ball, determined not to show her pain. Her refusal to do so both angered and excited him, but she didn't care. She'd always had that kernel of defiance deep inside that would probably be the death of her.

"I wouldn't sleep with your brother, Harlan. You're my husband. I wouldn't do—"

He kicked her again and again. "You're a whore, just like your ma was! Both me and Sonny slept with *her,* and you're no different, no matter how high and mighty you pretend to be."

Through her anguish, Susannah felt an anger building that had begun years before and had just kept growing. "Well, you're wrong," she managed to say, but refused to beg.

He grabbed the bodice of her dress and pulled her to her feet. His breath had the putrid stench of stale whiskey as it washed over her, and she tried not to gag.

"I'll do what I damn well please with that boy, whether he's mine or Sonny's," he said with menacing softness. "And you can't do a goddamn thing about it. I can cut off his ear if I want. I can burn his little pecker if I want."

He shoved her against the wall and strode to the door. "As a matter of fact, I think I'll go right over to that nigger whore's, get the boy and do jes' that."

For years Susannah had endured Harlan's abuse, but he'd never threatened Corey before. Wincing with each step, she followed him into the other room. Each breath she took was an agonizing effort. He'd cracked her ribs, she was certain of it.

The front door opened and Corey stood there, clutching his blanket. "Mama?"

Oh, God . . . "Corey," she said, urgently, "Corey, *go to Louisa's. Now.*"

Harlan grabbed the boy. "You stay here, boy. You hear me?" Clamping his calloused fingers around Corey's chubby arm, he yanked the boy inside.

Corey whimpered and shivered as silent, frightened tears coursed down his cheeks.

Susannah didn't dare take her eyes off her husband. "Let him go, Harlan." She forced herself to stay calm, not wanting to frighten Corey any more than he already was.

Harlan gave her an evil smile, took out another cigar and lit it, puffing hard to get a good fire. "Or what, Susannah? What you gonna do if I don't let him go?"

"So help me God, Harlan Walker, if you hurt him, I'll kill you." She shook with anger, her stomach twisting into knots.

With a laugh, Harlan ignored her threat and, dragging Corey with him, went to the cupboard and pulled out his whiskey.

Susannah knew he thrived on her fear, her pain. Suddenly all she could feel was anger bubbling up inside, threatening to absorb her.

She'd never understood why it was all right for him to hit her, why no one found it despicable that he could knock her around whenever he pleased. She'd long since stopped telling anyone what she went through; everyone except Louisa apparently thought she either deserved it, or was exaggerating. But for him to turn his bullying, abusive behavior toward their child was criminal. She wouldn't allow it. She *couldn't* allow it.

"This has always been between the two of us, Harlan," she said, forcing a calm into her voice that she didn't feel. "Don't start including Corey, he's just a child. He doesn't deserve it."

"Papa hurting Corey," Corey whimpered.

It was all Susannah could do not to fly at Harlan and yank Corey from his grasp.

Harlan pulled the child up by the arm. When Corey was dangling helplessly in front of him, he thrust the burning cigar close to his face. "Shut up, boy. You shut up, you hear? Else I'll burn your eyes out."

Corey began crying, deep hiccoughing sounds that tore at Susannah's heart. She rushed to her son, but before she reached him, Harlan had flung him away. Corey landed on the floor with a thud.

Susannah cried out and ran to where he lay. The wind had been knocked out of him, and he was gasping for air. She drew him into her arms, soothing

4

him with her touch. She glanced at Harlan, who was sitting at the kitchen table, swilling down his whiskey.

Corey clung to her, innocently pressing his knees into her sore ribs. Susannah bit back a moan. Pushing aside her own discomfort, she hurried into the bedroom and closed the door.

A miserable headache had settled in her eyes, and her body hurt so much it was hard for her to draw a normal breath. Gingerly she lowered herself and Corey into the rocking chair and tried to find a position that didn't cause her body to scream with pain. She pulled Corey's legs from around her and cuddled him sideways on her lap, his head against her breast. She rocked him until he was quiet, but kept her gaze on the door, expecting Harlan to come in any minute.

This can't go on. For years, Harlan had mistreated her, and then he had begun to abuse her physically. At first, she had convinced herself that if she could learn to curb her wayward tongue, Harlan would not beat her. But Louisa had made her see that it wasn't her fault, that she did not deserve the beatings, the rapes. And she had finally understood that it was something *in* Harlan that made him the vicious animal he was.

Susannah looked down at Corey, saw that his thick eyelashes were still shiny with tears. Her heart beat erratically. She couldn't let Harlan start abusing her son.

She would take him and go away. Louisa would go with them, take care of Corey while Susannah worked to make a living for all of them. She could get a job sewing.

Certain he was asleep, she rose from the rocker, grimacing against her newest injuries, and put him in his crib. He continued to hiccough and sob occasionally as he slept. Of all the pain she'd endured over the years, the one in her heart as she watched her child's restless sleep was the worst. Children shouldn't have to go through this. Children were special gifts from God—why would He allow this to happen?

She glanced up, catching her reflection in the mirror that hung over Corey's dresser. She barely recognized herself. A fresh bruise, from where he'd most recently struck her, began to blossom on her cheekbone, crawling toward her eye; she could feel it swell. The bruise on her chin throbbed, the ache reaching up into her head. Her eyes were dull and her hair hung in lank strands about her face.

Tears of frustration and anger wet her cheeks, and she wiped them away, wincing at the pressure of her own fingers against her injuries. She clung to the side of the crib, dreading having to face her husband again.

As if he'd read her thoughts, Harlan shoved open the bedroom door. "Get out here, whore," he ordered, his voice slurred from drink.

In spite of her bite of fear, Susannah said, "Be quiet, Harlan. I just got him to sleep." She hurried from the room, but Harlan grabbed her arm.

"You're turning the boy into a sissy," he sneered. "No son of mine will be a pansy!"

Trying to ignore his pinching fingers, she retorted, "Oh, so now he *is* your son." She could have kicked herself for provoking him. When would she ever learn?

He slammed her against the wall next to her sewing table, covering her with his thick, hard body while his fingers encircled her throat. He pressed his thumbs against her windpipe and Susannah forced herself not to panic. "Tell me, bitch," he said with a smirk that curdled her blood, "if I kill you, whose gonna look after that pretty little boy of yours?"

Black spots danced before her eyes. God in heaven,

what *would* happen to Corey if Harlan killed her? Of course she didn't want to die, but her death would mean nothing if Corey ended up being cared for by his father. She snaked her hand to her sewing table, searching for her newly sharpened scissors. Finding them, she gripped them in her fist. She had to stay calm, had to show no fear.

Harlan pressed harder, and the dark spots before Susannah's eyes thickened. She clutched at the scissors, and with more strength than she had ever thought she possessed, she plunged them deep into his chest.

"Bitch!" His eyes went wide with shock, his mouth went slack. Stumbling away, he looked down at the shears, and, as if in slow motion, brought both hands to them, and tugged at them until he pulled them out.

Susannah groped the wall behind her, gasping for breath as he came at her, the bloody scissors in his fist.

His face was filled with hate and his mouth moved, but no words came out.

She sidestepped him, ducking around him as he lunged at her. She ran for the door, but he grabbed her skirt, tugging her toward him, pulling her to her knees. She scrambled, frantic to get away. Suddenly the pull on her skirt loosened. She turned and found him lying still. Blood oozed from the wound in his chest, turning the front of his shirt dark red. He was no longer gasping for breath. She was certain he wasn't breathing at all.

She continued to stare at him. Her insides quivered. He lay there, huge, lifeless and yet still menacing as his dark, sightless eyes stared up at her. Odd, she thought, strangely detached, his eyes looked no different in death than they'd looked in life.

Cold and dead, Honeybelle, her mother had always said. *Harlan's eyes are cold and dead.* As a child,

Susannah hadn't understood how a man's eyes could be dead if he wasn't. Over the years, she began to understand that Harlan Walker had a black soul.

Now his face, bloated from drink, looked macabre. His lips were thick and slack. She could see his scalp beneath his sparse, thinning hair. Once, years ago, she'd thought him handsome. But that was before she'd discovered what a mean son of a bitch he really was.

With shaky fingers, she pushed her hair behind her ears. Her gaze found the bloody shears. As if Harlan would rise from the puddle of blood in which he lay, she made a wide circle around him and crept to where he'd dropped the scissors, picked them up and went to wash them off.

Her fingers continued to shake as she dipped the scissors into the basin of water on the dry sink. Rust. They'd get rusty if she didn't clean them.

Fear had weakened her; hysteria swelled within her like a balloon. God, what was she doing, taking the time to wash off a pair of scissors!

She and Corey had to leave. Had to get away. What would Sonny do if he found her like this? If anything, Sonny was worse than Harlan. Yes, Harlan was loutish and a brute, but Sonny . . . Sonny was slick, clever and cunning. She'd *never* have peace if Sonny discovered what she'd done.

"But, Honeybelle, where will you go?" Louisa's pretty black face was pinched into a frown.

Susannah finished packing and snapped her valise closed. "I don't know, and I don't care. We just have to get as far away from here as possible."

Louisa paced in front of her. "Yes. Yes. You gotta get away."

Susannah hugged the tall Negro woman who'd been

her friend since before her own mother had died. "I wish you could come with us."

Louisa snorted. "Now, wouldn't that look dandy? How could you hide with a big, black Negra woman along side? No," she added with determination, "I'll stay here and watch that pissant Sonny. If I find he's gone lookin' for y'all, I'll get news to you somehow, Honeybelle, but you gotta let me know where you are."

Susannah glanced back at Harlan's body. "And . . . and him?"

"I'll take care of that, never you worry." Louisa lifted the sleepy Corey from the sofa and handed him to Susannah.

Susannah cuddled Corey close, gathered what she would take with her, and with a fierce determination new to her, left her past behind.

Angel's Valley
Sierra Nevada Foothills
September 1867

From beneath the rim of his hat, Nathan Wolfe scanned the street in front of him. He sure as hell didn't know what he expected to find. Every town he'd stopped in from St. Louis to Sacramento had greeted him with the same message. If Susannah Walker was there, no one knew about her.

But he knew she'd come this way. He had proof she'd taken the train out of St. Louis. He supposed she could have headed south, but his gut told him that she'd want to hide. Where better to hide than in mountains that were nearly impassable?

A commotion across the street in front of the grocer's caught his attention. A young woman carrying a large package and holding the hand of a small child was fighting off the advances of Eli Clegg, the town drunk. Nate had seen him the day before, staggering about, accosting every woman he met. He appeared harmless. Nate watched and listened, mildly interested.

"C'mon, Red," the drunk whined. "Ya cain't avoid me forever. I know where ya live, ya know."

The woman tried to tug her arm free, but Clegg held her fast. "And I've got a shotgun at home that I'm itching to use, Mr. Clegg. Take your hand off me or I swear next time, I'll bring it with me and use it."

Clegg giggled, a high-pitched, drunken sound. "Ooooh, ya scare me, Red."

The boy with her started to whimper and cry.

"You're scaring my son, Mr. Clegg."

The drunk briefly switched his gaze to the boy. "Where's his pa, Red? Why ain't he here to lay claim to his property? If'n ya was mine, I shore wouldn't let ya leave my bed."

"Well, you'd have to chain me to it, Mr. Clegg, now please, just leave us alone."

Through the sarcasm, Nate heard the edge of panic in her voice.

"Oh, I'm 'fraid I cain't do that, Red."

Nate swore. Clegg was getting nasty. He pushed himself away from the wall of the livery and crossed the street just as Clegg was pressing in for a kiss.

Nate grabbed Eli's shoulder and pulled him away. "The lady asked you to leave her alone."

Squirming under Nate's grip, Clegg glared up at him, his face obscured by the strands of black beard that weaseled unevenly out of his sallow skin. The sour smell of stale whiskey radiated from him like bad air. "Who'n the hell are ya to tell me what to do?"

Nate shoved the drunk toward the bench that sat under the grocer's windows, sending him sprawling. "Mr. Clegg, I'm your worst enemy if you don't quit bothering this lady."

Clegg shifted nervously on the bench, leaned over and spat, missing the ground and hitting his dirty and badly scuffed boot. "How'd ya know my name?"

"Just get along and leave her alone," Nate ordered.

It was a request that Clegg appeared unable to ignore. Mumbling something under his breath, he stood, teetered a moment until he got his footing, then staggered down the street toward the saloon.

Nate glanced at the woman, but couldn't see her face or her hair, for her bonnet obscured both from his vision. But when she turned, he found himself looking into a pair of beautiful brown eyes. She tried to smile at him, but it faltered. He wasn't surprised; most women found him intimidating.

"Thank you," she managed to say, before taking her child's hand and scurrying away.

Nate watched her leave, stiff and self-conscious. When she disappeared inside the dress shop, he crossed the street to the livery to get his mount. The woman bore watching. He'd ask around, find out who she was. But hell, could he be so lucky as to have finally found Susannah Walker?

Susannah was grateful to be rid of the cumbersome dress she'd been hauling around, and even more thankful for the money she'd gotten for it. It was wonderful that Lillian Graves, the owner of the dress shop, needed a dressmaker; Susannah was happy she allowed her to work at home.

As she and Corey stepped onto the sidewalk, the man who had scared off Eli Clegg came out of the livery and rode past her. He didn't acknowledge her . . . which suited her fine.

She knew that not every stranger in town was there to spy on her, but she couldn't help feeling suspicious. Fear of discovery had become a familiar, albeit unwelcome, companion. This man had come to her aid, and then gone away. So why couldn't she shake off the feeling that she had not seen the last of him?

Still frowning, she clutched Corey's hand and walked to the livery where Kito, the Negro blacksmith, was waiting to take them home.

"Ouch! Mama hurting Corey's hand."

Until then, she had not been aware that she'd been clutching her son's hand so tightly. "I'm sorry, honey." She relaxed her hold.

"You all right, Miz Susannah?"

Grateful for his concern, she touched his arm, her fingers grazing the deep, ragged scar on the inner surface of his forearm. "I'm fine, Kito."

She'd healed that wound and countless others, especially the ones that gouged into the hard muscles on his back. They shared a history, yet neither spoke of it.

"Did Mr. Barnes bring over my groceries?" She strained to look into the back of the wagon and found it empty. She'd often wished she had some chickens or a cow so she wasn't always doling out her hard-earned money for eggs and milk, but at least she had her vegetable garden.

"Yes, Miz Susannah. I kept them inside, in the shade." He left, returning with a box filled with grocery items Susannah had ordered earlier. He put it carefully in the corner of the wagon.

As he helped her into the buckboard, she asked, "Who was that man who just rode out of here?"

Kito shook his head. "Jus' passin' through, so he says."

"Did he tell you his name, or maybe where he was from?"

Kito's deep, baritone chuckle expressed his humor at her question. "Most white folk don't tell a Negra nothin' worth knowin', Miz Susannah." He limped around to the driver's seat and hoisted himself beside her.

14

Nodding absently, Susannah lifted Corey onto her lap. As the wheels creaked and groaned over the rutted road, she thought back to the day, months before, when she'd first arrived in Angel's Valley.

Of all the dusty little mountain towns she'd ridden through, looking for a safe place to hide, Angel's Valley was the one to which she'd been drawn. Nestled in a valley where the mountains ran on and on, enfolding granite and clouds and evergreens and even, on occasion, thunder, the town seemed lost in a breathtaking tangle of tree-studded hills.

The grocer, Ed Barnes, had been quick to tell her Angel's Valley had once been a mining town. Raw. Wild. Lawless. "See that tree?" All smiles and puffed-up chest, the grocer had pointed to an ancient oak, whose gnarled limbs reached grotesquely outward and skyward. "The lynchin' tree. Many a thief met his Maker on that tree, yes indeed."

Everyone took pride in the town's gruesome history. It made Susannah think the town had gotten its name because those poor hanged men had been transported to heaven by the angels.

Despite its name, the town was not the perfect place she'd come looking for. Sometimes Angel's Valley was a moody hollow between the giant, swelling hills, where long shadows moved fast and dark across the snow covered peaks. Despite her fitful nightmares, she'd felt safe. So far, anyway.

As they drove into the yard, Max, the big black dog that had been left behind by his previous owner, loped up to them, barking a greeting.

Susannah lowered Corey to the ground, then jumped down herself. "I just baked bread this morning, Kito. Don't leave until I can give you some."

"I'd like that, Miz Susannah." Kito stepped to the ground and carried Susannah's supplies to the cabin.

He put her provisions away while she fixed him a basket of fresh bread and molasses cookies.

As she watched him leave, her thoughts went to Louisa. Every time she was with Kito, when he picked her up to take her into town, or after he'd dropped her off, she thought about her friend back in Missouri, and wished she were here with them. The impish matchmaker in her even wondered if Louisa and Kito would get along. With a rueful smile, she realized that Louisa had the kind of personality that frightened most men away. However, Kito wasn't most men. If anything, she thought, mildly amused, he was big enough to take down most men. Surely he could handle a smart-mouthed woman.

After fixing a small supper for herself and Corey, she bathed him, told him a story, and tucked him into bed. She went into her own room to undress, hating this time of day. There was no dusk here; the sun disappeared behind the western hills, and suddenly it was dark.

She turned out the lamp and crawled into bed, listening to the cold wind as it howled around the cabin, clamoring for a place to get in. Like a frenzied beast, the branches of the mountain alder that stood near the cabin scratched and clawed at the roof.

She huddled under her covers, dreading sleep. For with sleep came the nightmares, leaving her frantic and laden with fear. And she was always running . . . running. Awake or asleep, she was running. Each morning she awakened more exhausted than when she went to bed. And with her exhaustion came that dread that perhaps this was the day she'd be discovered. She yearned for sweet restful dreams and wondered if they'd ever come.

Who . . . who . . . who . . . The great gray owl that

had taken up residence in the oak tree in her yard asked her the same old question.

Who, indeed, Susannah thought, rolling onto her back. Who had she ever been but someone's property? Someone's chattel? Someone's whipping post?

Even now she didn't dare be herself, for if someone should discover who she was, she'd lose everything. Who would ever believe she had killed her husband in self-defense? Who but Louisa would even understand that in that moment when Harlan was choking her, she had only thought of her son? Had stabbed Harlan because it was the only way to keep Corey safe?

The wind kicked up again, rattling the window-panes. Susannah was growing accustomed to the sounds of the mountains. So different from those of the plains. She hadn't meant to journey so far, but as she and Corey had traveled over the long, flat land, over the vast space where the sky never ended, she had known she wouldn't be safe until she found just the right place. And a person couldn't feel safe in the flatlands. There were no big rocks, no hills, hardly a tree to hide behind. Then she'd seen the mountains. High, mysterious, with hidden clefts and valleys. The mountains were perfect.

Susannah had relaxed and was just drifting into sleep, when she jerked to a sitting position, her blood pounding in her head. She'd heard something. She waited, straining to hear over the beating of her heart. There it was again. . . . Startled, she discovered it was Max. He was barking, but it sounded anxious, and muffled, as if he were far away.

Clutching the covers to her chest, she looked at the window and listened, wishing she could hear better over the sound of her own fear. Max continued to yelp, furious, frustrated sounds.

Shivering from head to toe, Susannah groped for the shotgun, scrambled from the bed and crept to the door. On shaky legs she crossed to Corey's room and lifted aside the curtain that covered his door. He was safe and sound asleep, curled up in a tight little ball, his quilt pushed down to the end of the bed. Susannah covered him, then stood a moment just watching him sleep.

She went back into the main room, listening again. Max continued to bark, but softly now, less frantically. And he sounded closer, near the door. A shadow passed by the kitchen window, going toward the porch, sending Susannah's heart into her throat. With the shotgun raised and her finger on the trigger, she moved to the door and listened.

Footsteps sounded on the porch.

"Who's there?" She was surprised her voice didn't quiver and crack.

"It's me, ma'am."

She frowned, and held the shotgun tighter. "Who are you?"

He cleared his throat and shuffled his feet. "I . . . ah, I helped you get rid of Eli Clegg outside the grocer's this afternoon."

Susannah's heart sped up in both fear and surprise, for she remembered. "What do you want?"

"If you'll open the door, I'll tell you."

What did he take her for, a fool? "I don't think so, mister. And . . . and what have you done to my dog?"

"If you won't open the door, then meet me at the window, on the east side of the cabin."

Susannah expelled a frustrated sigh, but went to the kitchen window and waited for him. He arrived, Max at his heels. She lifted the window a crack and rested the nose of the shotgun on the sill, keeping her finger

18

on the trigger. "My gun is pointed at your head. Now, what do you want?"

"I don't want to scare you, but I followed Eli Clegg out here tonight."

Frustration edged with panic spread through her. "Out . . . out here? Why did he come out here?"

The stranger glanced around, then reached down and scratched Max's ears. That action alone surprised her. Max was very picky about who touched him. "I heard him being egged on at the saloon earlier this evening."

Susannah swallowed hard. "To . . . to come out here?"

"Yes, ma'am."

She was awake now, fully alert. "Why should I believe you? I've been here for months, and he's never been out here. He only bothers me in town."

"How do you know he's never been out here?"

That question shot a fresh jolt of fear through her. "I'd like to know what proof you have."

"Well," he began, scratching Max's ears again, "your dog, here, was locked in the shed with some steak bones to keep him quiet."

She narrowed her gaze. "How do I know *you* didn't do that?"

"As you can see, I don't need to bribe him." She heard the smile in his voice as he continued to stroke the dog.

"That's no proof," she shot back.

The stranger stood, pulled off his hat and dragged his fingers through his hair. "Clegg is sleeping off a drunk outside your bedroom window."

She gasped. "My—" She whirled around and raced to her bedroom, stumbling over the rocking chair to get to the window. She hissed a curse as pain shot

19

through her foot, then limped to the window and pulled it open. She peered outside—and found Eli Clegg slumped against a tree, snoring deeply. Lord, how could she have missed *that?*

She staggered to the bed and sank onto it, feeling violated and angry, and not just a little bit scared. When she'd composed herself, she went to the kitchen window, where the stranger still stood with Max.

"I guess I should thank you, again. Would you . . . would you get rid of him, please?"

"That was my intention, ma'am. I'll take him to the saloon. Someone ought to know where he lives."

Susannah heard him order Max to stay, then he disappeared around the side of the cabin. She left the window, feeling a clot of tears press into her throat at how helpless she really was. *Damn.* How could she be alert and watch for Sonny Walker if she couldn't even tell when a drunk was peeping into her windows?

Going back into her bedroom, she went to the window to make sure Eli and the stranger were gone. Relieved to find that they were, she slipped on her flannel dressing gown. She glanced outside, wondering how long she'd slept before she'd been awakened by Max's barking. It didn't matter. She couldn't return to bed now, she was too keyed up to sleep.

After stoking up the fire, her glance went to Corey's room. A fierceness . . . a powerful sense of possession swept through her. She would endure anything for her son. How she loved him! She had thought she was safe here, that nothing bad would happen. She'd always been on the lookout for Sonny, but she also knew he was far too clever to follow her himself. She had no doubt that he'd hired someone to do it for her.

After all the times she'd had to fight off his indecent advances when Harlan wasn't around, she knew he wouldn't just give up. Even if Louisa had been successful in getting rid of Harlan's body, Sonny would know that something had happened, for they saw each other daily. If he thought for a second that Susannah had been involved in getting rid of Harlan, he'd loudly proclaim her the culprit, for he knew it was the quickest way to have her returned to him. Send the law after her. Announce to the world that she was a murderess. Then, when she was returned and ready to be hanged for her crime, he'd step forward, "gallantly" coming to her defense, perhaps bargaining with the law, whom he had in his pocket anyway, to release her into his custody. And it would be done. Sonny had always been the clever one. And her life of misery would start all over again.

She went to the stove to make herself a cup of tea, listening to the sounds of silence. She loved the solitude. She avoided the townsfolk in Angel's Valley as much as possible, preferring to stay away from their prying eyes.

Maybe it was guilt that made her feel that way, after all, she hadn't been completely honest with them when she'd moved in, telling them her husband had never returned from the war. If she had her way, she'd stay away from town entirely, but she needed supplies on occasion, and she had to make frequent trips into the dress shop.

When the sun crept over the eastern ridge, Susannah was still awake, fighting the ghosts in her past. Corey woke up feisty, having slept through the clamor that had kept Susannah awake. After he'd eaten his breakfast, she changed him, got dressed herself, then stepped out onto the rickety porch. She pulled in a breath of warm, dry, pine-scented air. Even though they hadn't had rain for months, the river just down the hill still bubbled over the rocks. Above her, a red-shouldered hawk wheeled lazily, screaming into the windless sky.

Max loped up to her, his tongue hanging out over the edges of his teeth. Susannah smiled. Max always looked like he was smiling back at her. She bent down and scratched his ears, gently scolding him for his behavior the night before. She'd thought that having a watchdog around was the perfect solution to her problems. After last night, she realized there was no such thing.

Corey squeezed past her and scooted down the steps.

"Stay right where I can see you, Corey. If you mind Mama, we'll play a game later." Susannah watched his attempt to throw the ball for Max to retrieve, and laughed as he dissolved into giggles when Max ignored the ball and licked his face.

Her gaze went to the fallen tree that had been on the east side of the cabin since she'd arrived, and probably long before. Just looking at it made her tired. It would be perfect for firewood come winter, if she could get it chopped up. But she'd been putting it off.

With a rueful smile, she realized there were many jobs she'd put off, simply because she didn't know how to do them. She'd try, though. She'd grown accustomed to having every one of her efforts belittled, but now, she could try and fail, and no one would slap her or laugh at her. This new life, as hard as it was, was infinitely better than the life she'd left behind, or the one that had threatened to keep her there.

She carefully took the jiggly porch steps and knew that was another project she'd have to tackle. Corey never remembered her warning from one day to the next, and she was afraid one of these times he'd trip and fall, hurting himself.

You're a bad mother, just like Fiona was.

Susannah stiffened, and curled her hands into fists. No! She was *not* like her mother. It had been days since she'd heard that nasty voice inside her head; she'd hoped it was gone for good. Squaring her shoulders, she made up her mind to ignore the images and voices from her past and concentrate on building a good life for her and Corey.

She went around to the side of the porch, picked up the ax that leaned against the cabin and dragged it to the tree. For a moment, she stood still, listening to the sounds around her as her gaze traveled over the low ridge of hills that shielded her little valley from another. The hills were no longer a deep, rich green; they had abruptly turned a burnished gold that was slowly fading to brown. Up beyond the hills, below the snow line, the pine studded mountains were purple and black.

With a wistful sigh, Susannah turned to her task. She lifted the ax, grunting at the weight of it, and brought it down on the dead tree. The backlash from the contact created a dull ache in her head, and, unfortunately, she'd barely chipped the bark of the tree. Gritting her teeth, she whacked the tree again and again, finding a small measure of satisfaction in her slow progress.

Finally exhausted, she stopped and stretched. As she massaged a cramp along her spine, Max took off across the yard, barking furiously.

Alarmed, Susannah turned. Her alarm changed to fear when she saw a man on horseback coming toward her.

"Corey." She felt an urgency she could not conceal. *"Corey, go inside."*

Apparently Corey had noticed the rider, too. With eyes as big as saucers, he toddled to the porch, crawled up the steps and went into the cabin.

As the rider drew closer, Susannah recognized him as the man who had saved her from Eli Clegg—twice. Her cabin was off the beaten path. No one just "happened" to come by. She frowned, wondering what he wanted this time.

A reluctant memory shook her, reminding her that perhaps the world wasn't a big enough place in which to hide.

The man openly watched her. "Everything all right here this morning?"

"Everything's fine, thank you. It wasn't necessary for you to stop by again." Hoping to ignore him, she took another pathetic whack at the tree.

Max continued to bark.

"Excuse me, ma'am. The dog is spooking my horse."

She eyed him cynically. "I thought you had a way with dogs."

"I do, but my horse doesn't," he answered with a wry smile.

"Then perhaps you should leave," Susannah said dryly, and was surprised at her audacity.

He laughed, a rusty, unpracticed sound. "Now, that's what I like. A woman who stumbles all over herself, professing her gratitude."

Again she attempted to ignore him, hoping he'd go away, but Max continued to snap and snarl at the stranger's horse. Since it didn't appear that he was going to leave her alone, and to prevent Max from getting kicked, she finally ordered the dog to go to the cabin. He continued to growl, but obeyed, loped to the porch and curled up in front of the door.

She gave the stranger a suspicious glance. "Was that

all you wanted?" She hadn't meant to sound churlish; fear often did that to her.

He nodded toward the dog. "In spite of last night, he's really a good watchdog."

Susannah glanced at Max. "Until last night, I would have agreed with you."

"Don't be too hard on him. He feels bad enough already."

Susannah couldn't stop the chuckle that escaped. "Now, how can you tell that?"

"Well, just look at him. He feels all guilty and ashamed." The stranger expelled a sympathetic sigh. "He could have invented the expression, 'hangdog.'"

She looked back at Max, whose head was buried between his front paws. She thawed measurably, but tossed the dog a scolding look anyway. "Good. Let him suffer a while."

They were both quiet for a moment, then he said, "I'd be happy to chop up that tree for the price of a hot meal."

The offer caught her off guard. She leaned on the ax and studied the man. Though he was massively built, he sat astride a horse with ease. His voice was deep and pleasant. Not unkind. It didn't matter. Susannah had learned long ago that when a man wanted something, he could easily charm the venom from a rattler. Then you got what he *really* wanted. She brought her hand up to shield her eyes from the sun and studied the stranger.

"Now, why on earth would you want to do that?"

"It'll take you until Christmas to get that tree chopped into firewood."

"Well, fortunately, I don't need the wood until then," she answered, going back to her task. She wanted him to go away. Be gone. Get lost. It sounded ungrateful, but she didn't care.

25

Forcing her muscles to obey, she gritted her teeth and hacked away at the dead tree, wishing desperately that she could chop through the damned thing at least once before she toppled over, exhausted.

When she finally stopped and turned around, the stranger was leaving.

"Good," she said to herself, relieved. "Good."

"Mama?" Corey stepped outside, onto the porch.

"It's all right, darling. You can come back outside." She watched the man disappear into the trees, praying he was gone for good.

"Mama, look! Max catched the ball!"

Crossing to the porch, she sat down on the steps and tried to still her pounding heart. "That's good, sweetheart. Here," she urged, holding out her hands and forcing a smile, "throw it to Mama."

He giggled when she fumbled and had to go to the corner of the porch to retrieve the ball. When she returned with it and playfully tossed it at him, she saw how the sun caught the highlights in his golden hair, and she felt a catch in her throat. Oh, he was the most precious thing in the world to her. Everything she'd gone through since the day he was born had been worth it. Everything . . . She took no pride in killing Harlan, and running away had made her appear weak and unwilling to face the consequences. But she knew if she had it to do over again, she'd change nothing.

The next morning, she literally couldn't move. It had only been twenty-four hours since she'd foolishly attacked the tree, and now she was paying the price.

The muscles from her knees to her ears screamed with pain, but she groaned into her pillow and rolled out of her double bed.

She'd often thought about getting rid of the bed and

taking the extra single one that was stored in the shed. She slept only on one side of it, anyway.

That isn't the reason, though, is it?

No, she thought. That wasn't the reason. She would never share a bed with anyone again. Not ever! Bad memories forced their way forward, and Susannah felt nausea well up in her stomach. She took a deep breath and scolded herself for remembering, even briefly, the revulsion she'd endured. Every day she tried to shove the memories farther back into the attic of her mind, but every day, something would trigger them, and they'd come rushing forward.

After dressing, an act that hadn't been painful since she'd been kicked around by Harlan, she dragged herself into the kitchen where Corey was already sitting on his stool at the table.

"Bekfist, Mama." He banged his spoon on the table.

Susannah winced and shuffled to the stove, feeling as ancient as the mountains around them. "Of course, sweetheart. Breakfast, it is."

During Corey's morning nap, she went out to tackle the tree once more. Unfortunately, she couldn't even lift the ax.

She glanced toward the brush, where the stranger had come from the day before. She prayed he wouldn't come by again. It angered her that someone had violated her privacy. Whether she could use the help or not wasn't the point. She didn't want anyone around.

But, she thought on a long sigh as she marched around the log, she couldn't cut the tree up, either. She wondered how in the devil she was going to get the job done. Making a face, she kicked the tree and felt yet another pain shoot from her toes into her shin. Cursing her stupidity, she sat on the log and rubbed her throbbing foot.

Max bounded off the porch, his sudden departure startling her.

Still holding her foot, she turned, and her heart leaped against her ribs. It was *him* again.

He dismounted, bent down and scratched Max's ears. "Hello, fella. Is she still wrestling with that tree? I get the feeling she's a bit stubborn, don't you?"

Max was slobbering all over the stranger's pant leg. Susannah glared at her dog, hoping to make him feel guilty. He didn't appear to notice she was there.

"I'll get it done before Christmas," she said tartly.

"Ah, but which Christmas are we talking about?"

She detected a slight smile in his voice again, but she surely didn't see one on his face, or in his storm tossed green eyes. And now that he was practically standing next to her, she remembered his size. Although he was a big man, it was his face, rather than his size, that brought her a dash of fear. His nose appeared to have been broken more than once, and a scar cut a jagged path across his forehead. He wasn't handsome, and although she still felt a niggle of fear, she also felt a measure of comfort in his rough, no-nonsense looks. But it didn't matter. He was a man, and she was wary.

Never one for small talk, Susannah demanded, "What do you want this time?"

He gave her a slow, careful perusal before he glanced away, toward the fallen tree. "Why won't you let me help you with that?"

"And why do you continue to believe I need your help?"

He took off his hat, revealing a thick head of tobacco brown hair capped with sun bleached streaks. "Because you can't lift the ax, you've been circling the tree like an Indian appraising a wagon train, and you nearly broke your foot."

She glared at him. "You've been spying on me?"

He shrugged. "I saw you struggling as I rode in." His half smile brought just the slightest warmth to his cold eyes.

His eyes had always frightened her. . . .

As she willed the memory to fade and die, she realized the stranger was still scratching Max's ears. She continued to feel the bite of anger at the dog's defection.

"I'll chop up your tree for nothing, ma'am. You don't even have to feed me."

She gave him a skeptical look—the cold eyes, the way his tanned skin was pulled over the sharp ledges of his cheekbones, the mouth she guessed rarely smiled. "I can't imagine why you'd want to do that."

Again, the rusty half smile. "I could use the exercise."

Susannah's legs and arms still burned from her foolish attempt at physical labor. She stood and took slow, mincing painful steps to the porch and sat on the steps, relieved to be off her feet. She knew she'd never get the tree chopped up by herself. She could really use the help, and he was persistent.

She glanced at Max again. She'd be a fool to trust a dog's instincts. It was tempting to stick with her resolution to refuse the man under any circumstances. And she wouldn't feel right unless she paid him, but she had precious little money for that. But he'd only asked for a meal. She continued to vacillate back and forth, then . . .

Is that all he wants from you? A free meal?

She shoved the question aside. She didn't have to like him or trust him to allow him to chop her tree into firewood.

She stood slowly, swallowing a groan. "All right. You can chop up the tree." She crossed the porch, then turned and looked at him. "Stop at the door when you're finished. I'll give you something to eat."

He picked up the ax. "You don't have to do that; I said I'd do it for nothing."

Again, as before, his height and size made her want to cower, but she forced herself to stand firm. "We have to eat, anyway. You might as well join us."

Nodding, he went around the side of the cabin and disappeared.

Against her better judgment, Susannah stepped inside and went to the window. She watched him chop, the muscles in his back and his arms bunching into hard bulges beneath his shirt as he worked. She was surprised that watching him didn't repulse her, hadn't sent her stomach churning or made the hair on her neck stand on end.

Briefly, a picture of Harlan, sweaty and bare-chested in his baggy overalls, hovered in her mind, but she pushed it away.

She pulled in a deep breath and went to the counter to mix up a batch of biscuits just as Corey came out of his room, dragging his blanket.

"Hello, darling. Did you have a good nap?"

He didn't answer her. Instead, he pulled his stool to the window, climbed onto it and stared outside. "Why is big man chopping tree, Mama?"

"Because he offered to, sweetheart."

"Why?"

Susannah repressed a smile. *Why* had become his favorite word. "Because Mama can't do it by herself."

"Why?"

"The tree is too big, that's why."

Susannah noticed the play of emotions that scampered over her son's sweet face. He'd never had a good relationship with men. Poor little thing had never had a chance. She didn't want him to grow up fearing them, though. The only way to prevent that was to hide her own fears.

As she watched Corey rub his eyes, she was struck, as she always was, with the frightening worry of her situation. Despite it all, she had to stop thinking about what was past and concentrate on the future.

"Big man chopping tree good, Mama."

Susannah slid the biscuits into the old, cast iron oven, then joined Corey at the window. The stranger chopped with ease, swinging the ax as though he were born to it. He'd removed his shirt, the power in his chest and arms evident beneath the fabric of his undershirt.

She shook her head, remembering how hard it was for her to even talk to a man without feeling threatened. And this man hadn't even done anything threatening. Just being within five feet of her was threat enough.

The memory of Harlan intruded again, and she knew that it was a man's size that bothered her. She knew only too well the power behind a fist or an open hand. But sometimes it was his smell. That smell often stayed in her nostrils until she thought she would choke. Men smelled so different. So . . . bold, or something. It was hard to describe. When she'd been just a girl, she hadn't minded the smell. In fact, at first she'd equated it with safety. Then everything had changed—

No! She wouldn't let herself remember.

She and Corey stood and watched the stranger work until Corey started tugging at his clothes. Susannah noticed that he'd soaked through his flannel diaper, for the flour sack overalls she'd made him were wet.

As she lifted him off the chair, she said, not really expecting an answer, "When are you going to learn to go pee like a big boy?"

Having just turned three before they left Missouri, Corey was still a baby, but Susannah was aware that other children his age already knew about not soiling their underclothes. She remembered one of the ranchers' wives telling her to let Corey run around outside during the summer with only a shirt on, leaving his privates naked. "That way," the woman had said, clearly feeling superior, "he can do his little business anywhere he pleases, and you won't have any of that awful laundry to do."

While Susannah cleaned Corey up, she shook her head with disgust at such a notion. Why, that would teach the child nothing. He'd be no better than the dog.

But as she rinsed the diaper in the pail she kept under the porch, she wondered how old Corey would be before he finally decided he was too big to wear what babies wore.

She finished making lunch, relieved that Corey hadn't found it necessary to go outside and watch the man work. With sudden clarity, she realized she didn't have to worry about Corey absorbing her fears; unfortunately, he had a few of his own. Hopefully, over time, he'd forget about them. But as she watched him, his expression grave as he studied the stranger, she knew he hadn't forgotten them yet.

Nate washed up at the pump before going to the door. He was tempted to tell the woman to forget the meal, but damn it, he could smell meat and cabbage, and his mouth watered. He was hungry, and he didn't want to leave. Not yet.

She came to the door before he got to the porch. "Oh," she said, sounding surprised. "I was just coming to get you."

He studied her again as he moved toward her. She had dark russet hair that wasn't quite red, yet much more than brown. He remembered her eyes that first day he'd seen her in town. Big and brown . . . He'd always been a sucker for big brown eyes.

He swore to himself. No wonder Walker wanted her. No man in his right mind would let a woman like this leave, no matter what she'd done.

He followed her into the cabin. Gaily patterned curtains covered the windows and hand-stitched pillows were casually strewn across the threadbare sofa and chair.

A serviceable cast iron stove stood in one corner, flanked by low cupboards and a dry sink. A dressmaker's form with a dress pinned to it stood by the window, appearing every bit like a matronly chaperone. On a window ledge beneath the sheer yellow curtains sat a row of tiny plants. A small, round table set for three stood nearby. Though it was a plain room, feminine touches were evident everywhere.

"Please," she offered, "have a seat. Supper is ready."

Nate nodded, continuing his scrutiny as he crossed to the table. Fluffy, golden biscuits were heaped in a basket. There was a bowl of steaming cabbage and carrots with chunks of beef. He took a seat across from her.

The woman lowered her head and gave a quiet prayer of thanks, then told him to help himself.

As he ate, he watched her cut up the boy's meat and cabbage. Only when the boy was eating quietly did she put anything on her own plate.

She was a beauty. And even though she was generously curved, there was a frailty about her. Or a sadness. Even the boy was too quiet. It had been a while, but he still knew children, and unless they were frightened or being punished, they were at least wiggly at the supper table. His own had been.

A brief, painful vision of his son, Jackson, flashed before him. Jackson squirming in his high chair . . . squishing his potatoes between his fingers . . . building a fortress with his green beans . . . dropping them, one by one, onto the floor . . .

Nate closed his eyes, willing away the memory. He brought his hand to his face and sucked in a breath, noting that his fingers shook.

"Are you all right?" Her voice was soft, as if she were afraid of interrupting him.

Nate cleared his throat. "I'm fine." But he studied the boy again. A child that age wasn't so quiet by nature.

He glanced over at the woman, and their gazes met. Briefly he caught the haunted, wary expression in her eyes, and he felt a pull so strong, he looked away. *Don't delve too deep.* He forced himself to remember why he was there.

"Bread, Mama," the boy said, reaching toward the basket. His arm hit his cup and it went over on the table, milk spreading like a sea of white, tunneling straight for Nate.

"Oh, Corey!" The woman sprang to her feet, pulled off her apron and stemmed the flow just before it reached the edge of the table. "Oh, you must try to be more careful, darling." She sponged up the milk, nervously glancing at Nate. "He didn't mean it. It was an accident—"

He reached out to tell her it didn't matter. Before he got the words out, she cringed and rushed toward the boy, shielding him, her eyes filled with terror.

Nate frowned at her exaggerated reaction. While she stood in front of the child, apparently unable to move, Nate rose from the table and finished cleaning up the mess.

"You know, son," he said as he went to the dishpan and rinsed out the milk soaked apron, "when I was a little boy, I was always spilling my milk. And when I had a little boy of my own, he spilled his milk, too. I think it's just one of those things little boys do."

Nate returned to the table and righted the cup. The woman stood behind her son's stool, her hands protectively on his shoulders. The boy shivered uncontrollably, his eyes wide with fear.

"How about if we pour just a little bit into the bottom?" Nate splashed a bit of milk into the boy's cup. "Now, you wanted some bread?" At the boy's shy nod, Nate lifted a biscuit from the basket, slathered it with jelly and handed it to him.

He sat and continued with his meal. "Sit down, ma'am."

The woman sat, but Nate noticed that she ate very little.

When they'd finished their meal, she brought him a cup of coffee and a piece of pie.

"Dried apple," she said. "Pies aren't my speciality. I hope it's all right."

Nate felt a brief pain in his gut. Dried apple pie had been his wife's favorite. Another pang of guilt, another reminder of a life gone awry.

The child went out on the porch to play with the dog. His laughter brought Nate memories of Jackson again. Jackson's laugh as Nate tossed him high in the air . . . Jackson's giggle as his mother fought to put on his pajamas . . .

The memories dug at the scab that had formed over Nate's buried feelings. Even though he was sure the pie was delicious, he forced it down, unable to taste anything but the bitterness of his own loss.

When he'd finished, he stepped out onto the porch and lit a cigarette. He could hear the woman talking softly to the boy as she called him in for his nap. It wasn't long before she joined him on the porch.

"You thought I would hit your boy. Why?"

The woman gasped quietly, but said nothing.

"Why would you think I'd hit him?" He flicked his cigarette away, then turned and studied her. "Or you, for that matter?"

She turned away from his searching gaze. "I . . . I didn't think that."

"The hell you didn't."

"It doesn't matter," she answered. "It doesn't concern you."

He reached in to pull out another cigarette, then changed his mind. He was smoking too much these days. Out of frustration, no doubt.

"You're right about that. I'm sorry I interfered." The quiet hung heavily between them. He thought briefly of his meeting with the sheriff earlier. Nate had asked a few innocent questions and discovered she was Susannah Walker, all right, even though she called herself Susannah Quinn. Sonny Walker had warned him that she might use her maiden name. She professed to be still waiting for her husband to return from the war. A handy little lie, but a smart one. She obviously knew Walker was after her.

He pushed himself away from the porch railing. "Well, I guess I'll be leaving. Thanks for supper, ma'am."

"Thank you for cutting and stacking my wood."

Actually, he was anxious to leave. But as he rode toward Angel's Valley, he knew he had to come back to her cabin and further earn her confidence.

He remembered the first day, after he'd offered to cut up her tree and she'd refused him, he'd retreated to the bluff above her cabin and watched her through the telescope. He'd seen her pretty face as she'd smiled and laughed with the boy. She hadn't been all trussed up like most women he knew. Soft curves had pressed through the fabric of her plain cotton dress, and he'd suspected that she wasn't wearing a corset.

Then, he'd been pretty certain she was the woman he'd been searching for; he could feel it. His visit to the sheriff had just solidified his own gut feeling. Yet, she wasn't what he'd been led to expect. "A vicious, murdering bitch," which had been Sonny's words exactly, was not how Nate would describe her. When she didn't know he was watching, she was a mixture of sweetness and fire. She had a quick tongue, but she was also vulnerable and sad. And beneath it all, he detected a woman strong enough to do whatever was necessary to protect herself and her child.

Ah, hell. He had a job to do. Remembering the effect he usually had on women, he knew he had to tred softly. His sheer size was intimidating, but he couldn't help what he was—a man scarred by life, a man who'd lost all tenderness, a man who found it hard even to smile.

Then, as he'd studied the woman, the boy had turned and stared in his direction, directly into the lens. Nate had felt as though he'd been punched. He'd fallen to his knees, pressed the heels of his palms into his eyes, allowing his pain to devour him.

Even now, he could still remember his torture when he'd looked into the child's eyes. Five years. It had been five years since he'd learned that his wife and son had been killed, and yet, it could have been yesterday.

He still prayed for the day when the raw edges of his pain would quit cutting him to pieces and become a dull, aching memory. But even if the pain went away, he knew the guilt never would.

Yeah, he had to go back and see Susannah Walker. He'd been paid well by Sonny Walker to do a job, and he needed the rest of the money. He shook his head, disgust making him frown. If anyone had told him ten years ago, when he'd been a new husband with a pretty young wife, that one day he would become a heartless, callous bounty hunter, he would have laughed them off the face of the earth.

2

She slogged through the water, the muddy bottom sucking wildly at her feet. Behind her, Sonny gained steadily, his slick, indecent smile pressing her on. Her gaze was glued to the opposite bank, to where Corey reached for her, crying, calling her name. She had to get to him; she had to protect him. She flung herself forward, touching the dirt on the shore. It crumpled beneath her fingers, seeming to slide away, leaving her farther from land than she was before.

She clawed her way to Corey, her lungs bursting, her ears ringing with his cries. Lunging for the shore again, she touched a booted foot. She clung to it, pulling herself out of the water. She glanced up into her savior's face, and her blood ran cold. Harlan stood before her, dangling Corey in front of her, bloody scissors poised at her son's throat. Panic—raw, liquid and cold—spread through her, and the smell, so familiar, so cloying, gagged her. . . .

Like a whip crack, Susannah was alert, the nightmare still crawling over her heart. The smell clung in her nostrils as though it were real. It was always there and always the same, especially if the dream held visions of Sonny. Pressing her hands to her chest, she sat up and glanced around the room, grateful to be awake, but dismayed that the nightmares continued to haunt her.

Her bed no longer inviting, she threw on her flannel wrapper, stepped into her slippers and went into the other room to heat some water. It was barely dawn. At one time, rising early had been a habit. Now, when it wasn't necessary that she get up before the sun, she couldn't stand to stay in bed.

After making a fire in the stove, she checked on Corey. The images from her troubled sleep were still vivid, almost real, and she tried to shake the memory of them away, for they gave her a sharp thrust of guilt. She and Corey would always be running, wouldn't they? She knew they would eventually have to leave this place in search of another, safer one. She didn't dare stay too long anywhere, and, as she thought about the stranger, she wondered if perhaps they'd stayed in Angel's Valley too long already.

She left Corey's room, made herself a cup of tea and sat in a chair near the stove, thinking about the man's verbal assault on her the night before. She'd been forced to defend herself against a life she'd hated, been forced to lie about something she wanted everyone to know—that a man has no right to inflict pain on his family.

Other memories crept in as well. Her abject fear when Corey had spilled his milk, and her surprise when the stranger hadn't responded like she thought he would. *The stranger.* Odd, they hadn't even exchanged names, yet he'd been around a good part of the day.

He'd mentioned a son. She envied the woman who was married to a man who did not bully his children. This man, this stranger, had treated Corey's mishap as if it were the most natural thing in the world for a child to do. She instinctively knew it was, but Corey had not had a natural upbringing. She would blame herself for that for the rest of her days, in spite of finally having done something about it.

She often wondered if she would have ever dredged up the courage to leave had Harlan not started threatening Corey.

Again, her thoughts went to the man who had chopped her tree into firewood. She wondered why he had come into their lives, why he felt such a need to protect them. Why would he care if Eli Clegg wanted to peep into her bedroom window? Why would he care if she couldn't get a stupid tree chopped into firewood? She also wondered why she was so anxious to have him gone, but deep inside, she knew. She was afraid he'd been sent by Sonny to spy on her. Eventually he might come himself, but Sonny always had others take care of the preliminaries.

But this stranger who had come into her life wasn't the sort of man Sonny would call upon for help. She knew the kind of people Sonny associated with. She was certain she could spot the kind of man he'd send after her. Surely it wouldn't be a man who was so tender with her son, it made her want to throw herself at him in gratitude. And it wouldn't be a man who would willingly do a job for her without getting paid—or at least trying to get her into bed as payment. That was Sonny's style. What honest, decent man would take Sonny's dirty money and chase down a woman?

No, her suspicions were just a natural part of her guilt. After all, it wasn't the first time she'd had such a feeling. Foolish as it was, when she first moved here, she'd thought Eli Clegg, himself, had been sent by Sonny because he made such a pest of himself.

"Mama?"

She put her teacup on the table and opened her arms for her son. He crawled into her lap and they sat together, listening to the sounds of the morning as it awakened around them.

"What do you hear, sweetheart?"

Corey snuggled close, eager for the game they played so many mornings. "Corey hear birds."

"What do they sound like?"

He whistled, a clear, disciplined sound. She'd been stunned the first time she'd heard him.

"Anything else?" She smelled his hair, adoring the scent.

Corey sat very still. "Corey hear el'fants."

Susannah laughed. "Now you're teasing Mama," she answered, giving him a quick hug.

Later, after they were both dressed, Corey sat at the table, playing with a set of building blocks while Susannah tried to fix the locked wheel on her sewing machine.

Max barked, and Corey crawled down from the chair and toddled to his bench that stood under the window.

"Big man coming, Mama."

Frowning, Susannah's hand stilled over her machine. *Now* what did he want? The more she saw of him, the more her suspicious nature told her he had ulterior motives for stopping by.

Crossing to the window, she stood behind Corey, watched the stranger dismount, hunker down in front of Max and scratch his ears. When he glanced toward the window, Susannah's stomach twisted anxiously.

As if with a mind of their own, her fingers found the

handkerchief she'd tied around her hair, and removed it, smoothing back the curls that fell around her face. She went to the door, opening it just as he stepped onto the porch.

"Good morning, ma'am." He stood before her, tall and roughly handsome, his hat in his hand.

Despite her generous feelings toward him earlier, Susannah crossed her arms over her chest and appraised him. His hair was neat, as if he'd used his fingers as a comb. He hadn't shaved, for dark stubble reached up, hiding the slightly sharp ledges of his cheekbones and the rolling cleft in his chin that she'd noticed the day before. His shoulders strained at his shirt, and she remembered her reaction to him as he wielded her ax. Something warm expanded inside her, and again, the revulsion didn't come.

She nodded a greeting, attempting to stay aloof even though her pulse thrummed. "Did you forget something?"

He cleared his throat. "Actually, no. I've . . . ah . . . I've come to apologize for my behavior last night. I had no right to question you the way I did. It wasn't any of my business."

Telling him he was right was a temptation, but she didn't. "You came all the way out here to apologize?" She tried not to sound skeptical, but she failed. Her own words rang cynically in her ears.

"Yes, ma'am. And . . ." He looked away briefly, then said, "I know you haven't asked for help, but I noticed how badly your steps need repair. In fact," he added, gripping one of the splintered columns that held up the slanted roof over the porch, "these posts don't look like they'd hold up that roof in a high wind." He found her gaze and caught it. "The same thing would apply. I'll fix them for an occasional meal."

Hesitating, Susannah narrowed her gaze and gave him a firm stare. "Why would you work for just food? Surely you can find a job that would pay you."

"I have one waiting for me. Until then . . ." He shrugged. "I have some time to spare."

She fought the converging feelings inside her. He'd looked at her boldly when he talked, not allowing his gaze to shift. That had to mean something, didn't it?

Scolding herself, she glanced away, nervously fingering the buttons on her dress as she surveyed the splintered and weather-torn surface of the porch. Yes, it needed repair, but how could she even *think* about letting him do the work? Despite his kindness, he could still be there to spy on her.

But what if she was wrong? What if he was just what he said he was—a stranger passing through with some time to kill? She needed the porch fixed. Oh, but it was a hard decision for her to make. After he left the night before, she'd been happy to see him go. Relieved, even. It was too hard to trust anyone. It complicated her life.

Max loped to the porch, and the man spoke to him softly. Again, she knew she'd be foolish to trust the instincts of a dog, but again, she did.

"All right," she answered cautiously. "You can pick up what you need in town. Tell them . . . tell them I'll come in and pay for it later." She didn't know if she had enough money tucked away, but she'd scrape it together somehow.

He turned to leave, then stopped and gave her that same rusty, seldom-used smile. "And who shall I tell them will pay them later?"

For a brief moment, she sensed a trap, then knew it was either her guilty conscience or her imagination. "Susannah . . . Quinn. And, just who is going to be working on my porch?" she asked, surprised at the playful tone in her own voice.

"Nathan Wolfe." He extended his hand.

Susannah stared at it, reluctant, remembering other hands, not as large, but perhaps as powerful. Her gaze traveled to his face, to his eyes. Something in them gave her confidence. Slowly she took his hand, then quickly pulled hers away as a strange, pleasant warmth moved up her arm, to her elbow.

She clamped one hand over the other and looked away, puzzled by the lingering feeling. When she glanced up, he was already riding toward the road.

The pleasant sensation was quickly replaced by a queasy one that reminded her who she was, and why she was there. She almost called to him and told him not to bother. But he was gone.

Still wrestling with her anxiety, she went into the cabin. Her solitude had been infringed upon, and she had a sense of foreboding that she would never get it back.

As Nate sawed wood for the steps around the side of the cabin, he could hear Susannah's throaty laugh as she played in front with Corey and the dog. She was good with the boy, better than his wife, Judith, had been with Jackson. But Judith hadn't been as wholesome or as healthy. She'd been petite and delicate.

How many times had he wondered what his life would have been like if it hadn't been for that damned war? Hell, he'd spent years mulling it over in his mind. The war had changed his life forever. No longer did he have a wife and son to love and care for. He had thousands of acres of beautiful land, but no one to share it with. It lay fallow, blowing and drifting with only the wind as guidance. Like him. He was an outsider wherever he went, and he wanted it that way. No entanglements. No emotions ripping him apart.

But now, as ridiculous as it was, he felt left out of Susannah's little circle. Seeing the boy still made him ache in places he'd long thought were dead and cold, but part of him craved the time to spend with the boy. In spite of the fact that the memories hurt, he missed fatherhood. Out of necessity, he'd been damned good at it. He'd been a far better father than a husband. . . .

He swore, the dark curse a mere hiss on his tongue. Who in the hell was he trying to fool? What good would it do to get Susannah Walker's confidence? He'd only have to dash it later. In spite of everything, he considered himself an honorable man. And he'd already taken money from Walker. Whether he liked it or not, he had to finish the job.

He was getting soft, letting a woman and a boy get to him. And he still didn't know how he would implement Sonny's plan to get them back to Missouri. Susannah—Quinn, Walker—whatever the hell she wanted to call herself, didn't trust him. With damned good reason, of course, but she didn't know that yet. She hadn't come to her decision to let him work for her lightly; he'd seen the wary uncertainty in her eyes.

He'd paid for the supplies himself, not wanting anyone to connect the two of them. God, how he hated this bounty job! All of his life he'd fought for the underdog. It sickened him not to. And here he was, taking money—a lot of money—from a slime like Sonny Walker to track down a woman and a boy.

When he'd taken the job, he thought it would be easy. A murderer was a murderer, right? And murderers needed to be brought to justice. But Walker didn't want him to bring the woman back and turn her in. He wanted her brought to *him*. A warning bell should have sounded in Nate's head, but at that point he wouldn't have listened, anyway. All he saw was the money. Lots and lots of money. Money he needed to finally put his ranch in running order again. He wanted to go home, even if there was no one there but his old friend and caretaker, Nub Watkins, to greet him.

Despite his rationalization, he felt a wave of disgust that he'd sunk to such an all-time low to get what he wanted.

He lifted the wood he'd just sawed into his arms and walked around to the front of the cabin. Susannah had her back to him. Occasionally she turned to the side, and he saw the fullness of her breast as it pressed against her dress. His gaze lingered there and a pinch of hunger tweaked at his current state of celibacy.

She laughed as Max wrestled Corey for a stick. The sound was foreign to him. He'd hardly seen her smile, much less laugh. It was a purely feminine sound, lusty yet warm, provocative yet filled with mirth.

A thought struck him as he watched her. She reacted like a child herself, almost as if she'd never had a childhood of her own.

But she wasn't a child. Even though Nate didn't think she was yet twenty, she had some of the signs of having already lived a lifetime. That fragile vulnerability he'd seen in the depths of those big brown eyes the day before told him she'd seen more hardships than any young girl her age had a right to see.

And she was always alert. Always wary. She held herself aloof around him. But there was no reserve about her now, no pretense, no wariness. She was just being herself, and he found it appealing.

Suddenly she turned and their gazes met. The joy slid from her eyes and from her soft, luscious mouth, and she stopped laughing. She broke the connection first, dropping the ball to the ground and nervously wiping her hands on her dress. Corey ran across the grass and hid behind his mother's skirt. The only one who appeared happy to see him was the damned dog.

"Don't let me keep you from your fun." Nate grimaced at the gruff sound of his own voice. Hell, he could intimidate without even trying. It had become one of his best honed qualities.

"No . . . no," she said, hurrying to the steps. "I have to start dinner, anyway. Corey," she said, turning briefly, "maybe you should come inside with Mama."

Corey shook his head. "Corey stay out and play with Max, Mama."

"I can keep an eye on him." Nate saw the indecision on Susannah's face; his offer didn't appear to sit well with her.

She relented, but he could tell it was a hard fight.

The boy played quietly just out of Nate's vision, yet Nate felt him there. Heard him, too. He could actually whistle. Occasionally he turned, finding the boy pretending to saw through a piece of wood with a twig. He was sorry he'd offered to watch him, for memories of Jackson haunted him again.

"Don't hit! Don't hit!"

Nate turned quickly, thinking Corey was talking to him. He opened his mouth to say something, then watched what the boy was doing. He held two sticks, beating at one with the other. Something unpleasant lodged in Nate's chest.

"Corey help Mama," he said, holding one stick aloft. "Papa bad to hurt Mama." He snapped the other stick in two and left it on the grass.

Nate cursed under his breath and finished sawing the lumber for the steps. He knew very well that children had vivid imaginations, but what he'd just witnessed wasn't the sort of thing a three-year-old child would make up. Flying elephants, animals that could talk, those were the imaginings of children, not a father beating a mother. He was afraid those scenes usually had their roots in reality.

He went to his saddlebags and removed a piece of the sandpaper he'd purchased, then began sanding the wood. He glanced at the boy, and his hand stopped, for the boy was aping him, using a leaf to rub a small piece of wood the size of a building block.

Nate's hand shook and he felt a tug at his heart. At that moment, Corey had looked so much like Jackson, it had stolen Nate's breath away.

Slowly, almost reluctantly, for Nate despised the emotions that floundered inside him, he tore off a piece of sandpaper and tossed it in the boy's direction. Corey, so somber for a child, stared gravely at him with his big, brown eyes, then finally took the paper. Nate resumed sanding the boards and out of the corner of his eye, watched the child study his movements, then mimic them.

He stopped for a moment and ran his fingers along the wood. It was smooth. He glanced at Corey. Nate's stomach churned and his hands shook again, for the boy was touching his small piece of wood with his chubby fingers, aping Nate's movements.

With effort, Nate finished sanding, stacked the pieces against the cabin, then crossed to the oak tree and sat, resting against the trunk. The images he'd held captive in his mind for years began to stumble over one another to get out, and it hurt, damn it. It hurt.

Jackson had been a gift that Nate was certain he hadn't deserved. When he was gone, Nate knew that God was punishing him, that Jackson's birth had been a mistake. And Nate had carried the blame with him ever since. Somewhere, deep inside him, he'd always felt that had Jackson been born to another, more worthy man, he'd still be alive.

He glanced over at Corey, who had just settled himself alongside the stump of the tree Nate had chopped up the day before.

Again, feelings burrowed deep into Nate's insides. He pressed his head against the tree trunk, then wiped his forehead with the sleeve of his shirt. Without a smile or a look of acknowledgment, the boy did likewise.

Nate sighed, extended his legs, and crossed his arms behind his head. Corey did the same.

Nate closed his eyes and fought the heavy emotion that clogged his throat. How many days and weeks before he'd gone off to war had he spent alone with his son, his wife too weak to join them? Out of necessity, they'd had such a special bond. God, how he'd hated to leave. But Judith had assured him she'd gained her strength after the miscarriage. She'd assured him they would be fine. . . . She'd *assured* him!

And every day he'd been gone, he counted the days until he would return. He'd felt guilty leaving, but that guilt had been nothing compared to the guilt he felt when he learned they'd been out gathering berries, and had been killed by marauding Indians. *That* guilt would never leave him. Never. He should have been home, protecting them. He should have been . . .

He cleared his throat, which was thick with emotion, and crossed one ankle over the other.

Corey uttered a choking sound and Nate looked over at him just as he attempted to cross his ankles, too, but his chubby legs weren't quite long enough, and he had to bend his knees.

With a wistful smile, Nate shook his head, then picked up the jar of lemonade Susannah had left for him. He took a swig, then wiped his mouth with the back of his hand. Without looking at Corey, he reached out and offered him some.

The boy rose and crossed slowly to Nate. He stopped just out of Nate's reach and examined him with his big, serious eyes. With slow and deliberate steps he moved close enough to pick up the lemonade. Putting the lip of the jar to his mouth, he drank. It dribbled down his chin, onto his shirt, where it left a wide wet circle. He didn't take his eyes off Nate as he carefully put the jar on the ground. His chubby forearm came across his mouth, as if to wipe it dry, then he returned to his tree stump. When he sat, his position was exactly like Nate's.

Nate felt a fierce, not unpleasant tugging. Affecting a yawn, he stretched his arms high over his head. Corey yawned and stretched, too. They studied one another, Nate feeling a warmth tunnel deep inside where, for five long years, it had been so damned cold.

Still watching Corey, Nate jiggled his eyebrows up and down. Corey's mouth twitched, but he didn't quite smile.

Nate wiggled his ears—something he hadn't done in years—and Corey giggled softly, exposing strong, white baby teeth and a devilish dimple in one cheek. The warmth inside Nate expanded.

He stood and stretched again, still watching Corey. "Well," he said with another yawn, "guess it's time for a little nap."

Corey's smile faded; he shook his head firmly. "No nap." He went back to work, busying himself with his piece of wood.

Nate shoved some nails into the pocket of his shirt, picked up the hammer and the boards for the porch, and went to repair the steps, a smile lingering where for so long he'd had to force one to appear. For the first time in years, he felt a sense of relief, of sorts. Even pleasure. And peace.

Susannah stood at the window and clenched the hem of her apron, bunching it into a wrinkled mass. She didn't like what she saw. A fierce wave of possession shook her. Who was this man to vie for her son's affections? Corey was *hers*. She'd watched the exchange between them, amazed at Corey's boldness. She'd almost gone out and hauled him away, into the house, to keep him safe. She hadn't taken him and run from Missouri just to have some stranger lure him away from her.

Her good sense told her Nathan Wolfe had done nothing wrong. Her good sense whispered that because Corey was able to react toward the stranger without fear, he hadn't been permanently affected by what had happened before. But her feelings and emotions kept getting in the way of her good sense.

As she hurried to the stove and lifted off the skillet of soup and dumplings, she realized that she'd never be able to forget the past. But that was all right. Someone had to stay alert and remember it so that what had happened before would never happen again.

The door opened, and Corey ran into the room. "I do wood like big man, Mama," he chirped.

Susannah quickly rinsed a cloth and washed his hands and face. "I saw that, sweetheart." When she finished, she stepped out onto the porch and saw Mr. Wolfe at the pump, washing up. She wanted to look away as he removed his shirt, but she couldn't.

Muscles rippled in places she hadn't known there were any. There wasn't a place on him that wasn't solid and firm, as though he'd spent his life working with his back and arms. The hair on his chest drew her gaze, for it was thick and brown, but concentrated in an expanse across his breasts, then dwindling slightly as it grew toward his navel. Nothing like Harlan's sparse growth.

In spite of her inability to turn away, she still felt a jab of fear, for a man undressing before her had always meant just one thing. She'd never gazed on a man's body with interest before—she'd tried not to notice it at all.

He must have felt her watching, for he turned and looked at her, sending a frenzy of nervous butterflies into her stomach.

She cleared her throat and pushed a stray curl behind her ear. "Dinner is ready."

He nodded, turning away to drag a piece of soap through the hair on his chest. Susannah's mouth went dry. How strange. How very strange that she even wanted to look at this man. But she watched anyway, hypnotized.

Harlan had been big, but he'd slowly developed a paunch over the years. The mere thought of his body had always made her sick with a frightened nausea that she was never able to stop. Though he'd gone soft, he'd still been strong enough to beat her up.

Nathan Wolfe certainly was powerful enough to hurt her. His tight, corded muscles looked carved from sandstone, and the blood vessels that ran the length of his arms appeared like blue veins of granite. But despite his strength, Susannah hadn't seen him use it other than to chop wood.

She remembered the brief glow of pleasure she'd felt earlier when she'd taken his hand. She wasn't used to these feelings; she didn't know how to evaluate them much less cope with them.

When he ducked his head under the pump to wet his hair, she quickly went inside. She shouldn't have been watching him at all. She didn't understand why she had, for every day she swam against the current of fear that claimed her emotions where men were concerned.

She was sorry she'd asked him to stay. His presence would suffocate her. And the ease with which he seemed to attract Corey frightened and angered her.

Mr. Wolfe knocked at the door before entering, a gesture that surprised Susannah. She lifted Corey onto his stool, then went to dish up their food.

As she watched Mr. Wolfe split a biscuit, slather it with butter and share it with Corey, she remembered the dinner the night before. He hadn't so much as scolded Corey for spilling his milk. What kind of man was this? Her feelings were such a jumble.

"Thank you for watching Corey," she finally said, hoping to change the flood of her emotions.

He took another biscuit, devouring half of it. "I hope I didn't scare him."

"Scare him? Oh, no. You didn't—"

"I think it's my size," he broke in conversationally. "And maybe the scar across my forehead." He made an exaggerated frown and to Susannah's surprise, Corey giggled. "Got that in a fight with a grizzly."

Susannah gasped and pressed a hand to her chest. "You didn't."

He smiled. "No, I didn't. But it's a better story than the real one." He gave Corey a quick wink. "If those things don't scare him, then maybe my growl of a voice will. I usually frighten children and animals without even trying." He gave her a crooked smile. "Women, too."

"I thought you had a way with animals," she answered, feeling a fluttering in her chest.

He swallowed a mouthful of dumpling. "I mean other animals. Coyotes. Bears. Mountain lions." His eyes twinkled slightly. "All they have to see is my ugly mug, and they hightail it into the trees."

"You're not ugly," she answered softly, truly meaning it.

"Tell that to my horse."

She felt herself smiling. "Your horse?"

"He's happy he's always facing the other direction when I sit on him so he doesn't have to look at me."

Her smile widened. "You have a very clever horse."

He studied her for a long, quiet minute. "And you have a very pretty smile."

It disappeared, and she stared at her lap, confused. No man had ever spoken to her this way before, never given her a compliment, honest or otherwise.

"I noticed your ring." His voice sounded casual.

Swallowing hard, she tried not to twist the band. "My . . . my husband is still missing. From the war," she added quickly. Strange how much easier the lie came after many tellings. She looked at him then, and saw the doubt in his eyes.

"You don't believe me."

He leaned back against the chair and laced his fingers across his flat stomach. "Why wouldn't I believe you?"

She was unable to keep from toying with her ring. "You seem skeptical."

Again, he studied her before he spoke. "If I'm skeptical, it's because I think any man who wouldn't return to such a beautiful wife must be either dead or crazy."

His words flustered her. "He's not dead," she answered a little too quickly. "I . . . I know he'll come home soon." She abhorred all the lies and wished she could end them.

Corey scrambled down from his stool and went to play with his blocks near the fireplace.

Susannah started to clear the table. She and Nathan reached for Corey's plate at the same time and their fingers brushed innocently.

Susannah pulled away, startled by the warmth of his touch, and the current of pleasure that raced up her arm. The plate clattered to the table.

"I won't bite, Susannah."

Heat raced to her cheeks, then stole over her scalp. Flustered at his almost teasing tone, she forced herself to look at him. His eyes held a wary gentleness that was meant to soothe. Strangely, he had no way of knowing what she was feeling was not fear, but something else altogether, something much more frightening to her: a physical attraction that she'd never felt before and didn't understand.

3

Upon rising the next morning, Susannah heard Max moving around on the porch, his paws clicking against the boards. Smiling, she stepped to the door and opened it. Max lifted his head and woofed, his tail whacking happily against the porch floor.

She stepped outside and bent to scratch him. "Good morning, you handsome devil."

"Thank you. And, good morning to you."

Susannah gasped and stood, looking into the face of Nathan Wolfe as he climbed the porch steps. "Oh . . . I . . . I didn't know you were already here."

He leaned against the porch railing, flicked his cigarette away, and gave her a half smile. His gaze moved slowly over her. "And here I thought you were talking to me."

His teasing unsettled her, giving her an odd feeling in the pit of her stomach. Little things about him—his gentleness with Corey, his willingness to work, the warmth of his touch—confused her.

Remembering how she was dressed, and how little it took to arouse a man, she tied the sash to her dressing gown tightly around her waist, then pulled the lapels closed over her breasts. She gave him a quick glance; he still watched her.

"I don't ravage women," he said wryly as he pushed himself away from the railing and started down the steps.

A hot flush warmed Susannah's chest and worked its way slowly into her face. "How lucky for me," she snapped smartly. She went inside and purposely slammed the door harder than was necessary, angrier with herself than she was with him. Constantly remembering how her life was before was ruining the life she had now. Harlan and Nathan Wolfe were about as different as two men could be.

With a slow shake of her head, she went into her bedroom to dress. Old sorrows were hard to bury. As much as she wanted to, she'd lived with Harlan too many years to just shut him out of her thoughts. He continually glided in, slithering about her memory like the cold, clammy snake he'd been.

Had she responded so smartly to Harlan, she would have been punched, kicked or . . . or raped. It had always been a vicious circle. Her response to something he'd said or done would anger him, his own anger would arouse him, then she'd be at the mercy of the punishing end of his fist, or the hard toe of his boot, or . . . or the other. And despite her desire to protect herself against the other, her pregnancy with Corey had slipped through her defenses. But she wasn't sorry. Oh, God, no. She wasn't sorry she had Corey.

Now, regardless of her desire to have Nathan gone, she spent an inordinate amount of time dressing. Still, when it came time to fix her hair, she barely glanced at herself in the mirror. For too long, she hadn't liked what she saw. Black eyes . . . split lips . . . bruises along her jawline. And she couldn't even remember the last time she'd actually looked at herself without clothes, but at least those bruises had been easy to hide.

She fastened the last hook on her blue cotton dress and opened the bedroom door. Momentarily, she stood as if frozen. In her mind, what she saw was Harlan bending over Corey, like he'd been that day she'd had to kill him. She felt a cold rush of panic.

"What are you doing?" She tried to keep her voice calm as she hurried to them.

Nathan must have sensed her fears. "Don't get your knickers in a knot, woman. I'm just changing his diaper. What does it look like I'm doing?"

Susannah's relief turned to anger. She roughly pushed him aside and finished the job, ignoring her shaky fingers.

"You . . . you don't have to do that. It's not your responsibility."

He stood beside her, his thigh nearly touching her hip. "Sorry." He didn't sound apologetic at all. "But he was wandering around outside naked as the day he was born. I picked him up and brought him into the house and had to step over his wet diaper and pajamas to get to the door. He was obviously looking for you." He was quiet a moment. "He found me."

There was a cutting comment on the tip of her tongue, but she bit it back. She finished pinning the diaper, then pulled Corey close, ignoring his attempts to get free.

"Mama," Corey whined, pushing at her chest.

Reluctantly, she put him down. Without glancing at

Nathan, she went into Corey's room and got his clothes. When she returned, Nathan was gone and Corey was just toddling toward the door.

"Corey, let me get you dressed, honey, then we'll both go outside and play." She was relieved when he came to her willingly.

But she fought an internal battle. Nathan Wolfe had quietly and effortlessly charmed her son. Her first instinct was to put a stop to it. She had to wonder if it was because she was afraid of the ghosts from her past, or the devils in her future.

Nate hammered the new railing to the cabin, then checked the soundness of the posts that held up the slanted roof over the porch.

There wasn't much left to do, unless he could convince her that both the porch floor and the roof needed replacing. They did, of course, but somehow he knew she still wanted to get rid of him.

All morning his thoughts had been on Susannah. Something ugly kept clawing at him, ugly enough so that he didn't want to examine it further, for then his own reasons for being there would make him feel dirtier than he already did. But what had bothered him were her unnatural reactions to normal, everyday situations.

When Corey had spilled his milk, Nate had seen both Susannah's and Corey's reactions before, in other people. The stark fear and the chilling panic. The rigid body stance. Corey's uncontrollable shivering. Then there was the little scene Corey had played out with the two pieces of wood. . . .

He'd been in homes where beating one's wife and children was an everyday occurrence. Some men did it because they felt they were within their rights to do so. Others abused their families out of personal frustration. Some men boasted about "letting the woman know who's boss," but that was often just talk. Still others, the most despicable kind, found pleasure and arousal in it.

A bubble of anger festered like a sore in Nate's stomach, and he tasted the bitter tang of bile. Susannah had most definitely been slapped around, perhaps Corey had, too. Nothing. *Nothing* he'd been told about her appeared to be the truth. There were times when he wished he'd never stopped in St. Louis on his way home from the war, but by then, *home* was just a word. It had no meaning. And, damnit, Sonny Walker was smooth. Nate bet he could charm the fangs from a grizzly if he put his mind to it. Nate had put out the word that he was looking for work. He wanted enough money to make it home, and he didn't really give a good goddamn what he did to get it.

He'd met Sonny Walker in the saloon during a poker game. Afterward, when he'd cleaned Nate out, they'd struck up the deal.

Walker had warned him that she was a "clever bitch, too damned smart for her sweet britches." Time and time again Nate wondered if she was putting on an act for him. If she was, she was damned good at it.

Now, Nate was in a hell of a spot. He'd gotten part of his payment in advance, and he didn't take money from anyone without finishing the job. He had to quit thinking about Susannah as if she were a victim. What Walker did with her or to her once Nate got her to Missouri wasn't any of his damned business. Ah, but hell. There was that churning in his gut, warning him that to take her back to Sonny Walker would be a big, stupid mistake. But he couldn't afford to think about it.

He was checking the lumber stacked under the

kitchen window when he heard Susannah and Corey leave the cabin.

"Can we put our feets in the water, Mama?"

"Sure we can, sweetheart. Remember the place where the water is warm? Now, take Mama's hand, and we'll practice skipping. Do you remember the horsey song?"

Nate watched them retreat, Corey hopping clumsily beside his mother. Susannah held Corey's fingers with one hand, and with the other, lifted her skirt to her knees and skipped gaily down the hill, singing the words to an inane song about a horse that could fly.

A crushing warmth invaded Nate's gut. If Susannah was acting, she'd missed her calling, because he had yet to catch her out of character.

Max, who had been curled up in the shade, stood, shook his muscular body, then loped after them. He stopped, turned and looked at Nate, appearing confused as to where his duties were.

"Go on, boy," Nate ordered. "Keep an eye on them."

Max sprinted away, disappearing into the brush.

As Nate studied the remaining lumber, he realized he didn't have enough to rebuild the floor of the porch. Susannah wouldn't know the difference if he went into Angel's Valley and purchased the wood himself.

He headed for town, then detoured slightly, taking the path to the river. He just wanted to make sure they were all right, that's all. But when he heard Susannah's laughter, a strange, not unpleasant twinge in his chest gave him momentary discomfort as he listened to the unbridled happiness in her voice.

Moving on, he also heard water trickling and splashing over the rocks. Then he saw them. Pulling his horse to a stop behind a grove of manzanitas, he watched, and although he knew he was acting no more nobly than the peeping Eli Clegg, he couldn't pull himself away.

Corey, whose clothes were folded neatly on the grass near the water, sat in a shallow pool of water, splashing and giggling. He tossed a stick downstream, and Max galloped through the stream, retrieved the stick and brought it back to the boy, who threw it again.

Susannah dangled her feet in the water, her dress and her petticoat hiked to her knees and her legs bare. Her arms were braced on either side of her, and her face was lifted skyward, her eyes closed against the sunlight. Dark fires shimmered off her hair.

"Mama! Come in! Come in! Come in!" Corey chanted, splashing rhythmically.

Pulling her feet from the water, Susannah drew her legs up and hugged them to her chest. "Oh, darling, don't tempt me," she said on a sigh.

Max hopped onto the grassy ledge where Susannah sat and shook himself violently, sending water spraying over her like a spring rain. She gasped in surprise, then her sweet laughter rang through the air again.

"Oh, Corey! Max got Mama all wet, anyway." She stood, unfastened the hooks down the front of her bodice, and stepped out of her dress, dragging her petticoat with it. She pulled her chemise off over her head, leaving her in a white camisole and drawers, which had already been rolled up over her knees.

Nate knew he should turn away. He also knew he wouldn't. Like a man thirsting for water, he watched as she stepped to the edge of the pool. Her fists were at her hips, pulling her camisole snugly across her chest. Even from where he sat, he could see the perfect outline of her shape beneath the thin garment. Her profile was magnificent. Her breasts were round and firm, jiggling deliciously against her camisole as she moved on the shore.

Nate's eyes went to her generous cleavage as she bent over to gently scold the dog for getting her wet. Her breasts swung beneath the white, lace-edged garment, and Nate felt a delicious bite of hunger deep in his loins.

He forced his gaze away, only to find himself memorizing her rounded hips and long, shapely legs. He could see the faint outline of her stomach as it moved beneath her drawers, and he followed it down to the joining of her thighs. There, he thought, his mouth dry as dust as his gaze lingered, there is where she would have a luxurious nest of brown curls hiding her secrets. Her magical, feminine secrets . . .

Max galloped toward him and barked a greeting, shaking Nate from his dangerous musing.

Susannah quickly crossed her arms over her chest. They stared at each other for a long, taut minute.

Nate broke the tense silence. "I'm riding into town. Can I bring you anything?"

She shook her head, her eyes wide and her lips still open in surprise.

Nate touched the rim of his hat and nudged his mount toward the road, knowing he should have apologized for watching her, but actually not the least bit sorry he had.

Susannah sagged to the grass, her heart thumping so hard she was afraid her ribs would crack. What had she been thinking, shedding her clothes when she *knew* Nathan Wolfe was close by? But she hadn't expected him to follow her. Spy on her.

She shuddered, a foreign mixture of pleasure and indignation making her knees weak and her stomach fluttery.

Max meandered toward her, his tail swishing the bushes and his "smile" intact.

"Don't you smile at me, you . . . you mongrel," she scolded. "You're useless. Positively useless. A raccoon would make a better watchdog than you."

He nudged her hand with his nose, prompting her to scratch him.

Susannah laughed in spite of her distress. Taking his ears in her fists and shaking them gently, she ordered, "Just keep away the bad guys, will you?"

After she and Corey had dressed and returned to the cabin, she formed the bread dough she'd mixed earlier into loaves while Corey slept. She kept conjuring up the picture of her and Nate staring at one another across the prickly manzanita. She also wondered how long he'd been there, peeping at her.

A flushing warmth heated her when she thought about it. She should be outraged. Her indignation should be thorough, for he had violated her privacy.

She moved her bread near the stove and spread a cloth over it. So, why wasn't she angry? Lord, she wasn't even upset. She was *crazy,* that's what she was. Nathan Wolfe caused entirely unfamiliar feelings to stir inside her. They were more than pleasant. But they scared her.

She picked up a camisole she'd made for a local rancher's wife, settled into a chair by the fireplace, and started some intricate hand stitching. Nathan had returned earlier and she could hear him outside, sawing more wood.

An hour had passed, and she was just putting the bread into the oven when she heard voices outside. Puzzled, she went to the window and glanced into the yard. She sighed, annoyed.

A buckboard had pulled up with an elderly couple in it. Nathan was listening as the man talked and gestured toward one of the wheels. Lord, the road near her cabin was becoming a thoroughfare. She pushed away her agitation, went to the door and stepped out onto the porch.

"Good morning, dear," the woman called from the buckboard, giving her a warm smile. "Isn't it just a lovely day?"

Small talk. Susannah was never in the mood for small talk. Pasting on a smile, she left the porch and greeted the sweet, frail woman with the kind smile.

Ma Walker had looked kind, too, remember? Oh, Susannah remembered only too well. But the kindness had vanished every time she'd done something to displease the old woman.

Susannah approached the buckboard. "Is something wrong?"

The woman started to get down, and Susannah took her hands, helping her to the ground. The skin over her knuckles was so thin Susannah could see the tiny blue veins winding beneath the surface.

"Oh, we have a shaky wheel, I'm afraid." Her face was flushed, and once she was on the ground, she fanned herself with a handkerchief. "We should have had it looked at in Angel's Valley, but my husband . . ." She paused, a bit embarrassed. "You see, Alvin, my husband, is so afraid for my health, he didn't want to take the time. He just wanted to get me home."

Susannah knew it was selfish, but she didn't want company, much less a sick woman whom she'd have to care for, no matter how brief their stay. She wanted Nathan to fix their wheel and send them on their way. The woman took Susannah's arm and started toward the porch, leaving Susannah no choice but to help her get there.

"Are you ill?" Susannah had to admit the woman didn't appear well.

"Not really," the woman answered, slowly taking the porch steps. "It's . . . well, it's just my heart. Not as strong as it used to be."

"I see. I'm . . . I'm sorry to hear that." Susannah *did* feel sorry for the woman, she just wasn't accustomed to company. And, too, the woman reminded her of Ma Walker.

Her first memory of Harlan's mother filtered through her thoughts. She'd seen the woman sitting in a chair by the fire with a quilt thrown over her knees.

"Fiona, her ma, is dead," Harlan had told his mother. "She got no place to go."

Ma Walker had reached out and clutched Susannah's tiny hand, enveloping it in her big, rough one. She'd seemed so happy to have Susannah there, and Susannah had been eager to please her.

But even that first night, when she thought Susannah was asleep, the old woman had whispered angrily to her sons that "the skinny little brat would be useless" to her. "I never said you could bring your whore's child here and I don't care if the slut *is* dead," the old woman had whispered sharply. "How do I know it weren't your seed? How do I know she ain't yours?"

"Goddammit, Ma—"

"Don't you blaspheme, Harlan Walker," the woman had scolded.

"Sorry, Ma," Harlan had answered contritely. "But she ain't mine, and she ain't Sonny's. The kid's ten years old. Fiona said the girl's pa died years ago. An' it's only been five years since Fiona moved here."

Because of all that, Susannah had tried so very hard to please her, wanting her to be happy Susannah was there. But that never happened. Over the next few years, she'd tried so hard to be the best little girl . . . but she had never been good enough, not for any of them.

Susannah's guest stopped on the porch to catch her breath. "Awful, isn't it? I can't even walk a few steps without feeling as though I've walked a mile uphill."

Susannah gave her a weak smile. Ma Walker had appeared frail and helpless, too.

She helped the woman inside and settled her on the sofa. Excusing herself, she went to Corey's room, feeling a warm sense of relief when she saw him still sleeping, his thumb in his mouth. She stood a moment at Corey's door, trying to gather her scattered thoughts.

She didn't want company, but they were here, and she couldn't do anything about it. For years she'd learned to make the best of a bad situation; surely she could do that now.

She turned from Corey's door and went to the stove. "May I fix you a cup of tea?"

"A cup of tea would be lovely," the woman said. "By the way, my name is Lettie Hatfield."

Susannah hesitated, for she still didn't like giving people her name. "I'm . . . I'm Susannah."

As Susannah prepared the tea, Mrs. Hatfield explained to her that she and her husband had been up this way for her sister's funeral.

"I'm the only one left now," Mrs. Hatfield said on a sigh. "But at least I still have my Alvin."

Susannah put the tea on the table beside the sofa and studied her visitor. That kind of expression, that look of love, stunned Susannah. Oh, she loved Corey to distraction and she'd loved her mother, but this love between a man and a woman more than puzzled her. A feeling of hunger gnawed at her, and it had nothing to do with food.

Corey came into the room, rubbing his eyes and dragging his blanket, changing Susannah's focus. The commotion had apparently wakened him early. She pulled him into her arms and sat down in the chair beside the sofa.

"That was a short nap, sweetheart. Are you still tired?"

Corey gave the other woman a shy look before shaking his head.

"What a darling child. You're so lucky," Mrs. Hatfield said with a wistful smile. "Alvin and I were never able to have children. Because of it, we grew to depend on each other. From the day we first met, almost forty years ago, he's treated me like his queen. The only thing missing from our lives was children, someone to care for us in our old age."

Susannah felt a twinge of sadness for the woman. Her life would mean nothing if she didn't have Corey. But then, she didn't have a man in her life who treated her like royalty, either. Dark, black thoughts of Missouri intruded, pressing at the doors of her memory. Susannah excused herself briefly, anxious for something else to occupy her mind.

Morning encroached on noon. Susannah pulled her bread from the oven, grateful at how it had risen. She still remembered one of the first loaves she'd ever baked, hard and flat as shoe leather. It had been so cold in the cabin, it hadn't risen. And no one had told her to keep it next to the fire.

Reflexively, she touched her cheek, the slap she'd received from Ma Walker still stinging as if it had just happened.

Stupid, wasteful girl!

Corey tugged at her skirt. "Outside, Mama?"

With a sigh, she glanced at the door. She wanted to keep him inside and entertained, but he was accustomed to being outside, and she couldn't very well explain to her guest that she didn't want her son near Nathan, because she was jealous of the attachment. Jealous and afraid . . . She reluctantly let him go out.

She stepped out onto the porch, dredging up the nerve to even say his name out loud. "Nathan?"

When he turned, she felt that same fluttery feeling in the pit of her stomach that she had earlier down by the river. He'd begun to work in earnest, for he had unbuttoned his shirt. She glimpsed the hair on his chest, and the fluttering inside her intensified. "Could you . . ." She swallowed, trying to moisten her dry mouth. "I mean, would you mind keeping an eye on Corey?"

He gave her that now-familiar half smile and waved, flustering her further.

While Mrs. Hatfield napped, Susannah made lunch: her fresh baked cottage bread, cheese, canned peaches and cookies. Glancing outside, she noticed Nathan was still working on the buckboard wheel. Corey sat beside him on the tree stump, playing quietly with several small blocks of wood. Mr. Hatfield stood by and watched Nathan work, talking incessantly, offering helpful little hints about how to fix the wheel. He went from one subject to another, barely stopping for breath. Susannah hid a smile, almost feeling sorry for Nathan. *Almost.*

She arranged a tray, covered it with a cloth, and put it out on the table on the porch. As she took the steps to the grass, she heard Mr. Hatfield's chatter, and Nathan's occasional grunting response. She stood behind them, waiting to be noticed, unwilling to

interrupt them—a gesture left over from days past.
Even Corey was too busy to look up.

Nathan had stripped to the waist and was bent over
the wheel, studying the axle. She pulled her gaze to the
safety of his shoulders, but the well-muscled expanse
proved no safer at all.

He stood, the wheel in his hands, and turned toward
her. Sweat streamed over him, forking into tiny
tributaries as it tunneled through the hair on his chest.

Feeling breathless, Susannah looked away, but not
before her gaze caught Nathan's and held, briefly.

Mr. Hatfield turned and smiled at her. He was a
wiry little man, full of nervous energy. "Well, little
lady," he enthused, "I've been giving your man here
some hints about fixin' wheels, but he's determined to
do it his own way."

Her man? Susannah felt a knot in her stomach.
"Oh, but we're—"

"Mama!" Corey slid off the tree stump and ran to
her. She scooped him up and they rubbed noses.

"Yessir," Mr. Hatfield continued, "I shoulda
stopped in that town back there an' had it fixed, but by
golly, my Lettie ain't feelin' too good, and I just
wanted to get her home. Nice we came across you
folks, though. Yessir, the Lord was with us, no doubt
about that."

Corey saw Max and squirmed in Susannah's arms.
She put him back on the ground. He picked up a stick
and chased after the dog.

"Corey," Nathan warned, "don't run with that
stick. If you fall, you'll hurt yourself."

Susannah resented his interference, but she
couldn't fault the message.

"And that's a mighty fine son you got there, ma'am.
Me and my missus never had children. Nope, never

did. Wanted to, though. Yessir, wanted to, just never did."

Out of the corner of her eye, Susannah saw Nathan's relief when Alvin Hatfield focused his chatter on someone else. She tried to smile, but the strange winded sensation she'd felt earlier when she'd looked at Nathan's chest hadn't left her.

"Your wife is resting inside." She pointed to the porch. "I have lunch up there for the two of you any time you're ready."

Corey came back from romping with the dog and hugged her leg through her skirt. "Me eat with big man, Mama."

"Oh, darling. I think you should come in and eat with—"

"It's all right, Susannah. He can sit with me."

She was no longer angry at Corey's defection. She was afraid, but she still couldn't identify her fears. Not wanting to create a scene, she surrendered. "Well, all right. If you're sure."

"Come on, Corey," he said, taking him from Susannah's arms, "time to wash up at the pump like a big boy."

A panicky feeling crept over Susannah, but she fought through it and simply stared as Corey eagerly went into Nathan's big, strong arms, against that wide, hard, hair-covered chest. . . .

Clearing her throat, she turned and gave Alvin Hatfield a wan smile as they walked to the porch. She climbed the steps and motioned to one of the two chairs at the table. "Please," she said, "have a seat. Help yourself. Here. I'll . . . I'll pour you some coffee."

Alvin Hatfield sat and smacked his lips when she whipped off the cloth. "Mighty nice, ma'am. Mighty nice. Oh, fresh bread, I see. Ain't nothin' as tasty as bread fresh from the oven." He helped himself to a piece of bread, slathered it with butter, and slapped some cheese on it. "You've got a mighty nice little family, ma'am. Mighty nice."

Her panic returned, and she could hardly finish pouring coffee into Nathan's cup.

"Mama! Mama!" Corey ran to the porch and crawled up the steps. "Me wash at the pump like the big man."

"Good, Corey. That's . . . that's good." She had to set Mr. Hatfield straight. She was about to tell him Nathan wasn't her husband, when she glanced toward the pump. That fluttery feeling in her stomach was still there when she and Nathan exchanged glances. He walked toward her, buttoning his shirt.

She turned away just as he stepped onto the porch and pulled Corey into his arms. Pressing her fingers to her throat, she found the pulse that throbbed in the little hollow behind her collar. It *had* pounded hard like this before, but never with pleasure. Always with fear. She took a deep breath and tried to still her runaway heart. When she looked, he and Corey were seated at the table, across from their guest.

Corey clapped his hands and reached for a piece of cheese, almost knocking over Nathan's coffee. Susannah held her breath, but Nathan just moved the cup out of Corey's reach.

"How 'bout some lunch, Corey?" Nathan's voice was patient. Susannah's stomach pitched and tossed.

She went to the door, listening and lingering before going back into the cabin.

"Bread and cheese! Bread and cheese!" Corey chanted.

Susannah looked back at them just as Nathan

73

handed Corey his bread. Emotions she couldn't describe rushed through her like a river overflowing its banks.

She watched Corey lift his bread to Nathan's mouth.

"Big man want some?"

To satisfy Corey, Nathan took a bite, then continued with his own meal.

Susannah had the strangest urge to laugh. Or cry. She didn't know which, but a huge lump had formed in her throat.

She stepped into the cabin, her glance going to the sofa where Lettie Hatfield lay, still sound asleep. Susannah went to her and knelt down beside her.

The woman opened her eyes and blinked, then smiled at Susannah. "Oh, I'm sorry," she said, starting to rise.

"No, please," Susannah insisted, putting a hand on her shoulder. "Don't get up. Obviously you need the rest."

Lettie sighed and briefly closed her eyes again. "I do get so tired."

In spite of her suspicions and her desire to have them gone, Susannah grew concerned. "Where do you live?"

"In Jonesboro, in the next valley."

"But . . . but that's over fifteen miles away." Susannah hoped the woman didn't detect the dismay in her voice. They couldn't possibly make it to Jonesboro before nightfall.

"It will be all right. Alvin can make up a bed for me in the back of the buckboard. He's done it before, dear." She drew her legs up and snuggled against the pillow.

Shock mingled with Susannah's dismay. She couldn't let this fragile old woman sleep in the back of a *buckboard*. Oh, but she didn't want them here, either.

She turned away, pretending to straighten the lamp on the table while she fought with her conscience. She didn't know what to do. That wasn't true. She knew what was right.

Finally, she turned to Mrs. Hatfield. "I think you and your husband should spend the night here, with us."

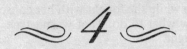

Lettie Hatfield slept most of the afternoon, and Susannah had started preparing dinner early. Although it had begun to rain, the cabin was snug and warm.

Susannah wasn't used to cooking for company. She'd never had any faith in her cooking at all, with good reason. Ma Walker had always said she was useless in the kitchen. No matter how much Susannah had practiced, nothing she did was ever good enough for the Walkers. But she'd gathered new confidence now, even if it had been cooking for just her and Corey. And . . . Nathan Wolfe, who gratefully hadn't complained.

Now, as she cleared away the supper dishes, she listened as Mr. Hatfield talked about the old days and his courtship with his wife. In all of her life, Susannah had never known anyone who liked to hear himself talk more than Alvin Hatfield.

Mrs. Hatfield was on the sofa, curled up with a

76

blanket over her knees, listening and smiling at her husband.

Susannah decided that if you loved someone, you could listen to that person forever, no matter how much he or she bored everyone else. All day she'd watched the couple, and now she felt a huge swell of envy. No one had ever cared for her like that. Not the way Alvin Hatfield cared for his wife. She'd had her mother, who was dead, and Louisa, who was still in Missouri, and Corey, who was just a child. They loved her, she knew that. But the feeling between Lettie and Alvin Hatfield was different, and Susannah wanted something like that for herself. It made her realize that her life was empty, barren and cold.

"So, Mr. Wolfe," Alvin Hatfield said, turning his attention to Nathan. "How did you and your little missus meet?"

Startled, Susannah froze. The bowl she'd been carrying to the counter slipped through her fingers and crashed to the floor. She stared at it, yet didn't really notice what she'd done.

It was the sound of Nathan's voice after the bowl hit the floor that finally made her move. She bent down, fumbling with the broken pieces, her fingers shaking so badly she was unable to pick them up.

"Susannah?"

The question in Nathan's voice made her look up. The concern on his face startled her. What had she expected? Anger? Hatred? Snarling lips?

He bent in front of her and put his hands on her shoulders. The warmth from his long, strong fingers seeped through her dress, into her skin.

He brought his lips close to her ear. "Follow my lead," he instructed. "Go sit down, Susannah. I'll clean this up."

She crossed to the chair, grateful to sit. She felt weak all over, for his gentleness still shocked her.

Alvin Hatfield clucked his tongue. "You women," he said around a chuckle. "Always thinking you've destroyed something that can't be replaced. That's the way my Lettie is, ain't it, Lettie? Remember the time you broke that old platter? Why, I think you cried for two days, and that wasn't because it was anything special, it had just been your ma's. It was already cracked and chipped; it was danged old."

"You just don't understand, Alvin. Women become attached to things that belonged to their mothers. It's all they have left, just memories," Lettie said quietly from the sofa. "Isn't that right, dear?"

Susannah glanced at her, then at Nathan, who was cleaning up the broken pieces. He looked up, and their gazes held for a brief moment.

"I think that belonged to *my* mother, didn't it, Susannah?"

Grateful he knew what to do, she nodded.

"See, Alvin? It isn't just me," Lettie Hatfield scolded softly.

Mr. Hatfield rubbed the bald spot at the back of his head. "Guess I'll never understand women." He reached across and patted Susannah's arm.

She noticed his gnarled and liver spotted hand and wondered if he'd ever used it to strike his sweet wife.

"So, little lady, how did you and your husband, here, meet?"

"Oh, he's—"

Nathan's booming laugh interrupted her. She glared at him and attempted to finish explaining, when Nathan interrupted her again.

"She wasn't quite fifteen when I first laid eyes on her." Nathan gave her a look of warning.

Susannah frowned. What was he doing?

"Fifteen!" Mr. Hatfield whistled. "That's pretty young, ain't it?" He winked at Susannah. "You musta had him hog-tied mighty early."

"Well, well, I—" *Follow my lead,* Nathan had said.

"I couldn't keep my eyes off her." Nathan sat down next to her and took her hand in his, giving it a gentle squeeze. His callused palm grazed hers, and she felt a jolt of heat. "One look into those big, brown eyes and I was lost."

Susannah squirmed under his touch but didn't pull her hand away.

He grinned at her, a look that to anyone else would have been intimate. "It wasn't an easy courtship, was it, Susannah?"

"I . . . I . . . I—" His touch continued to confuse her.

"I had to really woo her. I think I brought her dozens of roses before I discovered she was allergic to them. Remember, honey?" he asked, giving her a warm, lopsided smile. "You'd sneeze and sneeze, but would never hurt my feelings by telling me you couldn't stand to have them in the house." He chuckled, as if remembering, and gently rubbed the top of her hand with his thumb.

The warmth—the same warmth she felt whenever he touched her—crept up her arm. She tried to pull away, but he held her hand tightly.

"I think it was that night at the barn dance that you finally gave in and decided you might as well marry me, because it didn't appear that you'd ever get rid of me. Remember?"

She stared at him, feeling her throat work as she tried to talk. "The . . . the barn dance?"

Nathan nodded and briefly closed his eyes. "It must have been my army uniform that did it. It sure wasn't my ugly mug." He chuckled, amused. "I'd never been so bowled over by a girl in all my life," he reflected. "That was a special night, all right, but I think I fell in love with her long before that."

Mr. Hatfield grinned. "Sure sounds like you had it bad, young fella."

"Yeah, I had it bad, but I think I fell in love with her the first time I saw her." His gaze rested on Susannah.

Her heart pounded hard. "You . . . you did?"

"Don't you remember, sweetheart?"

That word directed at her was so foreign to her that she felt a wave of dizziness.

"You were outside, trying your darndest to chop up that tree." He laughed again, a soft, warm sound that gave her gooseflesh. He didn't look at her, though. His gaze was focused on the table. "You were just a bit of a thing, and could hardly pick up the ax, let alone use it. As I rode up, you hauled off and kicked the tree trunk with your foot. You sputtered and mumbled, hopped around on one foot while you held the other. I think you cursed the tree ten ways from Sunday."

Susannah sat mesmerized as he smiled and continued to study the table. Then he glanced at Mr. Hatfield.

"I knew then and there that she was the girl for me, but of course I had a devil of a time convincing her of that. She was so stubborn she wouldn't even let me help her chop wood. I knew she was the kind of girl who needed a long length of rope." He winked at Mr. Hatfield. "I wasn't sure she wouldn't hang herself with it, but I stuck around to make sure she didn't."

His gaze swung to Susannah and he searched her face. "Remember that day, honey?"

She nodded, unable to speak, the words *honey* and *sweetheart* sticking in her mind, making truth and fiction a jumble. Oddly, she knew that comparing her to an animal that needed tethering wasn't exactly complimentary, but she was too befuddled to react. "I . . . I do remember the tree."

He touched the cleft in his chin. "I'll never forget the night of the barn dance when I proposed. You wore that pretty gown of yours. Remember the one? All pink and white and frothy as a cloud?"

Unable to help herself, Susannah pictured them together, Nathan, tall, straight and handsome in a blue army uniform and her in . . . in a multilayered pink net dress with a low V neck and gold and pink cording fastened to each ruffle. It was a dress she'd often seen in her quieter, less violent dreams. One that had come into her mind after Louisa had told her about New Orleans, and the balls the white folks she'd worked for had given for their friends.

"It was the first time we'd touched, really," Nathan murmured, his voice interrupting her daydreams. "And we danced. Remember how we danced, honey?"

The endearment almost brought tears to her eyes. "We . . . we danced?" In spite of herself, Susannah had a picture of herself dancing in her special dress with Nathan. It was a ridiculous vision; she didn't even know how to dance.

"Oh, now, honey. You couldn't have forgotten that. It had started to snow, remember? We were dancing outside, away from the crowd." He tossed Mr. Hatfield a knowing grin. "I wanted to get her alone, of course."

Alvin Hatfield chuckled, enjoying Nathan's entertaining, though unbeknownst to him, fabricated, story.

"And it started to snow. Those big, soft flakes that just drifted lazily down." He moved his fingers over her wrist, pressing the soft underside.

81

Susannah allowed his touch to trigger the picture he'd painted, seeing big, fat snowflakes melting on his hair and his thick eyelashes. She could almost feel the warmth of his hand on her back, of her fingers against the rough wool of his uniform, of his legs as they moved on either side of hers, of their bodies touching . . . that casual touch that was not casual at all. She could see it. See them dancing together. Forever.

"I didn't even mind getting my slippers wet, did I?" she asked with a dreamy stare.

His fingers grazed her cheek, and she became fully alert. "No." He held her gaze. "You didn't mind at all. We danced in the snow until your pa came out and hauled us back into the barn."

For Susannah, whose life had been deprived of any sweetness and warmth, the fairy-tale story had taken root, and she thirsted for more.

She closed her eyes again, hoping to recapture the magic. She heard the slow lilting of the fiddle music in the distance as they danced together, close in each other's arms. They twirled under a snowy sky. They gazed into each other's eyes. He bent his head, nearly capturing her mouth. . . . But that went beyond anything Susannah could imagine.

She opened her eyes, blinking self-consciously. "It . . . it was a perfect evening, wasn't it?" She played the game, but pretending didn't come easy to her. Not that she hadn't had a few daydreams from time to time. She'd often had to escape into a world of her own to keep her sanity. But she'd never dreamed the kind of dream Nathan Wolfe had just put into her head. It was sweet. Too sweet. Nothing was ever that perfect.

She found him studying her, his eyes filled with a strange sadness. "Yes," he answered, his smile warm, "it was perfect."

Aware that it was all pretense, Susannah pulled her hand from his. What a fool she was!

"Well . . . well. I guess these people probably want to go to bed." She rose and went to Lettie Hatfield's side, relieved that the playacting was over. "Come, let me help you."

Lettie stood and took Susannah's arm. "I do hate to put you two out of your bed. Where in the world will you sleep?"

Susannah turned, her questioning gaze searching Nathan's face.

There was a long, heavy pause. "Susannah can sleep with Corey," Nathan finally said. "I'll get my bedroll and sleep outside."

"Outside?" Lettie Hatfield's voice was filled with dismay. "Oh, you can't let him sleep outside, dear," she said to Susannah. "It's still raining."

Susannah felt panic, the old, familiar panic closing in around her.

Nathan cleared his throat. "Well, I suppose I could sleep here, in front of the fire."

Susannah saw his tentative look, the careful stance. An involuntary shudder passed through her. She didn't know if it was fear, or gratitude or pleasure. . . . "Yes, why don't you sleep in front of the fire, Nathan?"

She knew something important had just happened, and it had happened to her. When the Hatfields were settled in her bedroom, and she was curled up next to Corey, she heard Nathan moving around in the other room. Although whatever had happened had happened *to her,* she knew in her heart that Nathan Wolfe was the cause.

Nate crawled into his bedroll and stared at the fire, grateful to be alone. Memories of Judith inundated him. Judith in her virginal pink and white gown, Judith smiling up at him, snowflakes melting in her hair and on her face . . . Judith sneezing over the roses. That's why he hadn't put roses on her grave, planting, instead, an incense cedar to shade the plot from the harsh summer sun. And the guilt of not being there to bury her himself kept his anguish alive.

For years he'd stopped his thoughts when they'd gotten this far. Tonight, they'd flowed without effort, but not without pain. It was odd that he'd pictured Judith in the pink dress, for although he'd bought her the material as a surprise, she'd never used it, tucking it away in an old chest in their bedroom. She'd asked for satin; he hadn't been able to afford it.

But Susannah . . . The memory of her childlike expression as he'd spun the tale had moved him. Once she realized what he was doing, she'd absorbed the story, pulling it in, making it her reality. He could read that in her eyes. Even before this evening, he'd begun to feel she had no happy memories. And, as painful as his memories were, he felt it would be worse to have no good memories at all.

For some strange reason, one of Judith's favorite poems came to him as clearly as if it were written before him:

> *I hold it true, whate'er befall,*
> *I feel it when I sorrow most;*
> *'Tis better to have loved and lost,*
> *Than never to have loved at all.*

He turned away from the fire and stared at the curtain that covered Corey's bedroom door. He could almost see Susannah curled up around the boy, protecting him even as he slept. He sensed that she would

fight to the death for Corey. He also felt she was just
learning to fight for herself.

What had really happened in Missouri that made
her pick up her son and leave without telling anyone?
That Harlan was dead was no mystery; Sonny Walker,
with the help of some hounds, had found the body,
buried in a muddy, shallow grave at the river's edge,
covered with leaves. He'd been stabbed. And Susannah, "the murdering bitch," was gone.

Nate still had trouble pinning the murder on
Susannah. Not at first, maybe, but now that he'd come
to know her, see her every day, he couldn't imagine
her doing it. Unless . . .

He swore and shifted to his side. He had to quit
thinking about it. He had a job to do, damn it, and one
way or another, he'd get it done.

But thoughts of Susannah crept into his head. The
story he'd spun tonight had been to soothe her, to
keep her from jumping out of her skin whenever the
babbling Alvin Hatfield asked her about her "family"
and her "man." But a part of his own story surprised
him. Judith had never so much as picked up an ax,
much less tried to chop a tree into firewood. That had
been something he'd done only for Susannah. There
was probably no deep, meaningful message, but he
did know that something was different between them.

Now and then he'd felt her gaze on him as he
worked, or when he washed up at the pump. He could
read a jumble of emotions in that gaze. Fear . . .
interest . . . curiosity. But always a wariness, despite
everything else.

His feelings toward her had changed, too. Pity for
what she might have gone through with Walker before
making her escape had been replaced by compassion.
And something else. Now, he found himself getting

lost in her liquid brown eyes. More often than he cared to remember, he watched her walk, envisioning the body beneath the clothing, wondering how she would feel tucked close to his chest.

Ah, hell. Who was he kidding? So she was a woman whose dreams were as ragged as a beggar's coat. So what? It wasn't up to him to change that. And he'd begun to feel too damned protective, too. He couldn't afford that, either, because it made him soft, and it could lead to something else. Something he was neither willing nor able to do anything about.

He had to stay focused on his goal, but it was getting harder and harder to do it. It was becoming obvious that the last thing he wanted to do was haul Susannah back to that bastard, Sonny Walker.

Harlan sat in the chair by the bed, watching as Sonny raped her. She tried to plead with him, beg him to pull Sonny off, but he just smiled at her, baring teeth that dripped blood. Sonny was ripping her apart, pounding into her, grunting like a wild hog, his breath sweet and cloying as it laved her face. She gagged. She was going to vomit. She turned to face Harlan, and he handed her a pair of scissors, also dripping blood. Sonny's hands, bloody as well, clamped her shoulders, and she screamed as that part of him inside her grew until it split her apart.

She fought him. Tried to free herself. The blood from his hands was sticky and warm, burning her skin like fire. The smell of him burned her nose.

He shook her shoulders. "Susannah!"

She surged from sleep, fighting him, desperate to get away. "No," she lamented, "please, *no!*" He pulled her against him and held her tightly.

"Susannah, wake up!" It was a harsh order, whispered close to her ear. His hand smoothed her hair, her back, her shoulders as he tried to quiet her.

She came awake fully, her breath wheezing, her heart pounding. Now she knew who held her; she knew his scent. A different scent from the one that haunted her dreams.

Relieved, she pushed against Nathan's chest. He released her, as if sensing her fears.

"Are you all right?"

His concern made her feel at once comfortable and ridiculous. She stared at the bed, trying to still her bounding heart.

"I'm sorry." She felt foolish and vulnerable, then remembered where she was. She whipped around. "Corey?"

Nathan's hand stilled hers. "He's been asleep in my bedroll for an hour."

The rain must have passed, for moonlight streamed into the room, carving his face in light. His eyes held pity, and she wondered what she'd exposed to him in her nightmare. She glanced away, ashamed and afraid at what it might have been.

He touched her arm. "Who are you afraid of, Susannah?"

She pulled free and looked toward the window. The trees moved against the moonlight, reaching upward like scrawny, bony fingers. Like Ma Walker's. She shivered.

"Everyone has bad dreams now and then." He stroked her arm gently. "By God, I know I do."

She took a shuddering breath and realized she was going to cry. Deep, ragged sobs clenched her chest and forced their way into her throat. Covering her face with her hands, she wept.

His arms came around her, and she went, hungering

for comfort, aching for someone to care. She leaned against him, her hands still covering her face, and continued to cry.

He stroked her hair, tentatively at first, then more boldly. "It's all right, Susannah. Cry."

His touch and the gruff purr of his voice soothed her. Not since she'd been a child had anyone comforted her so, and never a man. It was soothing . . . so different from anything she'd ever felt.

Pulling herself together, she stopped crying and drew away from the warmth of his chest. She felt odd, strangely skittish having him so close to her in the darkened room.

With his thumb, he wiped her cheek, the tender gesture causing Susannah's heart to ache with the poverty of need and she almost cried again. But she didn't. Instead, she took his hand in hers, anxious to touch it, feel its warmth and gentle strength. Anxious to know a man who didn't use his hand to punish, but to soothe.

Pressing her hand with his fingers, he brought it to his face; she touched the rough stubble of his beard. A moment, an ugly memory, encroached, and she tried to pull away, but he held her hand flat against his cheek until she no longer fought him. Her fingers, cold and clammy from her dream, warmed against his flesh. He began moving her hand slowly over his face.

"I'm just a man, Susannah, I'm not a monster. I would never hurt you." His breath caressed her fingers as he brought them to his lips.

She felt the tingle of his touch all the way to her elbow, but his words frightened her. She wanted to believe. But words, alone, weren't enough; they never had been.

He guided her fingers to the high, hard ledge of his cheekbone, then higher, to his forehead where she traced the scar, his thick eyelashes tickling her palm. "Who hurt you?" she asked, her voice soft.

"I got it during the war," he answered, continuing to hold her fingers.

He brought her palm to his mouth and planted a whispery kiss there, sending Susannah's heart into her throat and her pulse racing. Again, she tried to pull away, and again, he stayed her hand, pulling her toward him.

His face came close to hers and her breath caught in her throat. When his lips grazed her forehead, she gasped, unable to believe any man could be so gentle. As he planted slow, light kisses on her cheeks, she stiffened, but tried to fight it. She wanted to enjoy it. She wanted to, but . . .

His lips found hers. They pressed with an eager tenderness, and startled, Susannah pulled away. "No—"

The word came out a harsh whisper and she fought the nausea that squiggled into her throat. She was wild with fear until he released her, then she scrambled away from him.

With sad eyes, he studied her in the moonlight. "Who hurt *you*, Susannah? Who in the hell hurt *you?*"

She pressed shaky fingers to her lips, the fluttering memory of his touch still there, taunting her . . . haunting her. But she couldn't give him an answer. And even if she could tell him *who*, she'd never be able to admit the rest of it. "Please." Her voice was a ragged whisper. "Please. Just leave."

She waited until he was gone, then she curled into a ball, unable to control the panic. He was a kind man. A compassionate man. But if he ever found out what she'd done . . . what she'd been *forced* to do, he would change. He'd be as disgusted with her as she was with herself.

5

Susannah woke, disoriented. She reached out to touch Corey, then remembered what had happened the night before. She pressed her thumb and forefinger to her eyelids and allowed herself a brief moment of misery as she recalled the nightmares that had brought Nathan to her bed. The ones about Harlan she understood; the ones about Sonny she did not. Then again, she never tried to, for they were always vulgar and nauseating, and to examine them would undoubtedly make her as ill as in her dreams.

She felt a flush of anxiety as she slid from the bed and pulled on her wrapper. She was always so much more vulnerable at night, when it was dark. Her fears escalated, and new ones formed, preventing her from sleeping at all. All the ills of the world landed at her feet and nipped at her toes when she was sleepless in the dark.

She stepped into the main room, her gaze going to the door of her bedroom. It was still closed. Their guests were not yet up. Turning toward the fireplace, she saw Corey, tiny and sweet, still asleep in Nathan's bedroll.

A mixture of emotions swelled within her. To her surprise, the strongest wasn't envy. It was pain. Pain that one day soon, no doubt very soon, Nathan Wolfe would be gone, and Corey would again be without someone to look up to.

But for herself, she wanted him gone. Perhaps not for the same reasons as she'd had before, because she no longer thought of him as someone who'd come to spy on her. She'd decided if he'd been sent by the Walkers, he'd have done something about it by now. She was anxious for him to leave for other reasons altogether. She was beginning to like him, and that feeling was far more threatening. No one could know her secret, and the longer he stayed, the more tempting it was to unburden herself and share it with him.

She thought about her most recent nightmare, and Nathan's raspy, soothing voice and his affectionate touch as he'd awakened her. She would always remember that. Always. She would capture the memory and hold it against her heart forever.

But the other . . . His attempt to kiss her had been so tempting. She was curious to know what it would be like to be kissed that way. But memories were still too fresh . . . too awful. She rubbed her hand across her lips, as if doing so would dislodge the vile memory of Harlan's lips on hers, his tongue jutting into her mouth.

She looked toward the door just as Nathan came in from outside, carrying a pail of water. They stood without speaking, studying one another. A flood of emotions overwhelmed her; they were all pleasant, and she fought them.

Something deep inside her began to ache and she

clenched her fists to her chest, willing it away, willing herself to feel nothing. Years ago she'd learned it was safer by far to feel nothing at all. And now she was confused by her feelings, for over these last few days Nathan had prompted her to feel something other than disgust for herself. It should have made her feel good; it frightened her, instead.

He crossed to the stove and filled the coffeepot with fresh water.

Susannah hurried to him and tried to push him aside. "I can do that."

He held onto the pot. "So can I, Susannah."

Annoyed, she mumbled, "Just because they think we're married doesn't mean you have to continue the pretense when they aren't around."

He released the pot but didn't retreat.

Confusion tumbled over her. "I'm sorry. It's just that—"

"You don't have to apologize, Susannah. I understand."

He still stood beside her, his size and his warmth disquieting. She was suffocating with feelings of pleasure, and her eyes stung with tears of frustration. "Do you always have to be so damned understanding?"

He chuckled, a deep, warm sound that oozed over her like warm honey. "I can't seem to please you, can I?"

She wanted to apologize for her shrewish behavior. Instead she said, "I suppose I should thank you for saving my neck in front of the Hatfields last night."

"You can if you want to."

Puzzled, she turned. "Want to what?"

"Thank me."

His infamous half grin cracked his mouth, and his eyes were warm. Susannah felt herself thaw. She wondered, as crazy as it was, if she couldn't be half in love with him already. The way he treated Corey alone made her frightened for her feelings, and to have him look at her that way, like he had the night before . . . *Nonsense!*

"I still think they would have understood if you had explained that you're just doing a few chores for me. All that . . . that foolishness about the way we met—" She remembered the story, the easy way he pulled her into his tangle of sweet lies.

"I was trying to protect your reputation, Susannah."

She finished preparing the coffee, then turned on him. "My *reputation?* How will it look if that lie gets back to town? What in the world will those people think?"

Nathan shook his head and went to the window. "The Hatfields are going in the opposite direction. Everything will be the way it was once they're gone."

"But what if they . . . they run into someone on the road and tell them they've spent the night with us?"

Nathan went to the fireplace and stirred up the fire. "Then I guess everyone in town will think I'm your loving husband, finally, at long last, returned from the war," he answered, his voice edged with sarcasm.

She'd been slicing side pork, but slammed the knife down and glared at him. "That isn't funny. My . . . my husband could return any day now, then what? Would they declare me a bigamist and . . . and . . . and run me and Corey out of town?" She was furious with him, but she wasn't sure why. Of *course* he couldn't be her husband, and of *course* her real husband couldn't come looking for her, because, well, she'd killed him.

He glanced at her over his shoulder, arching an

eyebrow at her. "Get any more hysterical, and our guests will have something else to talk about."

She took a deep breath and turned back to the counter, pressing against it to still her quivering stomach. She searched for something else to say. "I hope Corey isn't the reason you're up so early."

"No, I'm an early riser. Like you are."

She tried to concentrate on what she was doing, but her hands shook. "Still, he . . . he can get pretty wiggly, and he was probably wet, too . . ." She could have bitten her tongue. How she hated reminding anyone that Corey was still in diapers! It made her feel like such a failure.

"I changed him before he crawled in with me."

Corey's diapers were in the bedroom where she'd slept. Heat flared into her cheeks. She wondered if he'd watched her, if that was the reason he'd heard her fighting her dreams.

"I . . . I'm sorry you had to do that." With deliberate care, she sliced some bread, working hard to cut each piece straight, for it was something she'd never been able to do.

"I didn't mind, but he's getting a little old for diapers, don't you think?"

She should have been angry and defensive, but she wasn't. She stopped slicing and piled the bread into a basket. "Yes," she answered, her voice barely audible. "I guess he is. But—"

"But, you want to keep him a baby for as long as possible, is that it?"

She whirled and stared at him. He had a smug expression on his face, as if he knew exactly what was on her mind. Well, he didn't. He couldn't. "No. That's *not* it. It's . . . it's just that . . ." Oh, Lord. How did she explain to the man that she wasn't equipped to stand up and teach her son how to pee? She felt heat stain her cheeks again, only this time it crept to the roots of her hair.

He pulled jam and butter from the cool cupboard in the corner and put them on the table. "I'd like to go fishing today."

The vivid picture of him watching her at the river's edge in her underwear heated her blood. "Who's stopping you?" she answered tartly.

He shrugged, still studying her. "I thought you'd want me to finish the porch and leave."

She coughed and cleared her throat, nervous sounds even to her own ears, and began putting together the ingredients for griddle cakes. She *was* anxious for him to leave, wasn't she?

"I guess I can't expect you to work all the time. After all, I'm . . . I'm not paying you."

"Good. Because today's the day. And I'd like to take Corey with me."

Alarmed, she stopped what she was doing, concentrating, instead, on the pounding of her heart. "Why?"

"Because," he said, searching her face, "it would be good for him to get away from you for a while. And good for you, too."

She wasn't sure if it was an insult or not. She bristled anyway. "What makes you say that?"

"Now, don't go getting your water hot," he answered. "Just take my word for it. It'll do you both a world of good."

"What makes you an expert?" She wanted him to expand on his background, tell her more about his son. His family.

He glanced away, refusing to meet her gaze. "Take my word for it," he said again, his voice soft, almost sad.

Something in his tone prevented her from pursuing the subject, although she was curious and tempted. She wanted to refuse his request to take Corey to the river with him. She wanted to believe she couldn't trust him with her precious child, and if she chewed on it long enough, she knew she'd reject the idea outright. She trusted no one with Corey but herself. She hadn't for a very long time. But was it fair? Hadn't Nathan proved to her that he could be trusted? *Maybe it's just an act.* Maybe. She was still torn between past memories and present realities. Ghosts and devils.

Suddenly Corey was awake, clamoring for his breakfast. When their guests came out of the bedroom, anxious to be on their way, Susannah shook off thoughts of Nathan and his cryptic answer. But as the morning slipped by, her brain still churned with questions.

The Hatfields left, and Nathan had Corey digging for worms, promising they'd catch a big fish for dinner.

Susannah's agony had been written all over her face. Nathan knew she wanted to refuse to let him take Corey fishing. He also thought her very brave to finally acquiesce.

But her surrender to let him take Corey fishing hadn't come easily. In the end, her apprehension had driven him to ask her to join them. She'd agreed, her enthusiasm evident as she promised to pack a lunch and join them at the river later.

"Corey? Time to go."

Corey stood, a wiggly earthworm between his fingers. "Worm!" He gave Nate a happy grin.

"Hey, that's a fat one," Nathan answered, taking

the worm and dropping it into the container with the others. "You ready to go?"

Corey nodded, wiped his dirty hands on his overalls, and grabbed two of Nate's fingers. Nate gave him the container with the worms in it, and picked up the two makeshift fishing poles he'd found in the shed.

The tiny fingers beneath his own sent a tightness into Nate's chest, a memory of other days . . . other streams . . . other picnics.

He forced it away, concentrating, instead on the moment he'd heard Susannah wrestling with her nightmares. He'd been in the room earlier, searching for a fresh diaper for Corey. He'd found Susannah asleep on her side, her covers pushed to the foot of the bed. No doubt that was what had awakened Corey, for the room was cold.

Susannah's nightgown had been up around her knees, her calves bare to his gaze. They were shapely and white, and she had dainty feet. But all this he'd known from the day before. Still, one look at a woman like Susannah was never enough. He'd stared openly at the lush swell of her hip and the ample breast that rested in the crook of her arm, and he'd again felt a stirring where one hadn't been for many, many years. And once she'd awakened, frightened and vulnerable, he'd been drawn to her further. For beneath the fear he saw a beautiful woman, all soft and warm and in need of comfort. And there was that fragrance, that sweet scent of woman that he'd missed for so long.

It wasn't that he hadn't had a woman since Judith died. He'd slept with women whose faces he couldn't remember, and whose names he'd never known. But even that had been a while ago. Not that he didn't miss the sex, it was just that he missed something else as well. Companionship. Closeness. Compassion. And passion. Ah, how he missed sweet, lusty passion.

Judith had always been eager, but not strong. Her sickly nature made it necessary for him to protect her. He'd even kept her safe from his strong, hungry needs, tamping them down, locking them away in a safe place in his mind.

Long before he'd gone off to war, he'd known they would never share passion. And he was a passionate man by nature, loving the intimacy one shared with a woman one loved. Judith might have been willing, but she'd never been able to give him a good, old-fashioned, sweaty roll in the hay. And he'd wanted it. He'd felt damned guilty that what they'd had together hadn't been enough.

He swore. It had been a hell of a long time since he'd felt the lusty bite of passion. Just the thought of it stirred the coals of his desire. Watching Susannah at the river, then asleep, had started him thinking this way. Ah, hell. It was before that. The first time he'd seen her trying to fend off Eli Clegg, he'd admired her abundant curves. He'd known that kind of woman before, not in the Biblical sense, but he could spot them. Often their enticing curves cloaked a rich, carnal nature. But something awful had happened to Susannah, and around him she was always wound up tighter than a pocket watch. He wondered if she'd ever in her life experienced good, lusty passion.

"The river!"

Corey's enthusiasm interrupted Nate's thoughts. "So it is," he answered, stopping at a boulder that sat near the water. He hunkered down and put a worm on each hook, then handed one of the poles to Corey. He took the other and they went to the riverbank and sat on an old log near the water.

Corey sat, whistling softly to himself, but when a fish took his bait, he got so excited he almost dropped the pole into the water. Nate brought him between his legs and helped him bring the fish in. It flipped back and forth on the end of the line, causing Corey to squeal with glee.

After the excitement of the first catch died down, they were quiet again. Nate felt Corey's eyes on him.

"What is it, boy?"

"Corey like sleeping by the fire." His voice was timid.

Nate hid a grin. Corey's *l*'s were *y*'s, like Jackson's, *like* coming out "yike." "So you like sleeping in my bedroll?"

Corey nodded. "Can Corey sleep there again?"

"Hmmmm. You'll have to ask your mama, Corey. I do have one rule, though. You want to know what it is?"

Corey gave him a sober nod.

"Nobody who wears diapers can use my bedroll." Out of the corner of his eye, he watched the boy's expression.

Corey looked down at his overalls, his face crestfallen. "Corey wears diapers."

"I see that," Nate answered. "But does Corey have to?" He could almost see the wheels churning in Corey's head.

All of a sudden, Corey gave him a determined glance and shook his head. "Corey no have to wear diapers."

Swallowing a smile, Nate ruffled Corey's hair. "Tell you what, Corey. Why don't we go over behind that bush. I'll show you what to do."

Nate could no longer hold in his smile as Corey hopped up from the log and tugged at his clothes. His bottom was already bare by the time they got to the bushes.

Susannah put the lunch basket on the ground and pressed her trembling fingers to her mouth. She'd almost called out to them when she heard Nathan talking to Corey about diapers and his bedroll.

As she'd listened to him, she marveled at the ease with which he did something that to her was so difficult. She remembered his comment about his own son and again wondered what had happened. How selfish she'd been, so wrapped up in her own past that she hadn't given a thought to his. She vowed to ask him about his son, but as she thought about it, she wondered if it was something too painful for him to talk about.

She bit her lip to keep from smiling as they rounded the bush. Nathan held Corey's diaper by the corner, and Corey swaggered along behind, no doubt feeling a new freedom in his overalls.

"Now," Nathan said, "it's all fine and good to do that in the bushes when it's an emergency, but—"

"'Mergency?" Corey interrupted.

"Yeah. When you can't make it back to the house or the 'necessary' in time. When we return, we'll give the ol' chamber pot a try."

"I go pee in the chamber pot!"

"That's the plan." Nathan rinsed the diaper in the river.

Susannah kicked at some twigs as she walked toward them, announcing her arrival. She had the handle of the lunch basket over her arm. Corey saw her first.

"Mama! Mama! I catched a fish and I learned to pee

standing up!" His cheeks were rosy and his eyes glistened.

Susannah had never seen him so exuberant. Tears stung her eyes, and she realized they were tears of joy. "All that?" she managed to say. "You've done all that since you got here?"

Nathan turned and gave her a careful look. He rung out the diaper and laid it on the boulder. "I hope you don't mind," he said.

Mind? How could she mind? "No. I . . . I don't mind, really." She felt herself blush. "If you must know the truth, I've been trying to think of a way to . . . to do that for months."

He gave her a sympathetic smile. "I kind of thought so."

She shifted her gaze from him and stared at the river. "Was it that obvious?"

"No, it wasn't that. I . . ." He sighed and slid his hands into the back pockets of his jeans, innocently drawing them tightly over his crotch.

Susannah's gaze dropped to the blatant bulge behind his fly. Instead of feeling the familiar sensation of revulsion, she felt a warmth burrow deep into her belly, then spread open like warm nectar bursting from a flower.

Clearing her throat, she looked away. "Yes? You were saying?"

He also cleared his throat and raked his fingers through his hair. "I remember how it is. I had a little boy once, and it was my job to train *him*, too."

"Corey hungry, Mama." Corey started rummaging through the lunch basket.

Susannah pulled out a chicken drumstick left over from the night before and handed it to him, grateful to have him quiet. She spread a blanket over the grass. "What . . . what happened to your son?"

Nathan sat and leaned against a tree. He was still for so long, Susannah was afraid he wasn't going to answer her.

"He died."

She gasped, her hand flying to her mouth. "Oh . . . oh, I'm so sorry . . ." A wealth of tears tightened in her throat. How on God's earth does one live with that kind of pain? She couldn't imagine . . . She didn't *want* to imagine . . .

"It happened while I was away, fighting the Confederacy. My wife and . . . and my son were out gathering berries. They were killed by marauding Indians."

Pain stung her eyes, and she knew it was tears. "Oh, Nathan. How awful." She studied him, searching for his agony. It was there, thinly veiled behind a blank stare. "How . . . how long has it been?"

He put a blade of grass between his teeth. "Five years."

She shook her head, unable to totally understand. "I . . . I can't imagine what . . . what you must feel . . ."

He appeared to study a spot in the distance. "They're up there, on the other side of the mountains."

Susannah followed his gaze. "They're buried up there?"

Nathan dove his fingers through his thick hair again, then rested against the tree. "Judith, my wife, is buried up north of here, near the Oregon border, outside a little town called Broken Jaw. I have land there. A ranch. It's where we lived." He let out a strangled sound, but when he spoke again, he was in control. "I didn't even get the chance to bury her myself. I wasn't there for her."

Susannah remembered the death of her mother—the last person to die that she loved. It was no longer painful, just a filmy distant memory. She thought about the Hatfields and the love they had for each other. The look on Nathan's face told her he'd felt that kind of love, too. "You . . . you loved her very much."

Again, he was quiet. Finally, he said, "Yes. She was a sweet, loving woman."

Sweet. Loving. Her chest hurt, and for some stupid reason she felt like crying. She knew why. He, like the Hatfields, had experienced something she would never know. Plainly, she was jealous.

"And your son?"

Again, Nathan was quiet for a long time. "My son, Jackson, was never found. They think . . . ." He took a harsh breath. "They think his body was dragged away by coyotes. There was . . . there was blood . . ."

Susannah cried out, his words stabbing her like knives. She could hardly speak, the horror of such a thing too much for her to bear. "Oh, N-Nathan," she said on a heavy, shaky sigh.

Her glance went to Corey, whose face and hands were smeared with chicken grease, and she felt a love that went so deep, her heart ached with each thundering beat. She would rather die a thousand painful deaths than see any harm come to her son.

She also had a new respect for Nathan.

"Mama, big man teached me to pee standing up," Corey chirped, unaware of the tension around him.

"Yes, dear, I heard." She tried to act calm as she wiped his hands and face, but talking about such intimacies with Nathan present made her blush, anyway. She spread out the picnic on the blanket.

Corey stood and squirmed, pressing his legs together. "Gotta pee again," he said, his little face pinched with discomfort.

Nathan was on his feet immediately. "I'm right behind you, whistler man."

She watched them disappear behind the bushes, feeling useless. She could hear Nathan's patient instructions, and felt a catch in her throat. In so many little ways she was truly grateful he'd come into their lives.

She pulled off a piece of chicken and picked at it, not really tasting it.

Corey rounded the bush, his little swagger intact. Susannah was so proud of him she wanted to squeeze him.

"Well," she said, filled with so much joy she was close to tears, "now you can finally wear your big boy underpants, sweetheart."

"Yeah." His eyes sparkled with pride. "An' you know what, Mama? You know what?"

His enthusiasm was catchy. "What," Susannah asked, unable to keep from grinning back at him.

"Big man have big thing and Corey have little one."

Heat flooded Susannah's face. "That's . . . that's . . ."

"Wanna see hims big one, Mama? Wanna see?"

Still blushing, Susannah threw a nervous glance at Nathan, who appeared to study the river with grave intensity.

"No! No, Corey. That's all right. Here, darling," she said, digging into the basket in the hopes of changing the subject, "have a cookie. Have two, sweetheart. Do you want some lemonade?"

She sneaked a peek at Nathan again. He gave her an embarrassed, lopsided smile. She tried to smile, but her lips were all wobbly.

"I'm afraid I've created a monster," he said around a smile.

Susannah didn't know what to say, so said nothing. She nervously popped pieces of a cookie into her mouth, then discovered, to her dismay, that her mouth was so dry she couldn't swallow them.

"He's made a big discovery, Susannah. You'll just have to get used to it."

Nervous perspiration prickled under her arms, on her forehead and at the back of her neck. She needed to change the subject. When she was able to swallow the wad of cookie crumbs in her mouth, she said, "He should really learn not to talk about such things in front of people."

"No, Susannah, don't make him feel it's a bad thing. It's natural for him to be intrigued with it for a while. If you punish him, or scold him when he talks about it, it will only make him that much more curious. Let it go. Ignore it. He'll get over it and find something else more interesting."

She tried to think about it as rationally as he had. She knew he could very well be right, but her past intruded, sending her different messages. She willed herself to stop thinking about the day she'd found Harlan bending over Corey. She wanted to do the right thing. And at this moment, Nathan's suggestion seemed right.

"Well," she said, intent on changing the subject, "isn't it about time for the two of you to catch some more fish?"

Nathan touched her hand. "Susannah? I want you to promise me something."

Her hand tingled beneath his. "If I can."

"If you should ever need to leave here for any reason—"

"What do you mean?" she interrupted, feeling herself tense.

"If you ever need me and I'm not here, come to Broken Jaw. I'll do everything I can to help you."

She pulled her hand away and turned toward the river. "Why . . . why would I need to get away?"

He didn't explain. "Just remember what I said, Susannah."

She would remember, but she wondered why he'd mentioned it in the first place.

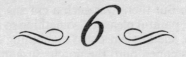

Corey was dry for the rest of the day. As night infringed upon them, Susannah's gaze was driven to Nathan's bedroll, which was rolled up and leaning against the wall by the fireplace.

And Nathan had fixed her sewing machine. He'd unscrewed the screw that kept the wheel in place and pulled out the delinquent piece of cloth. How simple it had been, and how easily he'd done it. She'd had to hide her feelings, for again, he was the first man to do something for her and not ask anything in return.

She'd just finished sewing a long seam in a pretty flowered print dress for one of Lillian's customers when she heard Nathan's voice outside, and Corey's answering laughter. Putting the dress aside, she went to the window and watched them come through the dimming light, Corey atop Nathan's shoulders, clinging to his hair.

A yearning settled near Susannah's heart—a greedy desire for something she had no right to wish for. But she couldn't help it. Nathan was the kind of father

Corey should have had. A bittersweet, pulsing joy swept through her as she watched them together. She'd never been in love, she wasn't even sure how it should feel. But there was such a craving inside her. Such sweet, painful pleasure, something so impossible to describe, she knew it could be nothing else.

As they stepped onto the porch, Susannah hurried from the window and busied herself with Corey's nightclothes.

The door opened, and Corey scrambled inside. "Mama! Mama! Big man make me a el'fant!"

Susannah looked at the smooth wood carving with the large ears, intricate tusks and skinny tail. "Why, Corey! What a wonderful toy. You be very careful with it, won't you?"

"Corey sleep with it."

Susannah found Nathan watching her, his eyes warm.

"When did you have time to make that?" She knew her own eyes spilled with gratitude.

He shrugged. "At night, when I couldn't sleep."

Reality hammered at her silly thoughts of being in love. She remembered that he had sleepless nights, too. His dreams were different. Sweeter, no doubt. Dreams of his wife and child. Not nightmares about bloody scissors and dead eyes . . .

With effort, she shrugged off her mood. "It's time for bed, Corey." He insisted on undressing himself and even went into her bedroom to use the convenience pail. Susannah decided it would be wise to put it in his room.

He went to Nathan, who sat at the table, and crawled into his lap. "Can Corey sleep in big man's sleeping roll?"

Susannah gasped. "Corey!"

Nathan ruffled Corey's hair. "Tell you what, little

108

whistler man, you stay dry for three nights," he said, holding up three fingers, "and we'll talk about it again."

Corey touched Nathan's big fingers. "I can count to three," he said, the *three* sounding like "free." He got to his knees and gave Nathan Wolfe a kiss on the cheek.

Susannah had to turn away. Corey's reaction to Nathan, especially the kiss, made her wish for things she knew wouldn't come true. Fairy-tale endings. They hurt. Oh, they hurt, these silly little daydreams she painted in her head. But it wasn't Nathan's fault. She knew that both she and Corey were starved for affection. She also knew that it wasn't Nathan Wolfe's responsibility to do anything about it.

"Come along, Corey," she said, hiding her emotion, "Mama will tell you a story."

After Corey was tucked into bed, she returned and found Nathan still sitting at the table, nursing a cup of coffee. Again, she felt the longing, the quest for something she'd never had.

He stood, drawing in a long sigh. "Well, I guess I should head for town."

An urgent panic hit her. "You . . . you're leaving?"

His expression was hooded. "You want me to stay?"

She toyed with the buttons at her neck, slipping them in and out of the holes. "I . . . it seems so foolish for you to ride all the way into town, then have to . . . to come back out here in the morning anyway to work on the porch."

They stared at one another. Susannah felt her heart pound against her ribs and her face flush with heat.

"I guess I could sleep outside, or in the shed."

Her hands twitched, and she wrung them together to still them. "That's . . . that's really not necessary." She held her breath.

"You want me to sleep in the house?" His question was cautious.

She motioned to the fireplace. "Where you slept last night is fine. Unless—" Oh, dear lord. "Unless you already have a room in town with a bed. I mean, the floor is so hard—"

"The floor is fine, Susannah. I'm used to it. Hell, I haven't slept in a bed for so long, I don't—" He cleared his throat and turned to prepare the fire for the night. "The floor is fine."

Susannah went into her room, closed the door and leaned against it, her body humming. She looked at her bed, wondering what it would be like to find him there, waiting for her. Her knees nearly buckled, and she dropped into the rocking chair near the window and started unbuttoning her dress.

She continued to stare at the bed, imagining Nathan Wolfe in it, the quilt folded down to his waist, his chest bare and warm. . . .

She shuddered and tried to shake away the delicious tremors in her stomach, but she discovered that she liked the feelings. Still, her imagination couldn't go any further. She wasn't sure if she was unwilling or unable to see beyond the image of him in her bed.

She stood and slipped out of her dress and her petticoat, then went to the mirror and studied her reflection.

Shocked, she found her eyes bright and her cheeks pink. She brought her fingers to her face and traced her skin. It was clear. No bruises. As she pulled the pins from her hair, she wondered what Nathan saw when he looked at her. She wasn't pretty. Ma Walker had always told her the least she could do when she worked outside in the garden was to wear a bonnet to protect her hair and her face from the sun. But she never had. Therefore, during the summer her hair often had a reddish cast to it, and she always had unattractive freckles across her nose.

She dragged her fingers through her hair, examining the color as it fell over her shoulders. It wasn't a color that would attract a man. And her eyes . . . She made a face at herself. All the really pretty women in the world had blue eyes. Yes, blue eyes and blond hair. Her eyes were too big. And too brown. And her lashes were so dark, they reminded her of a cartoon drawing of a cow she'd seen in a newspaper ad for fresh milk. *Drink milk from Daisy, the cow with the healthy udders.*

Screwing up her nose, she gazed at her chest. She'd felt like Daisy when she'd been pregnant with Corey. She unhooked her camisole and realized that even when she wasn't pregnant, she had unfashionably large breasts. She was no dainty, blue-eyed blond, that was for certain.

She glanced in the mirror again and felt a bubble of laughter, or maybe hysteria, in her throat. She didn't recognize herself. For so long, she'd felt ugly. *Been* ugly, all battered and sore. She touched her jaw, then her neck, tracing her collarbones, stopping at that hollow that pulsed beneath her skin. Her wrist touched her breast, making it tingle, and she gasped, shocked at how sensitive her nipple was.

Shivering, she hurried out of her underwear, again gasping with shocked pleasure as her drawers slightly grazed the place between her thighs. She pulled on her nightgown, turned down her lamp and crawled into bed, her eyes riveted on the door.

The next forenoon, Susannah stood on the porch, fanning herself with an old folded up newspaper as she watched Nathan work, bare to the waist, in the sun. Sweat streamed over him, and his shoulders were turning a dark shade of pink.

Her idle gaze lingered. She never tired of gazing at him.

"Gettin' pretty hot out here." He stopped working and wiped his forehead with a bandana he'd pulled from his back pocket.

She acted casual. "Up here, the October sun can be as dangerous as the sun in August." With the newspaper, she gestured toward his shoulders. "You're burning."

Shaking his head, he picked up the saw he'd been using and leaned it against the tree. "I never burn."

"Hmmmm," she answered. "Well, then that must be pink paint on your shoulders."

He chuckled, a sound she'd come to love. "Don't worry about it."

She pushed herself away from the sturdy new porch pillar, descended the new steps and walked toward him. "Whatever you say. Just don't come crying to me tonight when your shoulders are so tender you can't sleep."

He stood, feet apart and fists on hips, examining her approach, a tiny smile on his lips. "Can't I?"

Her heart did a little dipping dance before settling back in her chest. There it was again, that teasing. She felt herself blush, still unable to respond to it.

"Corey, um . . . I thought that maybe when Corey wakes up from his nap, we could take our lunch and eat it by the river. It's . . . it's cooler down there."

He wiped his dripping hair with the bandana, drawing Susannah's gaze to the thatch of dark hair under his arm. A little jolt of electricity rocked her, and she looked away.

"Sounds perfect," he answered. "I'll be done here by the time you're ready."

She hurried into the cabin and put together a picnic lunch. Corey woke, still dry. Susannah hugged him hard, then scooted him toward the convenience pail.

They meandered through the brush toward the river, Max loping on ahead and Corey sitting on Nathan's shoulders, his little tin pail gripped in his pudgy fist.

The minute Corey saw the shallow, swirling water near the warm spring, he started to undress, pulling his overall straps down and tugging at his shirt before Nathan even put him on the ground. And Susannah hadn't even had the blanket on the grass before he was naked and scurrying toward the water.

Susannah felt stiff and self-conscious, but Nathan appeared comfortable and at ease, lolling against an oak tree, chewing on a blade of grass. Forcing herself to relax, she leaned back on her elbows and closed her eyes, drawing in deep, purposeful breaths to try to erase images of Nathan from her mind. As usual, it didn't work.

And it wasn't any cooler by the water than it had been at the cabin. She felt sticky. Still, it was nice to just relax on the blanket with her eyes closed—
"Wha—!"

She sputtered and gasped as water hit her face, splashing over her neck and into her hair. She sat up, blinking and shaking her head. Corey stood in front of her, the empty tin pail dangling from his fingers.

"Corey cool Mama off." His expression was open, as if he were waiting for her response.

Susannah noted the wide, wet circle on her bodice, then sneaked a glance at Nathan, who appeared to smother a grin.

"You convinced him to do this," she scolded, not truly angry at all.

He radiated innocence, but his eyes shimmered. "Me? How could I have done it? I didn't say a word. Did you hear me say anything, whistler man?"

Corey giggled and squirmed, clapping his hands at his mother's animated reaction.

Blowing on a wet strand of hair, Susannah saw Nathan's grin before he coughed and covered his mouth. "You don't sound very innocent."

He gave her an expansive shrug and studied the bushes on the banks upstream.

She caught Corey's gaze, pressed a finger to her lips and took the pail from him as he splashed back into the water. With an air of nonchalance, she wandered to the water's edge, bent and scooped water into the pail. Holding it behind her, she gave Nathan a sweet smile as he turned his glance to her again.

He stepped back, suspicious. "Isn't it about time for lunch?"

"Not *yet,"* she said, tossing the water into his face.

"Why, you little—" He chuckled and reached for her, but Susannah scampered away, shrieking with laughter until he caught up with her.

He hoisted her into his arms and strode straight to the river.

"Oh, no, no, no," she said, squirming in his arms. "Not in the water, *please,* don't throw me into the water!"

"It's what you deserve, you devious little witch." He waded in until the water was at his knees. "You're at my mercy, now."

Another bubble of laughter escaped, then she looked up at him and grew very still. His green eyes, his crooked nose, his scarred forehead, which she'd wanted to touch again as she had that night he'd put her fingers there to trace it . . . his lopsided smile, all there so close. He smelled good, too. Not the rancid, choking smell she'd come to equate with a man. And she was in his arms. *In his arms.* The tingling she'd felt in her breasts the night before returned as the air cooled over her wet bodice.

She broke her own fanciful mood by turning her gaze away to stare at the water.

"You wouldn't throw me in, would you? I mean, I have shoes on and everything. You wouldn't want to ruin my shoes."

"No, I wouldn't ruin your shoes," he said, holding her easily in one arm.

She breathed a sigh, then felt his hand at her foot, sliding off her slippers. "Oh, no," she pleaded, biting back a smile. "That would be cruel."

His eyes were warm. "I guess it would, wouldn't it?"

Relieved, she laughed softly. "Yes, it would. I don't—"

He dropped her. The water oozed through her clothes, splashing into her face. She fell backward, her head disappearing under the water. She came up sputtering . . . to the sound of Corey's and Nathan's laughter. Max galloped in and pranced around her, yelping playfully.

Sitting in water to her waist, she pushed her hair off her face and out of her eyes. Once she could see again, she realized he was still standing over her. His eyes were warm and he had a wide, self-satisfied smile on his face.

She'd never seen this side of any man. Until Nathan, she'd never known that men actually teased and flirted and romped like children. She loved it. She was afraid she was starting to love him. "Think you're pretty funny, don't you?"

"Just trying to cool you off, Susannah." He started

for the shore, and Susannah lunged for him, grabbing his leg. He lost his balance and tumbled into the water, face first.

She laughed. Rich, healthy sounds that erupted from somewhere deep in her soul. It felt *wonderful.* Still laughing, she waited for him to get up and come after her again. Her laughter faded as she realized he hadn't moved. He lay there, floating facedown in the water.

Oh, God! What if he'd hit his head on a rock? She glanced at Corey, who was busy with a pile of stones and his tin pail, then she waded to Nate and tried to turn him over. He was deadweight.

Feeling a horrible sense of panic, she knelt beside him and pulled his head out of the water. "Nathan?" She struggled to get him up, hoisting him under the arms. "Nathan! Don't you dare drown. Do you hear me?" She put her hands on either side of his head and shook him, frantic for some response.

He shot out of the water, bellowing like a wounded bear.

Stunned and surprised, Susannah let out a sharp cry, relief flooding her—until she realized he was laughing.

She kicked at him, aiming for any part she could reach. "You wretch! You had me scared to death, damn you!"

He flopped into the water, laughing so hard she thought he might choke. And she wouldn't have cared if he had. She felt her lips twitch. Oh, yes she would. His laughter was contagious. Hers was quiet at first, just a shaking in her chest, then she felt the exuberance again, that deep-down hearty, healthy sound that felt so free. So good. So cleansing.

Corey had waded over to join them, gaily splashing them both and squealing with glee. And Max galloped and barked and dove, playfully attacking Nathan, who wrestled with him in the water.

"Susannah Quinn!"

Pushing her hair from her eyes again, Susannah tried to catch her breath.

"You there! Susannah Quinn!"

With Corey and Nathan and Max still rollicking in the water, Susannah froze and stared at the shore. "Oh, Lord," she whispered, her heart dropping to her knees.

She rose, her dress and petticoat so heavy with water she could barely stand. But that was the least of her problems. There, appearing proper and reproachful, stood her boss, Lillian Graves, the wife of the grocer, Edith Barnes, and Althea White, the minister's wife, who always looked like she was sucking on an unripened persimmon.

Today, Susannah was certain the sour fruit had exploded in her mouth.

"May heaven help me." With as much poise as possible, she picked up her water-laden skirts and slogged toward the shore.

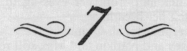

Althea White stared at her, her lips pinched and her eyes glistening. Her condemning gaze raked over Susannah's appearance and she arched a pale eyebrow at her. "We're *very* disappointed in you, Susannah."

Old feelings of disapproval spread through her like nausea. How would she ever explain this? "I'm sorry, we . . . I mean . . . we were just . . . it was so warm—"

"Why didn't you tell us?" Edith interrupted, her face flushed beneath her bonnet.

Susannah dragged herself to dry ground, then attempted to squeeze the water from her skirt. *Tell you what? That I have a stranger sleeping under my roof, with my three-year-old son as a chaperone?* "Tell you?"

"Dear," Lillian said, "we can understand that you might want to spend some time alone. After all, it's been three years or so since you've seen him. And to think all this time you were sick to death, thinking he was dead. My dear," she said, touching Susannah's wet sleeve, "we're so happy for you! Everyone is sighing with relief to know your husband has returned."

Susannah's jaw dropped. Her wet skirt slipped from her fingers, the heavy, wet fabric hitting the ground with a splat, pulling her dress against her shoulders.

"My—" She turned and stared at Nathan, who had just plunged Corey into the water, then lifted him into the air, sending the boy's peals of laughter ringing through the trees. She gazed downstream, and noticed that her slippers were bobbing and weaving in the current, destination unknown.

"Yoohoo! Mr. Quinn!" Edith chirped, smiling and waving.

Susannah watched as Nathan brought Corey to his shoulders and waded toward shore. "Beg pardon, ma'am?" He turned to Susannah, as if waiting for an introduction.

Susannah swallowed a groan, then introduced him —by first name only—to the three women.

Edith's smile was so wide her eyes were almost shut. "Well, Mr. Quinn, we are just *so* happy you've come home. Aren't we?" She nudged Lillian, who smiled weakly in his direction. Althea White still appeared to be sucking on sour fruit.

Susannah discovered Nathan could be very charming when he wanted to be. And she guessed he now wanted to be, for the three women gazed up at him as if he'd hung out the moon, just for them.

Nathan continued to chat with the women as he put Corey on the grass. Susannah looked on, still too stunned to speak. He reached for Corey's clothes, then whispered something into his ear.

Corey shook his head. "Corey went pee in the river."

Susannah rolled her eyes heavenward but still couldn't find her voice. What would she have said, anyway?

While Nathan dressed Corey, he chatted with the ladies as if they were all sitting in someone's parlor, drinking coffee and nibbling cookies.

"We're about to have a picnic lunch, ladies," Nathan said, "would you care to join us?"

Edith tittered. "Oh, my no. We don't want to intrude, do we, ladies?" Without waiting for an answer, she went on. "We were so worried about Susannah, living way out here, all by herself with just that mongrel dog to watch over her. As you know, Mr. Quinn," she said with a little wink, "Susannah is a mite stubborn."

Nathan was attempting to wring out his own clothes as his gaze caught Susannah's. She clearly saw mirth in his eyes. "Oh, don't I know it."

Susannah had difficulty standing, for her wet skirt hung around her like a wet sack of flour. But that hardly mattered. She couldn't believe what was happening, or *how* it had happened.

"Edith," she ventured. "How did you . . . I mean, who told you about . . . about Nathan?"

Edith pressed her gloved hands over her black and pink cotton dress, as if ironing out a wrinkle. "Why, it was my Ed who told me. He'd been in Oakville to pick up some things for the store, and had run into a man named—" She turned to Althea and Lillian. "What was his name, again?"

Lillian, who had been very quiet, answered, "Hatberg? No, Hatfield."

Althea nodded briskly. "Hatfield. Alvin and Lettie Hatfield. Her sister died a week ago Sunday. My Homer officiated at the service."

"Oh, yes," Edith went on. "That man, Hatfield, told

Ed how you and your husband had taken them in and let them spend the night." She leaned close. "Ed told me how sickly the woman was."

Susannah felt immediate concern. "Was she worse? I mean, had he stopped to take her to the doctor or something?"

"Oh," Edith said, trying to remember. "I don't think so." She shook her finger at Susannah, giving her a mock scolding. "And we had to learn about your husband's return from a total stranger."

"I'm sure she would have told us sooner or later, Edith," Lillian said. "They really need some time alone, don't you think?"

The words "time alone" sent Susannah's heart dancing in her chest again.

"Oh, I know that. But as part of the community, I wanted to welcome Mr. Quinn." Susannah started to correct her, but Edith forged on. She was grateful Nathan hadn't introduced himself. There would be no explanation for each of them having a different last name.

Edith droned on. "There'll be an apple-paring party at the Stedersons' ranch one week from Friday night. Heavens, Lillian, that's ten days away. That's enough time for them to be alone."

To Susannah, she said, "Everyone's agreed that it's the perfect time to celebrate your husband's return. We expect to see you there."

A buggy rattled over the road above the river. "Woohoo! Kito, we're down here!" Edith's voice rang loudly.

As the women hiked to the road, Lillian shot Susannah an apologetic look. Susannah smiled back, not at all sure just how she was supposed to respond. In truth, she felt as though someone had just hammered another nail in her coffin.

Picking at her wet skirt, she listened to Corey announce that he was hungry.

"But we're all wet, darling. Let's go to the cabin and change. Lunch will taste better if we're dry."

"No! Corey not wet. Corey hungry."

Susannah slumped to the blanket. Opening the lunch basket, she took out a biscuit and a piece of cheese, handing them both to her son.

Nathan sat in the sun, his shirt already beginning to dry. Susannah tried to avoid his gaze, but she couldn't. She knew, with certainty, they were both thinking the same thing.

"Now what do we do?" she asked, trying to cloak her panic. "You were the one who was so sure the Hatfields wouldn't run into anyone from Angel's Valley."

Nathan crunched on an apple.

Angry that he didn't respond, she admonished, "This is all your fault, you know."

He appeared surprised. *"My* fault?"

"Of course it's your fault. You should have put Alvin Hatfield straight right off. Instead you . . . you spun those dumb, silly stories about how we met." She flushed, angry that she still kept that memory so close to her heart.

"And what prevented you from explaining the truth?"

His voice was quiet; it unnerved her. "I tried to explain a couple of times. Something always interrupted me."

"But you could have, Susannah."

"No! No. I didn't know what to say. How to say it. I'm . . . I'm not that strong," she admitted.

He leaned over and grabbed her wrist. "Yes, you are. Damn it, Susannah, don't sell yourself short.

Look at what you've done! You're raising a child alone and doing a fine job. You're—" He stopped, breaking eye contact.

She thirsted for more. "I'm . . . I'm . . . what?"

His eyes were cautious when they returned to her face. "You're a lot stronger than you think you are."

She lifted her face skyward and closed her eyes. "We're tiptoeing around the problem, Nathan. How do we get out of going to the party?"

"We don't."

She blinked and stared at him. "We don't? What do you suggest we do, go and pretend we're married?"

He tossed the apple core at Max, who caught it and devoured it. "Would that be so bad?"

She sagged against the picnic basket. "One little fib. That one little fib is going to get us into more trouble." She sat up again. "We can't do that, Nathan. Sooner or later the truth will come out."

"When?"

She drew her feet under her, cringing as they settled against her wet underclothes. With nervous fingers, she removed the pins from her hair and threaded her fingers through the wet mass.

"When?" he demanded again. "When your *real* husband comes home, Susannah?"

She felt weak, sick. He deserved to know part of her secret. But only part. "I . . . my husband is dead." He took her hand, but she pulled it away.

"Tell me about it, Susannah."

She shrugged and tried to laugh. The sound was nervous. Forced. "That's all there is to tell. He died about six months ago. I . . . I needed to find some place that didn't keep reminding me of what we had. Our life together." It was the truth, although she hoped Nathan had taken it to mean she'd needed to get away because she'd missed Harlan so much, not because she'd had to—Oh, God, how she hated thinking about what she'd done!

"Then, why the lie, Susannah?"

She hugged her knees to her chest with one arm, pressing them hard against her fluttering heart, then with her free hand continued combing her hair with her fingers to dry it. "I didn't want people to bother me."

"People?"

She shrugged again, but this time she gave him a guilty smile. "Men, actually. If they thought I was waiting for my husband to return, they would leave me alone."

"Because you wouldn't be available." He waited a beat. "Not like a widow."

Relief spread through her. She'd convinced him. "Exactly." She glanced at Corey; he was asleep.

"What do you want to do about the dance, Susannah?"

She raised her face skyward again, her damp, heavy hair drawing her head back. She studied the sunshine as it spattered through the leaves. "I don't know."

"I could leave, be called away on some kind of emergency," he suggested.

The thought of him leaving left her with a heart full of sadness and fear. She shook her head, knowing that she never wanted him to leave her at all. "That would only save us from the dance. They'd still think you were—" She gasped and covered her mouth.

"What is it?"

She stared at him, her eyes wide. "There are two people in Angel's Valley who know you aren't my husband."

Nathan narrowed his gaze. "Clegg?"

She nodded. "And . . . and Kito, the blacksmith."

"I didn't say anything to him. Just that I was passing through. That shouldn't—"

"But I did. That day you pulled Eli off me, Kito took Corey and me home. I asked him if you'd told him who you were, or why you were in town." She shook her head, feeling dismal. "He knows, Nathan."

Nathan touched her hair, continuing to comb through it after she'd stopped. She jumped but didn't pull away. "So, what have we got, then? The word of a drunk and a Negro?"

She bristled. "Kito is a fine man."

"I'm not saying he isn't, Susannah. But his word probably wouldn't carry any more weight than Clegg's."

She realized that what he said was true. "I don't think Kito would say anything, anyway. He's my friend."

"And no one listens to Clegg, am I right?"

She nodded, then sighed, worry still pressing on her heart.

"'Ah, what tangled webs we weave.'"

His voice was like a seduction. "What's that from?"

"Shakespeare," he said around an embarrassed smile. "The rest of it is something like, 'when first we practice to deceive.'"

She realized how little she really knew about him. My, he read *Shakespeare*. She'd heard of him, of course, but she'd never had the opportunity to see anything but small, traveling circuses, and then only when she could sneak away without Ma Walker discovering she was gone. And once Ma Walker died, well . . . Harlan never took her anywhere, and he rarely let her out of his sight. But she'd worked hard at learning to read. Louisa, dear soul that she was, had learned from her former master when she'd been just a girl and a slave, and had taught Susannah everything she knew. But Susannah's skills didn't include anything so complicated as Shakespeare. "I've never read Shakespeare." She felt stupid. Inferior.

"Ah, don't worry about it. He's not always readable."

His hand continued to stroke her hair, and she tried hard not to give in to the pleasant sensation. "In our case, he was right, though, wasn't he? Tangled webs of deception." She said it again, letting it roll around on her tongue. "It's very fitting."

His thumb caressed her cheek, causing her heart to beat faster.

"Susannah," he said, his voice almost a whisper. "I'm going to kiss you."

She closed her eyes and stiffened, but didn't pull away. She wanted his kiss. She wanted to see how it would feel, to see if she could really stand to have him invade her mouth that way.

"Hey."

She blinked.

A smile cracked his mouth. "Don't think about it so hard. It's not supposed to be a chore. It's supposed to be a pleasure."

She relaxed a little and tried to smile. Gently, as if he expected her to sprint away, he nipped at her lips with his. Oh, she liked how he felt, all warm and nice. And he smelled clean. She could feel his stubble; it didn't bother her. She even liked the prickly sensation as he moved his mouth to the corner of hers, dragging the stubble across her lips.

Warmth dug a path inside her, shoveling away her fears. She touched his cheek, nudging his mouth back to hers, opening her lips, responding to his pressure.

The warmth expanded within her, rich with a sweet nectar that caused her to gasp with pleasure.

He kissed her harder, slanting his mouth over hers. His hand left her face and trailed to her neck, then grazed her breast. The tightness gathered in her nipple again as it had the night before, and she touched his shoulder, unable to keep the tiny sound of pleasure from creeping into her throat.

He pressed his tongue against her lips, gripping her arm as he did so.

Suffocation fell upon her like a blanket. She felt the ground spinning, and she pulled her face away from his, whimpering her fear.

He released his hold and rested his head against her shoulder, breathing hard. "I'm sorry, Susannah. I didn't mean to frighten you."

She rubbed her arms, feeling cold, and angry with herself for allowing Harlan Walker's disgusting treatment of her to intrude on what she now could have.

"No." She stood and picked up the picnic basket. "It's my fault, not yours." She had to get away from him before he saw something in her eyes she didn't want him to see.

Nathan watched her scurry away. *Ah, Susannah.* He'd just begun to untangle her own web of lies. Walker had beat her, he was sure of it now. He shouldn't have grabbed her arms, but it had been a reflex. Hell, he hadn't even been thinking about the Walker boys, only Susannah, and how much he'd wanted to kiss her. And she kissed like a woman who'd never been kissed before, at least not with any tenderness.

Thoughts of her life prior to her running filled Nathan with so much anger, he tried to force them away. But the picture of Susannah being hit set fire to his gut. Until she was willing to talk about what she'd done, he had no way of knowing what had happened to Harlan Walker. Whatever it was, Nathan was beginning to believe the bastard deserved it.

But who was he to pass judgment? He was the hunter and she was his prey. He couldn't follow through. He couldn't drag her back to Sonny Walker. Hell and damnation, he couldn't do it.

Corey turned on his side and sucked noisily on his thumb. Nathan feathered the boy's fine, golden hair off his forehead, recalling the change that had come over Corey since he'd arrived. Maybe he'd been good for the boy. He knew the boy had been good for him. The pain of Jackson's death was still there, but, as he'd hoped, the sharp edges were gone. The dull ache would never go away. That was all right, too.

He glanced at the river, seeing Susannah's look of shocked surprise when he'd dropped her. And her laugh . . . robust. Full-bodied. Full of life. Like her. He wouldn't have dared play that way with Judith.

Ah, Susannah, he thought again. What a work of art she was. Not a sixteenth century nude Caravaggio or Rubens, where the women were overly plump and dimpled, but a sleek, smooth marble statue, whose insides were smoldering with untapped desire. And healthy enough for a good old-fashioned roll in the hay. For some reason, he couldn't get that image out of his head.

He swore. Who was he kidding? If she ever discovered who he was, she'd use him for fish bait. He wondered when it would happen. How it would happen. He only knew for sure that it would, eventually, happen. The constant feeling of dread in the pit of his stomach intensified.

* * *

Nathan rapped on her bedroom door. "Susannah?"

She'd just pulled on her nightgown and was uncoiling her hair. She stepped to the door, opening it slightly.

He appeared contrite. And outrageously handsome. His chest was bare. "My shoulders are sore."

To hide the pleasure of seeing him stripped to the waist, she chided, "I won't say 'I told you so.'"

He winced as he flexed his back. "You already have."

She pulled the door open and scooted past him, aware of the warmth that radiated from his body. "Sit at the table. I'll get the salve."

She took the ointment from the cupboard and went behind him, swallowing hard as she examined his back and shoulders. Admitting to herself that she wanted to touch him, she took the lid off the salve, dipped two fingers in and spread it over one burned shoulder.

"Ouch!"

"See? I told you the sun was hotter up here," she scolded as she gentled her motions. She was sorry he was uncomfortable, but not at all sorry that she was given the chance to touch him.

She wanted the chore to last. "Have you always been a rancher?" She hit a particularly pink spot, and heard his sharp intake of breath. "Sorry," she said, and truly was.

"For the last two years I've been digging posts for the railroad."

"Hmmm." That kind of work explained the sharply delineated muscles in his back and shoulders. She was tempted to grip her fingers around his upper arm and squeeze.

Her desire for him darted through her. She also wanted to press herself against his back, wrap her arms around his waist and run her fingers through the hair on his chest. Her desire thickened, and she felt weak.

"Are you done?"

She jumped at the interruption into her thoughts. "Almost," she said, moving to his other shoulder. She'd left her room in haste, forgetting her wrapper. Now, her breasts were loose beneath her nightgown, and her nipples tingled. Each movement of her arm dragged the soft cloth over them, further intensifying her longing.

She moved away and took a dizzying breath. "There. We're done."

He turned his gaze on her, his eyelids heavy, his nostrils flaring slightly. "I think we've just begun."

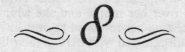

8

Susannah's heart trembled in her breast and heat sizzled through her.

Nathan took her hand, drew her around in front of him and pulled her onto his lap.

She fought for breath, and what breath she had came out jerky and she felt winded. With tentative fingers, she touched his chest. The hair, crinkly and curly, caressed her palms. She sucked in a breath and swallowed a moan of pleasure. His skin was warm and firm.

Swallowing hard, she pushed her fingers through the hair, her movements becoming greedy. She loved the feel of it against her palms. She dragged her gaze to his face and saw the desire in his eyes, the storm brewing there no longer cold, but hot as an August wind.

He touched her waist, drawing her close until she rested against him. He groaned, moving her breasts back and forth across his chest before he reached up to touch one through her nightgown.

Susannah stiffened, and he stopped, misreading her

reaction. She touched his hand, pressing it against her breast. He caressed it through the soft fabric, examining its shape, weighing it in his hand. Then he dragged his thumb over her nipple and she whimpered with pleasure, resting her forehead against his.

His breath mingled with hers as their lips touched, clung. His tongue brushed her mouth and she opened for him. New pleasures careened through her, lighting here, then there, finally coming to land in a mysterious place deep in her pelvis, a place, that although inside her own body, was unknown to her until this moment.

She rested her arms on either side of his neck, careful not to touch his sore shoulders. He fondled her breasts, electrifying her, making her ache and feel swollen in places that had only been numb before. A frantic sense of hunger tumbled through and she collapsed against him.

He stroked her hair, combing his fingers through it as he brought it to his face. "Ah, Susannah, Susannah," he whispered. "Your beauty takes my breath away."

Her heart pounded and heat rushed over her as she pulled him to her, feeling his hot expulsion of air as it penetrated her gown and engulfed her skin. She was heady with desire, as if she'd just had a sip of wine on an empty stomach.

She moved on his lap, feeling him thick and hard beneath her, and she pulled away, her need for him dwindling as quickly as it came. She stood and stared at him, then glanced at his crotch.

His size shocked her. Frightened her. She brought her hands to her cheeks; they were still warm. "I'm sorry," she whispered, "I'm sorry. So sorry. I wanted to . . . I . . . I thought I could—" She stumbled to her room and shut the door. As she crawled into bed, she shook with fear, waiting for him to come after her and force her. Then she knew he wouldn't. He wasn't Harlan. He was Nathan. Sweet, gentle Nathan.

But she'd disappointed him and hadn't meant to. She had truly wanted him. But the act itself still scared her. Just the thought of it had cooled her down faster than a tumble in a snowbank.

The more she thought about it, the more she realized Harlan hadn't deserved the pleasure of dying. She'd conveniently ended his misery, but hers would go on and on. In the deep, dark recesses of her heart, she wished his punishment could have been painfully drawn out over the next one hundred years, and she would have insisted on ruling the sentence herself.

Dismounting in front of the smithy that was adjacent to the livery, Nate listened as one of the local ranchers berated Kito.

"I told you I wanted it done yesterday, damnit," the rancher growled. "You damned free niggers ain't worth hog piss. I'll have your job for this."

Kito trembled, a nervous grin on his lips. "Yessuh, I'm sorry, suh, I'll have it done 'afore you leave town, suh."

The rancher stormed from the livery, pushing past Nate without acknowledging him. Nate caught the hate in Kito's gaze as it followed the rancher out the door. "'Morning, Kito."

Kito stood silent for a moment, then, with a limping shuffle, went to the forge, pulled out a strip of hot iron and rested it over the anvil. With a huge ball peen hammer, he began to shape the metal, the muscles in his arms and shoulders gleaming with sweat.

"Y-yessuh," he said with a stutter, "it's a fine morning."

Nate raised an eyebrow. The "down guilty" look

didn't sit well on someone Kito's size. Somehow Nate felt there was a different man lurking there, beneath the servility. Needing an ally, he wanted it to be Kito, and not Eli Clegg.

"Are you available to haul some lumber for me today?"

"Yessuh," he said, his lips quivering around his strong, white teeth. "Jus' let me know when you're ready, suh."

As Nate pulled Susannah's package from his saddlebag, he said, "You've heard the talk about Susannah and me?" He turned and caught Kito's masked look.

Kito bobbed his head. "Yessuh, I heard."

Nate took a deep breath. As he expelled it, he prayed he was doing the right thing. "It's not true, you know."

Kito kept his eyes downcast. "Nosuh."

Nate swore. "Cut all the bowing and scraping, and talk to me like a man. That damned Sambo impersonation doesn't work on me."

With a pair of tongs, Kito removed the steel to a bucket. The water inside bubbled and hissed as it cooled the metal. He still avoided Nate's gaze. "Suh?"

Nate had worked with escaped slaves during the war. He'd learned to force them to look him in the eye. He'd discovered that out of necessity, they'd become artful and clever, assuming a servility that had been expected of them. Nate also learned that this act was one way they kept "Old Master" from learning what was really going on inside their heads.

"I saw your expression, Kito. If looks could kill, that rancher would have had a knife carved into his back, making a hole big enough to pull out his spine."

Kito stepped so close, Nate could smell his sweat, in which there was no whiff of fear. The man's black-coffee eyes were the same color as his face, and the whites glistened in the dim light of the smithy. Sweat beaded at his hairline, coursing over his forehead, and his temples. It dripped from his chin, and ran in thick streams over his enormous ebony chest. His arms, thick as tree trunks, were crossed, accentuating the bulging muscles. He lowered his eyes, but not before Nate saw the derision.

"All right." Kito's deep, baritone voice held no trace of servility. He met Nate's gaze and jabbed one thick, soot-blackened finger at Nate's chest. "I ain't got nothin' to lose with you, 'cause you got somethin' to hide. I don't know who you are or why you're here, but you hurt that girl and her baby boy, an' I promise I'll come after you. I'll fin' you, rip off your head and spit down your throat."

Although the servility was gone, there was still a thick, southern quality to his speech. Nate matched his glare, refusing to look away. "I wouldn't hurt her." Damn it, he meant it.

"You bes' not," said the Negro on a hiss of breath.

"We understand each other, then?"

Kito stood before him, a proud, magnificent giant of a man, and studied him, unsmiling. "I sure as hell hope so. For your sake." He waited a moment, then added, "Suh." However, the word came out sounding nothing like a polite form of respect.

Nate shoved the package under his arm, left the smithy and crossed the street. As he walked toward the dress shop, he felt Kito's stare boring into the back of his head. Maybe it was his imagination—or his guilty conscience. Either way, he knew that if Susannah found out why he was there and didn't get to him first, Kito would do a commendable job of maiming him for life. Neither prospect pleased him much.

* * *

Sitting slumped in her sewing chair, Susannah stared at her machine. The machine wasn't the problem this time, it was the dress lying on it. It had belonged to her mother. It was the only thing she'd salvaged after the gossip mongers learned her mother, "the Whore of Baldwin County," had died.

She remembered watching in horror as they'd descended on the house like a flock of vultures, picking the house clean. The sheriff had understood her shock, but had done nothing to stop them. "Little miss," he'd said, "what would you do with all this stuff, anyhow?"

She hadn't known until years later that every whore who died in their community had her belongings taken from her. It was justice, she'd been told. For years the whores stole the men, making them faithless husbands. Upon death, a whore's property belonged to the women whose husbands had been lured away. But Susannah had sneaked in and taken the dress before any of the old crones had seen her.

Even then, the dress wasn't safe. After she and Harlan had married, he'd tried taking it away from her as punishment when she hadn't pleased him. But she'd fooled him. The first time she'd seen him rooting around for the dress, she'd taken it and hid it under the false bottom of an old trunk that was filled with his mother's clothes.

Now, as Susannah studied the white cotton voile with ribbon motif and pastel flowers, wrinkled, smelling of mildew and devoured by moths, she wondered how she could possibly restore it enough to wear it to the apple-paring party. If they actually went, that is.

She poked her finger through one of the holes she'd discovered, testing the sturdiness of the fabric. She did have that bit of grosgrain left after doing the last dress for Lillian. She stood and held the dress out in front of her, studying the haphazard pattern of the moth holes. Maybe she could—

Hearing Kito's creaky wagon, she flung the dress on her sewing chair and went to the window. Her pulse trembled at the base of her throat as she watched Nathan haul lumber from the wagon to the side of the cabin. New, exciting emotions scrambled into her throat, filling her eyes with tears of joy, of anticipation.

They had avoided each other since the night she'd spread ointment on his sunburn. She still felt awful that she couldn't give him what he wanted, but he hadn't brought up the subject, and she was grateful.

When Nathan finally came inside, she turned away to wipe her eyes, then gave him a questioning look. "Well?"

He nodded. "I talked to him."

She pressed her fingers against her throat. "And?"

Nathan snorted a laugh. "He'll keep quiet, all right."

"Did you threaten him?" she asked, angry.

"Me? Threaten *him?* Haven't you noticed? He has arms like tree trunks."

Relieved, she said, almost to herself, "Yours aren't so bad either."

He crooked an eyebrow. "What was that?"

She dismissed the question with a wave of her hand. "I have a good friend I'm just dying for Kito to meet."

"Oh, so you're a matchmaker, are you?" He studied her warmly from across the room.

Self-conscious under his scrutiny, she shrugged one shoulder. "I don't suppose it will ever happen. She's in—" She stopped herself. Did it matter if she told him? She didn't think so. "She's in Missouri. I don't expect I'll ever see her again." It made her sad. She loved Louisa very much. To her relief, Nathan said nothing, didn't question her further.

Returning to her sewing table, she picked up the dress and studied it again. She felt Nathan behind her.

"What are we going to do about the party, Nathan? It's less than two days away."

"What do you think we should do?"

"Darn it," she spat out, crushing the dress in her fists. "Why do you answer my question with a question?"

"Why do you answer *my* question with a question?"

She felt a smile coming on but stopped it. "Nathan, this is serious." She turned and gazed up at him. "What will we do?"

He reached down and touched the dress, running his fingers over the wrinkled voile. "If we went, were you planning to wear this?"

Embarrassed at her paltry wardrobe, she pulled the dress away. "It . . . it was my mother's. It's old, but there's nothing wrong with it that I can't fix. And yes," she added defensively, "I was planning to wear it."

"Then by all means, let's go to the party."

Her insides quickened. "Do you really think we should?"

He shrugged and left her, going to the window. "I don't know why not. It can't make our situation any worse than it already is."

Susannah frowned. It wasn't the answer she'd hoped for, but then again, she was letting her hopes interfere with reality. After all, what they truly had *was* a "situation," and it was already as bad as it could get.

"Nathan, I don't know how to dance. That's going to look pretty stupid, don't you think?"

He turned, snagging her gaze. "That's easy enough to remedy."

She swallowed hard. "What do you mean?"

"I mean," he said, coming toward her, "I'll teach you."

"You . . . you will? But . . . but there's not enough time."

Grabbing her hands, he pulled her to her feet. "I'll teach you a couple of different steps. The most popular ones. If they play something you don't know, we'll sit it out. All right, now, put one hand here," he directed, placing her hand on his shoulder. "I'll hold the other one in mine, like this."

Susannah stood close, a willing, eager pupil. Her pulse raced and she felt weak in the knees. "N-now, what?"

Nathan cleared his throat, all business. Putting his hand at her waist, he answered, "I'll teach you the waltz first. The steps are slow and easy."

He murmured the tempo into her ear—*one*-two-three, *one*-two-three—and she followed, stumbling over his boots whenever she allowed his nearness to interrupt the rhythm. And his nearness was truly an interruption. How could she explain such a thing to a man who had danced before, held a woman close before? Could he do this without becoming aroused?

For her, it wasn't possible. Nothing in her daydreams had prepared her for the sensation of moving against a man whose mere touch sent her pulses soaring anyway.

She tried to concentrate on the dance. She *tried*. A heaviness gathered low in her belly, warming her, seducing her, urging her to press against him. She was more than grateful that he held himself away from her.

What she felt wasn't normal. If it were, every couple who had ever danced together would end up rolling around in the hay, or pressing together in a darkened garden. She sensed that babies would be born nine months from every barn raising and apple-paring. Oh, my, yes. There was definitely something wrong with her. Pulling in a deep breath, she asked, "Are all dances so slow? Maybe we should learn a faster one."

"One thing at a time, Susannah." His voice was husky against her ear.

"But . . . but they're bound to play something fast. What will we do?"

He stopped and held her away from him. "We'll beg off. Use Corey as an excuse. Don't worry," he urged, tipping her face to his. "I'll take care of it."

She gazed up at him, her body still flushed and humming. "Somehow," she managed to say, "somehow, I think dancing fast would be safer."

He grinned at her, that half grin she'd come to cherish, then pulled her close. "Somehow, I believe you're right."

Melting against him, she felt him, hard and ready, against her stomach. Surprised, she raised her head. "You . . . you feel it, too?" She heard the breathlessness in her voice.

He arched an eyebrow. "It's pretty damned hard to be this close to you and not feel something, Susannah."

She swallowed the knot of emotions in her throat and concentrated on the tension in her belly. Rubbing her chin against his chest, she whispered, "How do people do this out in public?"

His hand pressed her closer. "Not everyone feels this way, Susannah."

She moved her fingers to the back of his neck, threading them through his hair. "Then . . . then why do we?"

He cursed; it sounded like a caress. "Damned if I know. I'll tell you one thing, though."

She pressed against him, feeding the hunger. "What's that?"

"We'd better not dance this close on Friday night."

She swallowed again, then tried to catch her breath. "Maybe . . . maybe we should practice dancing farther apart."

"All right," he agreed. "Let's try. And a little small talk couldn't hurt." He moved her away from him, resting his hand on her hip. There was enough room for someone to squeeze between them.

She felt cheated. "Small talk?"

He gave her a stupid smile. "Well, Miss Susanny. Fine night for a dance, dontcha think? Look at that moon, wouldja? Yessiree, that there moon looks like a lemon pie. Ummm, now don't that make you hungry fer a slice of lemon pie, Miss Susanny?"

She collapsed against him, laughing at his foolishness.

"Come on, now," he urged. "Practice small talk."

"Oh, no," she said, shaking her head around a smile. "I can't—"

"Come on," he coaxed.

"Oh, all right." She grinned up at him, batting her eyelashes. "Well, I do declare, Mr. Wolfe man—that were yore name, weren't it, Mr. Wolfe man? I swan," she said, tittering foolishly, "I gets to these dancin' parties an' I forgets my own name. Seems unlikely I could remember your'n. But you're right, Mr. Wolfe man, it sure is a fine night for an apple-parin', but that moon don't look like no lemon pie to me. To me, it looks more like my aunt Tilly's round, white behind."

He shook with laughter. "That's the idea. Now, remember that when we dance at the party."

She loved to listen to him laugh. It was still rusty, but now she knew why. And what she wanted to do most in the world was make his laughter be as natural to him as breathing.

Staring up into his face, she mused, "Well, at least this way I can look at you."

The color of his eyes changed, darkening with desire. "And when you look at me like that, I want to kiss you until you faint, then drag you off to the hayloft."

Their merriment was gone; desire returned. "How . . . how could we dance in the hay?"

His sensual lids hung over his eyes. "It would be pretty hard. I guess we'd have to find something else to do."

The warmth in her belly expanded. "What . . . what would we do?"

"We could lie in it, like a young man and a young woman just discovering forbidden pleasures," he answered, running his hand over her hip.

His touch made her brave; it also made her ache with need. "Just . . . just lie in it? Is . . . is that what new lovers do?"

They'd stopped all pretense of dancing and stood, barely touching one another. She throbbed and ached in places only Nathan had awakened; she knew he felt something, too.

"No," he said on a whisper, "I'd probably touch you here." His fingers grazed her breast, sending the nipple tingling.

"And . . . and what would I do?"

"Ah, being the sweet, young virgin you are, you'd push my hand away, hoping I'd try again, and again."

"And would you?" His thumb continued to circle her nipple, and she knew she'd collapse in a heap on the floor if he moved away.

"Being the randy young buck I am, I wouldn't stop until—"

"Mama?" Susannah felt a tug on her skirt. Corey stood beside her, staring up at her, a puzzled expression on his face.

Flustered, she bent and hugged him. "Why, darling. I didn't hear you. Did you have a good nap?"

She glanced up at Nathan, who had turned and walked to the window.

"Corey hungry," he announced.

Susannah looked up just as Nathan turned. Their gazes locked. *So is Mama,* she thought, wondering how she would survive the party.

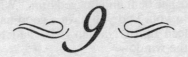

9

Strains of "Little Brown Jug" were carried on the wind for miles before they reached the Stedersons' ranch. Susannah's emotions ranged from excitement to fear to dread as the buggy, which Nathan had rented, clattered over the rough trail that led from the road to the ranch house. There was a bite in the air, and thick, dense clouds sank into the tops of the hills, a prediction of rain. Or snow. She shivered, even though she wore an old black cape and Nathan had draped a buffalo robe over their knees.

She curled her hands in her lap to keep from wrinkling her dress. It had turned out quite well. She'd carefully washed it in rosewater, hung it outside to dry in the wind, then sewed tiny pink grosgrain rosettes over all the moth holes, enhancing the deeper pink roses in the fabric itself. After tracing a rosette with her nail, she pressed her fingers through the front closure at her throat to make sure it wouldn't gape open. She'd discovered, to her dismay, that she was far more well-endowed than her mother had been.

Nathan's gaze rested on her. "You look beautiful, Susannah. Doesn't she, little whistler man?"

Corey sat between Nathan's legs, too busy "helping" him guide the team to respond.

She tossed Nathan a swift glance, not truly believing his words, but grateful, just the same. He'd said them earlier, too. As she'd emerged from her bedroom, feeling flushed and nervous, she'd found him watching her from across the room. It felt odd to have a man in her midst who didn't berate her, who actually complimented her. A pain, like rough twine, squeezed her heart. She was going to feel mighty lonesome when Nathan finally left for his other job.

Susannah's gaze was drawn to the Stedersons' home, which was fast approaching. It was the largest home in the area, for not only was Lars Stederson one of the most successful ranchers in the state, but he and his wife, Maybelle, had eight children. And Maybelle was pregnant with their ninth.

Susannah tried to think of anything but the party. It didn't work. Dancing with Nathan would be the least of her problems. Or, maybe not. Lord, she was beginning to wonder which problem would erupt and make a fool of her first, the fact that she and Nathan weren't married, or the fact that she couldn't dance with him without feeling a fierce arousal.

After the first lesson, when Corey had interrupted them, Susannah had hurried to her room and checked herself in the mirror. Her eyes had glistened, her cheeks were flushed and the pulse at her throat had fluttered hard against her skin. All signs she'd noticed before, but only with Nathan.

Now, as her gaze wandered over the sprawling lawn where several buggies and buckboards were parked beside a thicket of eucalyptus trees, she felt a blister of panic replace the memories of arousal. There would be no more practicing. No more hiding in her room when she could no longer hide her feelings.

"Nathan, I can't do this."

He gave her knee a fatherly pat. "Sure, you can. No one knows but the two of us, Susannah."

She drew a shuddering breath. "The tangled webs just keep growing bigger and more impossible to undo, don't they? Like knots in a skein of yarn."

"It'll be fine, Susannah. Just paste a smile on your pretty face and pretend you're having a good time. Who knows," he added, tossing her one of his heart-stopping smiles, "maybe you will. And remember, if things get tough, think about small talk."

"Lemon pie moons and stupid smiles." She sighed, the bubble of panic fading.

"And your aunt Tillie's behind," he reminded her.

A little snort of laughter escaped before she could stop it. "And Aunt Tillie's behind."

Briefly closing her eyes, she focused on what she had to do. After what she'd been through this past year, attending a party with a man like Nathan should be a pleasure, not a trip to the lynching tree. But that was how she still felt; tried and convicted by her own guilt. She had to do this, though. At this point, she had no choice.

Ed Barnes stopped sawing on his fiddle and pointed the bow at Nathan and Susannah. "Folks, we ain't playin' 'Matrimonial Bliss' for nothin', you know. C'mon, now, dance!"

Susannah gave him a weak, answering smile. *Couldn't the floor just open up and swallow me whole, instead?*

"Hey." Nathan nudged her arm. "Don't look so glum. We'd better dance."

Clenching her hands in her lap, she studied the

other couples on the dance floor, which was really the Stedersons' living room with all the furniture pushed to the walls. Concentrating on the music, Susannah tried to catch the beat. "Is this a waltz?"

"Yeah." He stood and pulled her to her feet. "A nice, slow one."

Susannah swallowed a groan and went into his arms. Everyone cheered, forcing heat into her face. At least this time she was certain her embarrassment would override the arousal she knew would come when he held her in his arms.

And she was right; at least she forced herself to concentrate on her surroundings. She kept an eye on Corey, who was being entertained by two of the Stederson daughters. She scanned the room for people she knew. She found many, but also discovered some new faces. Couples she didn't know.

Nathan swung her in circles, toward the patio doors that stood open. "We'd better do some serious dancing, or people will begin to talk."

Serious dancing meant arousal. "Oh, Nathan, I don't think I can—"

"Small talk, Susannah. Remember?" He whirled her onto the plank board patio. The air was cool, but it felt good, for the house, with everyone dancing and milling about, was warm.

Susannah relaxed against him. Nathan put both his arms around her, instructing her to do the same, then pulled her close. They rocked together, finding a rhythm of their own. Susannah felt the kernel of desire, but discovered she could hold onto it, enjoy it, keep it level.

"Well shucks, Miz Susanny, take a gander at that there moon."

She smiled, then peered at the sky. As Louisa used to say, it was as black as the devil's armpit. Not a

147

moon or star in sight. "I think you've done gone blind, Mr. Wolfe man, sir," she teased back. "That sky is blacker'n the backside of a skillet."

He pulled in a deep breath, pressing her even closer. "Safer than talking about the hayloft."

Closing her eyes, she rubbed her palms across his shoulders. She could feel the ridge of him against her belly. It hastened her own need. "Are you sure people can actually dance and not . . . not feel this way?"

His hand roamed her bottom, then slid to the safety of her back. "Believe me, Susannah. I've danced with dozens of women. I haven't had the urge to bed that many."

Her pulse raced, desire exploded inside her like an overripe fruit. "And . . . and you want to bed me?"

He took another deep breath, letting it out against her hair. "More than you'll ever know."

Her heart pounded in her ears and her legs felt heavy. "Why?" she asked, her voice sounding tinny in her ears.

He spun her around again, out of the light from the house, to a darkened corner of the patio. They stood, toe to toe, their arms still around each other. "Because you're sweet and pretty, and don't even know it. Because you're a wonderful mother. Because your body is ripe for loving, and I want to be the one to love it. And," he finished, kissing her forehead, "because you make me want to laugh again."

She thought of his wife and son, and the edge on her desire diminished. "Oh, Nathan." She pressed close, listening to the thundering beat of his heart. She wanted to make him laugh, make him happy again. She wanted in the worst way to tell him her deepest, darkest secrets, but in doing so, she would surely drive him away, and the one thing she wanted most in the world was to have him close. Always. She loved him.

It was as simple as that. But she hadn't been honest with him. She would be, soon. But not yet.

She breathed in his scent, capturing it in her lungs. No, not yet. The time would come soon enough. She wasn't the sweet, wonderful woman he thought she was. When he discovered the truth, he'd leave, no doubt shouting "good riddance!" at the top of his lungs.

"I wonder how Corey's doing."

Sighing against his neck, she answered, "I suppose we should go in and find out."

"I think we should wrap him up and take him home."

Home. For a fraction of a second, she felt a frantic caution. "We can't leave before they serve lunch, Nathan. It wouldn't be neighborly."

He moaned, pressing her bottom against him. "And, what time do they serve lunch?"

She closed her eyes, allowing her need for him to engulf her. "Around . . . around midnight." She brought her hands to his chest and rubbed, imagining it bare.

"God, woman," he said on a groan. "Do you want me to do that to you?"

Swallowing hard, she answered, "If you like."

"Don't tempt me." His voice was gruff, husky.

She took his hand and slid it through the closure at her bodice.

"My fingers are cold." It was a soft warning. He grazed her nipple. It tightened.

"Warm them, then," she ordered, her voice catching as he nimbly found a way through the top of her chemise to her bare flesh.

She clung to him, her knees weak as he fondled her. She found him still hard against her stomach, and couldn't stop herself from moving against him, rubbing back and forth. She shook, her breath a rickety, unstable sound in her throat.

He explored her breast as a blind man might, touching every surface, weighing it in the palm of his hand. "I want to see you. God, Susannah, I've dreamed of it." He pressed against her. "I'm ready to burst. Here," he said, drawing her hand downward and holding it over him. "Feel it."

She touched the hard length that pressed against his jeans, wondering at her heightened desire. She'd been forced to do this before, and had never liked it. Or wanted to do it. But this was Nathan, and she *wanted* Nathan. She stroked him, gently squeezing as she imagined what he would look like.

Pulling her hand away, he groaned into her hair. "We've got to stop, Susannah."

She was in such a delicious, carnal haze, she barely heard him. Deep in her belly she felt a throbbing, a pulsing that pulled all of her nerve endings together. She was swollen; she knew if he touched her there, he'd find her wet. She also knew that what she felt now she'd never felt before.

"Well, there you two are!" Ed Barnes shouted back toward the door. "They're out here, folks! Come on, now," he ordered, "folks are waitin' on you. Time to toast the lovebirds."

When he left, Susannah stood against Nathan, frantic to catch her breath while she fixed her bodice. "Ready to face the neighbors?"

He stepped away from her and sucked in greedy breaths of air. "You'll have to give me a minute."

A shutter had been opened, and light poured out onto the patio. Glancing down, she understood his problem before he turned away.

"All right." He turned back and took her arm, examining her. "You feel properly put together?"

She gave him a shaky smile. "What I feel is anything but proper."

"Come on, Susannah. If there was ever a need for small talk, it's now," he warned.

Leaning into him, she chirped, "Well, now, Mr. Wolfe man, sir, I got me a mess of skinned possum in my shed, and my aunt Tillie cooks up the sweetest grits in the county. Wanna come fer supper? I promise she'll wear somethin over that big, white behind of hers."

He laughed. They both relaxed and went inside to be scrutinized by the neighbors.

～ 10 ～

As they rode home, it began to snow. Big, thick, dry flakes floated quietly on the windless air. Corey was asleep in Susannah's arms, covered by the buffalo blanket.

"Now, was it so bad?"

Nathan's voice warmed her and she stifled a sleepy yawn. Huddling closer, she answered, "I guess it could have been worse." She tucked her free hand beneath the blanket; it landed on his thigh. She was quick to remove it.

"Put it back, Susannah."

She placed her palm over his leg, feeling the warmth of him seep through his jeans into her hand. Sensations stirred within her again, and she curled her hand around the inside of his thigh, where it was warmer still.

The snowflakes thickened. "I hope we don't miss the cutoff to the cabin," she mused, a little worried.

"No," he answered. "It's right there. See? The double oak trees."

Max's greeting guided them into the yard. Susannah hurried into the house to put Corey to bed. He woke up long enough to use the pot she hid under her bed. Nathan came in and fed the fire just as she was taking Corey toward his room. The child stopped.

"Can Corey sleep in big man's sleep roll?"

"Oh, Corey, I don't think—"

"Well," Nathan interrupted, "I did promise you didn't I, little whistler man?"

Corey nodded, fighting to stay awake. "Corey hasn't peed his bed for this many nights," he said, holding up seven fingers. "Big man say I could sleep in his sleep roll if I didn't pee my bed for 'free nights," he finished, holding up three fingers.

Nathan glanced at Susannah, his eyebrow raised.

She bit back a smile. "He's got you there."

"I can't believe he's been keeping count." Chuckling, Nathan unfurled his bedroll in front of the fireplace.

Susannah found it hard to swallow as she watched him. He was so perfect with her son. So competent in areas that she didn't understand. She could play with him, teach him games and songs, but she had no sense about the father-son routines of a three-year-old boy. She would never have known how much she'd needed someone like Nathan if he hadn't arrived.

Nathan stood. "Get your pillow, little whistler man."

Corey scurried into his room, emerging with his pillow and his blanket, and scooted into the bedroll.

Nathan adjusted the homemade screen in front of the fire, making sure no sparks could fly out.

Susannah gnawed her lower lip. "Do you think he'll be safe there?"

"When he falls asleep, we'll move him away."

She was jittery, trying to pretend nothing was going

to happen. "You . . . you think of everything, don't you?"

He gave her a disquieting look. "I can't possibly think of everything, Susannah, but I'm thinking of something very important right now."

She let out a whoosh of air and toyed with the closure at her bodice. "Nathan, I—"

"Come on," he whispered, drawing her toward the door. "One last dance."

She made a halfhearted attempt to stop him. "Outside?"

"Outside. In the snow. We wouldn't want Lettie and Alvin Hatfield to think we're liars, now, would we?" He tugged her old cape close around her and led her outside. It still wasn't windy, and the snowflakes were falling softly to the ground.

He coaxed her off the porch and onto the gravel, which had a fine layer of snow on it. Pulling her close, he hummed against her ear, and they swayed together.

Susannah was falling deeper and deeper in love. It frightened her, almost more than the intimacy she knew was going to occur.

"N-nice night for a dance, Mr. Wolfe man. And . . . and look at that moon—"

"No small talk, Susannah," he whispered, pulling her closer. "Think about us, together in your bed."

She tried, but somehow she couldn't imagine such a wonderful thing. They moved together, rocking back and forth, their arms around each other. Snowflakes melted on her hair, dripping slowly onto the collar of her cape.

"Think about me undressing you, peeling off the layers that cover your magnificent body." He reached up and stroked her breast, pressing his hand inside once again, where he'd been before.

His arousal grew against her stomach, and she, in

turn, found all of her sensations centered in that place between her legs, that place she'd feared for so long was dead. That place she'd feared, period.

"You . . . you're going to undress me?"

"Umm-hmm." He nibbled her earlobe and she shivered with anticipation. "If it weren't snowing, I'd undress you right here, in front of God and everybody. There are many exciting places to make love, Susannah. A bed is at the bottom of the list."

"Wh-where else besides a hayloft?" That had sounded exciting enough.

"In the sunshine, naked on a blanket of leaves."

She thought about it, deciding it wouldn't be what she'd choose. "But, wouldn't the leaves scratch my bottom?"

He flicked his tongue in her ear, sending shivers over her skin. "Not if you were on top."

Again, a rickety breath. "Me? On top?"

He chuckled against her ear. "Ah, Susannah, you have so much to learn."

Nestling close, she asked, "Where else?"

"In the river."

Oh, my . . . "How . . . how does a person do it in the river?"

"We face each other; you put your legs around my waist and we float."

She rubbed her cheek against his shirt. "I think I'd like that."

"We'll try it. Maybe tomorrow."

Blood pounded in her ears. "And . . . and then, what?"

He laughed again. "Have you no imagination, woman?"

"No," she said, shaking her head. "Not when it comes to this." And she meant it. She might just as well have been a virgin.

"Come on, then." He whisked her back into the house, helped her off with her cape and led her to her room. He lit her lamp, then brushed snowflakes off his shirt and hair.

She stood, helpless, wanting him so much . . . so very, very much.

He came and stood before her, reached around and removed the pins from her hair. With his bandana he wiped the strands that were wet from the snow, then he pulled the heavy mass over her shoulder.

"Cinnamon. Your hair has always reminded me of dark, rich cinnamon. You're a beautiful woman, Susannah."

That he found her pretty thrilled her. His hands went to her bodice and, with skillful fingers, unfastened the closure, pulling the dress down over her arms. The look of approval in his eyes gave her a measure of pride.

She glanced down and found her breasts quivering over the top of her camisole. When he bent and planted kisses there, she almost collapsed.

He reached behind her and unfastened her sash. She stepped out of her dress, standing before him in her petticoat, feeling very vulnerable.

"Don't be afraid, Susannah," he whispered, bending to kiss the throbbing pulse at the base of her throat. He untied the laces on her camisole, pulling it open, freeing her breasts. He touched them. "Beautiful. God, how beautiful." His voice was filled with reverence.

Shrugging out of her camisole and petticoat, she stood in front of him, unable to raise her eyes to his.

He drew her to the bed, made her sit on the edge, then spread her thighs, kneeling between them. He kissed her breasts, drawing the nipples in, loving each separately.

The most exquisite feeling flooded her, and she pulled him close, running her fingers through his hair, pressing her thighs against him as if she were afraid he would escape. She felt one of his hands untie her drawers. Feeling a twinge of fear, she tried to push him away.

He pulled her to her feet. "It'll be all right, Susannah. I won't hurt you, I promise."

She wanted this. She *did*. Her drawers fell to the floor, and she stepped out of them.

"Come here," he whispered, tugging her toward the bed.

She frowned. "But . . . but you aren't even undressed."

"I know," he said around a sultry half smile. He pulled off his boots and drew her with him to the bed, pulling her against him, spoon-style. The roughness of his clothing aroused her; the fact that he was dressed and she wasn't excited her.

His arms came around her, and he stroked her breasts with one hand while the other moved over her stomach. He dipped a finger into her navel and she gasped, pressing herself against him. His hand snaked lower, feathering over her, barely caressing her. She wanted him, for she ached down there, where he wouldn't quite touch her.

"I . . . I . . . I think you should touch me there," she said, her breath snagging in her throat.

"In time, Susannah." His fingers stayed there, just above the place that throbbed. She squirmed against him and opened her legs, inviting him in. He dipped into her, grazing a spot that was so rich with sensation, she nearly choked, her need was so great. His fingers circled her, dipping and stroking, nudging the spot that sent her soaring.

Against her ear, he whispered, his own voice a

shaky rasp, "You're wet, and swollen, and oh, so ready, Susannah."

If she could have spoken, she would have agreed. But she thrust her leg to the side, urging him to continue. And he did. He stroked her until she felt a tensing in her pelvis, and all at once she couldn't control it, nor did she want to. She jerked at the sensations that tumbled through her, stiffening as they reached a peak so incredible, she whispered his name, trying to keep from screaming.

She floated down from her climax, feeling boneless. Turning in his arms, she clung to him, one leg riding his hip. Tears pressed, and she didn't stop them. "Thank you for that," she said, when she could finally speak. He was still hard beneath the fly of his jeans.

"I'm going to get undressed, Susannah."

She gave him a half-shy, half-provocative smile. "Is that a warning?"

He touched her chin. "I don't want to scare you away." He got off the bed, and Susannah crawled under the covers.

"Will you toss me my nightgown?" It was a soft request.

He gave her a lopsided smile as he unbuttoned his shirt. "Nope."

She made a face and stuck her tongue out at him.

He shrugged out of his shirt, then started unbuttoning his jeans. "Do that again, and I'll show you what else it's good for."

She knew what he meant, and briefly, memories stirred, and she had a sick feeling in her stomach. It vanished as she watched him undress. He'd been beautiful bare to the waist. Naked, he was magnificent. Hard and masculine. And he was ready for her. Desire and anticipation raged inside her as she observed that part of him. It was hard, and so thick and long that it bobbed slightly as he came toward the bed.

He turned down the lamp and slid in beside her, pulling her gently into his arms. "Touch me, Susannah."

She ran her fingers through the hair on his chest, feeling the hard muscle beneath.

"Lower, Susannah."

She swallowed hard and moved her hand beneath his breasts to where the skin was sleek and hard, but no hair grew.

"Lower, Susannah."

With tentative fingers, she explored his hair-covered navel, then spread them lower, into the thick thatch of hair that surrounded him. As she touched him, she felt her own desire growing again. She took her hand away and pushed against him, riding the ridge, pressing it against the spot he'd discovered earlier.

When her breathing became erratic, he moved over her and entered her. She took his length, could feel him expanding that place that had always been tight, had always hurt. But this time, it did not. He was still for a moment, as if waiting for her to decide. She enveloped him, wrapped her legs around him and held him close.

His hands found her bottom, and he rocked against her, deeper and deeper, with an intensity that shook her. She hadn't imagined there could be such bliss, such ecstasy, but when she felt herself coming again, she bit his shoulder to keep from crying out her pleasure.

He surged against her, stiffening above her. She swore she could feel him all the way to her soul.

When they were huddled together under the blanket, Nathan said, "Don't hold back, Susannah. Don't feel ashamed to let yourself scream, cry, shout when you feel that pleasure coming."

She was cuddled in the crook of his arm, one hand stroking his hard, muscular hip. "I had no idea it could be like this."

"I know," he answered, caressing her breasts.

She stopped and hoisted herself up on one elbow. "How did you know?"

His fingers tunneled through her hair, dragging it over her shoulders. "I can tell when a woman has never been satisfied, Susannah."

She sat, cross-legged, beside him. "How?"

His fingers danced along her inner thigh. There was a rushing sensation where he'd just pleasured her. "When a woman has been on the brink but has never been satisfied, she's itchy, anxious, like she's going to jump out of her skin when I fondle her."

He fluffed her triangle of hair, sending another jolt through her. "How else can you tell?"

He was quiet for a moment, then said, "When a woman is not a virgin, but has been treated badly by a man, she draws back, afraid it's going to happen again with any man she meets."

Her heart thudded in her chest. "And which am I?"

He pulled her down to him and held her close. "Your husband, whoever he was, didn't treat you with the respect you so richly deserved, Susannah."

She felt tears threaten. "Oh, God. Is it that obvious?"

He held her, stroking her gently. "I'm glad the son of a bitch is dead. If he hadn't been, I'd have killed him myself."

As she lay wrapped in the warmth of Nathan's love, she began to have some hope for a future with him.

Maybe what she'd done wouldn't send him away. Maybe if she explained what she'd been through . . .

But something still gnawed at her. Thoughts of Sonny still wiggled into her sweet, new life, and when they did, they weighed heavily on her heart.

Nate lay awake, waiting for her to stir. He wanted her again, but he knew she needed her rest. He left the bed and lit the lamp, lowering the flame until there was just a soft glow in the room. Turning back to the bed, he stood and studied her as she slept. Beautiful. She was beautiful. A twinge seized his heart, and he pressed his palms against his eyelids.

It wasn't fair, what he was doing to her, but God forgive him, he couldn't help himself. Never in his life had he felt such helplessness with a woman. God forgive him again, but not even with Judith, whom he'd loved, had he felt the weakening sense of desire he'd felt with Susannah.

He slid into bed beside her, his root springing to life the moment her warm skin touched his. She rolled over and faced him, a smile on her face.

"Can't sleep?"

"Didn't want to. I'd rather watch you."

She hiked herself onto an elbow and studied him, her eyes warm, her breasts bare to his gaze. "I was having a sweet dream, for a change."

Caressing her breast, he watched the nipple change. "I'm sorry I woke you, then."

She closed her eyes, her face dreamy. "Don't be. It was about you, and as lovely as it was, I'd rather be awake when I'm with you."

Touching her made him harder than ever. By her expression, he knew she could feel his length against her leg. They exchanged glances.

Her hand slid beneath the covers, her fingers touching him. "Do you mind?"

Whipping off the covers, he gave her a crooked smile and answered, "Please. Be my guest."

Through a lust-filled haze, he watched her examine him. She moved the skin away from the bulbous tip and he steeled himself against the pleasure, lest he spend.

"What a clever little wrapping," she said, only half in jest.

"My own invention," he answered through clenched teeth.

She gave him a shy laugh, then continued to stroke him. "I've never wanted to look at a man's . . . thing before."

He chuckled, still floating on the sensual river. "'Thing'?"

With shy fingers she reached below and fondled his balls. His mouth was dry, his throat tight with control.

"I know the real word, Nathan, I just can't say it."

Desire raged through him, and he loved it. He wanted it to last, but if she continued to stroke him, he knew he'd explode. "Why——" He swallowed hard. "Why can't you say it, Susannah?"

To his relief and dismay, she stopped. "Ma Walker told me I'd go to hell if I said it."

The hard ridge of his desire softened. "She said you'd go to hell if you said 'penis'?"

Nodding, she answered, "That, and . . . and other words for it."

He shook his head, filled with rage for such a witch. "They're just words, Susannah. Words can't send you to hell. In fact," he added, "those very words can be very exciting, if shared with the right person."

Her expression told him she didn't believe him. He

settled onto the bed, drew her into his arms and caressed her. With a deep sigh, she pressed her softness against him, throwing her leg over his.

He reached between them and touched the petals of her sex, drowning in her eager reaction. He stroked her until she shook, until she pleaded, until she was nearly at the edge. Then he bent and whispered naughty things in her ear, words that when spoken between lovers, only intensify the desire. She squirmed against him and sought his stiff root, guiding it eagerly into her fertile home.

They made love with wild abandon. When Susannah reached her orgasm, Nate reveled in her unbridled release.

Wearing only her camisole cover and drawers, Susannah ran across the cold, wet grass and into the warm water. "Last one in has to make supper!"

Nathan, in his long underwear with Corey riding on his shoulders, bounded in after her. "Not fair! You had a head start, woman."

Susannah huddled down in the warm water, noting that steam rose from the surface as it hit the colder air. *"Brrr.* Do you really think this was such a good idea?" As she'd lain with him in the early hours of the morning, she'd agreed to take a brisk swim before it got too cold. After all, she'd thought, they could swim without desiring one another, for she was completely satisfied. That was then.

This was now. As the hard, muscled ridges of his body became evident beneath the wet fabric of his underwear, she realized that satisfaction was a baffling thing, for although they'd made love early in the morning, and he'd satisfied her, she wanted him again.

Nathan swung Corey from his shoulders and put him in the warm water. "Don't look at me like that, Susannah."

She scooted close, her buttocks floating just over the rocky bottom, only her head poking out of the water. "How am I looking at you?"

Over the weeks since he'd arrived, his rusty smile had vanished, replaced by a heart-stopping lop-sided one. He used it now, and she felt her heart stop, midbeat, before it clattered away in her chest again.

"Like a cat, drooling in anticipation of being stroked."

She swallowed a laugh. "I'm not drooling."

He reached over and ran his thumb along the sides of her mouth, his touch electric. "You could have fooled me."

With the back of her hand, she playfully swatted his away. "That's not drool, that's water."

Corey bobbed in the water beside them; Nathan had tied a sash around Corey's waist and attached it to his own so he would never be far from him.

She floated away, beyond Nathan's reach, only to discover the toes of one of his feet between her legs, twitching against the slit in her drawers.

"Don't you want to be stroked?" he asked, his voice like silk.

Shuddering at the wealth of her feelings, she decided that two could play the game. Riding his leg until her toes reached his groin, she touched him, desire thickening her blood when she discovered he was already hard. "Don't . . . don't you?"

Only his eyes changed. "I'll give you an hour to stop that," he threatened, his voice husky and compelling. He reached beneath the water and claimed her foot, rubbing the sole seductively. He then pulled her toward him and drew her legs on either side of his hips.

She floated just above the mass at his groin, knowing that if she touched it she'd be lost. He'd taught her that drawing out their pleasure made the pleasure that much more intense.

Beneath the surface of the water, one of his hands claimed her breast, and he rubbed the nipple through the wet fabric of her camisole cover. She felt the shock all the way to the place between her legs, and she bucked, accidentally pressing against his groin.

He groaned and returned the pressure. They sat together, their hunger mounting.

Unaware of their physical discomfort, Corey splashed beside them.

"Maybe this wasn't such a good idea." She watched Corey tug on the sash as Max galloped toward them, sending water every which way.

"Don't be so sure," he answered, his smile raffish.

"But, we can't *do* anything," she argued, trying to quell the ache between her thighs.

He drew her close again, but this time he moved his hand down over her stomach to the slit in her drawers. "Oh, Nathan," she said on a shudder, "don't . . . don't do that. I'm—"

"I know," he said. "You're already so hot down there the water's boiling."

She laughed, feeling a little embarrassed, for she knew it was true. "This isn't fair," she protested on a halfhearted whimper. The place between her legs *was* hot and insistent, craving his touch. She had no strength to push him away. With Corey and the dog splashing nearby, she clung to Nathan's shoulders and gave in to his touch.

Desire built within her like a storm gathering strength. Then he pushed her away.

She stared at him. He was grinning like a fool.

"Oh," she scolded, "you did that on purpose, you . . . you rat!"

His chest moved as he chuckled. "I couldn't very well finish the job, could I?"

She was still on fire. "Then you shouldn't have started it, you . . . you *worm."* She splashed his face with a rush of water.

He laughed out loud. "Oh, Corey, we'd better watch out. Your mama's on the warpath."

"You bet I am," she warned, unable to swallow her smile. She put her feet against his chest and shoved, laughing with glee when he fell backward into the water.

Nathan had untied the sash so Corey wouldn't go under with him, and the boy sat in the water, clapping and laughing as Susannah and Nathan tussled.

Nathan's head bobbed up and he gasped for breath, still laughing at Susannah's attempts to drown him.

"You *beast!* Don't you dare laugh at me!" She went at him again, pummeling him with her fists, lashing out with all her strength only to discover that the water softened her blows. And the fight did nothing to dissipate her desire. It only made her want him more.

After she'd flailed at him long enough, Nathan grabbed her wrists and stared at her, still smiling his heart-stopping smile.

"How do you feel now, Susannah?" He didn't wait for an answer. "Do you know how you look? You look like a woman who's in such heat, if she doesn't get satisfied, she'll splinter into a thousand pieces."

She was breathing hard, streamers of wet hair plastered to her face, neck and shoulders. And he was right. She was so hot she knew she'd die if he didn't make love to her.

They bobbed together until they caught their breath.

"Now you know why we did this, don't you?" His voice was seductive, sultry.

Still trying to hold onto a piece of her dignity, she said, "No. Why don't you tell me?" Immediately she knew the question was a mistake.

He grinned, but his eyes were dark. "Because now we can go back to the cabin, put the little whistler man down for his nap and have some good, hot, sweaty sex."

She shuddered and looked away. "I . . . I'm sorry I asked."

He stroked her one last time, and she felt a twitching that drove her to the edge. "No you're not," he argued.

"Mama! Corey cold!"

Grateful for the interruption, Susannah took Corey's hand, waded to the shore and wrapped him in a towel. Nathan followed them out of the water, but Susannah tried to ignore him as they made their way to the cabin.

"Hey, this is nice," Nathan said. "I like the way you move, Susannah-love. Your butt jiggles real sweetly when you walk."

Her cheeks flamed and she tried to stiffen her step and tighten her bottom. "You watch something else, you evil man," she answered, her mouth twitching into a smile.

She fed Corey lunch and put him down for his nap, trying to tell herself that Nathan was wrong. But her body told her otherwise. As she stepped through the curtain that hung over Corey's bedroom door, she found Nathan feeding the fire. He turned, his look heated and intimate.

"Was I wrong, Susannah?"

She wanted to tell him he was, but she couldn't. She wanted him. She *needed* him. Lord help her, but she loved him. "No," she whispered.

In two strides Nathan was beside her, pulling her toward the bedroom. Once inside, they tore at each other's wet underthings, anxious to touch, to feel.

"You're cold," she said on a shaky whisper, hand stroking his firm buttocks.

"Not here," he argued, drawing her hand around to the front.

She moaned as his lips claimed hers. The kiss was deep and wet as they shed the remainder of their clothes and toppled onto the bed.

He entered her, driving deep, and within moments they climaxed together. They lingered there, but soon crawled under the warm covers and explored each other until their desire for each other rose again.

He'd never had such great sex, yet he knew that with Susannah, it would only get better. He bent and kissed her and she responded with an open mouth, although she didn't wake up.

He slipped from the bed with reluctance, found dry clothes, and went into the other room. After checking on Corey and finding him asleep, he pulled out paper and tobacco and rolled himself a cigarette. Checking his pocket, he found the ad he'd taken off the door of the mercantile the last time he was in Angel's Valley.

Tilting the paper toward the light, he read the inquiry again: *Challengers needed! Meet the Moose! Big Moose McKay, the famous bare knuckle boxer, arrives in Sacramento on November 1st. Good money to the man who stays in the ring the longest.*

Good money. Those two words, more than any others, had drawn Nate's attention. He folded the paper and returned it to his pocket. He'd made his decision. There was no way in hell he'd turn Susannah and Corey over to Sonny Walker. But he'd already sent the money on to Nub Watkins, his ranch foreman, to begin repairs. Before he could do anything else, he had to pay Sonny back. He didn't want to owe the bastard anything.

He had another, more immediate, concern. He hadn't kept in touch with Sonny Walker, which was his mistake. That meant that at any time, the man could appear himself. He'd wired Walker the day he'd learned for certain that Susannah was here. Once he'd gotten to know her, he wished to hell he'd waited. Sonny knew she was here.

Now Nate had to abandon her when he wasn't sure it was safe to leave her alone. But in his mind, there was no other way. It was just the way he was. He had to wipe the slate clean before telling Susannah anything.

He stepped out onto the porch and lit the cigarette. The smoke lingered, dissipating in the hushed air. The snow was falling again, although it wasn't as heavy as it had been the night of the dance. Being snowbound with Susannah would be a treat, but it was one he couldn't afford, not now.

The door squeaked behind him. "Nathan?" She stepped outside, pulling her flannel wrapper around her. "What's wrong?"

He flicked the cigarette away and caught her to him. She came to him, melting against him. She felt so damned good, all soft and warm and ripe. . . . "Nothing. I went to check on Corey, then had a cigarette."

She snaked her arms inside his shirt, against his skin. "It's strange, but I don't like waking up alone anymore." Nuzzling his chest hair with her nose, she

murmured, "Come back to bed, just for a little while."
She gazed up at him. "Please?"

He bent and took her mouth, kissing her with deep,
wet kisses. Picking her up in his arms, he took her
back to bed, anxious to explore her further, yet
regretting what he ultimately had to do.

～ *11* ～

Susannah opened one eye and looked toward the door. It was barely dawn. The previous day was still vivid in her memory. It had been a perfect day. In her secret daydreams, she, Corey and Nathan were like a real family. Corey adored Nathan, and Nathan treated Corey like his own. And she loved them both.

Now, she was cold; she was alone in the bed. Turning toward the window, she found Nathan standing there, staring outside. Despite the warm memories of their day together, her stomach clenched, telling her something was happening. He had all the signs of a man on the move.

As if sensing she was awake, he turned, but said nothing.

She swallowed a fierce disappointment. "You're leaving."

He studied her. "It's time."

Realizing how awful she looked in the morning, she squirmed under his scrutiny. Her hair was all tangles.

Harlan had told her that after she'd slept on it, it always looked like the back end of a horse, and that the freckles across her nose stood out like mouse shit.

"Corey . . . Corey will miss you."

"And, will you?" He crossed to the bed and sat on the edge, tugging back the quilt she had tucked to her chin. He pulled it down, exposing her breasts. The cold air tightened them, pebbling her nipples.

She hoped he didn't see the rampant pain in her heart. "I won't lie. I don't know how to be coy. Yes, I'll miss you . . . very much."

With a regretful sounding sigh, he flipped the quilt back over her bosom. "I have a job waiting for me, Susannah. I also have a lot of things to sort out."

"About your wife?" She was certain he still thought about the family he'd lost. She often caught him staring off into space, his expression troubled and filled with pain.

"Yes," he answered on a nod.

"And . . . and me?" she asked hopefully.

He sighed again, swearing under his breath. "Hell, yes."

Whatever that meant. She couldn't tell if it pleased him to think about her or not. She gazed at the window as faint streamers of light slanted through onto the floor.

"I'll try to come back."

She threw the bedding aside and stepped from the bed, naked. Aware that he watched her, she scrambled for her dressing gown. "Don't make any promises you can't keep, Nathan."

"Susannah, I don't know what to say."

She tied the sash around her waist, pulling it tighter than was necessary. "Don't say anything more." She tried to ignore the knot in her throat. "You don't owe us an explanation. You've . . . you've done more than I could have expected as it is."

She walked briskly past him, pulled open the bedroom door and stopped. "Just tell me one thing."

"What?"

Unable to face him, she asked, her gaze focused on the door, "If you knew you were going to leave anyway, why didn't you go before . . . before the night of the party?"

The silence that hung between them was palpable, stretching to the point of pain. "I thought it would be best this way. For you, for Corey . . . for the gossip mongers in Angel's Valley."

She'd hoped he'd tell her it was because he'd wanted to make love to her, but she wasn't really surprised at his pragmatic answer. She was a fool to let her feelings for him affect her. But she certainly couldn't blame Nathan; he hadn't forced her to fall in love with him.

Frowning, Louisa Washington rubbed her sore butt and watched the hay wagon clatter out of sight. But she wouldn't complain; it had been a free ride from the remote train station. Huffing a sigh, she brushed the hay off her black linsey-woolsey skirt and straightened the neckline over her generous bosom. Well, she was here. Now what? Another wild-assed frontier town where she'd probably have to play the down guilty nigger in order to find out what she needed to know. Lord, she had to be crazy as a Mizzoura bedbug to come all the way out here. She'd just been blamed lucky she could talk her way out of trouble, because she'd found plenty of that between Missouri and California.

She straightened and looked around. Where in

blazes was everybody? The town was nigh onto dead. Adjusting the brim of her straw hat to keep the morning sun from blinding her, she looked toward the livery. A tall, massively built man stood in the wide doorway, his hands in his back pockets. She studied his fine lines, feeling a thread of interest. Lord a'mighty, he was a big one. She focused on his limping walk as he moved about. No matter. Legs were nice, but they only got a person around.

Arching a curious brow, she checked her neckline once more and sauntered his way.

He turned, watching her approach with interest— or so she wanted to believe.

She walked up to him, dropped her shabby valise to the ground and put her hands on her hips. Her gaze wandered up the length of him until she met his eyes. 'Course, she had to tilt her head back to do it, him being so tall and all. His face was mean, threatening. His black-coffee eyes were hard. He didn't scare her; his menacing appearance only made him more interesting. She let her gaze flick over his chest and shoulders, drawing in a quick breath as she did so.

"This your place?"

He crossed his arms over his chest and studied her, taking in her generous bosom. "I'm the smith here, for the time bein', anyway."

My oh my, she thought, feeling a rush of pleasure. A voice that rumbled like thunder. "I'm lookin' for someone. Think you can help me?"

He lifted a leather apron off a hook by the door, wrapped it around his hard, flat middle and tied the thongs in the back. "Not unless you tell me who it is."

She swallowed a smile. A quick mind. She liked that. She appreciated a challenge. Most men didn't leave an impression on her any stronger than a fart in a whirlwind. "Your woman know you talk to strangers?"

He met her brazen gaze. "Ain't got no woman."

Louisa warmed to the idea. "I can understan' why," she baited. "Who'd want a worthless cripple like you?"

Giving her a lazy grin, he answered, "An' who'd want a mouthy bag o' wind like you?"

Ignoring the remark, she smoothed her skirt, shaking the dust from the hem. "I'm askin' after a white gal with a little boy."

He snorted a laugh. "You might narrow it down a bit."

"Name's Susannah. The chile's name is Corey."

He turned away, straightening the latch on the door. "What you want them for?"

"That's my business, not yours," she answered tartly.

"An' if I know her?"

She felt a twinge of excitement. "I'm a friend, come all the way from Mizzoura to visit."

He laughed, a deep, quiet booming that washed over her, leaving her weak and a little breathless—a state she definitely was *not* accustomed to.

"Well, la-de-da. The fine lady's come all the way from Mizzoura to visit."

She bristled. Something else she wasn't accustomed to doing, for usually nothing anyone said to her bothered her a whit. "Are you gonna take me to Susannah or not?"

"I got plenty of work to keep me busy. I don' have time to haul you around."

"All right. Jes' point me in the right direction. I ain't too proud to walk."

His eyes glittered. "Ah, hell. See that buckboard?"

He flung his steely arm sideways, exposing bulging muscles and veins.

"I see it," she quipped, mesmerized by his body, "I ain't blind, you fool."

Continuing to stare at her, he shook his head. "How'd you get here all the way from Mizzoura with a mouth like that?"

She pulled a haughty face, picked up her valise and tromped to the buckboard. "What I do with my mouth ain't none of your concern."

Chuckling again, he followed her. "Hell, I jes' might like it to be."

She felt a glorious warmth whirl around inside her. Lord a'mighty, she could learn to live in a place like this with a man like that.

But as they started out of town, she glimpsed a man on horseback that she recognized, and any pleasure she'd felt was washed away by fear. Quietly urging the buckboard forward, she swore she'd kill any man who would hurt her sweet Honeybelle.

Susannah stood on the porch, staring at the trees through which Nathan had left an hour before. The snow had already begun to melt; there was little left anywhere. With both Nathan and the snow gone, the last few days hadn't seemed real. Had it not been for the pain in her heart, she might have believed it had been.

Pulling her shawl around her, she leaned against one of the new pillars. Of course she wanted him to return to her. She loved him. And he'd given her the self-respect Harlan had robbed from her. Even if he never came back for her, she'd still have that.

Hugging herself, she thought about the night that had just passed. He'd made her feel . . . so much.

She'd felt wanton and he'd encouraged it. They'd loved fiercely, openly. Now he was gone, leaving her with a new, turbulent need.

Her body still hummed as she recalled the many times he'd reached for her in the night. She'd gone willingly, even though she knew in her heart he would soon leave her. She was just happy that he'd left her with something.

What sleep she'd gotten had been dream-free. Nightmare-free. The first in months. And although she already missed Nathan, she felt whole.

Glancing at the nice new porch, she wondered how long she'd be able to enjoy it. Nathan had worked so hard. In some ways, she felt he hadn't been real, but someone she'd dreamed up to save her from a life too dreadful to imagine. And now, she realized that without him, she was vulnerable again. She'd thought of him as her protector. Now, she had an urgent need to pack up and leave this place. Run again. But hadn't she known it would eventually come to this?

A buckboard clattered over the rutted path toward the cabin, sending Max into yelping fits. She shaded her eyes to get a better look. "Kito?"

"Mornin', Miz Susannah. Brought you company."

Puzzled, Susannah peered at his passenger. Her heart leaped with joy. "Louisa! Oh, my darling dear!" She flew off the porch, meeting Louisa halfway. They embraced, clinging to one another, swaying from side to side.

Susannah pulled away, her eyes brimming. "I don't believe it. Oh, I just don't *believe* it." She took off Louisa's wide-brimmed hat and devoured her with her eyes.

Reaching up and touching Louisa's soft black hair, she whispered, "How I've missed you!" Their eyes met, and they both smiled, albeit sadly, remembering how they'd parted.

"You are still the most magnificent woman I've ever known, Louisa Washington." Susannah gazed into the black almond shaped eyes and felt a fierce tug of love. "You're even more beautiful now than you were when I left."

Although Louisa's eyes were filled with love, she gave Susannah a skeptical glance. "Ain't you looked in a mirror yet, Honeybelle?" she scolded softly.

Susannah hugged her again. "How did you get here? When did you leave?"

"There's enough time for that," Louisa answered, rubbing Susannah's shoulders.

Susannah closed her eyes and clung to Louisa. "I'm so glad you found Kito."

Louisa released her and turned to the buckboard. "Oh, that the no-account's name?" she asked, her voice lacking any signs of interest.

Susannah felt a stab of disappointment. She'd so hoped—Well, it wasn't the end of the world. At least Louisa was here with her.

As Kito made a turn in the yard, she said, "Kito, can you stay a few minutes?"

His gaze rested on Louisa. "Have to get to work, Miz Susannah. Gotta get everything done before nightfall. Tomorrow, I ain't got a job."

"Oh, Kito, I'm sorry. What happened?"

"One of the ranchers got me fired," he answered without remorse.

"What will you do?" Susannah asked, concerned.

"Don't worry 'bout me, Miz Susannah. I'll find me somethin'. I always do."

Louisa sized him up, then down, her hands on her hips. "Yessuh, you best git to work, then, you no-account cripple."

Susannah gasped, her hand flying to her mouth. "Louisa!"

Kito snorted a caustic laugh. "If that mouth of yours don't get you into trouble, I can't think of anything that will."

Susannah gaped at them. Why, they'd just met and they sniped at each other like . . . like . . . She couldn't even think what. She was just *so* disappointed. . . .

As they stood quietly and watched Kito disappear through the trees, Susannah put her arm around Louisa's waist. "He's really a fine man, Louisa. You shouldn't make fun of his limp."

Louisa stifled a laugh. "I don't give a damn about his legs, Honeybelle. Hell, legs don't mean shit. It's what's hung between 'em that counts. And," she said, tweaking Susannah's cheek, "I think I just might like what's between his." She picked up her valise and moseyed toward the cabin. Reaching the porch steps, she turned and shook a finger at Susannah. "An' you'd best close your mouth, Honeybelle, lest you catch yourself a mess of flies." She stepped onto the porch. "Now, I gotta go in and see my li'l man."

Susannah stared after her. And closed her mouth.

Louisa's presence dredged up all of the memories Susannah had hoped to bury. Now, along with fresh fear, she felt remorse. There had always been a thread of guilt at what she'd done to Harlan, but she'd reminded herself she'd done it for Corey's sake as well as hers. And she'd had no choice. Still, the fact that she ran had made her feel a bit like a coward. She often had to remind herself that in this case, the law was not on her side no matter what. She'd had no choice but to run.

"So, are you going to tell me what happened after

Corey and I left, or do I have to drag it out of you?" Susannah stood at the stove, frying side pork. Louisa, finally agreeing to let Susannah cook the breakfast, sat at the table, Corey cuddled against her bosom.

"Strange things happened, Honeybelle."

Susannah felt a wash of apprehension. "Strange? How?"

"Well, I swear that pissant Harlan was colder than a wagon tire when I went to find ol' Andrew to help me haul the bastard's body away."

Susannah's apprehension mushroomed. "What happened?"

"When we got to your place, he was gone, and—"

"He was gone? What . . . what do you mean, gone?" She carefully removed the crisp pieces of pork and put them on a plate, aware that her hands were shaking. Black thoughts of Harlan catching up with her at the train station, pointing an accusing finger at her, shouting "murderess!" at the top of his lungs . . . These were visions she couldn't shake.

Behind her, Louisa said quietly, "I don't know, Honeybelle, all I know is that he wasn't there when I returned with Andrew."

Susannah let out a shaky breath of air. "He . . . he couldn't have been alive." She turned and found Louisa watching her. "Could he?"

"I don't have a clue, Honeybelle, but if he was, he weren't alive for long."

Susannah gripped the edge of the counter next to the stove and tried to catch her breath. She swallowed and ran one hand over her face, upset and angry that she had to think about these things now, after trying so hard to forget them. The raw panic from her nightmares coated her insides.

"Why . . . why do you say that?"

"'Cause next thing I heard, Sonny and a pack of hounds found Harlan's body buried under two feet of Mizzoura mud, down by the river."

"Who put him there?" Nothing Louisa said made sense to her.

Louisa shrugged. "Damned if I know, Honeybelle."

Susannah turned toward Louisa, narrowing her gaze in thought. Louisa would have done anything for her and Corey. Anything. Was it possible that she could have—?

Shaking the thought away, she asked, "What did Sonny do?"

"He didn't go to the law, if that's what you're wonderin'. Not right away."

"Oh, it wouldn't have mattered, Louisa. He's been paying Sheriff Morley off for years."

"But Sheriff Morley was killed by a stray bullet soon after you left, Honeybelle. The new law ain't likely to let the likes of Sonny Walker stick him in his back pocket."

Susannah gave Corey a piece of meat. He devoured it and begged for another. "What are you saying?"

"Sonny'd never send the law after you. I think, though, that he *has* sent someone. That's why I'm here."

Susannah's shoulders sagged and she dropped into a chair. "I knew it. I knew I'd never be free of that bastard."

Louisa reached across and took Susannah's hand. "I'm afraid Sonny hisself might even be on his way here."

Fear chilled her insides and she gripped Louisa's fingers. "How did he know where to find me?"

"I don't know that, Honeybelle. I'd guess he prob'ly had someone on your tail right off."

Susannah pulled her hand from Louisa's and gnawed absently on her thumb. Oh, how she wished Nathan were here! "We'll have to leave."

"Where would we go, and how'n hell would we get there?"

Susannah's mind was whirling. Nathan's ranch, up near the California-Oregon border. It would be a long ride, and they'd have to travel at night, but Nathan had told her that if she ever needed to leave, to come to him. She'd deal with the repercussions later. "I know a place."

Louisa put Corey on the floor. "Fine, Honeybelle, but how would we get there without everyone knowin' about it?"

She took a deep breath, expelling it slowly. "Kito will take us there. We'll leave at night."

Louisa's interest was piqued, for her eyes lit up. "He'll do that for you?"

Susannah thought back to the bond she and Kito had forged many months before. It wasn't that he owed her something; she just knew he felt he did. "Yes. I think he will."

Louisa raised an eyebrow at her. "An', why will he?"

Susannah went to the stove and poured hot cake batter onto the griddle. "When I first moved in, I discovered him hiding outside in the shed. He was beat up real bad, his back was torn to ribbons and . . . and maggots had already started to eat at his flesh." She shuddered at the memory. "One of his arms had been so badly gouged, I could almost see the bone."

"Who was he hidin' from?"

Susannah flipped the griddle cakes. "At first he wouldn't tell me. Then, one day three men came to the door, searching for, as they put it, 'a filthy buck nigger.' They gave me some cockeyed story about how he'd killed a family of whites over in the other valley, and they were trying to find him."

"Why didn't you believe them?"

Susannah laughed, a humorless sound. "They were the mangiest men I'd seen in a long time." A wry smile curved her mouth as she remembered. "They reminded me of men Harlan would have called his friends."

"An' they never returned after that?"

Susannah shook her head. "Later I heard they'd been arrested for bank robbery and murder. As it turned out, Kito had been the only witness. They'd beat him to a pulp once, but he'd gotten away. They were going to make darned sure he didn't get away again."

"Well, if he can help, we'd best get to plannin', Honeybelle. I know Sonny was still home when I left, 'cause he was due in court for somethin' to do with Harlan's will."

Susannah remembered the strongbox she'd taken when she left. It contained a bunch of papers she hadn't bothered to examine. "His will?"

Louisa nodded. "But that don't mean he ain't right behind me. Knowin' Sonny, he hurried 'em through."

Susannah nervously picked at the hem of her apron and chewed the inside of her cheek. "I didn't even know Harlan had a will."

"I guess whatever's mentioned in it is rightfully yours, Honeybelle."

Although the room was warm, Susannah rubbed her arms. "Harlan had very little worth having."

"Well, what's important is us gettin' out of here before Sonny comes ridin' up." Louisa put Corey on his stool, and filled his plate.

Susannah said nothing; she was too sick to her stomach to speak. She'd hoped they'd found a home here, but she should have known it wouldn't happen. Her sense of foreboding grew. She'd killed Harlan, she would bet her life on it. And if Sonny was on his way here, he was coming because he knew she'd done it and he was going to make sure she was punished for it.

12

Susannah had packed up her sewing machine, her and Corey's clothes and the box that had belonged to Harlan. It was all that they'd brought with them; it would be all they took when they left.

While Louisa cleaned the insides of the windows, Susannah took a mop to the porch and washed it down. She was just returning from the pump with another bucket of water when Max barked. Turning, she saw a man on horseback ride into the yard. The familiar feeling of dread returned.

"Max, heel." She put the bucket on the ground and the dog returned to her side and sat, pressing close to her legs.

"Excuse me, ma'am." He gave her a wide, charming, overly enthusiastic smile.

Slick. He was too slick, and he was a breed. Her stomach churned a warning. This was Sonny's kind of man. Swallowing her anxiety, she gave him a brisk nod, wishing she had her shotgun handy. "What do you want?"

"I'm looking for Nate Wolfe."

Prickly pins attacked Susannah's stomach. She also couldn't ignore the fact that he had called Nate by name, which meant he knew she and Nate weren't really married. Which brought up more questions that she didn't want to ask. "What do you want him for?"

Continuing to smile, he pushed his hat back on his head, giving him a rakish, cavalier look. One he'd practiced to perfection, no doubt, and one, she thought, filled with scorn, that probably worked on most women.

"I have a message for him."

She couldn't quite decide if she felt relieved or not. Surely if this man worked for Sonny, he wouldn't tip his hand. "May I ask from whom?"

He spread his hands expansively, his smile even more dashing. "Why, from me, of course."

"And, who are you?"

"Name's McCloud. Is . . ." He glanced around. "Is Nate here?"

He acted like he knew Nathan, but she wasn't going to fall for it. She wasn't about to let anyone know Nathan had left, leaving her vulnerable. "He's . . . he'll be home shortly. Can I tell him what this is about?"

He gave her a cocky grin, yet his eyes were deceptive. "Tell him it's about his family."

Susannah's stomach dropped. "What . . . what about his family?"

"Tell him his family wasn't completely wiped out."

She pressed her hand over her mouth and fell to her knees, his words ringing in her ears. As she watched the stranger leave, she pushed one hand against her belly, the other still over her mouth. She swallowed an urge to vomit. She'd wanted to ask what he meant; she should have, for her own peace of mind. But any desire to learn that his wife was alive made her feel ill. God, but she was a selfish, wretched creature!

"Honeybelle?" Louisa stepped off the porch. When she saw Susannah on her knees, she rushed to her. "What is it? What's wrong?"

Susannah took a deep, shaky breath. "Did you see that man?" When Louisa nodded, she asked, "Have you ever seen him before?"

Louisa frowned. "I don't think so. I didn't get much of a look at him, but . . . Why?"

Susannah was reluctant to talk about Nathan. It was too complicated. Perhaps on the drive north to . . . Her stomach twisted again. Could she really go up there, to his ranch, after what she'd just learned?

Then again, she thought, allowing Louisa to help her up, maybe the man was lying. But why would he? No, she thought, her shoulders sagging, no doubt it was the truth.

"What is it, Honeybelle? You look like you just lost your best friend."

Susannah hugged Louisa's waist, wishing she didn't feel so sick. "I'll tell you all about it one day real soon. I promise."

"What time's that man supposed to be here?"

Susannah slanted her a glance. "'That man' has a name. It's Kito."

"I know his name, chile, I just ain't ready to use it."

Despite her deflated spirit, Susannah smiled. "I'd always thought you two would be perfect together."

They climbed the porch steps. "Now, don't go gettin' any fancy-dancy ideas, Honeybelle," Louisa scolded.

Susannah nodded, already distracted. They had nowhere else to go. Despite the news she'd just learned, she would have to take her friends and go to Nathan's. It didn't mean she had to stay, but surely Nathan would help them find a safe place.

As she finished packing, she thought about her foolish hopes and dreams. She should have known better. She wasn't a flitty-headed schoolgirl, she was the mother of a small child and couldn't afford silly daydreams about fairy tales and other things that would never come true.

She just hoped she could mask her feelings when she saw Nathan. The last thing he needed was to be reminded of his indiscretions. The last thing she wanted him to see was how much she still loved him, and always would.

"Miz Susannah? You sure you wanna be tucked under all them blankets?"

Susannah put Corey on a quilt on the floor of the buckboard and lay down beside him. He squirmed, murmured, then stuck his thumb into his mouth, the elephant Nathan had carved him tucked against his chest. Before Susannah pulled the covers over to conceal them, she said, "It's our only hope of making it out of here, Kito. With you and Louisa on the seat, it will appear like it's just the two of you."

Louisa snorted. "Yeah, and how far'll we get without bein' stopped, Honeybelle? Lord a'mighty, the two of us'll stick out like catfish at a shrimp feed."

"Just keep that paper I wrote handy. It will answer most questions. And don't get all flustered and forget that you and Kito are on your way to work for a Mr. Dillman who lives up in Broken Jaw. No one has to know the man doesn't exist." She was reluctant to use Nathan's name, just in case—well, she didn't want to get him into trouble even before they arrived. Glancing at the moon, grateful it was bright enough for Kito to see the road, she ordered, "Now, no more arguing, Louisa. Let's get as far as we can before daybreak."

She whistled for Max, who bounded up into the wagon, then pulled the blankets over her and Corey, enveloping them in darkness.

He sat at a table near the far wall, his poker winnings tucked safely into the flat, leather wallet he'd slipped into the inside pocket of his jacket. Dressed in his traveling clothes, he hadn't given the appearance of a seasoned gambler, which he was. And the week's growth of reddish beard further concealed his looks.

The barkeep moved toward him, his steps hesitant.

"Yes? What is it?" His voice was terse, impatient.

"The . . . uh . . . man you're looking for is waiting outside in the alley, sir."

He rose and exited through the door that led into the alley. A man walked toward him, swaying slightly.

"You Sonny Walker?"

When Sonny nodded, the man drew close and extended his dirty, gnarled hand. "Eli Clegg." Sonny ignored it. The man was weasel-faced and a drunk; stale booze and filth emanated from him like a rotten aura.

"I need some information," Sonny announced.

Clegg bobbed his head. "I'm yer man. Nothin' goes on in this town without me knowin' about it."

"I'm looking for a young woman and a boy. The woman may be going by the name of Quinn. The boy's name—"

"I know who ya mean." Clegg snuffled a wet laugh and scratched his groin. "I seen her nekked—"

Sonny grabbed the bandana around Clegg's neck and twisted. "If there's one thing I can't stand, you miserable drunk, it's a peeper."

Clegg clawed at his hands, making pathetic, choking

sounds in his throat. When he was released, he fell against the wall of the saloon and slid to the ground. With nervous bony fingers, he stroked his throat. "No need to choke me," he groused.

"There's a twenty for you if you'll show me where she lives."

As Clegg rose, he coughed, a sloppy, wet sound as he dislodged the snuff-colored saliva from his lungs and deposited it on the ground. "Fer another twenty I'll tell ya whose livin' there with her."

Sonny's heart raced, but he kept a bland facade. "If I think it's worth twenty, you'll get it."

Clegg spit again, the brown, syrupy wad splattering against the saloon wall. "Friggin' big fella."

Sonny's blood pounded in his ears. "Nathan Wolfe."

Clegg giggled, a high-pitched, annoying sound. "That's the fella. If he ain't screwin' her, I'll eat my shorts."

Hatred welled up in Sonny, oozing through him like poison. Double cross. He'd been double-crossed! With immense control, he led the drunk out of the alley. "Take me to her place, and the extra twenty is yours."

Sonny felt Clegg's surreptitious glance on him, but ignored it.

"What you want with the woman, anyways?"

Sonny's jaw was clenched to the point of pain. "She's got a couple of things that belong to me."

He watched Clegg swallow and wipe his mouth, his hands shaking. From his jacket pocket, Sonny pulled a silver flask and handed it to the drunk. Clegg took it, uncapped it and drank, not wasting a drop.

Nate nursed his jaw, wincing as he moved it back and forth. At least it wasn't broken. Which was more

190

than he could say for his nose, he thought, as he tried to pull air in through it. He kneed his mount, urging him forward. It wasn't easy to stay in the saddle, considering how sore he was. Sore, but content. By sheer grit and determination he'd stayed in the ring with Moose McKay long enough to earn him what he needed to pay Sonny Walker. Even if it *had* taken him four nights of pounding torture to do it. He tried to laugh, but the split in his lip prevented even a smile.

The familiarity of the trail made his heart race. Thoughts of Susannah hadn't been far from his mind, but as he rode into the yard, he felt an uneasy caution.

"Max?" He whistled for the dog. "Here, boy!" Nothing.

Pulling the horse to a stop, he dismounted and tossed the reins over the porch railing. Glancing around him, he bounded up the porch steps, stopping at the door a moment to listen. He heard nothing. A feeling of dread inched up his spine. Opening the door, he stepped inside. "Susannah?" Again, silence. Silence and an obviously unoccupied cabin. The feeling of dread spread like ripples on a pond. "Susannah? I'm here."

A husky chuckle floated out from the bedroom. Sonny Walker appeared in the doorway, leaning casually against the jamb. "Is that anything like, 'Honey, I'm home'?"

Ripples of dread became whitecaps. "Where's Susannah?"

Walker stalked him. "That's my question, you turncoat. I paid you good money not only to find her, but to keep me posted." He stepped close, and although he was shorter than Nate, he was a formidable opponent.

"Whoa," he said as he searched Nate's battered face. "I'd hate to see the other guy."

Nate automatically touched his face, grimacing at the reminder of his bruises. "Where is she?"

"That's my question, Mr. Wolfe. You failed me. Why did I ever think I could trust you? I don't even *know* you that well." Walker appeared genuinely distressed.

Ignoring him, Nate stepped away and checked the rooms. Everything was there except Susannah's sewing machine and their clothing. Something or someone had tipped her off. He hid his relief.

"What happened, Mr. Wolfe? She get to you?"

He turned and found Walker right behind him. Ignoring him again, Nate went to the window and stared outside.

"She has that ability, you know. Hell, she got to me often enough. She had a hard time keeping her hands off me."

Nate didn't rise to the bait. "I don't believe you."

Sonny's caustic laugh sent needles of ice down Nate's spine. "You wanted to believe you were special, didn't you?" He put his hand on Nate's shoulder. Nate shook it off.

"Where is the bitch?" Walker's voice was cold, hard as rock.

"If I knew, would I have come here for her?" He hoped, prayed she'd remembered his advice and gone north.

Walker spat a curse. "You're a fool. I was told you were tough, like me. I was told *nothing* got to you. That you were mean and empty enough to shoot your own dog, then hand feed it to the wolves. That's why I hired you. But," said on a rough sigh, "I understand what you're feeling."

Nate angled a hard look in Walker's direction. "You do, huh? You have no idea what I'm feeling."

"Listen to me!" Walker shoved Nate's shoulder,

forcing him to look at him. "I *know* the bitch. I've known her since she was a kid, damn it. Her ma died, leaving her to fend for herself. And, by God, she did a damn fine job of it. How could someone with her beauty survive, unless she used it? Does she stand demurely by and wait for someone to throw her a bone or a crust of bread? Hell, no. She's had that body since she was fifteen, Mr. Wolfe. And she's known how to use it since then, too."

He punched Nate's shoulder, as if they were comrades. "She's an actress," he said, coaxing, urging Nate to believe him. "She's survived by her beauty and her wit for years. She plays men like a pianist plays Chopin. She was hell-bent on surviving, Mr. Wolfe, and to do so, she honed her craft and became a consummate actress and a damned fine whore."

The word *whore* made Nate's skin crawl. He hissed a curse. Walker was too damned logical. Nate hated logic, especially when it involved his feelings for Susannah. "That bastard brother of yours beat her."

Sonny snorted a laugh. "Of course he beat her. He *had* to."

Nate felt the revulsion churn in his stomach. "No one deserves to be beaten."

"All right," Sonny conceded, "maybe not. Maybe Harlan used force when he should have used reason. But that was his way, don't you see? He was a brute. A big, dumb, stupid brute. He didn't know any other way of handling her. And believe me," he added, his voice sincere, "she needed handling."

Nate studied the landscape, watching the clouds cling to the hills like smoke. "If she's so damned clever, why did she marry Harlan and not you?"

Walker chuckled, as if accepting the backhanded compliment. "Because Harlan might have been big and stupid, but you see, we don't have the same daddy, Harlan and me. And Harlan's daddy left him something Susannah wanted."

In spite of it all, Nate was curious. "And, what was that?" He could feel Walker's eyes on him. "Well?" He turned and glared at him. "Are you going to tell me, or am I supposed to guess?"

Walker smirked. "You probably won't believe me."

Nate turned away, studying the hills, damning himself for ever getting involved with Sonny Walker. "Try me."

"Stock in a Texas cattle firm. Worth a fortune."

Nate turned, unable to hide his surprise.

"See?" Walker gave him a sly smile. "I knew you wouldn't believe me."

Nate bit the inside of his cheek, trying to digest the tidbit of news. He knew that Texas was opening up, but the timing was wrong. "If Harlan's father actually had such stock, he got it long before the rest of the country got wind of it."

"That he did. Harlan's daddy was no fool, even though Harlan was." Sonny Walker moved away, toward the kitchen window. "I think Harlan's brain was joggled when he was born. Ma told me once that he'd been pushing to get out of her belly for three days before anyone came to help her."

Damn. Too logical. Far too logical, even for Sonny Walker. "So, you're telling me that when Susannah left Missouri, she took the shares with her?"

On an acerbic laugh, Walker answered, "Yeah. She took the whole damned strongbox."

Nate dug the heels of his palms into his eyes. Had he really been duped? He still couldn't believe it. He'd seen the fear, the wariness, the sadness in her eyes . . . Damn. He'd *seen* it himself. But Sonny had told him she was a conniving little bitch. He hadn't seen that. Hell, maybe she'd been so good, he wasn't able to tell.

He slammed his fist against the wall, making the windows shudder. God, but he'd drowned in her eyes . . .

"And, that's not all she took," Walker said, interrupting Nate's thoughts.

"Christ, man. Don't tell me there's more."

"Just thought you ought to know the rest." He took a turn around the cabin, touching the fireplace utensils, the sofa, the kitchen table and chairs, obviously purposely prolonging Nate's anguish.

It worked. "Damnit, the rest of what?"

He stopped and stared at Nate with a gaze that was disquieting, empty. "She took my son."

Nate felt a cold wash of disbelief. "What do you mean, 'your son'?"

"Corey's mine, Mr. Wolfe." He gave him a halfhearted shrug. "Do you really think Harlan could have produced such a handsome child?"

Nate spun away, his fists clenched, his gut knotted with fury. Envy. Jealousy. He turned toward Walker, swallowing the bile that rose in his throat. "I don't believe you."

Walker's gaze was sympathetic. "She really sucked you in, didn't she?"

Nate shook his head, his ears ringing, his heart pounding. "I don't believe you," he repeated.

Walker sighed. "Mr. Wolfe, why would I say something like that if I didn't have proof?"

Nate could barely hear over the thundering of his heart. "What kind of proof?"

"When Harlan was thirteen, he got the mumps really bad. His balls swelled up like goose eggs. At the time, the doc told Ma he'd seen that happen before, and when it does, especially if the boy is in his teens, he'll shoot blanks. No friggin' chance of spreading his seed."

Nate swallowed, trying to dislodge the lump in his throat. "That's not always true."

Walker sighed again, as if working on his patience. "No, I suppose not. But believe me, Mr. Wolfe, Susannah got me into bed just once. *Once,"* he emphasized, shaking a finger at Nate. "And nine months later, she had a bouncing baby boy."

"It could have been Harlan's," Nate argued weakly.

"What the hell difference does it make? She got me into bed, damnit, isn't that proof enough that she's a slut and a bitch? Hell. Do you know what her ma was? Do you?"

Nate shook his head. He was almost afraid to hear. "No."

"A friggin' *whore.* 'The Whore of Baldwin County.' Harlan and I both crawled between that woman's thighs. And the apple doesn't fall too far from the tree, Mr. Wolfe."

Nate's stomach churned and he felt a headache coming on. He pinched the bridge of his nose, wincing at the pain. He'd forgotten his bruises from the fights with Moose McKay in the wake of Sonny's revelations.

"So now that you know what she's really like, you can't possibly want to protect her anymore. Where in the hell is she, Mr. Wolfe?"

Nate remembered where he'd told her to go if she was ever in trouble. God, had he been a sap, or was Walker still feeding him a line? Too much of what he'd said could be verified. The stock, Susannah's mother, Susannah's life as an orphaned street urchin . . . Damn. A kid didn't survive on the streets without learning to be artful, crafty . . . sly. And someone with Susannah's beauty could get anything she wanted. Make a man believe in her every word. There were two names for women like that. *Actress. Whore.* In his mind, they'd suddenly become the same.

Still, he remembered things about Susannah that made him distrust Walker's rantings. And damnit anyway, he didn't want to believe him.

His gut knotted again. He couldn't let Sonny Walker find Susannah. He wanted to find her first, and settle this once and for all.

"I don't know where she is. If I knew, I'd tell you, Walker." He was lying, but his anger—at Walker, at Susannah, at himself—covered the lie. He dug into his pocket, pulled out a wad of bills and threw them on the table. "Here. The advance you paid me."

Walker stared at the bills, then looked up at Nate. "You're still in my employ, Mr. Wolfe."

Nate raked his fingers through his hair. "Not anymore."

Walker gave him a sly smile. "Don't you want to get even with her?"

Just the way he said the words led Nate to believe not everything he'd told him was the truth. "I don't want anything more to do with her," he lied again. "And the next time I see you, I'll rip out your guts and strangle you with them."

Walker stepped away, giving Nate a false look of hurt. "Why, Mr. Wolfe. I'm crushed."

"Go to hell." Nate grabbed his hat and strode to the door. He was going home. To Broken Jaw. He hoped she was there. He wanted some answers, but he was so angry, he wasn't sure he could ask the questions.

13

From the edge of the aster- and windflower-studded meadow, Susannah studied Nathan's ranch. The smell of lilacs wafted toward her, reminding her of her mother's favorite perfume. She thought it odd that she would remember her mother at a time like this. Snapping cicadas rasped all around them. A woodpecker rattled a tree in the distance and a raven swooped down upon the flower-blanketed grassland, soaring into the sky with lunch gripped in its beak.

The ranch was nestled in a copse of Douglas firs, many of which were, Susannah guessed, hundreds of feet tall. On the way out from Broken Jaw they had ridden through groves of oak trees where a few men were stripping the bark, laying it carefully in the backs of wagons.

A nervous fluttering, like the butterflies that skimmed the sea of flowers before her, settled in Susannah's stomach as her thoughts returned to the ranch. From her vantage point, on a sloping hill at the edge of the meadow, she could see the house and all the outbuildings. Fresh lumber and shingles were stacked in the yard, as though someone was ready to do some repairs. The barn was in need of repair. Her gaze wandered slowly to the house, and the fluttering in her stomach continued.

The message she'd received from the breed about Nathan's family still clanged in her ears. She hardly dared breathe, much less go the last stretch and knock on the ranch house door.

"Well, Honeybelle? We gonna sit here all day, or are we gonna go in?"

Her gaze dropped to Louisa's lap, where Corey lay sleeping. Oh, Lord, now that she was here, she'd lost her nerve. "I don't know. I . . . I just can't—"

"You gonna tell me who this place belongs to now, Honeybelle? I've been askin' you the whole trip."

Susannah took a shaky breath. "Yes, I suppose you deserve to know. It . . . it belongs to a man I met in Angel's Valley. He . . . he came to my rescue more than once. He's the one who built the new porch. And he told me if I was ever in trouble, I could come here."

Louisa gently handed the sleeping Corey to Kito, who folded him in his huge arms. "Well, then, why are we sittin' here?"

Susannah slumped in the seat. "Because . . . oh, blast it!"

Louisa let out a huge sigh and took Susannah's hands in hers. "Did you fall in love with this man?"

Susannah nodded, forcing away the threat of tears.

"Then, what's the problem? The man'd be crazy not to love you in return."

She focused on the ranch house, but her thoughts were elsewhere. "Remember the day we left?" Out of the corner of her eye, she saw Louisa nod. "That man who came by, the one you said you didn't recognize, left a message for . . . for Nathan."

She twisted toward Louisa. "You see, Nathan was off fighting in the war when his wife and his son were reportedly killed." She swallowed, licked her lips and continued. "When he came home," she said, nodding toward the ranch, "he discovered that his wife had already been buried, but that his son's body had never been found."

"An', what did this man who came by tell you? That his wife and chile *weren't* dead?"

Susannah nodded, blinking away the moisture in her eyes. "He said . . . he said that Nathan's family hadn't been completely wiped out. How can I go up to the house, knowing that? For all I know, his wife could answer the door."

Louisa mumbled a mild curse. "How do you know the man tol' you the truth?"

"How do I know he didn't? Why would a perfect stranger lie to me?"

"Ladies," Kito broke in, "let me go up there and find out. Y'all stay here, by the wagon. Me and the dog'll go to the door."

"Oh, Kito, I don't think—"

"Jes' never you mind, Miz Susannah," he interrupted. He handed Corey to Louisa. Corey rubbed his eyes and woke, but sat quietly in Louisa's arms. He'd been such a good little traveler. "I'll figure somethin' out. If it looks bad, I'll say I'm tryin' to find somebody. If it don't, I'll say I'm lookin' for work. Either one ain't no lie."

During the ten days they'd traveled together, Susannah had learned it was useless to argue with Kito. He'd taken charge like any decent man would, taking unpleasant decisions out of Susannah's hands. They'd been lucky to make thirty miles a day in the buckboard, for often the hills obstructed the rutted roads, and more often than not, the ruts themselves caused them to lose time. He'd been patient with all of them, including the horse, who'd balked at the inclines and wanted to race down the descents. California's size had stunned them all, for it had seemed they rode on forever.

Although she knew she could have made the trip alone if she'd had to, she appreciated Kito's help and her admiration for him had grown each day.

Kito stepped down and called Max, who jumped from the wagon, loping beside him as he limped toward the ranch.

Susannah's insides were a quivering mass as she watched Kito step to the ranch house door. When it opened, she almost closed her eyes, unwilling to see a woman standing there . . . a woman who would be Nathan's wife. But a little, grizzled man stepped out onto the porch, closing the door behind him. She was almost relieved that it wasn't Nathan. She watched the exchange, straining to hear the conversation.

Suddenly both Kito and the man were walking toward the wagon. Her heart in her throat, Susannah nervously wiped her sweaty palms on her skirt.

As they approached, she studied the bowlegged little man. He was a midget beside Kito. She watched him come closer, wondering what she would say, wondering if she would even find her voice.

He stepped close to the wagon and squinted up at her. "You know Nate?"

Nodding quickly, she answered, "Yes. I . . . I know him."

"Know where he is?" the grizzled little man asked.

"No. No, I'd . . . I'd hoped he was here."

The man whistled through a gap in his teeth and studied her, swung his gaze toward Louisa, then at Corey. "Young'un yours?"

"Of . . . of course." Her glance went from Kito to

Louisa. *Who else would he belong to, you dolt?* She was getting more nervous by the minute, but she was relieved she could hold her tongue. It was at times like this when it usually started to wag.

"Well," he began, sucking in air through the hole where his two front teeth used to be, "I got me a sit-cheation here."

"A . . . a situation?"

He nodded. "I got a sick boy in the house. Sick in the head," he said, putting a finger to his own.

She grew tense with fear and excitement. "A boy? Nathan's boy?"

"Yep. You know 'bout Nathan's boy?"

With an answering nod, she said, "He . . . his body was never found. They assumed he'd been carried off by—"

"Yep," he interrupted. "That's the story. But Jackson weren't carried off by no coyotes."

Her heart galloped in her chest. "No?"

"Nope. He ain't talkin' much, but it appears to me like he's been livin' with the Yuroks."

"Yuroks?" She felt light-headed. Nathan's son was alive!

"Injuns. Live mostly on the coast." He swung his wiry arm toward the west.

"How can you tell?" *Oh, Nathan, Nathan, where are you?*

"When he's sleepin' he mutters a few words now and then. Sounds like Yurok to me."

"What about . . . about Nathan's wife?" She held her breath.

He took out a pinch of snuff and stuffed it against his cheek. "She's buried over yonder. What'd you hear about that?"

Flustered by his response, she stuttered, "I . . . not

much. I mean, a man came to my cabin before I left. He said Nathan's family hadn't been completely wiped out. I guess . . . I guess he meant the boy." She felt selfish relief.

The old fellow stroked his feedbag whiskers. "Who was he?"

She shrugged. "I didn't know him."

"He a breed?"

Her heart lifted in surprise. "Yes. He was a breed. Why?"

He scratched his chin through the thick, gray fuzz. "Was a scout for the infantry. Name's McCloud."

Nodding, she answered softly, "Yes. That's the name he gave me."

He took off his battered hat, scratched a spot at his temple, then shoved the hat onto his balding head again. "He knows somethin' 'bout all this. I knew it."

"All . . . all what?"

"I don't think Nate ever gave up hope that mebbe both of 'em might still be alive. After all, he weren't even here when Miss Judith was buried. Pretty danged hard to let a person go who you ain't even sure is dead. Woulda been better if he'd buried her hisself."

Susannah remembered how often she'd caught Nathan staring into space. Yes, undoubtedly he'd been thinking about Judith, hoping against hope that she was still alive. It hurt, but she couldn't blame him. "We'd like to help with the boy, if we could."

He sucked on his remaining teeth as he scrutinized her. "Ya don't look like his ma, but yer white." He spat a wad of tobacco juice out sideways. "Might help."

She glanced at Louisa and Kito. "May . . . may we all come to the house?"

He nodded expansively. "'Course. 'Course." He

pointed to Kito. "I kin use this fellow's strength to help me start repairs. And if he wants to stick around, I got me a heap of tanbark oaks that need strippin'."

"We saw men doing that as we rode through the oaks," she responded. "What is it used for?"

"Sell it to tanners. They use it to treat leather. Like I said, I could use the big buck's help."

The slur made Susannah bristle. "Sir?" When he turned, Susannah asked, "What's your name?"

"Nub Watkins, ma'am."

"Well, Mr. Watkins, I'm Susannah, the man's name is Kito. Her name," she said, indicating Louisa, "is Louisa. Please remember that."

Watkins shrugged, unaware of his crime and unbothered by her assault. "Sure. Sure. Don't make me no nevermind."

Susannah tiptoed into the bedroom, Max at her side. The boy, Jackson, lay on the floor, although the bed was made and the bedding turned down. It was inviting, but it appeared that the boy would have none of it. Max whined at her side.

"Max, heel." The dog shivered beside her, anxious to explore the room. She found Jackson staring at her. "Jackson?" Her voice quivered a little. He continued to study her and Max through eyes that were so much like Nathan's she nearly wept.

"My name is Susannah. I'm a friend of your father's. This," she added, "is Max. He loves children. I thought maybe you might want to rub his ears. He likes that, too." She waited for a response; there was none. His gaze roamed the ceiling.

Susannah took a deep breath, expelling it slowly. Scanning the room, she found a rocking chair in the corner. She crossed to it and sat. Max followed her. Perhaps Jackson just needed time to adjust. She wondered what memories he had of his mother and father. She wondered, too, her heart aching, if he really knew what happened to his mother. He'd been gone for five years. Did he remember English at all?

"Jackson, I'm going to tell you how I met your father." She ignored his quiet resistance. "He came to me when I needed help. First, he saved me from the hands of the town drunk. Then the drunk came out to my cabin and locked Max, here, in a shed so he could peep in my windows. Your father hauled the drunk into town and made friends with my dog. He . . . he built a new porch for my cabin, and chopped wood."

She paused, waiting for a response. When there was none, she went on. "He talked about you often. He loved you very much, Jackson. Very much."

Max nuzzled her hand, and she rubbed his ears. "At first I was angry with Max for taking such a shine to your father, because he was supposed to protect me. Max never liked anyone other than me and my little boy until your father came. I knew then that there was something special about him, for Max was very selective about who he let into my yard, and even more particular about who touched him."

She took in the room, finding the memories kept by a parent who had lost something more valuable than his own life. Handmade toys, a beautiful wooden top, a toy soldier . . . a carved wolf. "Your father made you many beautiful toys, I can tell. He made my little boy an elephant." She laughed, a soft sound filling the corners of the quiet room. "Corey loves elephants. He even tells me that he hears them early in the morning. Of course, he's teasing me. We know that elephants don't wander the mountains of California."

She glanced at Max, who was crawling slowly toward Jackson on his belly, his tail thumping against the floor. She also saw Jackson's hand move to his side, palm out, giving Max the chance to smell him. She felt a lightness near her heart and she quelled a smile.

When Max felt he'd been accepted, he sniffed Jackson's face, licking him lightly on the cheek. Jackson grinned, and again Susannah's heart squeezed with emotion, for it was Nathan's smile all over again.

Susannah stood. "Do you want Max to stay with you?" She wasn't sure Jackson understood, but when she moved toward the door, the boy hugged Max around the neck, keeping him by his side.

"I'll come for Max later, Jackson."

He appeared too engrossed in Max's affections to bother with her.

Susannah stepped into the great room. Louisa had already taken over the kitchen and had an enormous fire burning in the fireplace that occupied the center of the room. She was at the counter, mixing together what Susannah assumed to be cookie dough. In no time, the room would smell delicious.

"How is the boy, Honeybelle?"

Susannah poured herself a cup of coffee and sat down at the table. "I'm not at all sure he even understands English anymore." A small smile creased her mouth. "He understands love, though. He and Max are already fast friends."

"That was right smart of you."

"Smart? What do you mean?"

"To bring the dog in. Sounds like a perfect plan to bring the boy into the circle of his family again."

Susannah felt a bit self-satisfied. "I hadn't thought it out. It just seemed like a good idea at the time." She glanced around. "Where's Corey?"

Louisa turned from the counter. "Why, he was jes' here."

Feeling a sense of alarm, Susannah rose and went

toward the door that went outside. Out of the corner of her eye she saw that the door to Jackson's room was ajar. She'd shut it when she left.

Tiptoeing over, she peered in. She felt a jolt in her chest, for Corey and Jackson studied one another across the long expanse of Max's back.

"Corey?" When he raised his head, she said, "Come with mama, darling."

He shook his head. "No."

Susannah swallowed hard. She didn't want to forcibly take him out of the room. If she tried, he'd probably surprise her and throw a tidy little tantrum. He always did that when she least expected it. She went to him and lowered herself to her knees beside him. "Louisa is making cookies, darling. Don't you want to help?"

He shook his head firmly, his eyes never leaving Jackson.

Susannah softened. "Do you know who this is, Corey?" When he didn't respond, she continued. "This is Jackson. Nathan is Jackson's papa."

He looked mutinous. "Nathan is *Corey's* papa, too."

Susannah's hand flew to her mouth and she sank farther to the floor. He hadn't said a word about Nathan since the morning he'd awakened and found him gone. He'd wandered about the cabin for an hour, going to the window constantly to stare outside. Since then, he'd said nothing. Now—*this*.

She ran her fingers through his soft curls. "Corey, honey, I don't think—"

"He . . . Corey . . . stay," Jackson interrupted haltingly.

Susannah's mouth gaped open. "Jackson! You remember!" She scrambled to her feet and hurried to the door, anxious to tell the others. A backward glance at the two boys lavishing their attention on the dog told her it was all right for her to leave.

As she stepped into the great room again, she found Nub Watkins sitting at the table, noisily slurping coffee from a saucer. He glanced up at her. "How's things goin'?"

She nearly fell into the chair across from him. "You won't believe it. He spoke to me!"

Watkins sat up straight. "Say, what?"

Susannah nodded eagerly, glancing quickly at Louisa, who had just pulled fresh cookies from the oven. "I went in to get Corey, but Jackson said he could stay."

Nub's expression told her he didn't quite believe her. "Ya mean he up and said, 'Corey can stay'?"

"Well, he . . . it was quite hesitant, but he clearly said 'Corey—stay.'" She didn't think it was prudent to mention that Corey wanted Nathan to be his father. Although, she thought, her heart fluttering with pleasure, it was an interesting image. . . .

That night, Corey insisted on sleeping on the floor in Jackson's room next to the other boy. Nub dragged out another sleeping roll and unfurled it. Susannah just shook her head, wondering if Corey would grow up believing all men preferred the cold, hard floor to a nice, soft bed. It did give her a place to sleep, though. Since they'd arrived, she'd wondered if they'd all have to share the wagon.

Susannah stopped at the door and watched as Max curled up between the boys. She closed the door and found herself staring into Louisa's dark, scolding eyes. "What's wrong?"

"You think you should let them two sleep in the same room right off, Honeybelle?"

Susannah strolled into the kitchen, Louisa at her side. "Why not?"

Louisa leaned toward Susannah. In a hushed voice, she whispered, "The boy has been livin' with savages."

Susannah refused to absorb Louisa's fears. "So, do you think he's going to eat Corey during the night?" she whispered dramatically.

Louisa appeared stung. "Well, 'course not. But . . . well, I jes' don't want nothin' to happen, that's all."

Susannah hugged Louisa's shoulders. "Nothing will happen." And she felt certain she was right. But she cursed Louisa for planting the seed, for she slept fitfully, waking often to make sure everything was all right.

With morning came another problem. Susannah had second thoughts about being there when, and if, Nathan arrived. She'd known that he'd left her with many things to sort out. She had no idea what conclusions he'd come to. Perhaps finding her in his home where he'd loved another woman would be more than he could stand. And Nub didn't appear to be certain that it was Nathan's wife who was buried under the cedar tree. That left Susannah wondering if the woman, like the boy, had been abducted by Indians, and was possibly still alive. She forced the thought aside, for it made her feel jealous, and she hated the feeling.

She dressed quickly, went into the kitchen and found Nub building a warm fire in the fireplace. While the coffee cooked, she sat at the table, urging Nub to sit across from her.

"Tell me something about Nathan," she said, sitting forward eagerly. "Have you been with him long?"

Nub nodded. "Yep, was with the family when Nate was jes' a tadpole. They had money in them days, sent him to the best schools. His pa wanted him to become a lawyer, like him. Even sent him to some fancy college in the east, but Nate wanted to farm."

He laughed, the sound ending in a wet cough. "His pa hated the idea, but tol' him if he'd jes' finish them college courses, he could do whatever he wanted. So he did. His ma had died years earlier. Then, when his pa died, Nate bought this piece of land. Had plenty of money till he married that Judith woman."

He sounded truly disgusted. Susannah had thought that Judith was perfect. "What . . . what happened?"

"Oh, now don't go gettin' me wrong. Miss Judith was a fine woman, but sickly," he said, wrinkling his battered nose. "An' she come from money an' was used to spendin' it. See all them pieces of furniture?" He tossed his arm toward the other side of the great room. "Them's pieces Nate had special made and sent from back east jes' because Miss Judith wanted 'em."

Susannah hadn't really noticed the furniture. Probably because everything was shrouded in dust.

"An' now," he continued, his voice filled with dismay, "we ain't got the money to fix this place up like it should be fixed." He stood slowly, his knees creaking. "Gotta get them cows milked."

Kito came in from outside, and Nub pointed a finger at him. "You know how to milk a cow?"

With a deep, humor-filled chuckle, Kito answered, "I grew up milkin' cows, Mister Nub. Jes' lead the way."

After they left, Louisa came into the kitchen with a pail and scrub brushes. "That Mister Nathan of yours ain't lived here for five years, Honeybelle. Can you 'magine? That ol' rooster Nub tol' me Mister Nathan came back and planted a tree near his wife's grave, then up and left again. An' Nub practically lives in the barn. I'll bet this place ain't had a good cleanin' since that poor woman died."

Susannah agreed but kept her thoughts to herself, appearing cheerful as they gave the house a thorough cleaning. The furnishings *were* expensive, although they hadn't been cared for in many years. She polished a scruffy wooden corner cupboard only to discover that beneath the dust and dirt was a rich walnut front with iron butt hinges and brass knobs. The dishes behind the glazed door were delicate and ornate. They looked new; she supposed they hadn't been used in five years, either. Maybe longer.

Susannah was scrubbing down the kitchen floor when Jackson came out of his room, Corey and Max trailing behind. Susannah stopped working. "Good morning. Did everyone sleep well?"

Corey toddled across the freshly washed floor. "Gotta pee, Mama."

She gave him a hug, still indebted to Nathan for training him. "You remember where the necessary is?"

Jackson strode up to them. "Come," he ordered Corey, motioning for him to follow.

They went outside, and a cold gust of air lingered in the room, causing Susannah to shiver. They were far north, and it was early November. She sensed the air had a hint of winter in it.

She bent to her task, remembering the night she and Nathan had danced in the snow. Her body betrayed her, sending little slivers of pleasure throughout as she recalled the memory of Nathan teaching her to dance. Teaching her to love . . .

Her smile grew dreamy and she felt all warm inside. Yes, she really loved him. Could she keep it to herself when she saw him, or would her eyes betray her?

She stood and went to the window. She couldn't hear what Louisa was saying, but she guessed that, much to Kito's dismay no doubt, Louisa was scolding him for something, for her mouth moved fast and furiously and she waggled a finger at him.

Susannah shook her head, a grim smile curving her mouth. She didn't understand their relationship. Louisa was hard-pressed to show any gentle feelings at all, and Kito just rolled his eyes and shook his head whenever she walked away from him.

Louisa marched to the house and stepped inside, her brow wrinkled with worry and her mouth arched into a frown.

Susannah picked up the pail of dirty water, went outside and tossed it over a patch she'd discovered was the garden. To her surprise, there were winter vegetables growing there. When she came inside, Louisa was still scowling.

"Better watch out," Susannah warned, "or your face will stay that way."

"That ain't funny," Louisa muttered, going to the stove and stirring the oatmeal. "Those boys ready to eat somethin'?"

Just then, Jackson and Corey tumbled into the house and scrambled to get to the table.

"Did you wash your hands?"

Corey made a face, but left the table and went to the wash basin. Jackson gave Susannah a wary glance, then followed him.

While the boys ate oatmeal, biscuits and gravy, shoveling it in as though they hadn't been fed in weeks, Susannah nursed a cup of coffee, unable to keep from smiling. Nub had all but called her a miracle worker last night before everyone had gone to bed. It wasn't true, of course. She just blundered into things and somehow they turned out fine. And, she thought, giving the dozing Max a glance, it didn't hurt to have a dog around.

Hearing a strangled sound, Susannah turned. Louisa was at the window, staring outside.

"What in the devil—" Louisa clamped her fists on her hips and glared. "What's *he* doing here?"

Curious, Susannah rose and joined her at the window. There was a burgeoning in her chest, and her pulse raced at her throat. "It's . . . it's Nathan," she whispered, barely able to speak.

"Nathan? *Your* Nathan?"

Susannah could only nod, her heart bobbing in her chest like a rubber ball.

"Honeybelle," Louisa said, her voice filled with anger and dread, "that's the man who made a deal with Sonny 'afore I left Mizzoura. Oh, Lord!" Her hand flew to her mouth. "I saw him ridin' away that day I arrived in Angel's Valley, and it clean slipped my mind."

They both stared outside. "I know for a fact that he's the man Sonny sent after you."

Susannah's heartbeat changed, knocking frantically against her ribs. "Oh, Louisa," she said, her voice shaking. "You . . . you must be mistaken."

Louisa gave her head a furious shake. "I ain't mistaken."

Susannah bit her lip until she tasted blood. No! The silent scream tore through her, knocking aside the fluttery feelings of arousal, trampling the eagerness that had gathered in her breast at the sight of him.

Even after Louisa's vehement claim of certainty, Susannah wanted it to be a mistake. "If he'd been the one Sonny sent, why didn't he do something about it?"

"I don't know, Honeybelle, I jes' know what I know." She nodded with finality.

Susannah continued to stare at Nathan, still unable

to believe it. He'd deceived her. He'd made her love him more than she'd thought she was capable of loving, but he'd been sent to destroy her. She hurt, ached deep down in places she'd let him enter, in places she'd protected for years and years until he'd come along. Places that now felt violated and dirty because of his treachery.

She watched him approach and dismount. He greeted both Nub and Kito with warm handshakes. Nub spoke quietly, grabbed Nathan's arm, then nodded toward the house.

When Nathan turned, Susannah bit back a cry of alarm. The anger she saw in his eyes was stark, explosive . . . unforgiving. Or was it a mirror of what she felt in her own heart?

14

Susannah's own fury, which spread cold and harsh through her, prevented her from trying to understand his. It shook her, leaving her puzzled, hurt and angry, but confronting him would come later. For now—

Turning from the window, she studied Jackson, who had just shoved his plate away. She went to him and held out her hand. "Come," she urged, forcing a warm smile.

Skepticism made his features wary, but he took her hand and followed her to the door. "Max," he said, clearly and distinctly. The dog rose, stretched and followed them outside.

When the boy saw Nathan, he pinched Susannah's fingers.

"It's all right, Jackson. That's your papa." *Swine that he is.* She watched the emotions that flashed across his face, and wondered if he knew . . . if he remembered. He stood by her side, stiff as a statue.

One of the most difficult things she had to do was look Nathan straight in the eye. When she did, she was

215

startled to see the fading bruises on his face. Silent applause rang in her ears, for now he would know how she'd felt all of her married life. Her betrayal ran deep and acrid, like stagnant water in a forgotten underground well. Her chest ached, like she'd taken a blow to it, and her feelings swamped her.

Nathan's gaze rested on his son. She watched his face then, too. It was torn with anguish, agony . . . beseeching relief. His eyes glistened brightly. How she wanted to triumph at his pain!

With slow, halting steps, he came toward them. "Jackson?"

Jackson gripped Susannah's hand even harder, and at the sound of Nathan's voice, Max bounded off the porch, yipping and wagging his tail as he circled him. Nathan hunkered down and scratched the dog's ears, but his eyes never left his son's face.

Nathan gave Max a final swat on the rump, then came and stood in front of Susannah and his son, his gaze still on Jackson. He swallowed, his throat working frantically. "I see you've met Max."

"Max," Jackson said, his voice strong.

As if it were an order, Max loped back to the porch and sat at Jackson's side, his flanks shivering with excitement.

Nathan gave Susannah a swift glance. "He can talk? I thought—"

"I don't know how much he understands." She hoped her voice sounded normal. It was hard to speak around the treachery that crowded her throat.

As he gazed at his son, his face emanated a look of miraculous disbelief that turned swiftly to sadness.

"He doesn't know who I am."

"Give him time." Her throat continued to clog with emotions of her own.

The door opened behind her. "Papa Nathan!"

Susannah gasped, her fingers flying to her mouth.

Nathan's eyes burned into hers before he forced a smile for her son. "Well, hello, little whistler man. How've you been, boy?"

Susannah's stomach churned. What in the devil did he have to be angry about? At least her feelings of betrayal were founded in fact.

Corey went to the steps, scooting down backward. He toddled to Nathan and clung to his leg. The adoration on his face as he stared up at him almost broke Susannah's already battered heart.

Giving Jackson's hand a final squeeze, she pulled her fingers from his grip, took the steps and tried to tug Corey away from Nathan's leg. He clung tightly, squealing unpleasantly when she tried to get him loose.

Nathan reached down and took Corey into his arms. The child was quiet immediately. His eyes were hard and cold as he said, "Nothing is his fault. I'd be a heartless bastard if I blamed the child for the sins of the mother."

Susannah took a step back, feeling as though he'd struck her. She stood by the porch, trying to catch her breath and will strength into her legs so she could walk away.

Refusing to let him see the effect of his words, she narrowed her gaze at him and answered, her voice laced with frost, "How very noble of you." She took off across the yard, toward the small domed building on the other side of the barn, leaving him to fend for himself.

She pulled open the door to the building and stepped inside, anxious to get away, to be alone, if only briefly. The room was cool and dark, the only light slanting in through a small window, and the slight openings between some of the boards.

She shut the door, leaning against it briefly, willing her heart to stop clattering. Closing her eyes, she pulled the slightly dank smell of the room into her lungs, expelling it slowly.

When she was able to gather her scattered thoughts, she realized that what he'd said to her hadn't made sense. If he was who Louisa said he was, then he'd known about her crime from the very beginning. He knew she'd stabbed Harlan, because Sonny would have told him.

She spat a curse, angry that her feelings for him didn't die when she learned of his deceit. She'd been the grandest fool of all, allowing herself to be suckered in by his understanding, caring and . . . and loving.

But, why was he angry with *her?* That didn't make sense. *She* had every right to feel a horrible sense of betrayal. After all, he'd lied to her, lulled her into a false sense of security, made *love* to her, for crying out loud, then left her. His dishonesty hurt like no physical pain she'd ever endured. The only thing that hurt more was his revulsion. How superbly he'd kept it hidden—until now.

She pushed herself away from the door and stepped farther into the dank chamber. Puzzled by the unusual gadgets in the room, she walked toward the center where an enormous tin tub sat inside a large wooden base. The tub was deep, and looked big enough to bathe an entire family at one time. There was a faucet attached to the tub and tubing connecting it to a pump against the wall.

She circled the odd structure, intrigued. She didn't know how long she'd stood staring at it, but soon she heard the door open behind her. An anxious feeling spread through her chest.

"Honeybelle? What you doin' in here?"

Relieved it wasn't Nathan, she turned, wresting back tears of confusion. "I had to get away from him."

Louisa joined her at the tub, her brows furrowing as she studied the contraption. "Did he admit to bein' the one sent by that pissant Sonny?"

"We didn't even get around to talking about that," Susannah answered.

"Well, then, what happened?"

Susannah shook her head, her initial fury returning. "I don't know, and I'm tempted not to give a damn." She felt the betrayal dig a little deeper, scraping at her skin, exposing the nerves. "Obviously," she said, her voice shaking, "he's a far better actor than I'd ever given him credit for."

She grasped at straws. "Are you sure he's the man you saw with Sonny?"

Louisa took her into her arms. "I know it as well as I know my own name, Honeybelle."

Louisa smelled of cinnamon and bread dough, the comforting aromas cushioning Susannah's misery. "I should have followed my first instincts about the bastard, Louisa. I . . ." She swallowed. "I even thought he might have been sent by Sonny, but he wasn't the type of man Sonny or Harlan ever spent any time with. Oh, God," she said, tears cramming her throat. "He was helpful and . . . and kind, and gentle. *Damnation.*" She wiped her tears, swiping them away with angry fingers. "I've been trying to think of something that would have alerted me, but there was nothing. He was so good with Corey. And he did things for me, not asking anything in return."

She sniffed again, dragged out her handkerchief and wiped her eyes and nose. "He didn't ask for *anything.*" She shook her head, rubbing her face against Louisa's soft, woolly hair. "I'm angry, Louisa. Angry and hurt that he did this to me. Oh, God, I wish I'd never met the bastard."

Louisa continued to massage her shoulders. "Fill one hand with spit and the other with wishes and see which one fills up first, Honeybelle."

"You're a big help." Susannah sniffed again. "What's he doing now?"

"When I left to come down here, he was sittin' on the porch steps, Corey on his knee and Jackson beside him. And 'course that dog layin' at his feet."

"Of course," she answered, still drowning in self-pity. "He still has his little group of admirers, doesn't he?" She shoved her handkerchief into her pocket and straightened her shoulders. "Was he talking to Jackson?"

"Yes, but that boy was quiet as stone." Louisa let out an anguished sigh. "That li'l mister of mine is sure fond of that treacherous man."

She remembered how Corey had attached himself to Nathan's leg. "I'll have to work on Corey's choice in men."

Sighing, she gave Louisa a loving squeeze, then stepped from her embrace and walked toward the door. "In spite of what he's done to me, I want him to resume his life with Jackson. For . . . for Jackson's sake, anyway."

"That'll take time, Honeybelle."

Susannah rubbed her temples. "Oh, Louisa. Can you imagine how he must have felt when he discovered Jackson was alive? Can you imagine?"

"I imagine he's got a passle of feelins' to sort out."

Susannah remembered how Louisa had appeared to scold Kito earlier in the morning. "How about you? Have you some feelings to sort out?"

Louisa snorted and turned away. "My feelins' don't need no sortin' out."

"I saw you railing at poor Kito this morning. What was that all about?"

At the mention of Kito's name, Louisa's chin lifted a mutinous inch. "He gets my hackles up is all."

"Why?" Susannah asked on an amused laugh. "He's the most thoughtful, kind, gentle man I've ever known."

Louisa swung around. "Gentle and kind, maybe. Thoughtful? Huh! He knows I want him in my bed, Honeybelle. I've wanted that man from the first time I saw him, standin' outside the smithy, all sleek and black, muscles ripplin' on top of muscles." She sucked in a shivery breath. "He's got some fool notion that we oughta be married before we share a bed."

Susannah couldn't help laughing. "You make it sound like a crime. If that's the way he feels, why not marry him?"

"I fully intend to. I jes' don't want for him to have the upper hand."

Susannah's grin turned lopsided. "You never have liked *anyone* to get the best of you. However," she warned, "this might be the time to change."

The mutinous lines that creased Louisa's pretty face softened. "I know," she answered quietly, giving Susannah a sly grin. "I know."

They left the building together, arm in arm. Susannah's gaze went automatically to the porch. Kito stood there alone, watching them walk toward him.

Susannah leaned into Louisa, squeezing her arm. "Does the sight of him standing there, all sweat and hard muscle, do funny things to your insides?"

Louisa swatted her hand. "What he does to my insides is for me to know, you little tease."

But Susannah turned her gaze on Louisa and found all the symptoms there: the throbbing pulse at the base of her throat, the eyes wide and soft, the mouth slightly open, a smile of anticipation curling the corners . . .

"I think you've been smitten, Miss Louisa Washington."

"If you can see all that jes' by lookin' at me, Honeybelle, then you've learned a thing or two since you left Mizzoura."

Flashes of memory and desire penetrated Susannah's pain, pitching low into her gut. *If you only knew, Louisa. If you only knew.*

Louisa and Kito were married the following day, Kito having asked Nub and Nathan to bring out the first available preacher. Luckily for them, the traveling preacher was just leaving Broken Jaw. Louisa put up a token fuss at not being informed, but an intimidating word from Susannah silenced her.

For Susannah, who vacillated between wanting to confront Nathan and wishing he'd fall off a cliff, seeing Louisa so blissfully happy was painful pleasure. She wanted happiness for her friend, she always had. At one time she'd dared to dream that she, too, might find happiness with Nathan, but she no longer harbored such fanciful daydreams.

She still ached at the sight of him, in spite of her feelings of betrayal. Pleasure and desire just didn't die on demand. Though her mind fought them, her body responded, and she became as angry with herself as she was with him. They avoided each other. Her misery increased.

Nub had a small apartment at the back of the house which he insisted Louisa and Kito use. He informed them he'd always been more comfortable in the room off the barn, anyway. Years ago he'd put in an old stove, and it was always warm, cozy and quiet. He admitted that having the "young'uns" constantly under foot bothered him. This gave him the chance to get away.

That night, after Susannah put Corey to bed, she found Nathan on the porch, smoking a cigarette. Though it was the perfect opportunity to face him, she had to force herself not to run.

She studied his profile, regretting what had become of their love, remembering how his looks had both frightened and calmed her. The scarred forehead, the battered nose, the mouth with the rusty smile, the wide, hard, shoulders and flat stomach . . .

Memories of his deception tumbled in from nowhere, and she must have made a noise, because suddenly she found him staring at her.

He took a drag on his cigarette, the smoke swirling out as he spoke. "Nice wedding."

She swallowed, disenchanted. "Yes," she answered softly. "Thank you for letting them stay." She reined in her feelings, both anxious and afraid to confront him with her fears.

He shrugged, studying something off in the distance. "Kito's a good man. I can use the help. And the woman is a far better cook than Nub."

"Louisa," she instructed. At his questioning glance, she said, "Her name is Louisa."

He gave her a silent nod.

Susannah pulled her shawl around her, trying to drive away the chill. Though it warmed her arms, it couldn't touch the coldness in her heart. The silence between them stretched to the point of pain. She could stand it no longer.

"You must have had a good laugh at how easily I was duped," she said, her throat tight. "I'm surprised, with the money you were paid to find me, you didn't haul me to the law and collect the rest of it."

"I was tempted," he answered around a menacing snarl.

Coming from Nathan, a verbal slap was worse than the physical ones she'd endured from Harlan, for the point of contact was her heart, not just the superficial skin on her face.

He sighed, gruff and deep, then flicked his cigarette away. It burned only a moment in the darkness before going out. "How did you find out?"

"Louisa," she answered simply, refusing to offer him more information. "What were you planning to do with me after you took your *pleasure?*"

Pulling out a pouch and paper, he rolled himself another cigarette. He took a long, quiet drag on it, the smoke disappearing into the night. "It doesn't matter now."

She tried to laugh, but the sound clotted in her throat. "Of course not. Nothing matters now, does it? Has Sonny paid you in full?"

He snorted a laugh. "Eager for his company, are you?"

"No! And why would you even think that?" she asked, anger making her stomach churn.

His hand gripped the porch railing. "You really need it all spelled out for you?"

"Yes," she said on a hiss of breath. "I need it all spelled out for me."

He was quiet for a moment, then said, "Sonny told me why you married Harlan."

A blister of anger burst inside her. "Oh, he did, did he? And what, pray tell, did he say?"

"That you married him because you knew he was wealthy."

Susannah laughed, a hard sound, filled with disbelief. "I married that son of a bitch because he was *rich?*" Incredulous, she added, "Is that why I killed him, too? Because he was *rich?*"

"You took the strongbox with you when you left, didn't you?"

She continued to look at him as though he'd lost his senses. "How did you know about the strongbox?"

"I learned a lot from Sonny the day I stopped at the cabin. Oh," he said on a harsh laugh, "I was so damned anxious to see you. Hell, I'd even earned enough money to pay Sonny back the advance he'd given me to find you."

His words confused her. "You did? Why?"

"That hardly matters now. How do you think I got so beat up? I spent hours in the ring with a notorious bruiser just to prove to you how much I cared. All I wanted to do when I got to the cabin was take you to bed again and screw your brains out—"

She gasped at the hateful tone in his voice. "There's no need to be vulgar, Nathan. I'm fully aware of why you *screwed* me."

"But instead of you waiting eagerly for me," he continued through clenched teeth, "I found Sonny, waiting for *you.*"

Suddenly she was afraid. "He was there, waiting for me?"

"Yeah," he said on a silky breath. "Waiting for sweet little you. What were you going to do with the stock certificates, Susannah?"

"Is that what was in the strongbox? Stock certificates?"

He snorted another hard laugh. "You *are* good, Susannah. Sonny told me you were."

"Sonny!" she spat. "You're a bigger fool than I thought if you believe anything that . . . that horse's ass has to say."

"You're telling me you didn't take the strongbox?"

"No. I took it. Maybe it was a callous thing to do, considering the circumstances, but—"

His hard, humorless laugh interrupted her. "But what good were cattle shares to a dead man, right?"

"Yes, I mean . . . I mean, no. I mean—" Oh *damn*, she didn't know what she meant. "Nathan, is *that* why you're so angry? Because I took my dead husband's valuables?"

He grabbed her chin and pinched hard. She swallowed a cry of pain. "Oh, we haven't even gotten to the good part, Susannah."

She pried his fingers from her chin. When he finally let go, she rubbed her skin, knowing that in the morning she'd be bruised. *That* was something she understood well.

"We haven't even come to the part about Corey."

A warning bell clanged in her head, but she couldn't understand the meaning. "What about Corey?"

"I want you to tell me the truth, Susannah. God, but I *need* the truth!"

She straightened in front of him. "I've never lied to you, Nathan."

He shook his finger at her. "Don't be so quick to say that. When I first met you, you lied to me about your husband. You lied to everyone about your husband."

"Yes, but . . . but that was only to protect Corey and me."

"Once a person starts to lie, it becomes easier, don't you think?"

She narrowed her gaze. "I have never lied about another thing, Nathan. Especially not to you."

Again, silence was taut between them. "Sonny claims you seduced him—"

"I *what?*"

"—and nine months later, Corey was born."

Hysterical laughter tinged with disbelief bubbled from her throat. "Sonny told you *that?* And . . . and you *believed* him?"

He didn't avoid her horrified gaze. "He had proof, Susannah."

She fought for breath. Armed with Sonny's gift of subterfuge, he was turning the tables on her, and she didn't know how to stop him. "What kind of proof could he possibly have?"

"Harlan had the mumps when he was thirteen. The doctor said he wouldn't be able to father children."

"I . . . I knew he'd had the mumps . . ." A fragment, so small it couldn't take hold, teased the edges of Susannah's memory. But she knew it wasn't real. Only in her nightmares had Sonny Walker ever succeeded in touching her. "It's not true."

"That's it? A simple, 'it's not true'? Not very convincing, Susannah. Tell me. If it *is* true, then who is Corey's father?"

She turned away, fighting the urge to beat at him with her fists. "It *isn't* true, Nathan. Don't you think I'd remember if someone else fathered my own child?"

"I would think so."

She heard the sarcasm in his voice. "If you don't believe me, Nathan Wolfe, then you can go straight to hell."

He was quiet for so long, Susannah thought he'd gone inside. Instead, she found him watching her. She was alarmed by what she saw on his face. "You still don't believe me."

"I want to. God, Susannah, I want to—"

"But you can't?" The blister of anger erupted, and she slapped him hard across the face. "Believe Sonny's lies if you must. I'm sure he was very convincing. Oh, you are such a *fool,*" she managed to say, her voice shaking with rage. "I'd take Corey and leave right now if it wasn't too dark to travel."

She pushed past him, shoving open the door to the house. "Corey and I will be gone at first light." She didn't know where they would go, and she didn't care. She just wanted to leave.

She refused to beg him to listen to her. To believe her. She would never grovel. She'd gladly leave. She realized that every time her life hit a snag, she ran away, but she didn't care. At least she did something. No longer would she accept any man's abuse and do nothing at all.

She'd hardly slept, yet something awakened her. Briefly disoriented, she stared at the window, then remembered that when she'd gone into the bedroom the night before, Corey was asleep in the bed. She'd grabbed a blanket and curled up on the sofa. She tried to stretch; her foot hit the end of the couch.

It was barely dawn. Awake most of the night, she'd alternately fumed with rage and moped with despair at how quickly things had changed.

She saw a movement out of the corner of her eye and turned over, finding Jackson standing beside the couch. Her surprise turned to concern.

"Jackson? What's wrong?"

His face was contorted with frustration as he tried to speak. "Uh . . . Corey . . . uh . . . Max," he stammered, pointing toward the door.

Her sense of alarm propelled her off the sofa. She plunged her arms into her flannel wrapper and tied the sash as she followed him to the bedroom. It was empty.

She rushed outside, ran down the steps and crossed the wet grass to the necessary. Shoving the door open, her heart sank when she found it empty.

She whirled around, her throat working frantically as her fears mounted. "Corey? Max?" Her cries were met with silence. *"Corey! Max!"*

Jackson was at her side, looking up at her, concern etched on his handsome young face. She gently took Jackson's shoulders and bent to look at him. Trying not to frighten him, she asked, "Do you know what happened?" She knew she couldn't expect an answer, but she had to ask, just the same.

Jackson, understanding the question if not the words, shook his head.

Susannah started toward the house, breaking into a run as she neared the porch. She ran inside, nearly knocking Nathan over in her haste to get to Louisa and Kito's quarters.

Nathan grabbed her arm. "What's wrong?"

She yanked it away, ignoring him as she hurried past him.

He caught up with her, taking her arm again. "I said, what's wrong? You're as pale as a ghost."

"Louisa!" she shouted as she continued down the hallway. "Kito! Louisa! Is Corey in there with you?"

Kito opened the door to their quarters, bare to the waist. "What, Miz Susannah? What about the li'l mister?"

Louisa was beside him in an instant, nervously belting her robe. "Honeybelle? What's wrong?"

Susannah pressed a hand to her bosom, trying to still her pounding heart. "Is . . . is Corey in there with you?"

They exchanged glances. "We ain't seen Corey since las' night," Kito answered.

She pressed shaky fingers to her mouth. "Oh, God . . . He's gone."

Nathan roughly turned her toward him. "Gone? What do you mean, gone?"

Flinging his hands from her shoulders, she spat, "G-o-n-e. Gone. As in not in the house, not in the necessary. Gone."

Nathan shoved his arms into the sleeves of his shirt. It was the first time Susannah had noticed that he, like Kito, had a bare torso. Her gaze lingered briefly as a fresh streamer of memory wrapped itself around her heart.

"What about the dog?" he asked as he buttoned his shirt.

She stumbled toward the kitchen. "I called him. He didn't come." It was then that she realized Corey might not have simply wandered off.

She swung around, bumping firmly into Nathan. Glaring up at him, she brought her fist close to his face and warned, "If Sonny had something to do with this—"

He grabbed her wrist and returned her angry glare. "Sonny Walker has no idea where you are—unless you wired him and told him yourself."

Wrenching her arm from him again, she hurried into her room to dress, slamming the door in his face.

~ 15 ~

Late afternoon of the following day, Nate and Kito rode over land they'd already searched at least a half dozen times before. Though neither spoke, their gazes shifted nervously toward the sky. The night ahead of them would be cold. A child alone, defenseless against the elements and the animals, would not survive.

During the long hours of the search, Nate's mind often wandered to thoughts of Susannah. Hell. He had to force himself to think about something else, but even when he did, images of her snaked into his head, stronger than before.

She'd always been convincing. As the mistreated wife, cowering when she'd burned his hand with the coffee. As the sweet, young innocent who, despite having had a child, was virginal in her response to his lovemaking. As the guileless mother, adoring her child, enchanted by his perfection, becoming childlike in her play with him. And as the timid pupil, shying away from Nate's kisses.

It couldn't be an act, not all of it. Once he'd realized

that, she was so angry, he doubted she'd have cared that he believed her. Sonny Walker was a snake, he knew that. He had the feeling there was some truth in what he said, but he couldn't dissect it all and discover it.

He didn't doubt that Susannah had fended for herself from the time she was a girl. He didn't doubt that her mother had been a whore. Sonny had said that the apple didn't fall far from the tree. Nathan didn't believe that; he didn't want to.

But there was still that matter of Harlan's bout with mumps. If he couldn't father a child, who else could be Corey's father? That's what bothered Nathan the most. Logical choice would be Sonny. But if it were true, why hadn't he noticed even the faintest flicker of response in Susannah's eyes when he mentioned it?

He forced his thoughts to another equally painful subject: Judith. Poor Judith, dying painfully. Alone. A worry still niggled at him. In his mind, he knew it was Judith buried out there, deep in the dirt. But because he hadn't seen her body, hadn't buried her himself, a small part of him wondered that perhaps she, like Jackson, was still alive.

He'd spoken with the sheriff in Broken Jaw, asking that he be informed if the man who'd brought Jackson back to him ever came around again. It was a harsh, callous thought, but imagining Judith being forced to live with the Indians was more cruel than wishing her dead. Never mind the stigma that attached itself to white women who'd been made to live that way, Judith wasn't physically or emotionally strong. She wouldn't have survived the hardships, the rapes. And if she had . . . He sucked in a ragged breath, his guilt compounded.

With his smattering of knowledge of the Yurok language, Nub had questioned Jackson about his mother. Nate had even showed him the ferrotype of the three of them that the photographer had taken before Nate went off to war. Jackson appeared to know her, to remember her, but whatever else he knew was locked away in a place for which Nate had no key.

With an urgency bordering on frenzy, he had to know whether it was Judith lying in the ground under the branches of that cedar tree. Until he heard from someone who'd been at the burial, he wouldn't rest. Until he knew for certain, he couldn't return to the welcome turbulence of Susannah's passion.

Although once back on his land, where he and Judith had started their life together, he'd found her presence everywhere. Even riding up that first day he could almost see her bent over, working in her flower garden, the floppy brim of her big hat dipping down to protect her face from the sun. And now, guilt for what he'd felt for Susannah became the master of his conscience.

A soft, mewling sound was carried toward him on the breeze. He pulled his mount to a stop. "Listen," he said softly.

Kito pulled up beside him. "Sounds like a bawlin' calf."

"Or a bawling child," Nate amended, his heart racing as he nudged his horse toward the sound. His gaze snagged a board sticking up amid a tangle of brush. Why hadn't they seen it before?

Cursing, he quickly dismounted and ran to the site. He'd forgotten about this old well. Hell, it had been boarded up when he bought the place. Hurling a few of the rotten boards aside, he peered into the dark, abandoned hole.

"Corey?" Fear, like grasping fingers, pinched his

heart. Ragged sniffles and weak heaving cries met his ears. He sagged to the ground with relief. At least the boy was crying. He should have remembered this hole. He should have!

"Kito? Light that lamp and bring it over here. And bring the rope."

"Is he all right?" Kito called.

"Damned if I know. He's crying, anyway, but it's darker than the devil's doorway down there."

Kito handed Nate the lamp, and Nate, on his stomach, dipped the lamp into the hole. His throat clenched like a fist when he saw Corey's face, and the tears that tracked through the dirt that covered it. The child began crying in earnest.

Soothing him with words of comfort, Nate moved the lamp past him and found Max lying lifeless against the wall of the well. "Looks like the dog tumbled in after him."

"We ain't heard no barkin'," Kito mused. "Is he dead?"

Nate squinted into the darkness. "I can't tell. Corey? You hang on there, little whistler man, I'm coming down for you." Corey's cries were weak; Nate had to get down there fast.

"Let's get these boards cleared away," he ordered, ripping at the rotting wood, tossing it aside. When the hole was open and fading sunlight slanted over it, he grabbed the rope and tied it around his waist.

"Here," he said, extending the rest of the rope to Kito. "Lower me down."

Nub rode up, his horse all but skidding to a stop. "They down there? You find 'em?"

"They're here. Ride back and tell his mother. And bring the wagon," he shouted as Nub rode back toward the ranch.

Kito lowered Nate into the hole. At the bottom,

Nate picked Corey up and held him close. "How you feelin', whistler man?"

Hiccoughing through his tears, Corey grabbed Nathan around the neck and held on. "Pull us up, Kito!" As they started a slow, upward ascent, Nate glanced at the dog. He hadn't moved or made a sound.

Susannah hiked up her skirts and ran. When her lungs burned and she thought they would burst, she ran some more. She reached the spot as Nathan lifted Corey to the ground.

"Ohgod, ohgod, ohgod," she murmured, tears streaming as she panted the words. She flung herself down beside him and dragged him into her arms. He cried, ragged sounds that tore at her heart. She hugged him close. "Are you all right? Oh, my darling!" She kissed him, sniffling away her own tears as they mingled with his.

Closing her eyes, she simply sat on the ground and held him, rocking rhythmically back and forth as she thanked God for generously allowing her to keep her child.

"We'd better get him to the house, Susannah. We don't know how badly he's hurt."

Nate's voice found its way inside her head. Sniffing again, she took in Nate's appearance. He was dirty, smudged from head to toe with mud. His face was guarded, but she hadn't expected more. Nodding, she allowed him to take Corey from her. Nub and Jackson arrived with the buckboard, and Nathan lifted Corey into the back where Nub, or someone, had prepared a soft bed.

"You ride back with him, Susannah. No doubt Louisa is ready for you."

She climbed into the wagon. "Nathan?" When he turned, she asked, "What about Max?"

Nathan looked toward the hole. "He's down there."

She felt a rush of panic. "You're not going to leave him there, are you?"

"Susannah, I don't think he—" He growled a curse. "I think he's dead."

Jackson leaped from the wagon and scrambled to the hole. "Max! Max!"

Nathan grabbed the boy by the shoulders. "Easy, Jackson. I don't think Max can hear you."

Jackson shrugged off his father's touch, huge tears hanging in his eyes. "Max," he pleaded, his voice pitifully thin.

"Nathan," Susannah said softly. "You can't just leave him down there."

Nathan's gaze was hooded, but he motioned toward Kito. "Lower me down again. I guess the least I can do is bring him up."

As the wagon clattered over the field, Susannah held her son close but kept her gaze on Jackson as he stood stiffly beside the hole to the abandoned well.

Louisa ran toward them as they rolled into the yard.

"He all right, Honeybelle? He all right?"

"I think so, Louisa. He's scared, though."

The wagon stopped, and Louisa reached toward Susannah. "Give the chile to me, Honeybelle. I have the bed ready for him."

Susannah lifted Corey over the side and into Louisa's waiting arms, then hopped over the side herself. They sped to the cabin and put Corey on the bed. His dirt-smeared face was pathetic.

"I . . . I'll get some soapy water," Louisa announced, then left the room.

Susannah carefully undressed him, studying his little body. Her heart constricted when she saw the bruises he'd gotten from his tumble into the well. She winced when she saw the purple discoloration and the swelling on his ankle. When she gently touched it, he whimpered.

"Corey? Darling? Can . . . can you move your ankle for Mama?"

He shook his head, his mouth drooping at the corners and his lips quivering.

Susannah took the ankle, gently moving it with her fingers. Corey cried, but put pressure against her hand with his foot. Relief careened through her. It wasn't broken.

Louisa returned with the soapy water, and Susannah bathed her son, studying him from every possible angle. He was weak and bruised, and had a sprained ankle, but he was alive. *Thank you, God.*

But now she couldn't leave, and she'd had every intention of doing so. And Nathan wasn't such an ogre that he'd throw them out now, with Corey hurt.

Her thoughts went to the night before, on the porch, and her blood ran hot. Oh, men were so anxious to believe what other men told them. But she wouldn't have thought that about Nathan. He *knew* Sonny. Ah, she thought on a heavy sigh, obviously not well enough. Not as well as Susannah knew him. Sonny Walker had been a thorn in her side for years. Years and years and years.

Why was Nathan so angry that she'd taken Harlan's strongbox? She'd taken it because she knew that if worse came to worst and she couldn't find work, hopefully she could sell whatever was in there to feed her and Corey. What did it matter to Nathan, anyway? And marrying Harlan because he was *rich?* What a joke! She shouldn't have to explain to Nathan that it had been a matter of survival. At the time, she hadn't been strong enough to leave either one of them, but at least Harlan had offered to marry her. Sonny, on the other hand, had merely wanted someone to warm his bed.

She rinsed out the cloth she'd used to wash Corey and pressed it to her face, the cool dampness soothing her.

There were footsteps behind her. Turning, she felt the familiar fluttering in her chest as Nathan stepped into the room. He looked tired, haggard . . . and heart-stoppingly handsome in spite of his fading bruises. It didn't matter what had gone on between them, she couldn't prevent the feelings that tumbled through her at the mere sight of him.

He came toward her. "How is he?"

His concern for Corey warmed her. Briefly, she wondered if his concern would have been as great if *she'd* taken the tumble into the well.

"He'll be all right. He's got bruises and scrapes . . . and I think he sprained his ankle. I don't think anything is broken." She smoothed the cloth over Corey's forehead, dampening his curls. He was asleep.

"What made him go off like that?"

He stood by the bed, his nearness sending shivers through her. "I don't know. He . . . he's walked in his sleep only twice before—" She gasped slightly, remembering that both times had been before they'd left Missouri, when he'd awakened to the noises of Harlan beating her and her trying to fight him off. It was as if Corey couldn't stand confrontation, so if he ran far enough away, he couldn't hear it, therefore it wouldn't happen. Sort of like closing one's eyes before being hit by a runaway horse and buggy.

"You think he walked in his sleep?" he asked incredulously.

He stood so close, the first thing that met her gaze

was the fly of his jeans. The denim was worn there, as if what was behind it was too large to be cradled comfortably. Her mouth went dry, sending another shiver through her as she remembered. She gave him a quick glance, then lowered her gaze to the bed again. "I can't think of any other explanation. Unless he had to use the necessary and got lost."

With one long, strong finger, he lifted her chin, his thumb moving over the bruise he'd made the night before. "I'm sorry," he apologized, his voice husky. He dropped his hand to his side.

His touch awakened memories of desire, and she quietly cursed her lovesick heart. Antagonism festered and her throat ached with unshed tears for what they'd had and lost. "Don't give it a thought. I'm accustomed to much worse."

Something flashed in his eyes before he turned and strode to the door.

She shouldn't have brought it up. The painful memories of assault were hers and hers alone. "Nathan?" When he turned, she asked, "Max?"

He let out a ragged sigh. "Well, he's not dead. I think it would be best to put him out of his misery, but Jackson . . ." He dragged his fingers through his hair, rearranging it in a way that made him look boyish . . . and lost. "Jackson would probably never forgive me."

"What are you going to do?"

With a weary shrug, he answered, "Nub took him to the barn. We'll have to see if there's anything we *can* do. I don't imagine Jackson will leave his side."

"Nathan?"

He faced away from her, his thick arms bracing the doorway. "Yeah?"

"I . . . I guess Corey and I will leave as soon as . . . as soon as he's able to travel," she said quietly.

"Is that what you want, Susannah?"

With a hunger so deep her heart ached, she studied him. His head was bent, giving him an expression of weariness and defeat. She took a deep breath. "If you can't believe me, or trust me, then yes. It's what I want."

"Why don't we wait and see what happens." He turned, his face pinched with anguish. "I want to believe you, Susannah. I do. But there's still a part of me—"

He left without finishing the sentence, and Susannah had the deepest, saddest, most miserable urge to bawl.

Louisa forced her to leave Corey's bedside, but instead of going to sleep, Susannah went to the barn to see her dog. Her mouth twisted into a wry smile. *Her* dog?

She stood, watching Jackson dip a cloth in water and wring it into Max's mouth. Whatever happened, if, by some miracle, Max survived, she would have to leave him with Jackson. She'd never known a bond to be forged so quickly and deeply before.

"How is he, Jackson?" As before, she was sure he didn't understand the words, only the question.

A frown nicked his brow. With gentle fingers, he touched Max's head and said a word Susannah didn't understand. Glancing up at her, he repeated it, closed his eyes and placed his hands against his cheek in a gesture of sleep.

"I see," she said, not really sure she did. She bent down beside Max and stroked his ears. He'd been scraped badly, too. Someone, perhaps Jackson himself, had cut the hair from his wounds and cleaned them.

"You're doing a fine job, Jackson," she said, giving

his hand a confident squeeze. Before she could draw her hand away, Jackson gripped it.

"Corey?"

Nodding, she gave him a warm smile. "He'll be all right."

She left the barn and let her gaze wander over the range of mountains that protected them from the ocean. There was a faint dusting of snow on them, but she wasn't surprised; it was well into November. There was a bite to the air that bode of winter.

Out of the corner of her eye, she saw movement in a copse of incense cedars. She turned her head and saw someone kneeling. With a fluttering constriction near her heart, she realized it was Nathan. One knee on the grass, his arm resting over his other thigh, he was staring at something on the ground. The stricture around her heart tightened. He had the posture of a man communing with the dead.

Staying behind him, she moved slowly in his direction. She saw the slightly raised granite slab and understood. New emotions tumbled over the old, and she felt a brief but unconscionable wash of self-pity.

She crossed her arms over her waist, hugging herself tightly. The scene before her didn't surprise her, she just wished it didn't give her such a hollow feeling in the pit of her stomach.

As she watched him, his head bowed and his shoulders slumped, her self-pity disappeared. He looked so sad, so vulnerable. He was still wrestling with his feelings for Judith, and she wanted to understand. In some ways she did. In others, she wondered if he would ever resolve his feelings and his guilt. It made her angry.

Feeling like a voyeur, she turned to leave. Her foot snapped a twig.

"What do you want?"

She whirled around and found Nathan standing, feet apart, hands balled into fists at his sides, his expression commensurate to a thunderhead.

She felt part of her anger dissolve in the face of his pain. "I . . . nothing. I saw you here, and I—"

"And you what?" His voice was threatening.

"And . . . and I wanted to see where she . . . your wife . . . was buried." She swallowed hard, hating the suffering she saw in his eyes. "Oh, Nathan, I'm so sorry—"

In two long strides, he was in front of her, his hands clamped to her shoulders. "I want to hate you." His harsh whisper chafed her skin, bruised the fragile petals around her heart.

She stared into his tormented eyes, the remainder of her anger dissipating like smoke on the wind. "Oh, Nathan, I—"

His mouth came down on hers, hard, angry and as hungry as her own. He held her head with one hand, forcing the kiss, devouring her mouth, and swept her back and her buttocks with the other. He pressed her close; she felt the thick ridge behind his fly against her stomach. In spite of her answering response, she felt unclean having such sensations here, so close to his wife's grave.

"Nathan, not here, I—"

He lifted her up, bringing his shaft against the kernel of sensation that was buried in the folds of skin behind her drawers. He rubbed against her, tentacles of desire leaving her shaky and wanting more, yet she knew he was responding out of frustration, anger and pain, not out of any love for her.

His breath was ragged as he dragged his mouth from hers. "I want to undress you, throw you down on the grass and plunge myself into you." He kissed her again, sucking her lips, probing the soft underside with his tongue. She opened to tell him to stop, but his mouth devoured hers again, and in spite of herself, she answered his kiss.

She finally tore her mouth away to catch her breath. "Nathan, no. I—" She gasped as his hand found her breast, fondling it roughly. With a harsh groan, he ripped the front of her dress, sending the buttons flying. His hand dipped inside and she felt heat scorch a path from her nipple to her pelvis. He dragged one side of her dress and her chemise over her shoulder, freeing her breast. He pulled away briefly, gazing down at her, his thumb moving back and forth across the turgid nipple.

"Beautiful," he said on a husky whisper. "So damn beautiful . . ." He bent and took the nipple into his mouth, rubbing it with his tongue. With a groan of reluctance he raised his head and stared at her, his eyelids heavy with desire. He dragged up her skirt and petticoat and moved his hands to her buttocks, lifting her so that his thick need pressed against her. She clung to him, tears of frustration wetting her cheeks and her lips. She forced herself to remember where they were, but her reluctance for him to take her was all but gone.

He sank to his knees, bringing her with him, wrapping her legs around his waist.

She was drowning in sensations. Still, a seed of respect nested amid her desire, and she pushed against him, fighting the inexorable desire that expanded between her legs, where her womanhood cradled the hard, enormous length of him. He was angry, she knew that. And she sensed that he didn't *want* to want her.

"Oh, God, N-Nathan." She sobbed as she fought him. "I understand. I really do, but not here, not like this!" She was as close to the edge as he. She bit his chin and pinched him, but her efforts had become futile, as had her wish to do so.

He expelled a ragged, pain-filled moan.

"It's all . . . all right, darling." She knew everything he was feeling, for she felt it too. But they had to stop. They *had* to. She knew he would sink into a deeper pit of guilt if they didn't. "No, Nathan. Please," she pleaded, "you don't want to do this. Not this way . . . not here—"

He jerked away, the desire fading quickly from his eyes. He stood, dumping her to the ground.

"Get away from me." His voice was laced with misery.

With one hand she held her dress together over her bosom. With the other, she wiped her face, her tears continuing to drip from her chin. "Nathan, oh, Nathan, I understand—"

"I said go away!" His face was drawn with disgust and guilt as he eyed her desire tumbled appearance. "Only a whore would seduce a man on his wife's grave."

All remnants of her own desire scattered like buckshot in the wind and her anger surfaced. "What?"

"You heard me," he warned, turning away from her.

She glared at him, knowing his attack was in self-defense because of his own guilt. It did nothing to soften her own anger. "Oh, I heard you. More of Sonny's verbal vomit, no doubt."

"Are you saying your mother wasn't a whore?" It was more of an accusation than a question.

Susannah swallowed, unsure if she was angrier at Sonny for feeding Nathan so many insulting suggestions or at Nathan for believing them. "No. My mother was a whore. But that doesn't automatically make me one."

"Go ahead, Susannah. Convince me I'm wrong

about you. Damnit, prove to me that Corey is Harlan's boy. *Prove* to me you didn't sleep with your own brother-in-law, or someone else for that matter."

She saw red. Livid, bloodred. "You *ass*. I don't have to prove anything. That part of my life is as clear to me as the cloudless sky above us. And even if it weren't, what difference should it make to you? Why in the bloody hell do you care what I did years before I even met you? If it's so damned important to you, *you* find the proof. But you won't do that, will you? You only believe what you want to believe." With one hand still holding her bodice together, she got to her feet, amazed that she could stand without help.

"Meaning what?"

She riveted him with a hard glare of her own. "Why is it that with me, 'the apple doesn't fall far from the tree'? Yet with Corey, you don't 'blame the child for the sins of the mother'?"

She left then, striding across the uneven ground as quickly as she could, hoping to put as much distance between them as was humanly possible.

~ 16 ~

Nate watched her storm to the house, hating himself . . . hating her . . . He staggered to an old cedar and slumped to the ground, resting himself against the trunk. Yeah, she was right. He'd used analogies as they suited him. Corey was innocent; she probably was, too, but the question of who Corey's father was still gnawed at Nathan like a toothache. Because of that, he'd lashed out, using it as an avenue for his own guilt.

He'd wanted her with the urgency of a man being buried alive, gasping for air. He'd thought he could use her as he'd used other women, but found that he couldn't. In spite of what he wanted to believe about her, in spite of his itch and his craving for her, he couldn't just use her callously then toss her aside. He'd had no trouble doing that with other women after Judith died. But damnit, why wouldn't Susannah tell him what he wanted to know? What was she hiding?

A squiggle of sanity made him ask himself why it was so damned important.

He wanted her; he could admit that. He just didn't want to need her, but need her he did. He rubbed his hands over his face, digging the heels of his palms into his eyes. And he couldn't leave her alone. Even now, so close to Judith's grave, he'd wanted to take Susannah and bury himself deep inside her.

His gut flamed, shaming him. His need was so overpowering, he would have taken her here had not his guilt been stronger. He was no longer imprisoned by his love for Judith, only the guilt he felt at not loving her enough, and not being there when she'd needed him.

God forgive him, but he wanted Susannah still. Thoughts of her were etched in his memory, even in his heart. Had they been anywhere else on his ranch, he would have taken her for certain. And he'd want it to be angry and violent, but he knew himself better than that. Susannah, no matter what she was, was the kind of woman he'd been looking for even before he met Judith.

He lifted his gaze toward the cabin. Kito came toward him, his limping strides purposeful, his look threatening. When he reached Nate, he stood and looked down at him, his powerful fists clenched on his hips, his face barely masking his anger.

"What're you doin' to that gal?" Even without the words, he was a threat.

Nate glanced away. "You don't know the whole story, Kito."

"You promised me you'd never hurt her. 'Member that?"

Nate nodded, remembering well. "That was before."

"Before what?"

Nate sat with his elbows on his knees, his arms

hanging down between his legs, and studied the man. There wasn't a trace of Sambo left in his demeanor.

"Before I discovered she had so many secrets," he answered, unable to curb the angry edge to his voice.

"'Before I discovered she had so many secrets,'" Kito mimicked in a whiny voice.

Nate ignored him. "I learned that her husband wasn't the father of the boy, Kito. Why won't she tell me the truth?"

"I 'magine you asked her all nice-like," Kito responded, his expression grim.

Nate dragged his hands over his face. "It's not an easy question to ask politely," he rebutted.

"Do it really matter so much, Mister Nathan?"

Nate swore. "It wouldn't matter at all if she'd just tell me the goddamn truth!"

"An' how do you know she ain't?"

Nate slammed his head against the tree trunk, welcoming the pain. "Because there's proof that she isn't."

Kito shifted his weight off his bad leg. "Guess at some point a person's gotta have faith, Mr. Nathan."

To change the subject, he asked, "Has there been any word on this McCloud fellow?"

"That's what I come out here to tell you."

Nathan stood, unsure whether it was dread or anticipation that slammed at his heart. "Well? What is it?"

"He's in town. He'll meet you at the saloon in the mornin'."

Dust and smoke danced together in the streams of daylight that sifted into the saloon through the wooden slats that covered the windows. The room had a sour smell as stale sweat and cigar smoke mingled with the potent odor of rotgut whiskey.

It was barely noon; the room was quiet, except for the man behind the bar, and a table filled with early morning poker players near the door. Nate stood for a moment, allowing his eyes to adjust to the dim light. A man sat at a table in the back, his chair tipped against the wall, his hat nearly covering his eyes. Nate threaded his way around the empty tables and chairs until he stood in front of him.

"You McCloud?"

The man brought his chair to the floor and shoved his hat to the back of his head. He was a breed. Inky hair hung nearly to his shoulders. High, sharply ridged cheekbones marked his facial terrain like a craggy mountain chain. His eyes were the startling shade of whiskey aged in smoke. An expensive cigar was clamped between his strong white teeth.

"And if I am?"

Nate straddled a chair across from him. "Nate Wolfe," he announced, not bothering to extend his hand.

McCloud poured himself a shot from the bottle that stood on the table. By way of offering, he lifted the glass toward Nate.

"It's a little too early for me."

With an indifferent shrug, the breed removed the cigar from between his teeth and tossed back the whiskey, slamming the empty glass on the table when he was done.

"Your boy all right?" He kept the cigar between his first two fingers.

Nate nodded. "Do I have you to thank for bringing him home?"

"It was the least I could do." He circled the empty

glass with his forefinger. "I saw the whole thing happen five years ago."

Nate's insides went cold. "You were there?"

McCloud nodded. "Before you get any ideas, I think you should know that what you were told was a lie."

Nate leaned in close, gripping the rungs of the chair so tightly his knuckles went white. "What the hell are you saying?"

McCloud poured himself another shot but didn't take it. Instead, he appeared to study it. "I was a scout for Commander Phillips out of Fort Humboldt." His gaze left the glass and landed on Nate; it was filled with disgust. "Your wife and son weren't the victims of an Indian raid, Mr. Wolfe. They were victims of a careless mine explosion. An explosion planted by Commander Phillips's men to close down the passageway to the Alhambra mine."

Nate swallowed hard, barely hanging onto his fury. "Why don't you tell me exactly what happened, and how my family got involved."

McCloud tossed off the whiskey, then plugged the cigar between his teeth again. Closing his eyes, he took two deep puffs, accentuating the hollows beneath his stark cheekbones. "Damn fine cigars, these Caribbeans. Got them from a whore." He puffed again, then blew out a ring of smoke. "She was a little long in the tooth, but I like 'em that way."

Nate held the reins on his agitation, knowing the breed was drawing out the moment.

McCloud tapped out the ash on the edge of the table. "About your family, Mr. Wolfe. I don't know what they were doing there. Phillips thought he'd sealed the area off. Hell, the place was thick with blackberries and we found a basket nearby. I guess they could have just selected the wrong place to pick berries."

Nate rubbed his temples, trying to ward off a massive headache. "Then what happened?"

The breed spun the empty glass on the table. "We were ordered to leave, but about an hour later I doubled back. That's when I discovered your wife was dead, but the boy had disappeared."

Nate was reliving it again, pulling in the guilt, allowing it to eat at him. He wasn't able to suppress his feelings, nor did he want to. The guilt was deserved. "How did you know my son was alive?"

"I didn't think he was. The lieutenant in charge of the blasting ordered us to leave and concocted a story about the marauding Indians. When I found the boy gone," he continued, lifting one sharp, black eyebrow, "I searched the ground, found blood and realized he might have been dragged off by . . . by something. Coyotes, maybe. Hell, I didn't know. That's what I thought until a few months ago."

Nate's head continued to ache and spin; his stomach felt rancid with bile. "What changed your mind?"

McCloud shoved the empty glass between his thumbs. "I heard rumors about a white boy living among the Yuroks. They aren't my people, but I've had some dealings with them."

Nate massaged the knot in his neck. "Thank you for bringing him home."

The breed gave him a casual shrug. "I figured it was the least I could do. He hadn't been mistreated. Fact is, he'd been adopted by the tribe."

"And they let you take him?"

A grim smile cracked McCloud's mouth. "I had to do a little bartering."

Nate had to ask. "What about my wife? I was

wondering . . ." He sucked in a painful breath of air. "I've had a recurring nightmare that the woman buried on my ranch isn't her."

McCloud studied him, his unusual colored eyes carefully masking whatever it was he knew, or was feeling. "Put your mind to rest, Mr. Wolfe, it's her. Her body was identified by Doc Madison. He's probably got some records over there. I suggest you talk to him."

Almost relieved, Nate put his head in his hands. Maybe now he could put it all behind him. God, he hoped so.

"Your ranch looks a little seedy. Run-down."

Nate nodded. "I've been gone a long time."

"I'm a fair carpenter. Could you use some help?"

Studying the breed, Nate realized that giving him a job was the least he could do as payment for returning Jackson. "Can't pay much, but would room and board do?"

The breed shrugged. "Better than nothing."

Nate stood, studying McCloud only briefly before leaving the saloon and returning home.

Susannah mixed biscuits for supper, but could still feel the verbal slap from Nathan's attack the day before. Odd as it was, his anger and the way he chose to channel it had a deeper and more lasting effect on her than all of Harlan's slaps and punches. But she knew why. She loved Nathan; she'd loathed Harlan.

She glanced at Louisa, who was stirring dough for molasses cookies and humming softly, a smile creasing her generous mouth.

"Married life agrees with you."

Louisa gave her a sly smile, then returned to her chore. "I'm ten years older'n you, Honeybelle. Thirty's nippin' at my butt like a hound huntin' down a possum. In all my born days, I never expected to feel this way. But I'll tell you what, the minute I laid eyes on that man, I knew he'd be mine."

A tangle of emotions clogged Susannah's throat. She couldn't help but feel envious at Louisa's good fortune. On quiet nights, she could hear the sounds of their lusty lovemaking, and it made her ache for what she couldn't have. "You know how happy I am for you."

Louisa stopped what she was doing. "Why're you so danged stubborn, Honeybelle?"

Susannah dumped the biscuit dough on the counter, kneaded it a few times, then pressed it into a thin slab with her fingers and the heels of her hands. "Stubborn? What do you mean?"

"You know full well what I mean," Louisa scolded. "That scalawag of a man has all sort of crazy notions about why you married Harlan. Why don't you jes' tell him the truth?"

"If he'd wanted the truth, he wouldn't have been so easily taken in by Sonny. The worst part, though, is that he has some insane notion that Harlan wasn't Corey's father."

Louisa sifted another cup of flour into the cookie dough then mixed it in with her hands. "So you're jes' gonna let him come to his own conclusions, is that it?"

"He says he wants to believe me, Louisa. Why is it up to me to convince him? He worked for Sonny. He should know him well enough to realize when the bastard's lying."

"Why would he think Harlan weren't Corey's pa?"

"Oh," Susannah answered on a whoosh of air, "some crazy story about Harlan having the mumps when he was young, therefore rendering him sterile or something."

Louisa stopped working altogether. "Can that happen?"

"How should I know!" She felt immediate remorse. "I'm sorry, Louisa. None of this is your fault. But having mumps didn't make Harlan incapable of fathering a child. Corey's proof of that."

Louisa went back to her dough. "I see what you mean, Honeybelle." She pulled out a cookie sheet and began dropping miniature balls of cookie dough onto it. "But no person alive 'cept you and me and Sonny knows what went on in that Walker house."

With a tin cup, Susannah cut out biscuit circles and placed them on a baking sheet. "Well, *I* know I didn't sleep with Sonny, and *you* know I didn't sleep with Sonny. If Nathan can't accept my word for it, then we weren't meant to be together." She slid the sheet into the oven. "Maybe it would be best if we left, after all."

"If you leave, we'll *all* leave."

"No," Susannah argued, wiping her hands on a towel. "You and Kito have found a home here. I've never seen you both happier. I think it was a blessing that he lost his job in Angel's Valley. You'll both be so much happier here."

"We can be happy wherever you are, Honeybelle. You think I could let you take my li'l mister away again? Hell, no."

Susannah refused to argue. As much as she wanted Louisa and Kito with her, she knew that Nathan's ranch was the perfect place for both of them.

She went to the window and caught a glimpse of Jackson as he stepped into the barn. He hadn't come up to the house since they'd hauled poor Max out of the well.

She quickly prepared a lunch of cold chicken, bread and cookies, placing it in a tin pail with a handle. Hurrying to the back of the stove, she filled another smaller pail with oatmeal, lacing it with molasses and cream.

Crossing to the coat tree by the door, she lifted off her threadbare cape and slid it around her shoulders. "Louisa, I'm going out to try to get Jackson to eat something. When Kito comes in for lunch, would you bundle Corey up in a warm blanket and ask him to bring him to the barn?"

"What you plannin' to do, Honeybelle?" There was slight disapproval in her tone.

"Earlier this morning, after the doctor was here, Corey had insisted on seeing Max for himself. I promised him that if he took a good, long nap, I'd take him out to see the dog."

"You sure he should be moved?"

"Do you think I'd move him if the doctor had told me not to?" He'd assured Susannah that children were resilient, able to sustain tumbles that would surely break an adult's bones. But Corey did have a sprained ankle and was supposed to stay off his feet.

"Did you ask the li'l man why he went off like that?"

Susannah rotated her neck, hoping to work out the kinks. "Yes, poor little love. But I knew the answer even before he told me."

"Which was what?"

"He woke up and heard Nathan arguing with me on the porch. Whenever that happened between Harlan and me, Corey would wander off until he couldn't hear the noise anymore. I'd discovered it a couple of times, and believe me, it scared me senseless." She shivered. "Something dreadful could have happened to him. It almost did, this time."

Louisa gave her head a solemn shake. "Why didn't they hear the chile' cryin' way before they did, Honeybelle?"

"Odd as it may seem, the doctor thinks he probably

cried himself to sleep. And since the rest of us were sleeping, no one heard him."

"No injury to his sweet li'l head?"

Susannah gave Louisa a peck on the cheek. "No injury to his sweet little head, you old softy."

Susannah took the two tins, left the house and hurried across the cold grass, shivering as the chill easily filtered through her clothes. Stepping into the barn, she paused and listened as Jackson chanted an eerie, almost tuneless melody.

Padding noiselessly through the dimly lit barn, Susannah came to the room where Nub had put the stove. She felt the warmth immediately and peeked inside, finding Jackson curled up against Max's long body, chanting softly against the dog's ear.

The sight of the two of them almost broke her heart and she said a quick prayer herself for Max's survival. Jackson stopped chanting, and Susannah realized he was staring at her.

Smiling, she held out his lunch. "You haven't eaten since yesterday, Jackson." When he didn't respond, she opened the pail and pulled out a piece of chicken.

"Aren't you hungry?"

He moistened his lips and swallowed, eyeing the chicken hungrily.

Susannah sighed, put the chicken into the pail and placed it on the cold, dirty floor near him, then sat down across from him. "You have to eat, Jackson. You won't be any good to Max if you don't eat."

He rummaged through the contents of the pail, pulled out the bread and broke it into scraps. Then he took out the chicken and smeared grease onto a piece of bread and shoved it under Max's nose. Slowly, lovingly, he rubbed it back and forth across the dog's mouth.

Her heart lurched again. "Jackson," she said softly,

lifting off the lid to the other tin, "let's give him some of this." She took a spoon from her apron pocket, scooped out some of the oatmeal-molasses-cream mixture and put it on the inside of the lid. She handed it to Jackson.

With an understanding nod, Jackson took the food and placed it near Max's mouth. Susannah handed him the spoon and watched him feed her dog. About halfway through the tin of oatmeal, Max hiked himself up and slowly lapped up the rest of it.

Jackson grinned, his eyes glistening. "Max," he whispered, bending over to hug the dog.

Blinking back tears, Susannah cleared the emotion from her throat. "Now Jackson must eat," she ordered, pushing his lunch toward him.

Jackson gave her another smile, one so achingly familiar that it pinched her heart. "Your father will be very proud of you, Jackson."

He didn't understand her, but she didn't care. She was satisfied that he was eating. Still, when she thought about the struggle he and his father would have ahead of them, she felt a measure of sadness.

"Mama! Max all right?"

She turned and saw Corey's sweet face poking out from a bundle of blankets in Kito's arms. "Hello, sweetheart. Yes," she said, scooping her son into her arms, "Max is fine, thanks to Jackson."

She scooted against the wall, resting the bundled Corey on her lap. "Thank you, Kito." She held Corey firmly, but he squirmed, wanting to touch the dog. She moved closer, enabling him to caress the animal's hip.

"How's things in here, Miz Susannah?"

"They're wonderful, aren't they, Jackson?"

Jackson barely acknowledged them, concentrating instead on a second piece of chicken.

"We finally got Max to eat some oatmeal," she

explained. "It was the only way to get Jackson to eat, too."

Kito smiled, his dark eyes warm. "Sure am glad to hear it, Miz Susannah. Don't know what the boy'd do if that dog died."

Susannah's own smile softened as she watched Jackson eat. "I don't know either, Kito."

"Max sleeping?"

Giving Corey a quick kiss on the cheek, she breathed in the clean baby smell of him. Love expanded inside her. She hugged him until he squirmed. "Yes, darling. Max is asleep."

"Well," Kito said, stepping nervously from one foot to the other, "guess I'll get back to work. We fed the li'l mister a bite of bread and jam before we left the house, Miz Susannah."

"Again, thank you." As he turned to leave, Susannah said, "Kito?"

"Yes, ma'am?"

She let out an audible sigh. "I'm happy for you and Louisa. I'd thought all along that she'd be a good woman for you."

"You was right, Miz Susannah. She keeps me hoppin'. I didn't know what I was missin' till she come crashin' into my life, waggin' that saucy tongue of hers."

Susannah marveled at the smile that spread across Kito's face at the mere mention of Louisa's name. "I had my doubts in the beginning."

He chuckled. "I didn't."

"Not even when she talked so cruelly about your bad leg the day you brought her to the cabin?"

His chuckle deepened, rumbling up from deep within his chest. "I knew she didn't mean nothin' by it even then."

Susannah settled against the wall and put Corey on the floor between her legs. "How did you know?"

"Somethin' happens 'tween a man an' a woman that goes beyond words, Miz Susannah. Me'n Weesa felt it the first time we laid eyes on each other."

She frowned, remembering that those were almost Louisa's words exactly. Pondering them, she watched him limp from the room.

She hadn't felt that way about Nathan from the very beginning, had she? But now, just thinking about him made her heart pit-a-pat a little faster in her chest. Perhaps there had been something there; she'd just chosen to ignore it. Or she might have been too caught up in her fears to dwell on it.

Closing her eyes briefly, she rested her head against the wall. Whatever she'd felt had been one-sided, for were it not, Nathan wouldn't have been so eager to soak up every one of Sonny Walker's lies.

Jackson's sigh of contentment forced her thoughts to the present. He'd stretched out beside Max, his head on his arm, his eyelids heavy.

Corey continued to stroke Max's hip, but he appeared tired, too.

She studied the three of them. "Well," she scolded, her smile warm, "aren't you all just terrific company?"

"Sing, Mama," Corey requested, his voice husky with sleep.

With Corey in her arms, she struggled to her feet, crossed to Nub's cot and put her son down, making sure he was well covered. She took the blanket off the end of the bed and kneeled beside Jackson, draping the quilt over him. She stayed a moment, staring down at the face that was so much like Nathan's she wanted to cry. She brushed the tawny, golden brown hair from his forehead, her heart twisting when she saw that he frowned in his sleep.

"Oh, Jackson, Jackson," she said on a sigh. "What sadness must be locked away in your heart . . ." On an impulse, she bent and kissed his cheek, then touched the spot with the backs of her fingers.

"Mama, sing what the bird says," Corey ordered from the bed.

Rising from beside the sleeping Jackson, she gave him one last glance before returning to the bed. Corey held out his arms, and she took him onto her lap, again nuzzling his hair.

> Do you ask what the bird says? The sparrow, the dove,
> The linnet, and thrush say, "I love, and I love!"
> In the winter they're silent, the wind is so strong;
> What it says I don't know, but it sings a loud song.
> But green leaves, and blossoms, and sunny warm weather,
> And singing and loving—all come back together. . . .

She glanced down to find him asleep, his dark curly lashes fanned out on his cheeks. She hugged him close for a moment, savoring the feel of him in her arms before laying him back down on the cot.

It was then that she realized someone was standing in the doorway. She glanced up and her heart leaped against her ribs. "Nathan," she whispered, unable to contain the tangle of emotions that somersaulted through her.

17

Susannah's face held an abundance of emotions. All of them scraped against the raw edges of Nate's heart. "What's going on in here?"

She stood, her gaze wary as it lingered on him. "We finally got Max to eat something. And Jackson, too."

He stepped into the room, careful not to touch her as he walked past her, for if he had, he would have been hard-pressed not to attempt to drag her into his arms. Unfortunately, she didn't look all that receptive. It didn't surprise him.

He shoved his hands into his pockets and crossed to where his son slept, though his thoughts were still on Susannah: the song she'd sung, the womanly way she smelled, the sweetness of her lips, the rounded fullness of her breasts, her startled yet amazed reaction to her sensual awakening all those weeks ago, her natural, instinctive, delicious passion. . . . He realized with a sense of amazement that he could go on and on recounting her assets.

He gritted his teeth and swore again. To change the direction of his wayward thoughts, he said, "I didn't know Samuel Coleridge's *Answer to a Child's Question* had been set to music."

"I don't know anything about that. My mother used to sing it to me when I was little. For all I know, she made up the tune herself."

She was still holding herself aloof. With his guilt about Judith's death and burial finally put to rest, he was anxious to get on with his life. After his visit with the breed, Nate had stopped to see old Doc Madison. He'd identified Judith's body five years ago, and put Nate's tortured mind to rest.

As he'd ridden home, Nate realized how possessed he'd been. He also knew that if he didn't set things right with Susannah, he'd lose her forever. The concept made him ache all over.

His thoughts meandered back to the poem she'd sung. "Your *mother* knew the poems of Coleridge?"

She glanced away, but not before he saw that he'd hurt her. "My mother wasn't always a whore, Nathan."

He wanted to ask what had happened to make her one, but he realized that what her mother was had nothing to do with her. It was a cleansing revelation. "Do you know the rest of the poem?"

Her cheeks flushing pink, her eyes still averted, she nodded.

> *But the lark is so brimful of gladness and love,*
> *The green fields below him, the blue sky*
>   *above,*
> *That he sings, and he sings, and forever sings*
>   *he,*
> *"I love my Love, and my Love loves me."*

He was silent, the words forcing an opening into his soul. How easy she was to love! He cursed Sonny Walker for painting Susannah with a dark brush, and himself for believing him. But no more. Susannah was a strong, proud woman. What he'd done to her could have broken her spirit. That it hadn't proved to him that he wasn't worthy of her love. But he wanted to be.

Cursing, he tried to focus on Jackson, but the picture of Susannah kissing the boy's cheek as he slept was engraved in stone in his mind. And the sound of Susannah's husky-sweet voice as she sang to Corey still rang in his ears.

Jackson stirred, snoring softly as he crowded the dog. The uncomfortable lump formed in Nate's throat again, but he welcomed it. He'd have withstood the pits of hell if that had been the only way to have Jackson returned to him. He forced a grim smile. In a way, he had withstood hell, both in the war and in his mind.

His glance landed briefly on Nub's bed where Corey slept. "Why is he here?"

Her fingers caught the edge of her apron and she twisted it nervously. "He wanted to see Max. Kito bundled him up and brought him out."

They stood in uncomfortable silence. Finally, she spoke. "What did you learn in town, Nathan?"

Ah, just the way she said his name, drawing it out with her soft Missouri drawl . . . He cleared his throat roughly. "Doc Madison verified that it's Judith's body in that grave."

She let out a soft gasp. "I'm sorry, Nathan. I'm sorry you got your hopes up only to have them dashed again."

He was convinced that she really meant it. Tears shimmered in her eyes and she caught her trembling lower lip between her teeth. Hell, she seemed more upset about it than he was. He felt relief to be able to put it all behind him.

With another explicit curse, he moved away and hunkered down next to the dog. She kneeled next to him, her fresh delicate scent teasing his nostrils as she stroked Max's rump.

"He ate a lunch pail full of oatmeal and cream," she said softly, tossing Nathan a tentative smile. "And the doctor checked him after he examined Corey. He said Jackson was doing everything *he* would have prescribed to keep the animal alive."

Her expression was plaintive, almost melancholy. "Jackson is a fine boy, Nathan."

"No thanks to me," he mumbled, feeling awash with self-pity.

"Perhaps not. But it's up to you to assure him that where he spent the last five years matters to you only because they kept him alive and took care of him. Not that he spent them living among people you think are savages."

Her words were like a blow to the stomach. "I wouldn't do that."

Her gaze bore through him, sharp and clean as a whittling knife. "No?"

"Of course not. He's my son."

She gave him a cynical smile. "You have a habit of jumping to conclusions, Nathan. Never mind what you've thought about me. I'll bet you punished yourself endlessly before learning that Judith truly died, wallowing in your worry that if she'd survived in an Indian camp, she could come back to you, but would be shunned by the rest of the world."

"What's wrong with that?" His defenses were up.

"Nothing, if your concern was purely for Judith, and not for yourself."

He rose and swung away, knowing there was truth in her words. Her hand settled on his arm; he felt her touch through the layers of his clothes. "I didn't say that to hurt you, Nathan. Just don't dwell on the past. Jackson is here now; take advantage of every minute."

He strode to the door, anxious to leave the temptation to touch her behind. "When did you acquire such wisdom?" Though the question was meant to insult her, he found he truly wanted to know.

She picked up Max's empty water dish, crossed to Nub's bucket and filled the dish with the dipper. When she put the full dish in front of Max, he struggled to his elbows and noisily lapped at the water.

"It's never easy to forget the past, Nathan." Her expression was open and unguarded. "I should know. A day doesn't go by that I don't think about . . . about what I did to Harlan. I killed another human being. He was a rotten, abusive drunk, but he was a human being. Don't you think my crime eats at me?"

She kneeled down beside Max and examined his wounds. "I think about it because my mind won't let me forget it. But I have to remind myself that if I hadn't . . . hadn't killed him, he would have killed me. And if he would have killed me, Corey—" She swallowed repeatedly, appearing to fight tears. "Corey would have . . . have been at Harlan's mercy. Or . . . or Sonny's. I couldn't let that happen, Nathan. I just couldn't." She glanced up at him, her soulful brown eyes wide and guileless and shimmering with unshed tears. God, he could drown in them. . . .

Blinking furiously, she glanced away, one shoulder shrugging helplessly. "There's nothing I wouldn't do to protect my son," she finished, a delicate shudder passing through her as she lowered her head.

He studied Susannah again. "Did you know your father, Susannah?" He had no idea where that question came from.

She shot him a quick, puzzled glance, one which slid away slowly. "No," she answered softly, moving her hands to Max's ears. "He wasn't around very long."

Nate snuffled a laugh. "Skipped out on you, did he?"

"No." Her gaze snagged his and held. "He died."

He felt like a heel for even asking the question. It wasn't any of his business anyway. She should have told him to take a flying leap off a cliff. She probably wanted to.

"Mama! Papa Nathan! Corey gotta pee."

Susannah scrambled to her feet. "Hold on, sweetheart." She went to him and lifted him into her arms.

Nate moved toward her, intent on carrying Corey to the necessary.

"No," she said, casting a glance at Jackson, "you stay here. We'll be fine."

"Susannah." When she turned he said, "Bring Corey to the shed with the tub in it before you put him to bed tonight."

"The tub? Why?"

"The warm water will soothe his bruises and help him sleep," he answered.

He watched her leave, knowing that he wanted to learn everything there was to know about her. And sensing, too, that whatever he learned would only make him love her more.

He glanced away from the door and found Jackson studying him, his expression grim.

Nate tried to smile, although his insides quaked with uncertainty. "Hello, Jackson."

The boy was no longer his charming, lovable, trusting three-year-old son. This boy didn't admire him. This boy's face didn't light up when Nate entered a room. This boy undoubtedly felt abandoned.

Another thought struck him. This boy had learned everything he now knew from strangers, from people who had probably plucked him from the jaws of death. Even so, a fierce sense of possession gripped Nate. Jackson had loved him once. Nate would make him love him again.

Until Jackson's return, Nate had rebuked a God that would so cruelly take his family from him. Now, though unsure how to proceed, he asked the God he'd deserted to listen to him again. He wanted what they'd had. He didn't care what he had to do to get it back.

His gaze caught the edge of something familiar leaning against the far wall of Nub's room. Smiling to himself, he crossed the room, pulled it away from the wall and brought it to where Jackson sat.

"Remember this, Jackson?" He hunkered down beside the boy and ran his fingers over his handiwork.

Jackson's face changed, his expression one of painful joy as he greedily touched the wagon that Nathan had made for him so many years ago.

Nate spun the wheels with his finger. "Still works," he announced, pride lacing his voice.

Jackson's eyes were bright with excitement. "Max," he said, his arms forming a carrier from the dog to the wagon.

Nate's smile spread and he felt a seed of excitement burrow into his chest. "That's a terrific idea, boy." He took the old blanket that Susannah had spread over Jackson and folded it, making a bed in the wagon.

Max was up on his elbows, watching them. He

barked, a weak, high-pitched whining sound of excitement when Nate carefully lifted him onto the cart.

Jackson took the handle and tugged, the wagon moving slowly over the dirt packed earth.

Feeling a warmth in his heart that expanded with such fierce happiness Nate thought he might explode, he followed his son outside.

They sat under the trees with Max, listening to the wind as it whistled through the leaves. Nate pointed to objects, familiarizing Jackson with the English names. It was a game; often Jackson said the word before Nate had a chance. His chest swelled with pride, for his son had a quick, eager mind.

Kito emerged from around the side of the cabin, lugging a basket of wet clothes. Louisa joined him, and when they stopped under the lines Nate had strung between the trees, she kissed Kito full on the mouth, then shooed him away.

Nate rose. "I'll be back, son. I want to talk to Louisa."

"Pa?"

Emotion, raw, painful and sweet rose through Nate. He turned, his eyes wet with tears. Jackson's face held the intensity of one on the brink of understanding. Nate rushed to him. "Yes, son," he answered, his voice breaking, "I'm your pa."

Tears streaked Jackson's cheeks. They reached for each other, and Nate pulled his son hard against his chest, his own tears wetting Jackson's hair.

"Pa . . . Pa . . . Pa . . ." It was a litany of relief, disbelief, comprehension.

Nate held him until Jackson pulled away. The boy's eyes shimmered. "Pa," he repeated around a huge, toothy smile.

Nate started to sit beside him, but Jackson gave him

a little push, nodding toward the clothesline. "Talk . . . to . . . Louisa."

Knowing his eyes brimmed with love, Nate gave his son's hair a teasing ruffle. "I'll be right back."

He strode toward Louisa, his breakthrough with Jackson giving him hope that he could still save what he'd had with Susannah.

Louisa struggled with a wet sheet. "Here," she ordered, handing him one end. "Hold this whilst I start pinnin' it to the line."

Nate took the sheet and pulled it straight. "Tell me something about Susannah."

"'Bout time you come askin' after her. From the way she's been mopin' around, I thought you'd already made up your mind."

"I may need a lecture, Louisa, but I don't want one. Tell me about her life."

Louisa finished pinning the sheet to the line. Nate handed her the end of another, holding it as he'd held the one before.

"Her ma died when she was only ten," Louisa began. "Poor Honeybelle. I learned that poor chile' was in the cabin alone with the body for more than a day."

If possible, her expression grew even more grim. "I also learned that bastard Harlan Walker'd come by to see Fiona, Honeybelle's ma, and found the poor woman dead.

"When Fiona got sick, she tol' me to watch after Honeybelle. Hell. No one in that town'd let a 'dirty nigger' raise a white chile. They'd let filthy trash like the Walkers do it, but not a Negra."

Nate's stomach burned. "She lived with them?"

"Yeah," she answered, snorting loudly. "Them pissant Walker brothers sweet-talked her into comin' to live with them and their ma." She spat a curse.

"That woman could've been a preacher were she a man, the way she proclaimed hellfire and brimstone."

She stopped working and gazed into the distance. "I tried to get Honeybelle back, but no court in the land would give her to me." She sniffed, wiping her eyes with the edge of her apron. "She had a miserable life, Mister Nathan. I came around as much as I dared, and as Honeybelle got older, she'd meet me in secret places, cryin' . . . cryin' . . .

"That white bitch filled Honeybelle's head with all sorts of nonsense meant to scare the bejesus out of her. Made her think God was mad at her for bein' pretty and nice."

Louisa pulled out a handkerchief and blew her nose. "As a young'un, she was worked to the bone. Nothin' ever satisfied that evil bitch. *Nothin'.* Then, Lord help her, she grew into a young woman, beautiful and ripe for the pickin', poor darlin'. She would've been better off if she'd been standin' behind the door when God gave out good looks. Instead, she was at the front of the line."

Nate's insides quivered with fury. He clenched his fists, willing himself to stand quietly and listen.

"The only good thing Ma Walker ever did was have an iron grip on them two boys of hers. They didn't dare fondle Honeybelle until she tol' them they could. 'Course, she never let Sonny touch the girl. Sonny was a cocky bastard, always mouthin' off to his ma. Harlan was her favorite, prob'ly 'cause he was soft in the head and let her lead him around by the nose. She's the one who made Honeybelle marry that skunk. Poor chile was only fifteen, still a baby herself.

"Things wasn't good. Harlan started slappin' her around after his ma up and died. 'Afore that, he was just plain mean, but he never hit her. Honeybelle quit comin' to see me then. I had to find her. I think she was afraid to talk about it, for fear of things gettin' worse if Harlan found out. She was also ashamed. She had some fool notion that it was *her* fault that Harlan beat her."

Louisa took a quick breath, plucked a shirt from the basket and pinned it to the line. "I jes' happened by that mornin' she stabbed Harlan with the scissors. I helped her get away. She mighta stayed and took the consequences, but she'd have been a fool to do it. No one in that town cared that Harlan slapped her around. Lotsa men did it to their women." Her eyes grew hard. "Seems it was a matter of *pride,*" she finished, her voice laced with anger.

"An', Mister Nathan, I only know part of the story. There's lots of it still locked up inside poor Honey-belle's head."

Finally, she turned to him. "Ain't you got somethin' better to do?" She nodded toward the trees. "Seems like that boy of yours could use some company. I done all the talkin' I'm gonna do."

Dismissed, Nate hurried back to Jackson. Outwardly, he was calm, but inside, he seethed with a frenzied hatred that nearly consumed him. Somehow, he would make Sonny Walker pay for the sins of his family.

That evening, as Nathan requested, Susannah carried Corey to the shed. Pushing open the door with her hip, she peeked inside. Her eyes went wide with amazement, for the enormous tub she'd discovered the day he'd returned to the ranch was full of water and steam rose from it like fog.

She eased around the door and pushed it shut with her foot.

Corey clapped his hands gleefully, then pointed at the tub. "Water, Mama."

His excitement was infectious. Susannah grinned at him and gave him a squeeze. As she drew closer to the tub, she felt the warmth radiating from the water.

"Is the little whistler man ready for a swim?"

Susannah jumped at the sound of Nathan's voice; she hadn't seen him on his knees beside one of the pumps.

"Corey swim!" He clapped again and wiggled in Susannah's arms.

Nathan stood, sweat glistening off his bare torso, tunneling through the hair, soaking the fur that surrounded his navel. Her heart drummed, her pulse dispatched flashes of memory to her brain. She studied every tightly honed muscle, remembering how they'd felt beneath her fingers. He reached up and rested the flat of his hand on the wall, and she followed the sinewy lines of his limb from his hair-dusted hands to the thatch of dark hair under his arm.

A shiver stole through her and her knees felt weak.

"Like what you see?"

She pulled her gaze away, ashamed to have been caught staring.

"All right, whistler man," Nathan said as he unbuttoned his fly, "it's into the tub we go."

Corey reached for Nathan, and only by sheer luck was Susannah able to hang on to him. She stared, for there, right smack in front of her, Nathan slid his jeans down his hips and stepped out of them.

"Nathan!" Heat plunged deep into her belly as she belatedly averted her eyes.

"You didn't expect us to take a bath with our clothes on, did you?"

He stood before her, tall, strong, beautiful and very naked. The heat she'd felt when she stepped into the room intensified, and she knew it wasn't coming from the water.

"Come on, Corey," he said, lifting him from Susannah's arms. Susannah stood, a bit dumbstruck, as Nathan undressed him. Like the brazen hussy he thought she was, she stared at him, at his groin. Though somewhat limp, he was not small. The place between her legs tingled.

As he took the steps to the landing on the edge of the tub, his manhood twitched, jutting out slightly from his bush.

"I suggest you get out of here while the getting is good, Susannah," he ordered, touching himself. "As you can see, the chap hasn't performed much lately but he has a damned good memory."

Embarrassment and desire swarmed through her like a thousand hungry bees. She struggled to get to the door, but even then, she had to have one last peek. She hadn't realized that he'd stopped on the platform and was staring at her.

He stepped into the water with Corey in his arms. "Come and get him in about fifteen minutes." His voice told her he was in control.

Swallowing a chaotic knot of emotions, she nodded, unaware that she'd been salivating. "I'm sorry, I . . . I . . . I . . . yes, I . . . will."

She stepped outside and leaned against the closed door, her heart bounding against her ribs and her emotions scattering like seeds in a whirlwind.

Unable to get the picture of him out of her mind, she hurried to the house and tried to immerse herself in her quilting. But her hands shook so badly, she quit after she'd pricked herself for the dozenth time with her quilting needle. Louisa walked by at one point and asked her a question, but she wasn't listening. Nevertheless, she nodded, which apparently was the proper response, for Louisa went on by. When she finally glanced at the clock that sat on the mantel, she realized she'd been sitting in a fog for nearly an hour.

She sprang up and hurried to the front door.

Louisa came out of her quarters, tying the sash of her robe around her waist. "Where you goin', Honeybelle?"

"I . . . I have to get Corey. I . . . it's past time—"

"What you sayin'? The li'l man's already in bed."

Susannah frowned. "What?"

"I asked you if I should get him, and you nodded. He's been asleep for nigh on thirty minutes."

Susannah felt a foolish rush of disappointment. Unconsciously she'd been anxious to have a reason to return to the shed. "I'm sorry, Louisa. I guess I was wool-gathering."

Louisa went into the kitchen and fixed herself a cup of tea, her gaze frequently resting on Susannah. "My guess is he's still out there, Honeybelle. I ain't seen him come in yet." A sly grin cracked her mouth. "I do believe he was in that tub without a stitch on, too."

Heat rushed to Susannah's cheeks.

Louisa's grin widened. "He said to send you out."

Susannah gasped. "He didn't."

Louisa's face was a mask of mock insult. "Would I lie, Honeybelle?"

Susannah eyed the door. "Well, I guess I should thank him for bathing Corey."

"Yes, Honeybelle. You do that."

Ignoring Louisa's wry comment, Susannah pulled on her cape and stepped outside. The night air was crisp and cold. Since she'd been there she'd smelled winter in the air, but it never seemed to arrive.

She marched resolutely to the shed, stopping to take in a quick breath before she opened the door. When she did, she felt another stab of disappointment. The room was empty.

She stepped inside. "Nathan?" When he didn't answer, she strolled to the tub, noting that it was still full. It looked inviting. She shoved up the sleeve of her dress and dipped her hand into the water, swallowing a pleasure-filled groan.

A cold gust of air hit her, and she turned as Nathan entered. Like a guilty child caught with her fingers in the cookie dough, she quickly stepped away from the tub.

"I thought you might enjoy a nice warm bath," he announced.

She felt a frustrating urge to scream; he was fully dressed. "That . . . that was very thoughtful of you."

He crossed to the wall behind her. "There are towels here, and soap." He gave her a crooked grin. "I'd join you, but I'm already as wrinkled as a prune."

Why was he being so accommodating? "Thank you," she said graciously. Before he got to the door, she asked, "Why did you build such an enormous tub, Nathan?"

His smile was brief. "Maybe I'll tell you about it sometime."

She watched him leave, then picked up a towel and soap and put them on the ledge. She undressed quickly, staying near the tub to keep warm. After uncoiling her hair, she pinned it to the top of her head with a single pin, then climbed the short ladder to the ledge. Feeling the chill in the room, she stepped into the warm water. She sat on the outcropping he'd built partway down the wall, leaned against the side, and briefly closed her eyes. The water caressed her and she expelled a long, luxurious sigh.

Hanging onto the shelf he'd built, she floated,

letting the water buoy her. She kicked her legs, scissoring them back and forth, loving the feel of the water as it pressed against the tender place at the top of her thighs.

She was floating sideways when a jetting stream of warm water shot against her there, and she gasped at the exquisite sensation. Lest she enjoy it too much, she hauled herself to the ledge, pressing her thighs together to prevent further temptation.

With a grim smile, she twisted on the seat and reached for the soap. Her hand stopped midair, for her gaze met Nathan's, who stood near the pipes.

He gave her a rather lascivious smile. "I thought you might need more warm water."

She knew she blushed, but her face was hot from the water anyway, so perhaps he didn't notice. Forgetting the soap, she crossed her arms over her bosom. "What are you doing here?" She'd intended to sound indignant. Her words didn't come out that way.

He stepped to the side of the tub. He wasn't smiling, and his expression was hot, blatant and sexual, but his eyes held a tenderness she hadn't seen since he'd left her in Angel's Valley. "I couldn't stay away."

$\approx 18 \approx$

And he couldn't. Under the guise of giving her more hot water, he'd come back into the shed when he was sure she was in the tub. Her torso had floated just beneath the surface, her pink nipples, tightened into pearls, poked through the water, the triangle at the joining of her thighs a perfect shade of rusty brown. Hips sweetly rounded, tempting. Legs long and shapely. Desire, thick and hard, had pounded through him.

Now, she had an innocent wide-eyed appearance, her hair perched slightly to one side on top of her head, wet tendrils clinging to her neck and shoulders. She modestly tried to hide her firm, ample bosom from his gaze.

"You're shivering," he announced.

She stared at the water. "You . . . you make me nervous."

"There's fire in you, Susannah. I want you so damned bad that my tongue aches." He stepped close to the tub and studied her over the side. The words "good enough to eat" entered his mind.

"That's . . . that's not very flattering." Her voice shook as she spoke.

He fed on her innocent discomfort. "Ah, but you have no idea what feats of pleasure I can perform with my tongue."

Color spread across her chest, over the breasts she tried so valiantly to hide from his view. "Why are you saying these things, Nathan? I'm not a whore, I'm *not—*"

"I'd never talk to a whore the way I'm talking to you."

She tossed him a rosy glance. "You wouldn't?"

The hope in her eyes touched something inside him. "No. I wouldn't waste my time."

He reached into the water, scooping it toward her with his hand. "I thought you might like to know that Jackson called me 'Pa' earlier today."

"Oh, Nathan, that's wonderful." Her gaze was warm as it clung to his. Tears of happiness shimmered in her eyes.

"I also had a long, very important talk with Louisa this afternoon."

She swirled her slender foot in the water. "About me, I assume."

"Yes, about you. Susannah, I hardly know where to begin. I've been a selfish, distrustful bastard. I want you to forgive me, if you can."

She was quiet for a long moment, then said, "All of this came about because of your talk with Louisa?"

"No," he admitted. "Actually, I've hated myself since the moment I started demanding answers to questions that weren't my business to ask."

"You hurt me, Nathan. Your deception, your lack of trust, your anger . . . Through it all, though, I couldn't stop loving you. I wanted to, but my heart wouldn't let me."

"Ah, Susannah," he whispered. They were quiet for a moment, but it was a comfortable silence. Finally, he said, "I want you to do something for me, for both of us."

She was wary. "What?"

His gaze rested on her triangle, the hair waving slightly as the water caressed it. His mouth went dry.

"Touch yourself."

She gasped, shooting him an angry look as she gathered herself in her arms and crossed her legs to close herself in. "I said I'm no whore, Nathan Wolfe."

What he'd learned from Louisa humbled him. He felt remorse. "I know that, sweetheart," he said softly, claiming her gaze. "But learning about your body by touching it doesn't make you a whore."

"It . . . it doesn't?" She unfolded slightly but still covered herself.

"I'm sorry for every awful thing I've ever said to you. And you were right. I used analogies to suit me."

"Analogies?" She unfolded a bit more, yet still held her arms against her breasts.

He smiled at her innocence. "Comparisons between you and your mother, and you and your son."

"Oh," she whispered with a little nod.

"Touch yourself, Susannah."

"No! Oh, Nathan, I . . . I've never . . . I mean, I can't . . . I mean, it's not right—"

"Specifically, who told you such a thing?" he interrupted.

She ducked her head and studied the water. "Well . . . um . . . everyone, I guess."

"Ma Walker?"

Her head shot up, her eyes filled with surprise. "How . . . how did you know?"

"I guessed as much after my talk with Louisa." He gave her a warm, encouraging smile.

Chewing on her lower lips, Susannah studied the water again. "From . . . from the time I moved there, she . . . she preached at me. When she wasn't scolding me or slapping me for not doing things the way she wanted them, she was lecturing me on the sins of the flesh, telling me my looks were a curse from the devil.

"As I got older, she . . . she warned me to stay away from her boys." She shuddered, her mouth pinched with distaste. "I didn't want them to touch me, Nathan, I *didn't*. And I never *ever* made them think otherwise. But . . . but she just wouldn't stop talking about things like that. And, she said that if I ever did anything sinful like . . . like touch myself, I'd be punished. I'd go straight to hell."

Pity dug deep into Nate's gut. "Do you still believe that?"

With another shy duck of her head she answered, "I don't know. I'm . . . I'm not sure."

"But I touched you there, Susannah. Did it feel wrong to you?"

Her eyes flew open and she stared at him. "Oh, no. No, no. It—" She caught her full bottom lip between her teeth again. "It felt wonderful."

Heat scorched him, thickening his blood. "Then why is it wrong to touch yourself?"

"I . . . I guess it shouldn't be, but . . ." She closed her eyes briefly and gave him a nervous laugh. "I just can't imagine doing such a thing, Nathan. Now that I think about it, it's . . . it's just so silly."

At least she wasn't angry or upset. "Just this once, Susannah. Feel your body. Get to know it. Run your hands over it; touch places you've never touched before."

She laughed again, that nervous, anxious sound. "Oh, Nathan, I couldn't—"

"Try. For me. Please."

She swallowed and closed her eyes again. Slowly she brought her hands to her breasts, tentatively touching them.

"Touch your nipples, Susannah," he instructed, feeling the stricture at his groin.

Her fingers grazed them and she let out a little gasp, her head moving to expose the exquisite, white expanse of her neck.

He longed to bury his face there, kiss her skin, lick off the water. He forced down his hunger but he started to undress.

"Oh," she whispered, "when . . . when I touch them I can feel it down . . . down between my legs." She gasped again, and a delicate shudder quivered through her body.

Nate gripped the side of the tub, feeling his control slipping. He was hard as a board.

Her eyes were closed as she moved one hand down over her navel, then to the top of her mound. She fluffed the hair with her fingers, hesitating at the entrance.

He swallowed hard. "Spread your legs, Susannah. Let—" He swallowed again, forcing control. "Let the water caress you."

"It . . . it did before," she said on a husky breath. "A stream of warm water t-touched me there."

"And how did it feel?"

"It . . . it felt good, Nathan. Too good." Her fingers were still poised over her opening.

"Let yourself go, Susannah. Don't think. Just feel."

She kept her eyes closed. He was certain it was in self-defense. As she pressed one finger inside, she inhaled sharply but didn't remove her hand.

Slowly she began to stroke herself. Her legs floated akimbo in the water as her body relaxed. Her sweet mouth was open slightly, her breath quick and uneven as lust swept through her. Suddenly she stiffened and groaned, trapping her hand between her legs.

Nathan shed the remainder of his clothes and climbed into the tub, grasping her from behind before her head went under the water. She clamored into his arms, hugging him tightly.

He stroked her warm, wet flesh, her beauty testing his restraint. "Now," he whispered against her hair. "Was that so bad?"

She gave him a nervous, breathy laugh. "No, but . . . but, Nathan?"

"Yes, love?"

"I'd rather we did it together," she answered, taking his earlobe into her mouth and sucking on it.

He groaned and lifted her over him as he sat on the ledge. Clamping her legs around him, she shuddered fiercely as she gathered him inside her. He mouthed her breasts, sucked her nipples and knew he would spend. And he did.

"I'm sorry," he apologized, holding her close.

"Don't be sorry, Nathan," she answered with a lazy, satisfied smile. "We'll just have to do it again."

She unpinned her hair and ducked under the water to wet it completely. "Hand me the soap, would you?"

He brought her between his legs and washed her hair, occasionally dipping down to caress her breasts with soapy hands. She pulled away long enough to rinse her hair, then he tugged her back against him.

"I'm not done bathing you," he growled into her ear, "but you'll have to turn around." She relaxed against him, her head lolling against his shoulder.

"Must I?"

"If I'm going to wash you, yes, you must." His blood ran thick again, his groin heavy.

She turned to face him, her knees on either side of him, her pelvis out of the water.

Swallowing a groan, he soaped his hands then stroked her thighs with his thumbs. Her head lolled again, exposing her neck, and she gripped his shoulders.

He worked his way to her delta, skirting her engorged center, concentrating on the dense patch of hair that covered her.

"You have a birthmark," he observed, leaning forward to kiss the crescent shaped mark just above her pubic hair while his fingers continued to move upward, inside her thighs.

She inhaled sharply and pressed forward, trying to reach his fingers, but he teased her, drawing out her desire, not wanting it to end, for watching her gave him nearly as much pleasure as touching her.

"Damn you, Nathan Wolfe," she whispered, her voice shaking.

He touched her then, his lathered fingers creating soapy bubbles that clung to her. He felt her knees shake so he slipped off the ledge, pulling her onto him again and they floated as one in the water.

She squirmed against him, anxious for him to finish what he began.

"Patience, love," he whispered as he pressed his mouth to hers. The kiss began tentatively, as if each were afraid that anything deeper would send them over the edge. But soon it became wet, slick, tongue against tongue.

Nate felt a stronger desire building inside him than he'd ever felt before. He gripped her buttocks, pressing her hard against him, and thrust deep, rocking against her until they both cried out their release.

Susannah stood by the tub, unable to keep from touching Nathan as he rubbed her dry. When he finished and was drying his hair, she tugged the towel from him.

"My turn," she said, still feeling a little shy. She dried the hair on his chest, dragging the towel down over his stomach to his groin, where she made a special attempt at getting him dry. He grew at her ministering.

"I'll give you an hour to stop that." He smiled the lopsided smile she'd grown to love.

She blushed, remembering that he'd said that to her once before. "I was just trying to dry you off."

His grin widened. "And I was just trying to wash you when I touched you in the tub."

Her blush deepened and she felt it heat her scalp. "All right. So I wanted to touch you."

He tossed her the clothes she'd worn and she stepped into them, a bit reluctantly. While he dressed, she asked, "Why did you build this tub, Nathan?"

He buttoned his fly, but couldn't hide the fact that he was hard again. "I built it for Judith. She wasn't well, Susannah. She never had been. She had arthritis, her joints swelled painfully. The warm water seemed to give her some relief."

Susannah attempted to remove more water from her hair, rubbing it gently with the towel. "You were very sweet to think of it, Nathan. You . . . you must have loved her very much." Thoughts of the dead woman summoned a bevy of feelings inside her.

"I loved her in a very special way, Susannah. She shouldn't have had a child; the doctor warned both of us that she wasn't strong enough to carry one."

"But . . . but she had one anyway."

He combed his hands through his hair. "Yeah. I didn't want her to get pregnant but she—" He exhaled, cursing as he did so. "She wanted to give me a son."

The knife of envy went deeper. "She must have loved you very much to risk her life for you."

He strode to the mechanisms on the far wall and twisted a knob. She heard the water escaping through a pipe under the floor.

"Yeah," he answered, "she loved me more than I deserved to be loved."

"Oh, Nathan, don't say that." When he returned to her side, she touched his shoulder, rubbing her palm against his arm. "You're beginning to sound like me," she chided, giving him a scolding smile.

He pulled her into his arms. "Do you think you've forgiven me enough to marry me?"

The question came out of nowhere. She opened her mouth then shut it, swallowing the threat of tears. "You . . . want to marry me? Why?"

He ran his thumb over her lower lip, then to her chin. "After what we've just done, you have to ask me that?"

Sex was one thing; love was another. Bolstering her courage, she said, "Yes, I have to ask you that."

Inhaling deeply, he studied her, his eyes warm. "It's more than what we've just done, Susannah, although I admit that if I live to be ninety, I'll never get enough of you that way. I'm as randy as a billy goat already."

He just wants me in his bed. "And?" she asked, hoping she was able to keep her feelings hidden.

He touched her hair, lowering his hand to the wet curl that rested over her shoulder. Her breast tightened, pebbling the nipple. "And you're beautiful and warm . . . and you make me want to smile and laugh again."

Through me, he wants to try to forget Judith. "Anything else?" she managed to ask.

He kissed her forehead, a fatherly gesture that

puzzled her. "And I want to make a home for you and Corey here, with me and Jackson."

He wants me as a buffer between him and his son. "I can live with that," she answered, forcing a brightness into her voice, "but . . . but is there any other reason at all?"

He held her loosely in the circle of his arms. "And I want to help you forget the past."

She focused on his chin, unable to meet his gaze. *He feels sorry for me.* She rested her head against his chest, her throat so tight with topsy-turvy emotions that she could hardly breathe. He hadn't told her what she'd wanted to hear.

"Well," she said, keeping her voice light, "how can I refuse an offer like that?"

"I'll make you happy, Susannah."

"Oh, Nathan, you already have." Tears impaired her vision. Standing on tiptoe, she draped her arms over his shoulders and kissed him. *And I'll love you enough for both of us.*

Susannah finished the letter to Lillian Graves, in which she'd apologized again for leaving Angel's Valley so abruptly. She'd tried to explain as little as possible, yet knew Lillian would understand if she mentioned Nathan and the ranch. She felt a wash of guilt at not having written her sooner.

She sealed the envelope, put it on the table, then gently touched the ivory silk fabric she'd purchased for her wedding dress. Her fingertips barely grazed it, for she was afraid she'd snag it. She and Louisa had gone into town and gotten it the day before.

"I shouldn't have bought this, Louisa. I could wear the one I wore to the dance back in Angel's Valley. It's perfectly fine."

"Hush that talk," Louisa scolded. "The man says

for you to get somethin' pretty, an' you got somethin' pretty."

Susannah continued to gaze at it. She'd fallen in love with it immediately. The bolt of silk had almost stood on end and waved at her when she stepped into the store. "How do I know he can afford this? I should have paid for it myself." She gently drew the back of her hand across the beautiful fabric again.

"That's nonsense, Honeybelle. A man wouldn't feel right lettin' his bride who has no family pay for her own dress, leastwise not Mister Nathan."

"But I've got a little money, Louisa. And I keep forgetting about Harlan's strongbox. Who knows, maybe those papers are worth something." She worried her thumbnail with her teeth.

"They prob'ly ain't worth the paper they're printed on," Louisa scoffed.

The longer Susannah stared at the fabric, the sicker she felt. It was natural for her to daydream; she'd done it most of her life. From the moment she'd seen the ivory silk, the dress she wanted to make from it became clear in her mind. She saw the silk fringe, the crepe de chine trim and the bishop sleeves, even the knotted band at the waist. The perfect wedding gown.

Turning away, she pulled in a quiet sigh. It was silly. It was wasteful. She couldn't do it. But she knew she'd get an argument if she said anything to anyone. She'd have to find a way to return it herself, and while she was in town, perhaps go to the bank and see if the papers in the strongbox were worth anything.

Glancing up, she caught Louisa's questioning gaze. "I'm sorry, Louisa. Did you say something?"

Louisa shook her head. "That man gonna want to wait till you make that dress? I've seen the way he ogles you. Lan' sakes, Honeybelle, I think he'll explode if you make him wait too long."

She briefly lowered her gaze to hide her smile. Nathan had vowed not to touch her again until they were wed. She'd thought it was a sweet, if misplaced, gesture. The hunger in his eyes was proof of that. So she wouldn't give her plans away, she answered, "I guess he'll just have to now, won't he?"

When Louisa left her to stir the pot of soup that had been simmering on the stove, Susannah ventured into Nathan's bedroom. After all, she thought, shoving aside the feeling that she was intruding, it would soon be hers, too.

Standing just inside the doorway, she let her gaze wander over the room. The furnishings were expensive. Even with her scant knowledge of furniture, she could tell that much. The bed, a large mahogany and pine four-poster, appeared at one time to have had a canopy, although now it was plain, and the coverlet a simple heavy quilt. An exquisite Chinese shaving stand occupied the wall next to the window and a mahogany and pine dressing table was tucked away in a corner, dusty from years of neglect. A mahogany chest-on-chest was next to it, one drawer slightly ajar. Beside the built-in country wardrobe, there was a blanket chest.

Susannah inched her way into the room, feeling like an intruder. She went to the bed and stared at where Nathan slept. The indentation on his pillow drew her gaze, and she pulled the pillow from the bed, lifting it to her face, drawing in a breath.

Clutching it to her, she crossed to the blanket chest, curious to know what was stored there. In the first two drawers, she found folded sheets and quilts, but in the bottom one, beneath an extra pillow, she discovered yards of soft pink netting.

She tossed the pillow aside then took the fabric from the drawer, unfolding it on the bed. She expelled a soft sigh. It was lovely—and it must have been Judith's.

She wondered if she dared use it. Would Nathan even know? Probably not. Would he care? That, she didn't know. But it would be so practical. . . . She heard the kitchen door close, then Nathan's voice, and she folded the material and laid it back in the drawer.

"There you are."

Despite her feelings of guilt, the sound of his voice sent her heart soaring. "Nathan!" She shut the drawer, drew up the edge of her apron and began wiping off the top of the chest. "I thought you and Kito were fixing the roof over the barn."

He watched her, a frown nicking his forehead. "We ran out of shingles."

She dropped the hem of her apron and went to him, relieved when he folded her in his arms. She pressed her nose against his shirt, smelling traces of the brisk, cold air that mingled with his scent. "You'd better get in to buy more before the rains come."

"Will I have to put up with a bossy wife?"

He was teasing, but there was something else in his voice she couldn't put her finger on. She traced the crooked line of his nose.

"I hope you're not angry that I'm in here."

"Of course not," he answered, his eyes warm. "Do whatever you want to with the room. You deserve that much. And more."

Her finger moved down over his lips to the bearded stubble that grew over the cleft in his chin. She kissed that spot, then let her lips rest there.

"I don't want to do anything with it, Nathan. I just wanted to see where . . . where—"

"Where we would eventually sleep?" When she nodded, he drew her closer. "I want you naked in my bed now, but I want to make an honest woman of you first. I also understand that you might want to get rid of Judith's things—"

"Shhh," she said, placing her finger over his mouth. "We don't have to worry about that now. It's more important that you get your outside work done before the rains come. I won't have you getting sick on me." Being in his arms triggered her desire, and she pressed close. He was hard beneath his fly.

He lifted her chin with a finger and kissed her with hungry urgency. She opened her mouth, and the kiss deepened further. They both shook with need.

With a sharp groan, he pulled away and gazed at her, his eyes dark with desire. "I must have been crazy to vow not to make love to you."

They rubbed against each other, heightening the pressure.

"Can't we move the wedding up? Like say, to tomorrow?"

Laughter danced on the fringes of his lips and in his eyes, but she knew he was serious.

"This abstinence was your noble idea, not mine. And anyway, my dress is nowhere near ready." She reached between them and cradled him in her palm.

He sucked in a breath. "I've said it before, woman. I'll give you an hour to stop that."

Memories of their lovemaking in the water aroused her so, she nearly climaxed where she stood. "In an hour, we'd both be naked."

He stilled her hand, bringing it to his mouth and kissing her palm. "Inside of a minute we'd both be naked. Now," he said, kissing her again, "if I don't step away from you, I'll go back on my word. I never do that, no matter how much it hurts. And believe me," he added, briefly pressing her hand to his groin again, "it hurts like hell."

Picking up his jacket, he gave her one last heated gaze before going to the door.

"Nathan?" When he turned, she asked, "You will be able to finish your work before the rains come, won't you?"

Again, something flashed in his eyes. "That's not something you should worry about, Susannah."

Frowning, she watched him leave. The lumber that had been in the yard when she first got there was gone; she hadn't seen them use it. She was curious to know what had happened to it. She left the bedroom and returned to the kitchen, the ivory silk fabric still lying on the table.

With gentle fingers, she caressed it, lost in thought. Suddenly she understood.

She found Louisa in the room where Corey slept. He'd just awakened from his nap and she was changing his clothes.

"Do you mind watching him for a while?"

"'Course not, Honeybelle. Where you goin'?"

"I have a letter to mail, plus a few other things to buy. I'll be back as soon as I can."

"Mister Nathan know you're goin'?"

"No, and please don't bother him. I'll take Nub with me." She bent down and kissed Corey. "Be a good boy for Louisa, sweetheart."

"You're up to somethin', Honeybelle, and I don't think I like it."

"Don't be silly. In my excitement to get the material for my gown, I forgot something. I can't start sewing on it until I get it. And as long as I'm in town, I might as well mail the letter to Lillian."

Feigning nonchalance, she went to the corner where she'd stored her things, opened the strongbox and stuffed the contents into her apron pocket. She went to the door, blew them both an exaggerated kiss, and left

the room. After pulling on her old cape, she slipped
into her gloves and snatched up her parcel and the
letter, then left the house. Once in the buckboard, she
transferred the papers from her apron pocket to her
purse. She left before anyone could ask her where she
was going.

19

With her purse and her parcel pressed close to her chest, Susannah left the bank, the president's words still ringing in her ears. The contents of the strongbox, some Texas cattle shares and other papers, had added up to a small fortune.

In spite of her elation, she cursed Harlan Walker. All the years they'd been married he'd pinched every penny. He'd taken her earnings as a seamstress, claiming them for his own, forcing her to hide some of it from him so she could buy sewing supplies. They'd nearly lived in squalor, and she'd just taken him at his word that they were poor. Fool that she'd been, she hadn't thought twice about the many nights he was out drinking and playing cards with his cronies, or how much money he'd spent on his own personal entertainment. She tried not to let the past eat at her, though. She was excited about her new wealth and was so anxious to tell Nathan about it that she could almost forgive Harlan for hiding it from her.

As she hurried across the street to the mercantile,

she realized that now, although she could afford the ivory silk, she wasn't sure she wanted to spend Nathan's money or her own on it. For too many years she'd been conditioned to scrimp. Considering what had to be done to the ranch, she couldn't justify spending an exorbitant amount of money on a dress.

The little bell over the door tinkled as she entered the shop and the aroma of freshly ground coffee seduced her. The owner, Mr. Glass, glanced up from the corner where he was sorting mail.

"Hello, again, ma'am. Didn't get everything you needed yesterday?"

Clutching her parcel to her chest, she crossed to the counter. She pulled out the letter to be mailed and handed it to him. "I've had second thoughts about it, I'm afraid."

He dropped the letter in a big canvas bag and frowned, concerned. "Something wrong with the material?"

"Oh, no. No, it isn't that. I . . ." Mr. Glass had spoken so kindly of Nathan, she realized that he'd known him for years. She decided to be frank. "I just feel guilty. It seems so, well, frivolous, to spend his money this way."

Mr. Glass began slipping letters into the slots on the wall. "Money didn't exchange hands, young lady. We made a trade."

"Really? What did he trade?"

The storekeeper peered at her over the top of his spectacles. "He brought me some prime lumber."

Susannah pressed her hand to her throat. "Lumber? Oh, no." So that's where it had gone. "Oh, Mr. Glass. I can't let him do that. He needs the lumber far worse than I need a silk wedding dress."

Mr. Glass gave her a private closed-in smile. "You're not much like Lady Judith, are you?"

"Lady Judith?"

He dismissed the question with a wave of his hand. "Didn't mean to defame the dead, but Judith Wolfe went through Nathan's money like blackbirds on a feeding frenzy. And he let her do it."

Susannah couldn't abide gossips. She felt a strange need to defend Nathan's late wife, even though she'd heard similar complaints from Nub. "I heard she was very ill. Surely she—"

"Yes, she was a sick one, all right. But from where I stood, it appeared to me that she played it for all it was worth."

Desperate to change the subject, Susannah asked, "Well, would you mind if I exchanged the fabric for the lumber? And . . . could you maybe throw in some shingles? Please?"

He studied her. "You sure that's what you want?"

"I'm sure, Mister Glass. And the sooner the better, all right? There's a leak in the barn roof that just *must* be fixed before the rains come."

"Of course," he answered, giving her a strange smile. "You got someone with you who could load it into the wagon?"

"No, I'm afraid not. I . . . I came in alone." She'd lied to Louisa about asking Nub to take her; she hadn't wanted anyone to know what she was doing.

"I'll take care of it then, ma'am."

"Thank you, Mr. Glass. I have a few other errands to run. I'll return in less than an hour. Will that be enough time to find someone to load it up?"

"Sure will." He chuckled and returned to his task, enjoying some private amusement.

Susannah left the store, thinking about the impression that Judith Wolfe had made on the storekeeper. In spite of the fact that the woman was dead,

Susannah found she was angry with her for taking advantage of Nathan. Slowly, a picture of Judith Wolfe began to form in Susannah's head, and she couldn't help but feel guilty about it, for Judith's selfishness came through as one of her strongest qualities.

As she passed the bank, she instinctively clutched her purse closer, as if guarding her newly found wealth.

"Well, well. Hello, Susannah."

She stopped midstride, her heart racing. "Sonny," she whispered, a shiver scooting down her spine.

"I've been searching for you," he began conversationally. He moved from behind her to face her. His eyes, often so dark and empty, held a strange fire. "Nate Wolfe is a hard man to find. You *are* staying with him, aren't you?"

Susannah shot a frantic gaze toward the street, alternately upset and relieved that she'd come in alone. "I . . . I suppose you've already told the sheriff what I did, and that I'm here." Her fear made her babble.

Taking her arm, he steered her down the street. "Oh, I won't turn you in, Susannah, not as long as you give me what I want."

She tried to tug her arm away, but he held it fast. Suddenly having learned her own worth, she understood why he wanted her. "You've come all this way for nothing, Sonny. I don't have anything you want," she said with false bravado.

He chuckled, an evil, familiar sound. "I have a room at the hotel. I'd advise you not to make a scene here on the street, or I *will* tell the sheriff you're wanted in Missouri for the murder of your dear, departed husband."

"It was self-defense and you know it," she managed

to say, trying not to stumble as he hurried her along the plank board sidewalk. "And I'm not even sure he was dead when I left."

"Really?" he asked smoothly. "What would make you think that?"

"Someone—" She was hesitant to use Louisa's name. "I was told that when they came to . . . to remove the body, it was gone."

"Ah," he said. "No doubt that nigger whore you were so close to. She'd say anything to make you feel better, don't you know that by now?"

The thought had crossed Susannah's mind. She'd been certain Harlan was dead; any reprieve was welcome.

They entered the hotel and Sonny smiled, tipping his hat at a couple who passed them at the door. Susannah knew only too well that behind that charming smile lay a clever, evil man. She had no idea what he would do, but she expected the worst. It made her stomach churn.

He stopped at the desk, his fingers pinching the soft flesh of her upper arm. "My key, if you please." Again, his voice exuded charm, causing the man behind the desk to throw them both a lascivious smile.

Susannah's skin crawled, and had the man really studied her, he'd have seen the fear in her eyes.

She managed to take the stairs without tripping. When they arrived at his room, he carefully locked the door behind them, pocketing the key. He tossed his fawn-colored Stetson onto the bed, then ran his long fingers through his golden hair, his gaze never leaving her face.

"I didn't think you could get more beautiful, Susannah, but I was wrong."

She hoped she was successful in hiding her revulsion. Sonny was a contradiction and had always been one. Outwardly, he was suave, immaculate, well dressed and cut a handsome figure. Inside, he was evil and ugly. Harlan, on the other hand, had been evil, ugly and dirty both inside and out. He hadn't the brains to pretend he was something he wasn't. She shuddered, remembering . . .

"Let me take your cape—"

"No," she said firmly, clutching it to her, hiding her purse beneath it.

He moved away, his arms up in a gesture of resignation. "All right, but you might as well sit down. You'll be here for a while." He waved a hand at the tufted velvet settee. She would have refused if her knees hadn't been so weak. She sat, still holding her purse to her bosom.

"A drink?"

She shook her head, trying to stay calm.

"Oh, but surely you still take a drink now and then," he mused, pouring one for himself.

"You know I don't drink, Sonny. It makes me quite ill."

He still studied her, swirling the amber liquid in a crystal snifter, a smirk lurking at the corners of his mouth. "I can remember when you liked a little drink, Susannah."

Feeling like a scrubwoman next to him, she nervously smoothed the folds of her patched and wrinkled calico skirt. His tone was conversational, yet she knew Sonny well and realized it was a trick he used to catch people off guard before he attacked. But she knew what he was doing; he was a master of intimidation and innuendo. "I have no idea what you're talking about."

"Remember Ma's funeral?"

A frown nicked Susannah's brow. "Of course. How could I forget?"

He smiled, his expression carnal. "I knew you'd remember."

Susannah didn't understand. "Why wouldn't I?"

"You *do* remember that Harlan suffered from a severe case of the mumps some years before we took you in, don't you, Susannah?"

It was the information Sonny had used to poison Nathan against her. She fought for control. "I remember hearing about it, yes, but what's that got to do with your mother's funeral?"

He threw his head back, laughing quietly. "Do you remember the punch you drank afterward?"

A vague uneasiness settled inside her. "That was almost four years ago. You can't expect me to remember that."

He laughed again, but this time there was an edge to it. "Playing dumb doesn't suit you, Susannah."

Forcing strength into her legs, she stood. "I don't have to listen to this—"

"Sit down, whore."

His words were like a slap, but she refused to be intimidated. "Tell me what you want, Sonny. I have to return to the ranch."

His suggestive gaze moved over her until the air between them was taut with friction. "Among other things, I want you."

"Well, the last person on this earth I want," she spat, "is *you.*"

He gave her a strange, almost ethereal, smile. "And I want my son."

She stumbled, the edge of the settee catching her behind the knees. She dropped to the seat, straining to keep from showing her fear. "He's not your son," she answered, quietly but tightly.

Sonny poured himself another drink. "No? Oh, but he is, my darling."

"Don't . . . don't call me that," she answered vehemently.

He stalked her. "Maybe you should seduce me one more time so I can shoot my seed into you, like I did before. You wanted me once, Susannah. I can make you want me again."

Her skin crawled and fear prickled her scalp, sinking into the roots of her hair. "I never wanted you."

He stood over her, his eyes never leaving her face, his eyelids heavy. "You have a birthmark in a very delicate place, Susannah."

Her heart leaped, but she kept her face passive. "A lot of people have birthmarks," she answered, although her voice shook.

His grin was frightful. "Ah, but yours is directly below your navel, hidden so slightly in the silky reddish brown hair that covers your—"

"Stop it!" She turned away from him, her head throbbing and blood pounding in her ears.

From somewhere behind her he asked, "How would I know that, Susannah, if I hadn't seen it for myself?"

Her teeth chattered and she clamped her jaw tightly. Her mind was cluttered with thoughts that still just skirted the hem of her memory, but she was beginning to feel a horrible sense of panic.

"Harlan *was* sterile, Susannah. Why do you think you never had another child?"

"Just lucky, I guess," she said as glibly as possible, but her throat was so tight she was barely able to speak.

He chuckled, sounding truly amused. "He wanted a child. Well, more importantly, he wanted a son. He asked me to do the honors, and faithful brother that I was—"

"I don't believe you," she hissed, turning to glare at

him. "I might have hated Harlan, but I loathed and despised you."

His eyes were dead. Empty. "But when you're drunk, you become your mother, did you know that?"

The Sonny of her nightmares leaped into her head, unraveling the fabric of safety that had protected her for years, exposing a truth that she didn't want to face.

Sonny leaned so close she could smell his breath. She gagged at the familiar, cloying aroma, pressing her fingers to her mouth. "What . . . what's that you're drinking?"

"Why, the same thing we were drinking the night after Ma's funeral, Susannah. Don't you remember how much you liked it? Don't you remember?"

It was the same odor from her nightmares. It was the sickening smell that clung to her nostrils each time she woke from one.

A flash of memory had her on a bed, both brothers standing over her. She remembered floating, slightly dizzy and nauseous from the sweet drink they'd given her. Then Sonny was on top of her, pushing himself inside . . .

She swallowed the bile that had climbed her throat and rested behind her tongue. She swallowed again and again until she could finally speak. "You raped me."

He raised a tawny eyebrow. "Rape, Susannah?"

She closed her eyes, but when the vision materialized as vividly as if it had happened yesterday, she opened them, blinking furiously to keep the tears at bay. "You . . ." She swallowed again. "You ripped off my clothes. My . . . my only dress . . . the buttons went flying . . ."

Emotion thickened in her throat and she couldn't speak, she could only remember the horror, the fear, the pain, the smell . . .

"You weren't a virgin, of course, but I liked to pretend you were. I enjoyed touching you, kissing your birthmark. It's the shape of a crescent—"

"Stop it!" She covered her ears, refusing to listen, praying the banging of her heart would drown out the sound of his voice.

He sat beside her, his fingers caressing her knee. "Your body responded like the true daughter of a whore that you are, Susannah. Your mother, Fiona, faked it," he said on a sigh. "Harlan could never tell, but I could."

She huddled on the settee, trying to curl herself into a ball, to protect that which he'd defiled almost four years before. "You would have had to get me drunk, you bastard. There was no way I'd have let you touch me otherwise."

"Convince yourself of that, Susannah. I'm sure it makes you feel better. But now," he added, still caressing her knees, "we have a son. That aside, I'm also entitled to everything that's in my brother's strongbox."

"Was that what Harlan left me in his will?"

He barked a laugh. "You? He left you nothing."

Whether it was the truth or not, she didn't care. But she wasn't about to hand him the certificates, either.

He misread her silence. "Don't feel too badly, Susannah. Harlan may not have wanted to give you anything, but I'm perfectly willing to share. Besides," he added, "I'm anxious to get you into my bed again."

She pinned him with a hateful glare. "I'd tell you I'd have to be dead first, but obviously, since you raped me when I was drunk, you probably wouldn't notice the difference."

He gave her a look of mock despair. "Ah, Susannah, you wound me."

She flung his hand off her knee and turned farther

from him. "Nothing would please me more," she answered on a hiss of breath.

He stood, crossed to the sideboard and poured himself another drink. "The courts have decreed that whatever belonged to Harlan is now mine, and—"

"I don't believe you," she interrupted.

He swirled the drink around in the glass. "Shall we go to the sheriff? Think about it, Susannah. With just a word from me, you'll go to jail. And that precious, curly haired child you protect with such vengeance will be mine—to do with as I please."

Her stomach roiled and her head continued to throb. She pressed her fingers against her temples. *Think.* She had to think. The threat of the sheriff made her quake, for although she could maintain until she was blue in the face that she'd killed Harlan in self-defense, no one would believe her. But worst of all, if she went to jail, Corey would be given to Sonny. It wouldn't matter whether he was the child's father or not, he was Harlan's brother, therefore next of kin.

The threat of losing her child was stronger than anything he could do to her and he knew it. "If you so much as touch Corey, I'll kill you."

He pinched the bridge of his nose. "Susannah, Susannah. Why are you fighting me so? To avoid this, all you have to do is bring me the strongbox, and you, your son and I can live in luxury."

She turned away so he couldn't see her face. "I . . . I gave Nathan the strongbox to hold for safekeeping. I don't want him to become suspicious—"

"Just get it, or you'll spend the rest of your life behind bars. Actually, I think I'd make a rather grand father," he speculated.

He moved behind her and rested his hands on her shoulders. Snakelike feelings slithered over her skin. "You missed your calling, Susannah." One hand stroked her neck, then her throat. "You'd have made a finer whore than your mother. High-class. Men would have paid much for you."

"I'm not—" She tried to move away, but his fingers gripped her throat, threatening to cut off her air.

"Don't pretend to be such a pious priss, Susannah. I clearly remember the look on your face as I rubbed that sweet spot between your legs. The look changed from one of fear to total and complete . . . rapture," he finished, leaning over and whispering the word into her ear.

The smell of the drink made her want to vomit, and she fought it. "No! I—" She gasped as he pressed against her windpipe.

"Deny it if you can, but I know what you really are."

She clawed at his fingers until he finally let go, then she stood, gasping for breath, gripping the arm of the settee for support. "Then why in the bloody hell would you want me?"

His eyes were filled with lusty promise. "That should be quite obvious. Now," he said, "bring me Harlan's strongbox, Susannah. If you don't, I'll tell the sheriff where you are and you'll lose that precious son of yours."

Her shoulders sagged in defeat and she quickly shored herself up again. Short of giving in to him, she knew nothing she said would change his mind, but she had to try.

"Nathan will help me, I know he will—"

Sonny's derogatory snort cut her off. "He can't help you. He double-crossed me, Susannah. He's harboring a fugitive. Hell, he's in as much trouble as you are. All I have to do is contact the sheriff—"

"No!" She didn't want to drag Nathan into this. She was sorry she'd even mentioned his name.

"I thought not," he answered, pleased with his threats. He grabbed her from behind, clamping her to him. "And don't think about doing me in, Susannah. I have a little insurance tucked away. Should anything happen to me, the truth about Harlan's death will fall into the hands of the law."

She fought her panic. "If you don't let me leave right now, someone from the ranch will come searching for me."

He released her and sighed. "Yes, you're probably right. You won't run from me again, though, will you?"

When she didn't answer, he gripped her chin, pinching it hard between his fingers. "No matter where you run, Susannah, I'll find you. Remember that."

She tried to pull away, but he held her fast. Pain shot into her jaw. Refusing to be cowed, she glared at him, hating him more with each breath she took.

"I don't like that look of defiance, Susannah. Just remember that if you cross me, I'll put you away. And if that's not threat enough, remember that when you're locked away in some dirty, dusty jail, Corey will be with me."

He shoved her away from him and strode to the window, appearing to study the street below.

An unsettling sense of dread shot through her as she nursed her jaw. His words were a bigger threat than the unexplainable bruise his touch would leave on her skin.

"You're worse than Harlan ever was. He was just mean; you're evil," she answered with quiet hatred.

He turned, giving her a nasty smirk. "I do what I can."

Uncontrollable stomach spasms left her weak. She felt pinned against a wall with no place to run. No escape possible. Turning toward the door, she said, "I need a few days to . . . figure this out."

He moved from the window and stepped in front of her, unlocking the door. He opened it with a gentlemanly flourish that she knew was all show.

"By all means," he said. "You have until the day after tomorrow."

She stepped out into the hall and hurried down the stairs, clinging to the bannister for fear her legs would give out.

Somehow she managed to make it to the wagon. The lumber and a stack of shingles were piled neatly in the back. She pulled herself onto the seat and gripped the reins, the action halting her shaky fingers. Though she'd been in town less than two hours, it had felt like an eternity.

～ *20* ～

Louisa was waiting for her on the porch, her fists on her hips and her expression thunderous. "Where you been, you shameful girl?" She hurried beside the wagon as it creaked toward the barn. "You like to scared the wits out of us. An' you were s'posed to take Nub with you. Why'd you go off alone, Honeybelle? With that pissant Sonny lurkin' around, it ain't safe for none of us."

The ride back to the ranch had given Susannah plenty of time to think. She tried not to dwell on the vile memories surrounding Corey's conception, but she couldn't help it. She knew now that Sonny could be Corey's father. And Nathan couldn't help her. She knew he would if she asked him to, but it would only embroil him in a mess that was hers and hers alone. He was already in enough trouble because he'd not followed Sonny's orders. And yes, he was harboring a fugitive—her.

She didn't want to leave. It seemed she always ran

307

when she couldn't face things, but she didn't know what else to do without getting Nathan into trouble. She loved him; she always would, and leaving him would be like cutting off a limb. But losing Corey would be like cutting out her heart. She couldn't live without a heart.

Pasting on a gay smile, she stopped in front of the barn, hopped down and handed the reins to Jackson. Their new ranch hand, the breed McCloud, who had brought Jackson home, was teaching the boy how to handle the horses. She watched him unhitch the team and lead them into the enclosure.

"There's too much to do around here to take Nub away for a few hours, Louisa. Nathan says it's past time for the rains, and there's still that leak in the roof. I learned to take care of myself a long time ago. I can't start relying on others now."

Louisa strained to look over the side of the wagon. "What's that lumber and them shingles doin' there?"

Susannah pulled her gloves off. "It's to fix the leak in the roof."

Casting her a suspicious glance, Louisa asked, "Where'd you get the money for that?"

She started for the house. "That's not important. What's important is getting things fixed around here before it starts to rain."

Louisa studied her as they walked to the porch. "I been lookin' for that fabric you bought yesterday. Can't find it nowhere."

"That's because I took it back," Susannah said softly.

Louisa gripped Susannah's arm, stopping her. "You *what?*"

"I took it back."

"But why?"

Susannah stepped into the house, Louisa still clinging to her arm. "We both know I don't need such a lavish wedding dress." As it turned out, she probably wouldn't need a wedding dress at all. The thought made her ache.

Louisa gave her a disapproving sigh. "Mister Nathan tol' you to buy it."

"But, do you know what he used to pay for it?" When Louisa shook her head, Susannah said, "The lumber and the shingles that he'd planned on using to fix the barn."

An expression of understanding relaxed Louisa's face. "So that's where it all went."

"Yes. Now you understand why I couldn't let him do that."

"Oh, Honeybelle, that man must love you somethin' awful."

Susannah turned away. No, she thought, he just assumed that every woman was like Judith, their needs fulfilled by material things.

Louisa glanced out the window. "Speakin' of that man . . ."

Susannah's gaze followed hers, and she saw Nathan striding toward the house. He looked as though he'd eaten a thundercloud for lunch.

McCloud had informed him there were shingles and lumber in the back of the wagon when he and Jackson had pulled it into the shed. Damn it, he hadn't even known Susannah had gone back into town.

He stormed into the house. Susannah's cape was still over her shoulders and her gloves dangled from her fingers.

"What's the lumber and shingles for?" He hadn't meant to sound so angry, but he couldn't take it back.

She removed her cape and hung it on the peg by the door. "It's for the barn, silly."

There was a nervous quaking in her voice, but he didn't stop to analyze it. "How did you pay for them?"

She made a fuss over straightening the other coats on the pegs. "The same way you paid for my fabric."

He frowned, letting her words sink in. "You know about that?"

She came and stood before him, her eyes wide, her face sweet. "I couldn't keep that ivory silk, Nathan. I don't *need* anything so grand. I'd feel guilty——"

"But I wanted you to have it," he interrupted firmly.

"I know," she said on a smile, then reached up to touch his chin. "That's what made the gesture so special. But it wasn't realistic. We . . . we needed the lumber and shingles far more than I need a fancy wedding gown."

He couldn't understand her. Women always liked expensive things. Giving them was the only way he could profess his love, for the words themselves always came hard. "But, Judith——"

She placed her fingers over his lips, quieting him. "I'm not Judith," she said, emphasizing each word.

His anger dissipated, and he pulled her into his arms. She stiffened and removed his arms from her waist. Something was wrong. He shouldn't have mentioned Judith's name.

He watched her cross to the corner by the stove and pull a pair of Jackson's overalls off the drying rack. "I shouldn't have brought Judith into this. I'm sorry I mentioned her. It's just that she was only happy when I bought her things." He gave her a helpless shrug. "I guess I thought all women were like that."

She continued to take clothes off the rack, fold them and put them on the table. "No, don't apologize. It's only natural for you to mention her." She turned toward him, and he saw the pain in her eyes. "But I'm not Judith, Nathan. I would ask nothing from you but your love."

He swung away, knowing he might lose her if he didn't say the words. God, but they'd always come so hard. . . .

"I do love you, Susannah." He turned toward her. "I love you and I want to marry you so you can't ever leave me."

Her eyes filled with tears and she pushed the drying rack to the floor as she ran from the room.

It wasn't the reaction he'd expected.

He was still standing, puzzled, when Louisa came in from outside, her apron filled with squash from the garden.

"She musta tol' you she took the material back," she observed, studying his face.

Nodding, he answered, "She did. But I don't understand her, Louisa."

Louisa dumped the squash on the counter then planted her fists on her hips. "You say somethin' to upset her? 'Cause if you did, I'll get Kito to rip your heart out through your mouth and don't think he won't."

He listened to the rhythmic cadence of her words and wondered if he'd live the rest of his days under the threat of Kito's brawn. Probably, he thought, with resigned sarcasm.

Louisa wiped her hands on her apron, then turned to clean the squash. "My Honeybelle ain't had a pot to pee in all her life, Mister Nathan. She sewed for other people until her fingers bled. An' she tried to squirrel a few pennies away, but that bastard Harlan always found her hidin' places. Took her money and drank it up," she said with a flourish of a knife. "Or gambled it away." She clucked her tongue angrily and cut the squashes in two, then scooped out the seeds. "If you ask me, I think she shoulda kept the ivory silk, but 'course no one asked me."

She turned, two squash halves in her palms. "She loves you a heap to give up the chance for the dress of her dreams just so's you can fix that blasted hole in the barn roof."

He was beginning to realize that, but her reaction to his admission of love still mystified him. Something else was bothering her; he'd find out what it was or die trying.

Susannah sat on Corey's bed and wiped her eyes with the corner of her apron. He loved her! Oh, God . . . he loved her. . . . It would have been hard enough to leave had he not said the words, but he had. And though she didn't want to, she still had to take Corey and go away.

Was she a coward for running again? Perhaps. If she could think of any way to deal with this without involving Nathan, she would. But now that Jackson was home, and he and his father were getting along so beautifully, she refused to jeopardize either of them.

The door swung open, hitting the wall. Nathan stood in the doorway, the thunderous expression back on his face. He strode to her and stood over her, his thumbs hooked into his pockets.

"I want to know what in the hell is going on here."

With a quick swipe of her fingers, she wiped the remaining moisture from her cheeks. "What do you mean?"

He lifted her chin, inadvertently touching her fresh bruise. She winced.

"What's wrong?" His voice was sharp as he released her and sat down beside her on the bed.

"Nothing," she answered, turning slightly away.

"Susannah." His tone was threatening as he pulled her toward him.

She refused to look at him, but he gently lifted her chin again, this time examining it.

"What happened?"

"Nothing," she answered a bit too quickly. "It's nothing, really." She tried to avoid his intense gaze. "I'm . . . I just get emotional when I think about . . . about us."

"No," he argued. "It's more than that. If there's something wrong, Susannah, I want you to tell me. How can I help you if I don't know what's bothering you?"

"Oh, Nathan," she said on a choking sob. "How I wish you could—"

"Damn it, Susannah, you're scaring the hell out of me. Tell me what's wrong." He tried to fold her in his arms but she pulled away again.

She wanted to tell him. Oh, how desperately she wanted to! She put her hands over her face and pressed her fingers against her eyes. "You can't help me, Nathan. No one can."

He took her in his arms. This time she didn't fight him. "Try me."

She huddled against him, wondering what she would do if she no longer had his strength to rely on. She hadn't wanted to involve him, but something stronger, maybe his admission of love, urged her to tell him everything.

"It's Sonny," she finally said.

He swore, holding her tighter. "I wondered when he'd show up. Tell me what happened."

She did, from the moment Sonny stopped her outside the bank to the last frightening threat. She related his specific interest in the strongbox and the contents, and her exposure to the law for Harlan's death if she didn't comply with everything he wanted. And his threat to keep Corey and have her sent to prison if she didn't submit to his every demand.

"And he could do that, Nathan," she said, shoring up her nerve. "He—" She took a deep breath. "He could do that because . . ." Her lower lip quivered and she bit down on it, hard enough to cause herself pain. ". . . because he *is* Corey's father."

Nathan's hand tensed on her shoulder. "What?"

She pulled away and curled into a ball on the bed. "At their mother's funeral they got me drunk. Sonny . . . Sonny ripped off my clothes and . . . and raped me. I remember now. Oh, God, Nathan, for years I've been having these awful nightmares where Sonny raped me. And . . . and there was always this gagging smell, even after I'd wake up. But it wasn't just a nightmare, Nathan, it happened. It really happened. It all rushed at me when I was in Sonny's hotel room. He . . . he was drinking some vile, sweet drink—the same thing he made me drink after the funeral. I remember everything that happened. Everything."

Tears stung her eyes again, and she dashed them away with her fists. "I won't blame you if you don't want me now. Everything you'd accused me of is true. And you can't help me even if you wanted to. Not now."

Nathan sat on the bed and stroked her shoulder. "Ah, Susannah. I love you to distraction and I'll always want you. Once we're married, Corey will be my son, too. And no court in the land would take the boy away from his mother."

She swallowed, relieved. "Not even if she's guilty of murder?"

"We'll settle that one way or another, don't you worry about it. But something's been bothering me." He pulled her to him again. "What's in the strong-box?"

"Well," she began, "I thought it was just a bunch of worthless papers, but I took them to the bank this afternoon and discovered they're some kind of stock certificates and they're worth a fortune. Can you imagine?"

Her purse was at the foot of the bed. She grabbed it and opened it. "Here. They're all here." She dug them out and shoved them at Nathan.

Nathan flipped through them, studying them. "You're rich, Susannah."

Hope stirred within her. "No. *We* are. And I'd wanted it to be my dowry, Nathan. We can fix up the ranch, we can—"

"This is what Sonny wants, isn't it?"

Nodding, she answered, "He claims they were left to him. That they're his."

"And the only way he can get them from you is to threaten to expose you for killing Harlan."

"But I *did* kill Harlan," she answered, her face pinched with emotion.

"That's been the consensus, hasn't it?"

"It's not a consensus, Nathan, it's the truth."

Nathan drew a few certificates from the pile and tapped them against his chin. "I've been thinking maybe we should go to the sheriff together and give him your side of the story."

Fear and horror turned her blood to ice. "Oh, Nathan. I . . . I couldn't. Sonny said he's already told the sheriff what happened. He's always had the law in

315

his pocket, Nathan. It wouldn't work. It wouldn't do any good. They'd just put me away somewhere——"

He gripped her shoulders. "We've got to put an end to this, Susannah. You can't go on living with it hanging over your head."

Her throat tightened. "It's better than a noose around my neck," she managed to say.

He gently ran his fingers over her chin. "Sonny hurt you, didn't he?"

She shrugged. "He . . . he pinched me."

Nathan continued to stroke her face. "Do you love me?"

She softened, her eyes filling with tears again. "Oh, Nathan. You know I do."

"Then you must trust me, Susannah."

She pressed his fingers firmly against her cheek. "I want to, darling. But we don't have much time. Sonny expects me to get back to him the day after tomorrow."

"That's all right," he said. "I'm afraid McCloud and I have been working on this behind your back. I hope you don't mind."

She sat up straight, intrigued and surprised. "What have the two of you been doing?"

"McCloud has been gathering information for me."

"About what?"

"About the Walker brothers and their unsavory activities."

Hope surged through her. "Will it do any good?"

"It will if we can get the right kind of information."

Again, she remembered what Louisa had told her when she first came to her cabin in Angel's Valley. "Nathan, Louisa was going to take care of Harlan's body that day. But . . . but when she returned with a friend to help her, the body was gone."

He studied her for a long, quiet minute, then stood and went to the door. "Louisa! Come in here."

Louisa stepped into the room, her expression cautious. "What's wrong, Mister Nathan?"

He took her hands, and Susannah saw the surprise that registered in her eyes. "Tell me exactly what happened when you went back to get Harlan's body and found it gone."

She shrugged. "Ain't much to tell. My friend Andrew and I had planned on burying the bastard, but he was gone."

Nathan drew away and paced the room, nervously dragging his fingers through his hair. "What could have happened?" He said it as though he were trying to recreate the incident in his mind.

"Someone had to have come in and taken the body," Susannah said, furnishing him with a possibility.

"Yes, but who would do this and not tell anyone?"

Susannah's spirits rose a bit more. "Why, Sonny, of course."

"And why wouldn't he tell anyone?"

Susannah and Louisa exchanged glances. "I don't know. Why?" Susannah asked.

Nathan continued to pace. "Because maybe," he said, deep in thought, "because maybe Harlan wasn't dead after all."

"But he was! At least . . . at least I thought he was. He hadn't moved, Nathan. And," she added, turning to Louisa, "you thought he was dead, too, didn't you?"

"I admit I did," Louisa said, pondering the question. "But I took your word for it, Honeybelle. I didn't get any closer to that bastard than I had to. Alive or dead, the man was snake piss."

Susannah brought her hand to her mouth, her spirits inching upward. "Oh, Nathan. Is it possible? I mean, could I have . . . have just wounded him?"

"Of course it's possible. It's *more* than possible. In spite of what he wanted everyone to think, Sonny had little love for Harlan. I imagine he was damned angry that Harlan had a strongbox full of wealth that he wouldn't touch. Not only that, he wouldn't share it with anyone, either. Not even his half brother.

"Suppose," Nathan continued, "suppose he happened by that morning and found Harlan on the floor, bleeding badly. And suppose that under the guise of taking his brother to a doctor, he actually took him to the woods and finished him off." He swung around, pointing to Susannah.

"You've already convinced yourself that you killed Harlan. Louisa," he said, shaking his finger at her, "is, in his mind, just a nigger. Excuse me, Louisa, I mean no disrespect."

Louisa nodded regally. "None taken, Mister Nathan."

"Even if she were to tell someone that Harlan's body was gone, who'd listen?"

Susannah paced as well. "Oh, Nathan, this is all just speculation. We can't prove anything."

"Not yet, but with McCloud's help, maybe we can. And we don't necessarily need the truth to get the truth from him," he added cryptically.

"Now, Louisa, you probably can't be a formal witness, but would you agree to tell the sheriff everything you know?"

She pulled herself up and tossed him a haughty look. "'Course I will. I'd walk through hot coals for my Honeybelle."

Nathan coaxed Susannah into his arms. "McCloud

will be here for supper. We'll get this settled, Susannah. I don't want you to worry about it."

Susannah nestled close, grateful he couldn't see the worry that remained in her eyes. With every breath she took, she wanted to believe Nathan, but she knew Sonny Walker better than anyone. And she privately couldn't believe he'd left anything to chance.

~❧ 21 ❧~

Another message for you, Mr. Walker." The desk clerk slid it across the counter, then returned to his books.

Sonny could feel his heart race. Staring at the envelope, he slowly turned it over, hoping not to see the same printing as he'd seen on the one he'd received just after Susannah had left. Cursing sharply, he dropped it on the counter. The writing was the same.

With a tense feeling of dread, he picked it up and slid his finger through the opening, pulling out the piece of paper with the tips of his fingers. As he read it, he found himself swallowing convulsively.

I saw what you did.

He crumpled it and stuffed it into his pocket. The one he'd received earlier in the morning had said, *You weren't alone at the river.*

Frustration and anger made him shake, fear made him sweat. He couldn't stand to sweat; it was for the weak.

Smoothing his hand over his hair, he nodded a quick thank you toward the busy desk clerk, then took the stairs, two at a time, to his room.

Once inside, he paced, remembering the day he'd discovered Harlan crawling toward him, blood oozing from a wound in his chest. He'd known immediately that Susannah had done it, for neither she nor the boy were anywhere in sight.

Harlan's eyes had been nearly glazed over, but he'd reached for Sonny, hope on his stupid ugly face, thinking that maybe he wasn't going to bleed to death after all.

Sonny had masked his glee, pretending to give a goddamn, and had helped Harlan into his buggy, shoving a towel against the wound to stem the flow of blood. On the premise of taking him to the doctor, he'd gone straight to the river and drowned him, putting an end to Harlan's suffering before he buried him in the shallow grave beside the water. No one had been around. He'd been alone, damn it! He was sure of it. . . . Still, the contents of the notes now burned in his brain.

Afterward, he'd returned to the house and searched it. Had Susannah not taken the strongbox, the contents of which he'd coveted for years and felt he deserved, he might not have sent someone after her. Even now he wondered why he persisted. Probably because he would never be truly safe as long as she was alive. Even if he somehow forced her to come with him, he knew her unwillingness would one day mean the end of his freedom. She was a loose end he couldn't afford. Despite it all, he was grateful to her, for she'd started the process that had allowed Sonny to finish his half brother off. Actually, he'd done him a favor by killing him. Put him out of his misery.

He went to the window, pulled aside the lacy

curtain and stared down into the dirty street. He wanted—no, he *needed*—to get out of there, but he had to get the strongbox from Susannah first. And, he thought, his frown turning to an evil smile, he had to get Susannah, too, for although he didn't want her, he had to get rid of her. Too bad, though. Perhaps he'd have her one last time before he disposed of her. His loins stirred at the thought.

Sonny's gaze moved over the buildings across the street, to the alley between them. A man was there, casually leaning against the brick, staring up at him. A sick feeling permeated his chest and he pulled back, startled. But before he scrambled from the window, the man gave him a wide smile and saluted him.

His heart banging against his ribs, Sonny flung himself against the wall. He dug his fingers into his hair, raking them through it, carelessly ruining the perfect lines. Creeping to the window again, he peered across the street. The man was gone. But again, as before, the contents of the notes burned in his brain. Was he the author of the notes? Had he been the one to see him at the river?

He pulled out his pocket watch to check the time, cursing his shaky fingers. The poker game started in ten minutes. Shoving the watch into his vest pocket, he crossed to the dressing table and poured himself a stiff shot of brandy. It went down quickly; he was forced to take another. The third shot finally took the ragged edges off his nerves.

He brushed his hair into place and left his room. As he hurried past the front desk, the clerk called his name. Sonny was tempted to ignore him, but the brandy had done its job, for he was no longer afraid.

The clerk handed him another envelope. On his way out the door, Sonny ripped it open and read the contents.

Harlan Walker does not Rest in Peace.

To learn how I know, meet me at the bridge at midnight.

He crushed the note and tossed it aside, the brandy numbing the fear he'd felt when he'd read the others. His false sense of euphoria began to crumble when he stepped into the saloon, for there, at the poker table, sat the man who had saluted him from the alley. The man he feared had seen him kill Harlan.

It was ten minutes to midnight when Sonny left the saloon. Two quick shots of whiskey perked him up, and he waited until he was well down the street before he allowed himself a wry chuckle. He reached into his breast pocket and lovingly patted his wallet, fattened with his winnings.

Fools. All of them were fools. How worried he'd been to discover the man from the alley at the poker table! He needn't have bothered to worry at all. He was a breed, and breeds were stupid and lazy and nearly always drunk. If he thought that by challenging Sonny to a game of poker he'd rattle him, the breed was mistaken. Poker was Sonny's game. He was a master at it.

And the other drooling idiots posed no problem either. The toothless codger with the feedbag whiskers, the one with the big nose, others whose faces he couldn't even remember. He'd cleaned them out. Of course, he'd cheated, but no one had guessed.

Continuing to feel invincible, he approached the bridge. Sonny knew who he expected to find. He smirked. The breed from the alley wasn't nearly as clever as he thought he was. Trying to scare him with those childish notes! And he was a lousy card player as well.

He had a sudden case of the jitters. Shadows

loomed out at him, reaching for him, and his heart sprinted in his chest. A thought exploded inside his head. What if, lurking in the darkness, the breed hid with his friends, intent on robbing him? Sonny pressed his hand to his pocket again, as if doing so would protect his winnings.

He slowed his steps and glanced furtively about him. He strained to hear; nothing reached his ears but the thundering of his own heartbeat.

Fear accelerated the effects of the whiskey, and he was immediately sober. "Breed!" He growled the name into the darkness, making certain the sound held no fear.

He continued forward, the outline of the bridge engraved in moonlight. Moving closer, he called out again.

A rustling noise sounded ahead of him, and suddenly someone stood before him.

Marginally relieved, Sonny moved ahead. "After the beating you took tonight, I'm surprised you'd show your face." He smirked, confident again. The moon slipped behind a cloud as he stepped closer. He peered into the darkness. "Let's get this over with, breed. Is it money you want? Hell, after tomorrow I'll have more than enough for both of us." He had no intentions of sharing.

"I don't want none of your blood money, you pissant."

A shock raced through him and he stepped closer. "You?" He felt such a careening sense of jubilation that he laughed out loud.

"I saw what you did, Sonny Walker."

"You saw nothing, you nigger bitch," he snarled, hoping to intimidate her.

She stepped back slightly, giving up ground. "I didn't come to fight with you. All's I want is for you to give my Honeybelle a little money to tide her over till she can fin' a job. An' I want you to leave her alone, y'hear?"

He snorted a laugh. "Or what?"

"Or I'll tell the law what I saw."

"Who'll they believe, nigger bitch? You or me?"

"I'll tell 'em, pissant, so help me God, I'll tell the law."

He wanted nothing more than to pitch the nigger off the bridge and watch her drown. "Listen to me, bitch. You tell that mistress of yours that I want her to meet me here with the strongbox at six o'clock tomorrow morning. If she doesn't bring it, tell her I'll find that kid of hers and drown him in the river, just like I finished off his pa."

The woman gasped. "You mean you killed your own brother?" Her voice was shrill, high with fear.

"That's what I said, didn't I? Now get the hell out of here and deliver my message before I decide to do the same thing to you."

She stood, unmoving and silent for a long, tense minute. Suddenly, she spoke. "You get that, Mister Nathan?"

"We got it, Louisa."

Shocked to hear another voice, Sonny froze and was immediately grabbed from behind. A pair of handcuffs locked his wrists together. He was spun around, and found himself staring into the face of Nathan Wolfe.

Hate oozed from Sonny like venom. "You stupid fool," he hissed. "It's her word against mine. Who's the law going to believe?"

Another man ambled up to him, one thumb tucked into his front pocket, the other producing a badge. "The law, Mr. Walker," the man said, "believes Louisa Washington."

Rage exploded in Sonny's head and he lunged for Louisa, lost his balance and fell, face first, into the dirt. He was picked up by his jacket collar and put on his feet. Dirt and grass mixed with the bile that pooled in his mouth, around his tongue.

The woman stood nearby.

"You weren't there," Sonny rasped angrily, spitting out the glob of mud and grass. *"No* one was there to see what I did!"

"I guess you'll never know for sure, Sonny," Nate said, giving him a little shove.

Another man came out of the shadows, reached inside Sonny's jacket and pulled out his fat wallet. It was the breed.

"Just so you know," he said, "you're not as good as you think you are. You've been duped, Mr. Walker. Duped but good."

He opened the wallet and took out some bills. "This two hundred is mine. You didn't win it, I virtually gave it to you. Suckered you into thinking I was too drunk to know what I was doing.

"And these," he said, taking out a few more bills, "belong to my friend Nub. Nub's got your typical poker face, doesn't he? I'll bet you thought he was just a toothless, ragged old man. *Tsk.* Never judge a man by the cut of his clothes, Mr. Walker.

"And," he added, lifting out a few more bills, "I think Brownie gave you this much, and Hank lost at least two hundred."

Sonny swallowed the angry bile and mud mixture that clung to the back of his tongue and watched the breed toss the empty wallet aside.

"You're a cheat, Mr. Walker," the breed said around a smile. "You cheat at life, and you cheated at cards. We let you win, of course. Personally, I think your technique could use some polishing. What do you say, Sheriff? Think he'll learn a new technique in prison?"

The sheriff shoved Sonny toward the street. "Afraid he won't have much time for card playing where he's going, Mr. McCloud."

"Oh, that's a shame. Don't you think that's a shame, Nate?"

"Nope," Nathan Wolfe said from somewhere behind him, "it's music to my ears."

"A toast to the newlyweds!"

Susannah was tucked close to Nathan's side, and she snaked her arm around his lean waist, giving him a squeeze. They touched champagne filled glasses and each took a sip, their gazes locked.

Nathan gave her a private grin. "I'll give you eighty years to stop looking at me like that."

Susannah's heart overflowed with love. She couldn't believe they were man and wife. It had been a month since Sonny's arrest, and three weeks since she'd appeared before the judge to tell her own story. After reviewing all of the information, which clearly indicated that Susannah had fled the scene of a crime even though she wasn't guilty of murder, the judge ruled in her favor. She was free.

She'd then insisted they finish the roof over the barn before they married, for it had finally begun to rain. It had rained every day since then, sometimes coming down in sheets, sometimes misting.

They stood before the roaring fire in the great room, their friends and family surrounding them.

Nathan's gaze heated her again.

"Don't look at me like that," she chastised. "This little celebration is bound to go on for hours."

"Think anyone would miss us if we sneaked off to the bedroom?"

"You—" She gasped as he nuzzled her ear. "You're making this very difficult, Nathan," she scolded softly.

"That was the plan." He kissed her cheek. "Your dress is beautiful," he said, bending to take her lips. The kiss was hot, filled with promise.

When they parted, she said, "I'm glad you didn't mind that I used the material you'd bought for Judith."

He studied her face, his eyes warm. "She never wanted my gifts unless she picked them out herself."

"Hey, Nate!" McCloud motioned to him, and Nathan pressed a kiss on Susannah's cheek, promising to be right back.

"Come on now, everybody," Louisa called from the kitchen. "Come eat this food before these young'uns devour it all."

Susannah tried to stifle a smile as she watched Corey and Jackson fill their plates. They inched toward a small table that Nathan had made especially for them, scooted carefully onto the chairs and began shoveling food into their mouths. Max sat in front of them, his tail thumping the floor as he waited for their generous treats.

The house was so crowded, Susannah was certain over half the town was there.

She watched Kito step to his wife's side, run his hand down over her buttock, then whisper something in her ear. To her surprise, Louisa giggled, then swatted Kito's arm playfully. Susannah would have thought that a giggle from Louisa was about as possible as a giggle from the dog.

Grateful to have a moment alone, Susannah crossed to a quiet window and gazed out over the fir studded meadow. Everything was such a beautiful wet shade of green. A year ago, she would never have believed her life could take such a wonderful turn. She was happy. She was in love. And she wanted to give Nathan a child.

He came up behind her and pulled her close. She rested her head against his chest.

"Are you happy?"

Turning, she put her arms around his waist and looked up at him. "I'm so happy, I could dance," she answered passionately.

He tossed a rueful glance out the window. "No snowflakes, I'm afraid."

"But I'll always remember the first time we danced together in the snow."

He grinned, touching her hair with gentle fingers. "After the Stedersons' party?"

She shook her head and gave him a lusty smile. "No."

Frowning, he answered, "No?"

She rested her face against his chest, listening to the thundering of his heart. "The first time I danced with you was in my mind, after that story you'd spun to the Hatfields." She gazed up at him. "I knew the story was about you and your wife, but . . . but it was so easy to picture myself there, pressed close to you, knowing there was love in your eyes as we danced outside on the snowflakes."

A chuckle rumbled up from his chest. "By the time I got done with that story, I wasn't sure how much of it was truth and how much was wishful thinking. I'd been drawn to you from the beginning, sweetheart, but that night—" He heaved a deep sigh and hugged her close. "That night was the turning point in my feelings for you."

She closed her eyes and cuddled closer. "Mine, too, but from the minute you came to my rescue, I'd thought about you. You were like no man I'd ever known. You hadn't asked me for anything in return for all the work you'd done. Your touch didn't repulse me, in fact, when you took my hand and introduced yourself, I knew something was different. From then on, every time I saw you my heart almost broke free from my chest."

They turned and watched their family and guests eat and drink with gusto. Noisy voices and laughter filled the house. "And here we are," Nathan said, sounding supremely satisfied.

"And here we are," Susannah repeated. She glanced at the window again, watching the rain, knowing they needed it, but wishing for something else just the same. "Nathan, does it ever snow here?"

"I'm afraid not, sweetheart."

She smiled at her foolishness. "Just wishful thinking, I guess."

"You know I'd make it snow just for you if I could, don't you?"

Her heart expanded with love. "I know. And I love you for it." She took his arm, and they strolled back into the noisy room.

They clattered over the rutted road in their new buggy. She was blindfolded. "Nathan Wolfe," she scolded, touching the cloth over her eyes, "just what are you trying to prove?"

He stilled her hand. "Don't remove it, darling. Trust me."

She gave him an indelicate snort. "It's a good thing I don't get sick from the motion."

The air was cold, far colder than when they left the ranch. "Won't you tell me where we're going?"

"It's not far now, love. Be patient." He squeezed her knee, then caressed it, snaking his fingers up under her skirt.

She gave his hand a playful swat. "Oh, no you don't. You get nothing until I find out where we're going."

The horses stopped, and her heart lurched. "Are we here?"

He left the buggy, then lifted her to the ground. "We're here." He removed the blindfold.

Susannah blinked at the sight in front of her. "Oh, Nathan," she said on a sigh. They were high in the foothills. It was snowing. Big, white flakes drifted down, making the world look like something out of a fairy tale.

"It's the best I could do," he said, taking her in his arms.

Her eyes filled with tears. She pressed against him, allowing him to guide her through the steps of a waltz. "You are the most wonderful man."

As they danced, she glimpsed the cabin hidden under the trees. "What's in there?"

He squeezed her bottom. "The makings of a splendid honeymoon."

Swaying with him, she murmured, "I suppose it's too cold to make love in the snow."

His chuckle was warm against her ear. "I don't think I could get the ol' chap up, sweetheart. But there's a bearskin rug inside that'll feel great on your bottom—or mine, depending on who's on top."

"Do you think it will be snowing in the morning?"

"I can almost promise you it will."

"Good," she said, anxiously tugging him toward the cabin. "Tonight let's try out the rug."

~ *Epilogue* ~

Spring 1871

From the newly built porch, Susannah watched the children play. Louisa and Kito's three-year-old son, Abasi, Abe for short, sat in the wagon, one-year-old Miranda seated safely in front of him.

Corey, a handsome six-year-old, waved to his mother as he pulled the babies toward the house. He whistled clear, clean notes, imitating the sweet warbles of many of the resident summer birds that nested in the trees around them. His music also served to entertain the smaller children.

When Miranda saw Susannah, she laughed gaily and clapped her chubby hands. "Mama! Mama!"

Susannah's heart melted at the sight. Sunshine glimmered off Miranda's cinnamon curls, turning them to flame. Her dimpled cheeks were pink with excitement. Susannah hurried down the steps and plucked her daughter from the wagon. They rubbed noses. "Were the boys good to you, sweetheart?"

"'Course we were," Corey said indignantly. "But

you gotta change her, Ma, she smells somethin' aw-ful."

Susannah sniffed. "Oh," she said, wrinkling her nose, "she does, doesn't she?"

Abe scrambled from the wagon and stood in front of her, appearing eager to speak. He was a handsome boy and already big for his age. Susannah had no doubt that one day he would be as big a man as his father. She could already detect strains of his mother's dry wit in his personality.

She put Miranda on a blanket on the porch and started to clean her up. "What is it, Abe?"

"I'm gonna get a puppy," he said, his dark eyes glowing with excitement.

Abe had been speaking clearly in full sentences since he was two years old. "I heard that. What are you going to call him?" Max had found a paramour at the next ranch. She'd recently had six pups.

"I dunno. Maybe 'Doggie.'"

Susannah laughed. "Well, you bring Doggie by when you get him, all right?"

Abe smiled and grinned, exposing his straight white teeth.

With some of the wealth Susannah had gotten as a result of Harlan's death, she'd given Kito and Louisa the means with which to purchase some land of their own, adjacent to the ranch. When they'd insisted on paying her back, she'd argued that she hadn't gotten them a wedding gift. Just having them close was all she ever wanted.

Glancing up, she saw Nathan and Jackson returning from the barn, Max loping along beside them. As always, her heart bumped hard against her ribs at the sight of her husband. They both waved at her.

"Hello, you two! Did you get everything done?"

They were building a new enclosure for the pigs. Some of their neighbors had let their pigs run free, and the result was destruction to everyone else's gardens.

"It'll be done in a few days," Jackson informed her. "Pa said I could finish it myself if I wanted to."

In the three years since he'd returned home, Jackson had become a different person. He rarely spoke of his life with the Yuroks, and everyone respected his silence. Nearly twelve, he was on the verge of manhood. His voice had even cracked on occasion. Although Susannah sensed he was happy, he was still a very serious child.

"So," Nathan said, sitting down beside Susannah. He kissed her, sending a rush of hot expectation through her. "What's happening here, my lovely wife?"

She brushed some hay off the front of his jeans.

His eyes filled with mischief. "I'll give you an hour—"

"Stop that," she said with a shaky laugh, then glanced at the children. "Corey informed me that your daughter 'smells somethin' awful.'"

"What? Not *my* daughter," Nathan roared dramatically. "Not my dandy little Mandy!" He bent down and sputtered against her bare tummy causing her to giggle sweetly. She kicked her plump legs and gripped handfuls of her father's hair.

A buckboard rattled toward them, over the grass. The horses stopped in front of the house, and Louisa waved. "You kids ready for some lunch?" She carried her new baby daughter, Kaya, against her bosom in a slinglike contraption Susannah had made.

Abe toddled to the wagon and struggled to get in. Louisa cuddled him close against her side and kissed the top of his head.

Louisa had softened since her marriage to Kito, but

she was fiercely protective of her children, a trait that brought out all the old qualities that Susannah had grown to love.

Susannah finished pinning Miranda's diaper and pulled down her dress. "Are you sure you want all of them, Louisa?"

"It's Friday, ain't it? Friday I get 'em all. An' don't expect me to bring 'em back till late, y'hear?"

Corey scrambled into the back of the buckboard. Jackson picked up Miranda and followed them.

"Jackson?" When he turned, Susannah said, "You really don't have to go if you don't want to." She knew he was often torn between playing with the younger children and spending time with the adults.

He looked at his father, then at her and gave her a knowing little smile. "Aw, I think I'll go with the rest. Pa says I can finish the pig enclosure over the weekend, and Nub's gone to visit his sister. Kito promised to teach me how to strip the bark from the oak trees. He says that once I learn, I can sell what I strip to the tanners myself. Anyway," he added around a sly little smile, "no doubt you'll be busy the rest of the afternoon."

Nathan clutched Susannah to his side. "You're a wise young man, son."

He chuckled a bit as he walked away, giving his father a backward wave. "Try to leave some water in the tub for the rest of us," he said as he pulled himself into the back of the wagon and settled Miranda on his lap. "It's bath night, remember?"

As they rode away, Nathan shook his head. "Is he trying to tell us he knows how we spend every Friday afternoon?"

Susannah smiled and snuggled against him, desire tightening her. "No doubt he's become observant with age."

Nathan dragged her off the porch and headed for the shed. "Observant with age? Hell, Susannah, he's only twelve."

She couldn't help smiling. "Twelve going on twenty."

"Well, we're not giving up our Friday afternoon bath," he said gruffly.

Susannah squeezed his waist. "Don't be silly. We don't have to give up anything. Jackson senses what's going on, and he's wise enough to understand. And it's because *you* are such an understanding father. Were it not for you, I would have worried myself to death when Corey discovered his privates, remember?"

"God, that seems like a lifetime ago." He gave her a lopsided grin. "He was proud of his 'little one.' Wanted to know if you'd like to see my 'big one.' Did you?"

She laughed, remembering. "Maybe I did. I just didn't know it at the time. I was so embarrassed I thought I'd burn up."

She caught his sudden grim expression. "Don't worry about Jackson, darling."

"I can't help it. I wish I knew what had happened to him those five years he was lost to me."

"Maybe one day, when he's older, he'll want to share it with you."

They continued to stroll to the shed. The sky, clear and blue, was so bright it almost hurt Susannah's eyes. The meadow was adrift with color; fresh wildflowers waved in the wind. Chickadees and warblers and buntings sang in the trees. The hills were drenched with oat and rye grasses, thick and green and succulent.

"I love summers here," Susannah mused. "Winters at the cabin are still wonderful, but summers here in the valley are spectacular."

He squeezed her hand. "I guess we could start a tradition of dancing on the meadow."

"Why not?" She dragged him toward the flowers, but he stopped her.

"First the tub, then the flowers."

She raised her eyes seductively, then rubbed against him. "No," she argued, continuing to tease him with her body. "First the flowers, *then* the tub."

His eyes darkening with desire, he took her in his arms and waltzed her toward the wildflowers. "I believe you're right, Mrs. Wolfe. I believe you're right. Nothing like making love outside, for all the world to see."

He rubbed her bottom, pressing it against his groin.

"I'll give you an hour to stop that," she ordered, melting against him.

Laughing together, they danced on the meadow.

> *But the lark is so brimful of gladness and love,*
> *The green fields below him, the blue sky above,*
> *That he sings, and he sings, and forever sings he,*
> *I love my Love, and my Love loves me.*

Dear Readers:

I hope *Dancing on Snowflakes* touched your heart. If I ever go off course and sideline the romance, I hope someone will tell me. I also hope that readers of historical romantic fiction realize that while there will always be a happy ending, getting there can often prove to be a painful trip. Which, to my mind, makes the ending that much sweeter.

Those of you who have read my stories before know that I rarely, if ever, write just one book, leaving interesting (hopefully!) characters undeveloped. They usually clamor for a story of their own, and I try to accommodate them. I have some characters in mind from this story, but I'd be interested in hearing from you, too. Some of my best ideas have come from readers.

Happy Reading!

Jane Bonander

P.O. Box 3134
San Ramon, CA 94583-6834

Julie Garwood

Prince Charming

Time and again, Julie Garwood has delighted critics —and millions of readers—with her exquisitely romantic love stories. Her bestselling novels have inspired such outpourings of praise as "destined to be a classic...a treasure" (<u>Romantic Times</u>), "belongs on my 'hands off or die!' shelf" (<u>Rendezvous</u>), and, simply, "another gem from Julie Garwood" (<u>Affaire de Coeur</u>). Her hardcover debut, SAVING GRACE, hailed by <u>Rendezvous</u> as "a wonderfully romantic and memorable story," was an instant <u>New York Times</u> bestseller. Now she brings us a very special new love story...

The Captivating New Novel from the
New York Times Bestselling Author of
GRAND PASSION

❧❧❧

Jayne Ann Krentz

TRUST
ME

❧❧❧

Available in Hardcover

from

POCKET
B O O K S

1004-01

Judith
McNaught

Jude
Deveraux

Jill Barnett
Arnette Lamb

A Holiday

Of Love

A collection of romances
available from

POCKET
BOOKS   1007-02